RSC
ROYAL SHAKESPEARE COMPANY

PART I
CONSPIRATOR

PART II
DICTATOR

BASED ON THE CICERO TRILOGY
BY ROBERT HARRIS
ADAPTED BY MIKE POULTON

Image: RSC Visual Communications

ROME
MMXVII

TICKETS FROM £16
WWW.RSC.ORG.UK/IMPERIUM

Supported using public funding by
ARTS COUNCIL ENGLAND

GRANTA

12 Addison Avenue, London W11 4QR | email: editorial@granta.com
To subscribe go to granta.com, or call 020 8955 7011 (free phone 0500 004 033)
in the United Kingdom, 845-267-3031 (toll-free 866-438-6150) in the United States

ISSUE 139: SPRING 2017

Granta, ISSN 173231, is published four times a year by Granta Publications, 12 Addison Avenue, London W11 4QR, United Kingdom.

The US annual subscription price is $48. Airfreight and mailing in the USA by agent named Air Business Ltd, c/o Worldnet-Shipping USA Inc., 156–15 146th Avenue, 2nd Floor, Jamaica, NY 11434, USA. Periodicals postage paid at Jamaica, NY 11431.

US Postmaster: Send address changes to *Granta*, Air Business Ltd, c/o Worldnet-Shipping USA Inc., 156–15 146th Avenue, 2nd Floor, Jamaica, NY 11434, USA.

Subscription records are maintained at *Granta*, c/o Abacus e-Media, Chancery Exchange, 10 Furnival Street, London EC4A 1YH.

Air Business Ltd is acting as our mailing agent.

Granta is printed and bound in Italy by Legoprint. This magazine is printed on paper that fulfils the criteria for 'Paper for permanent document' according to ISO 9706 and the American Library Standard ANSI/NIZO Z39.48-1992 and has been certified by the Forest Stewardship Council (FSC). *Granta* is indexed in the American Humanities Index.

ISBN 978-1-909-889-06-4

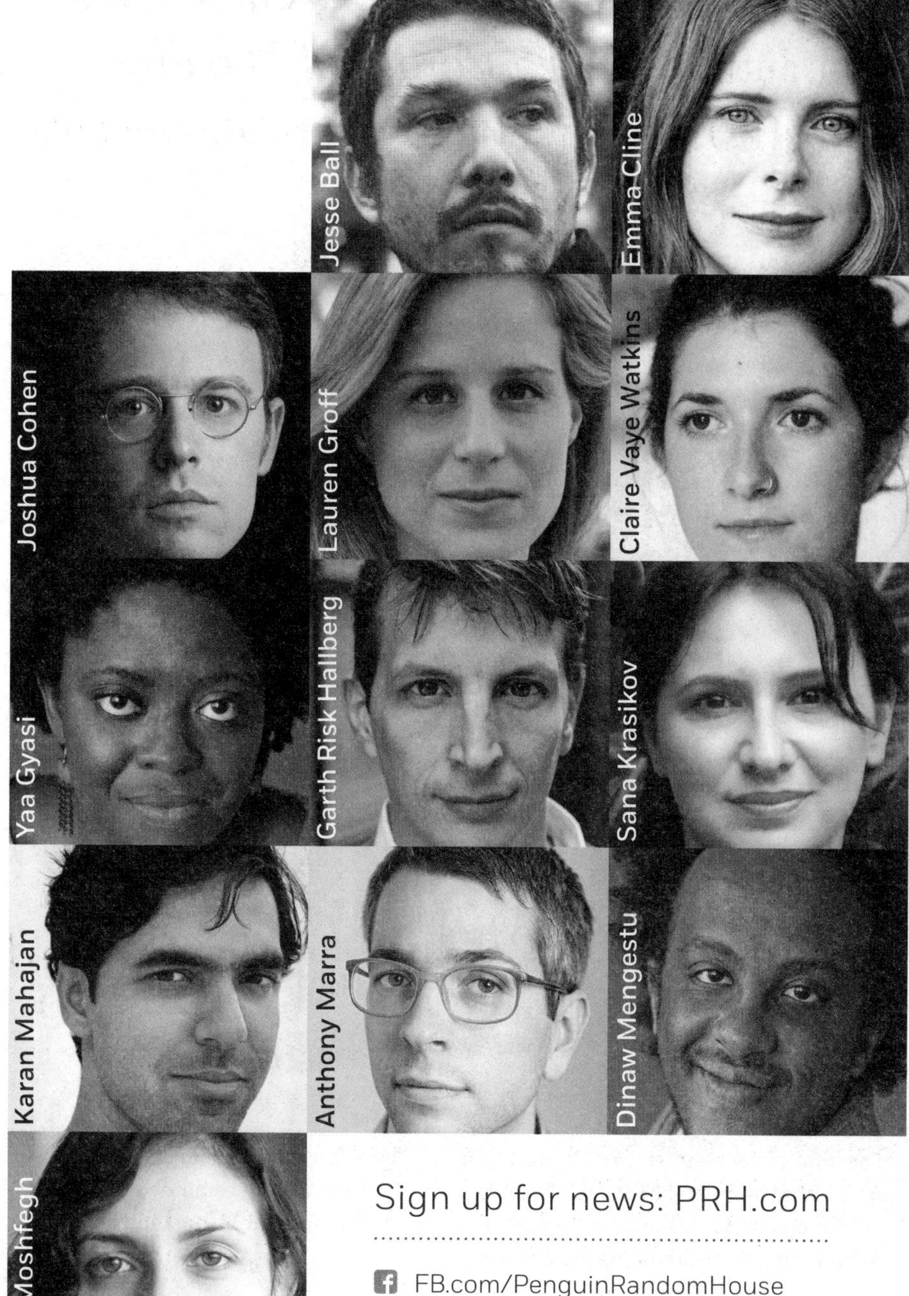
Jesse Ball
Emma Cline
Joshua Cohen
Lauren Groff
Claire Vaye Watkins
Yaa Gyasi
Garth Risk Hallberg
Sana Krasikov
Karan Mahajan
Anthony Marra
Dinaw Mengestu
Ottessa Moshfegh

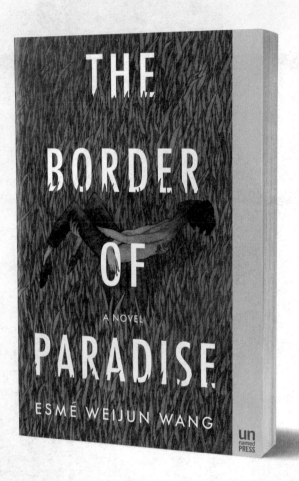

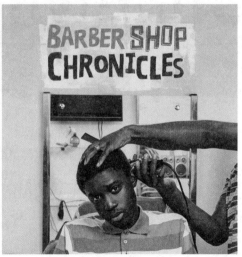

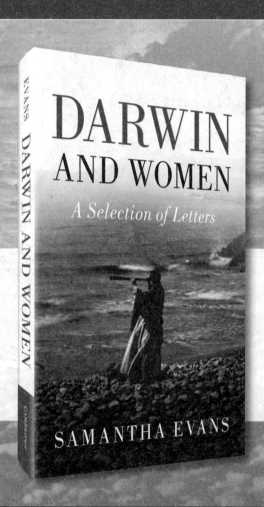

EVERYTHING

By Karrie Fransman

The first frame came from Egypt...

Born in Scotland

South African parents

THE FIRST MAP WAS DRAWN IN GREECE

OUR TIME SYSTEM DATES BACK TO 2000 BC TO IRAQ

The first mirror was made in Germany

The first photograph was taken in FRANCE

Cotton clothes first spun in Pakistan

The first paintbrushes in China

Russian Grandfather

Polish Grandmother

Dutch Grandfather

Lithuanian Grandmother

THE OLDEST BOOK IS FROM IRAN

THE FIRST DICTIONARY WAS FROM SYRIA

THE FIRST NOVEL WAS WRITTEN IN JAPAN

Tea came from China & grown in India

Google UK Invented by a Soviet immigrant to America

THE WEEKLY Newspaper WAS INVENTED IN GERMANY

FOUNTAIN PEN INVENTED BY A ROMANIAN

IS FOREIGN

Illustration by Karrie Fransman

litshowcase.org

CONTENTS

Introduction

In spring 1979 the first issue of *Granta*, a Cambridge student magazine dating back to 1889, was published in its new incarnation: a literary quarterly, in paperback format. Bill Buford and Pete de Bolla were joint editors. The title was *New American Writing*, and it featured work by Joyce Carol Oates, Norman Bryson, Tillie Olsen, Leonard Michaels and Susan Sontag, alongside pieces about writers – some in the vein of literary criticism, some mere notices or magazine articles – including Cheever, Updike, Bukowski and others.

The introduction began with a complaint about contemporary British fiction, which, the editors wrote, was 'neither remarkable nor remarkably interesting'.

'Current literature,' they merrily concluded, 'is unsatisfying simply for the sense it suggests of a steady, uninspired sameness, a predictable, even if articulate prattling of predictable predicaments.'

They were young and they were enthusiastic, and they had a point to make: that American fiction – 'challenging, diversified, and adventurous' – was not as well known as it should be in Britain, whose publishers were slow to pick up American gems. This neglect, they argued, was a sign of the dearth of debate, the lack of literary criticism and the absence of 'a place for the imagination to practise'. The new incarnation of *Granta* was launched to fill that cultural gap, and the editors would do it by bringing American fiction to Britain.

Granta took off, and within a few years the editors conceived the idea of a Best of Young British Novelists issue: *Granta* 7, published in partnership with Penguin in 1983, was the first issue of the Best of Young Novelists series. It was a much-fêted list, probably more so than any of the subsequent ones, including now-famous authors like Martin Amis, Pat Barker, Julian Barnes, William Boyd, Kazuo Ishiguro, Ian McEwan and Salman Rushdie. The concept was launched, and the second Best of Young British Novelists issue was published in 1993; the third in 2003; and the fourth in 2013.

Ian Jack was the editor of the first Best of Young American Novelists issue, published in 1996. A somewhat onerous system had been devised whereby five regional judging panels sent their own shortlists to a central jury. The panels famously missed some of the most interesting up-and-coming names – Nicholson Baker was absent, a decision Ian Jack described as 'insane and perverse' in his introduction to the issue. David Foster Wallace, Donna Tartt and William T. Vollman didn't pass the regional panels either, though many outstanding writers did: Sherman Alexie, Edwidge Danticat, Jeffrey Eugenides, Jonathan Franzen, Elizabeth McCracken and Lorrie Moore, amongst others.

'Who are the best young novelists in the United States of America?' asked the cover copy, immediately renouncing its own query with this caveat: 'A bad question. Writing can't be measured like millionaires, athletes and buildings – the richest, the fastest, the tallest.' One senses Ian Jack, sceptical and intelligent, in the copy. He gives in, of course – the rest of the blurb is a defence of the concept, which was said, at least, to pose 'a useful question'.

In 2007 we did it again. This time the judging process was simpler, with one panel consisting of Edmund White, A.M. Homes, Meghan O'Rourke, Paul Yamazaki, Ian Jack and me. We emailed back and forth (people were less worried about leaks and hacking then), and finally met in New York to discuss the shortlist. 'No list of this kind can offer anything approaching a final judgement,' Ian wrote in the introduction. 'That is up to posterity, if there is one.'

But still: it was a good list. Ian also mentioned the preoccupation with death in contemporary American fiction, noting that 'the dead', 'the memory of the dead' and 'the post-dead' made frequent appearances in the works we had read. He quoted Zadie Smith on American writing – 'why so sad, people?', she had written in her own preface to an earlier anthology of American writing. But what about Ian Jack's phrase above about the judgement of posterity: 'if there is one'? Why so sad, Ian?

The truth is that fantasies of the apocalypse have snuck into us like a virus, embedding themselves into the core of American writing. American dystopia was a strong theme in fiction ten years ago, and it seems strongly present still: pandemics, war and dysfunction predominate (though we noted a good bit of humour too). From the outside one feels the origins of that sadness are all too obvious – 9/11; war; coffins draped in American flags; PTSD; torture scandals; Guantánamo Bay; school shootings and gun crime; the war on drugs; the crash of 2008 ... Where is the good news? From bee death to the loss of manufacturing; from climate change to populism, it's all looking bleak.

But then it always did look bleak: here is a big troubled country with a free press – of course it's going to look bleak. Have you ever read a newspaper in a country with censorship? Try it – that's where you find the good news, the bland news, the happy stories.

This year's list has been a momentous undertaking. Ten years ago we read over 200 novels for the longlist. This time, submissions doubled. Rosalind Porter, *Granta*'s deputy editor, was on maternity leave, but carried on reading. Luke Brown, Luke Neima, Francisco Vilhena, Eleanor Chandler and Josie Mitchell read voraciously. Our Granta Books editors read too – Laura Barber, Bella Lacey, Max Porter, Anne Meadows and Ka Bradley all contributed. Alex Bowler, our publishing director, was hired when the longlist was more or less done, but took an interest in the process. I chaired weekly meetings, where we discussed and logged the merits of each book.

We decided to have an all writers' jury, reasoning that most fiction writers are now deeply engaged in other people's writing too; teaching, editing or publishing. We asked five writers we admire to be on it: Paul Beatty, Patrick deWitt, A.M. Homes, Kelly Link and Ben Marcus.

All lists are a reflection of the tastes of their judges. We are very aware of the authors who might have been on the list had the conversation gone slightly differently. Paul Beatty unfortunately had to drop out when he won the Booker Prize for his novel *The Sellout* – the calls on his time became too great to carry on. We can't know what influence he might have had on the final discussions. Some of us regretted Laura van den Berg, Tao Lin, Brit Bennett, Téa Obreht and Steven Dunn. Katy Simpson Smith and Maggie Shipstead could have made the list, too. NoViolet Bulawayo, a marvellous writer, unfortunately turned out not to be eligible, but she was part of our original selection.

For the first time ever, there are more women than men on the list: twelve to nine. Last time around we had nine women and twelve men; the first list had seven women and thirteen men. Progress, I guess – or chance. We didn't count until we were done. In 2007, immigrant writers were more prominent: seven had been born or raised in other countries. This time, only four of the writers were born abroad.

Every list is a compromise – of course it is. But then it takes on a life on its own. Tobias Wolff, a judge in 1996, the year of the famous misses, wrote this:

> It seems to me that we could make up another issue of *Granta* entirely of writers who aren't in this one, and lose nothing in quality. The idea of choosing twenty writers to represent a generation makes some sense in your country, but in ours, immense as it is, and teeming with young writers, such a process mainly exposes the biases of the judges, my own included.
>
> Which isn't to say that our list is not a fine one. It is. And on it you will find many writers of eccentric and even visionary gifts ... We read a great number of good books, and drew attention to some of them, and gave occasion for aficionados to celebrate their own neglected favorites by ridiculing our list. I'm proud of the unsatisfactory, incomplete job we did, and hope that its incompleteness, by stimulating outrage and disbelief, will awaken others to the wonderful range and vitality of the writers now coming into the fullness of their powers.

That was true then, and it's true now.

I want to thank everyone who made this issue possible – the judges, Patrick deWitt, A.M. Homes, Kelly Link and Ben Marcus, first of all. They were conscientious and deeply insightful, and very good company too. Josie Mitchell, one of our editorial assistants, was in charge of all logistics, and did it brilliantly. Daniela Silva, *Granta*'s designer, conceived the concept for the cover and commissioned and photographed the light installation. Anthony D. Romero of the ACLU kindly allowed us to meet in their boardroom – thank you for that. Mimi Clara helped with logistics, as did our publicists Suzanne Williams and Elizabeth Shreve. Agents and publishers have been uniformly helpful – thank you for all the generous support.

Most of all, however, I want to thank the writers on the list – because this, of course, is not just a list, it's also an anthology. Here is Ben Lerner, with the poignant story of Dale. Here is Greg Jackson, on the old politics of the left and the new politics of the right; here are Sana Krasikov, Karan Mahajan and Dinaw Mengestu touching, one way or another, on terrorism. Here is fantasy by Jesse Ball, Mark Doten, Jen George and Ottessa Moshfegh; and exciting new stories by Halle Butler, Emma Cline, Rachel B. Glaser, Lauren Groff, Yaa Gyasi, Catherine Lacey and Chinelo Okparanta. Here is Garth Risk Hallberg with another New York character; Anthony Marra on escaping fate on an Italian island; Esmé Weijun Wang on mental illness, racism and murder; Joshua Cohen on a soldier in the Israeli army; and Claire Vaye Watkins on a past relationship…

I want to write more, but I don't want to give the stories away. Read them, and judge for yourself. ■

Sigrid Rausing

Courtesy of the author

JESSE BALL

1978

Jesse Ball is an atheist, anarchist, novelist, poet and theorist born in New York. His works of absurdity have been published in many parts of the world and translated into more than a dozen languages.

A WOODEN TASTE IS THE WORD FOR DAM A WOODEN TASTE IS THE WORD FOR DAM A WOODEN TASTE IS THE WORD FOR

Jesse Ball

1

The woman wore a hat made of paper and a very plain but bleak costume, a kind of rebuke. It said that she was doing something you should be doing, or should have done. What was that?

She was pushing a wheelchair across broken pavement and she did not stop at cracks or breaks. She did not see them. The job to her was pushing the wheelchair between places. It was explained to her. You will push the wheelchair from this place, a place in the children's ward, to this place, a place in the zoo, and you will push it back. They did not say the pushing was the job, but she saw it so. What was in the wheelchair and its condition mattered less to her. Sometimes it was a girl, sometimes a boy. Or it might have been. Who could say? No one else had been there. The child could be delighted, tearful, insensate, incensed, insufficient, it didn't matter.

Whoever was in the chair that moment (had she even looked?) was bounced rather awfully by the cracks, and the wheelchair made some sort of slow but wild progress towards the double doors of the zoo building. The nurse felt the deteriorated pavement was her burden. She was trying to smooth it out with the large round wheels of the chair, but it had no effect at all, except that it hurt her hands and arms quite badly, and shook the chair nearly to pieces.

They called it a zoo, but it wasn't much of one, was it? She shoved the footplate of the chair into the spot where the doors met, slamming the chair forward into the doors and the doors buckled back, eliciting a small cry from the one in her tow, but the doors buckled just enough, and an opening brushed along the sides of the chair. They went through it, and then they were on carpet.

2

That was the moment – the wheels running easily on the woven fabric. He could feel something like magnificence – or the possibility of it, in his curled little body. He had clung to the chair as it bounced and threw him this way and that, but now he need do nothing. He was drifting through a place of shadows, and on either side windows had been cut into places no one had ever been – jungles and forests, deserts. There was anything you wanted to see, but you didn't know it was, and when you saw it you knew even less, but wanted more still. None of it meant anything to him, though, anything to him like going to the beaver dam at the extreme end. The beaver dam. He could think of nothing else. He would wake in the narrow cot of the cripple ward, and call out for water, and what he meant when he called out was, take me to the beaver dam, please. When they carried him to the lunch chair where he was forced to eat things he never would, he would mutter it again, by pressing his head into the table. Take me to the beaver dam. Someone finally noticed after days of this that they should do that. They should take him to the beaver dam. So on the chart it was written, weekly visit to the zoo, w. esp. attention to beaver area.

He tried sometimes to talk to the nurses about the beavers. He knew nothing really to say, but they knew even less, and though he tried as hard as he could to make them feel what he saw in the beavers, it was of no use. Their nurses' faces were painted shut, had always been that way. Not something wrong or bad, just the case.

There were four beavers in the pathetic little river that lay behind the plate-glass window. One he called Ganthor. One he called Stueben. One Mouselet. One Ganthor. He called two of them Ganthor because he hadn't yet decided which was which, and he thought it was more accurate that way. Still he knew one Ganthor was female. He just couldn't say how it worked, and the beavers moved so unpredictably, it was not easy to learn.

The beavers were known as being something like fish, but also they could cut down trees. He liked that. Unfortunately in the place beyond the glass there were only things that looked like trees, but no real trees. The things that looked like trees had been made to appear to have been cut in half by the beavers, but he knew they hadn't done it. As a salve to the beavers, small pieces of wood were brought to them in a cart, and Stueben would rummage there all day, but could never discover what to do beyond that. The other beavers had no interest.

Mouselet was quick and her nose was cleaner than the others. That was how he knew her. There was a point by the glass that she would approach, but none of the others would. That was another sign.

Ganthor maybe kicked with his feet while swimming a bit more than seemed necessary. Stueben rummaged. That was the beavers and their ways.

The nurse stood heavily, breathed heavily before the glass. Her heart was beating and she always felt it was someone else's. That was an illness people died from once: the sensation that your heart was someone else's, and the terror of having it beat near you. A heart that is overseen like that starts to flutter, and soon enough it stops, like a fish in a dry pail, smashing its silhouette, losing its nature.

3

He said, look, Ganthor is coming out of the dam. Look. But the nurse wouldn't look.

Ganthor wants to get to the other side because he likes it there better. Now there is Ganthor on the other side, and also over there, and they want to be together, so they meet in the middle.

This was another reason they were both Ganthor – they kept meeting in the middle who knew why.

Stueben had something wrong with his head, and when he would rummage he would sometimes stop and press his head against some sharp part of the wood, as if he were trying to discover what had happened. However long ago it had happened he was still trying to find it out. It did not look good for him.

Sometimes the beavers would come and line up near the glass. Mouselet in front, in her spot, either Ganthor anywhere behind her, and Stueben off to one side, kind of crouched. They would stand there and stare out and then it wasn't clear whose side of the glass was whose. The nurse hated it.

Oh, they're doing it, she would say, and curse quietly, massage her wrists, and turn the wheelchair around. That's it for the fucking zoo.

But today he didn't want to go, and when she turned the wheelchair, he tried to turn and keep looking at the beavers. He was sure they had seen him. He felt they had actually seen him through the glass. Could it be? He tried to cry out, and he did, he cried out, something he had never heard, this cry of his.

Behind him there was an enormous crash, and the nurse started to run.

4

The beavers waited, and bided their time. They got a feel for when he would come, and they tried to show him, through semi-ritualized behavior, what he needed to know. At the end of each performance they would gather to bow, and then they would resume from the beginning. However many times we have to do it, they would say to each other. However many times.

They spoke in the darkness of the dam about the time when he might call out and what they would do. It was a hope beyond hope, and sometimes Ganthor felt it would never happen. Ganthor would say, we are waiting for nothing, actually for nothing. And then Mouselet would hit her head against the ground, and Stueben would vomit, and Ganthor would piss. But they were sturdy as boards, and their strength came back each morning. However much was taken, it always came back, for there was no work for them to do but that – and there is always strength to do the work that is yours.

We love him, said Stueben one day. It is a matter of love. Ganthor said he did not love anyone. Ganthor agreed. Mouselet said everything is done through love, there isn't anything else, so . . .

But Stueben insisted it was different. I am not doing the job I should. There is something I can do in that woodpile that will reach him. I just know there is.

And when it comes, he said, when the moment comes, be ready Mouselet. You are the one to crack the glass.

5

CRASH!

CRASH!

CRASH! CRASH!

The nurse ran on, her paper garments ripping freely in her fear. She shoved the wheelchair haphazardly before her, and it turned, turned on its broken wheel, tangled her leg, and she fell past it, heavily on the ground, screaming her flapping tongue. The beavers came, and were among them. It was a madcap question, shouted into the face, and the beavers drove like arms through the air. The nurse was dead in moments; they turned from her, and they pulled the chair off the one who had fallen.

My love, they cried, my love, my dear, and they beat at him with their hands and feet, with their tails and mouths, with their eyes and noses, bristles, combs, beaks. They tore at him, revenged him, delivered him. He crouched under it, and his crippled legs were ripped away, and his twisted shoulders, his false little neck, his squinting eyes, the little dive of his hair about his ears, ripped away it all went. And there he was then, one of them, fresh and clean, his rough fur lapping at the edges of himself, his strong teeth, his flatness of whip, his sternness of leap and swim and cant.

They drew him up, and he held himself to them, and so happy they all were, so complete was their victory

they hardly knew – should they go back to the dam or somewhere else? Where else could there be? They looked at each other and they were so many but also so few. They were too old and too young. All the years left to them could not be crossed except by accident, but suddenly it felt – they were poised above, could somehow see the flat rush of time. But it curled and tore like heat at their eyes.

They were there together on the stupid carpeting and the sound they were making was the sound of beavers.

+

My friends, what I mean is, this life is shallow like a plate. It goes no further.

I love you all. Now I know you and I love you, and it doesn't matter for this life will kill us without knowing us and ruin our beautiful hearts without seeing them, and there is nothing breathing never nothing anything to breathe inside a stone. ■

Courtesy of Jerzy Rose

HALLE BUTLER

1985

Halle Butler is a Chicago-based writer. Her first novel, *Jillian*, was called the 'feel-bad book of the year' by the *Chicago Tribune*. She has co-written screenplays (*Crimes Against Humanity*; *Neighborhood Food Drive*), and is currently working on a second novel. 'The New Me' is an excerpt from that project.

THE NEW ME

Halle Butler

Feeling pretty good!

My chest clenches and my stomach bottoms out as if to say, 'Are you sure?' But I feel sure. Making some decisions today, no doubt about that! Not thinking about certain things today, no doubt about that!

I look at my face in the bathroom mirror, sallow and grayish, my teeth browning in the cracks, a kind of a low gum line on the bottom incisors, a kind of chapped, painted look to the lips, actual countable pores on my forehead, divided by a real wrinkle that starts between my once lush and still-masculine brows and tapers out halfway to my scalp. A not too unattractive face, when seen in my memory or maybe from afar (though when I see it reflected in windows, the eyes seem exceptionally beady and the jaw stern). Never mind. I'm not distracted by these things anymore. I tape a pillowcase over my mirror using packing tape from a time in my life when I needed it, when I moved and sent packages. There's a chunky white substance in the corner of the pillowcase, which I tell myself is laundry detergent (flashing back to middle school, Megan Lambert, tall and beautiful, laughing and turning red, saying that the stain on her cardigan was in fact laundry detergent, not semen, haha, what a joke. I'm like her now. Laughing. Haha).

I take a trash bag into my bedroom and go through my clothes: too small, hole, out of fashion, too bold, too ratty. It fills, and I put it in the hallway outside my apartment, and go back to my bedroom with a new bag.

I throw away a pair of brown loafers with holes in the bottoms, almost completely crystalized with sidewalk salt – last year's winter boots. I still have my cross-country shoes from high school, fifteen years old, but lightly worn. I hold them and close my eyes, visualizing their value in terms of use and pleasure. They go in the bag.

I toss a pair of stained underwear, and think about how I'm going to buy myself an attractive, soft pajama set. That's the kind of stuff I like now. A fourth trash bag of my clothing goes into the hall, to be taken downstairs in the morning when I'm feeling more rested.

I visualize myself getting coffee with Sarah tomorrow, really bonding and getting to know each other, breaking out of this two-year pattern of drinking, complaints, and misunderstandings. Maybe we could go out for breakfast, play cards, really listen – or better, not have anything to say. We could just exist together.

I text to see if she wants to get breakfast. 'Can't really spend money on restaurants right now but I have some beer I could bring over if you want.' The true opposite of what I'd planned, almost as if she's willfully unable to see how nice it might be: the silent, guileless pancakes.

'What if we just got some coffee somewhere? We could play cards.'

'Don't really like cards and honestly can't spend money on coffee.'

Well, okay.

I'm angry for a second, feeling that it must be a deep lack of imagination that holds Sarah back from fully understanding how wonderful my proposition is, and that I, if I am really in a position of being honest with myself today and every day moving forward, don't really need to be around people with that kind of stubborn lack of imagination, that inflexibility and unwillingness to let me take control (no one ever wants to do what I want to do, and I'm so permissive, so

'Oh okay!' all the time, so 'Tell me about your day' all the time, that again and again I end up doing things I don't want to do: acting the therapist, toeing my limit with alcohol even though I'm visualizing tea, pretending to be grateful at my workplace even though I want to be home). But, I don't need to feel this way. I want to be happy, and I want to nurture my friendships, and I want to be happy to see Sarah, so that's what I'm going to do.

I think about offering to buy her coffee, but then I feel like that's what she was angling for, and I'm not going to do that (be manipulated) anymore, so I let the text hang.

I am looking at clothing I could buy for myself and thinking about making some kind of salad when Sarah texts 'actually p bored rn can I just come over tonight?'

'Oh okay!'

I try to relax. I'm not drinking before she arrives, despite having several nice IPAs on hand from my recent Peapod order, and I have made a mustard vinaigrette to go on a spinach salad that we might share.

She shows up an hour after her text with four warm beers in her backpack. 'What's with the bags outside?' she asks. 'Oh, just doing a little house cleaning,' I say. She raises her eyebrows and nods, stepping over two boxes that I have filled with knickknacks from the living room, and a filthy rolled-up carpet.

She offers me a beer and asks for a cigarette. I give her one, ask if she wants anything to eat, indicating the salad in a large bowl on the counter. She says, 'No, I'm not going to eat that. I'm good.' I nod and say, 'Cool,' and put it back in the fridge uncovered. We sit in momentary silence. She blows breath out of her mouth, puffing up her cheeks either like a monkey, or like someone with deep world-weariness.

'Sooo, how are things with you?' I ask.

She makes an immediate mistake, thinking that, again, I will be interested in hearing a story featuring coworkers and family members I do not know.

I don't even try to listen, I just sit, grunting occasionally, 'Oh, yeah, Chris, he sounds awful,' trying to stay conscious, drinking quickly, hoping it might unlock some latent interest in the narrative. I try to interject, to change the subject to something broader that I might be able to participate in, but my attempt is reaching ('That's like that one movie'). She veers to a dark topic, a trauma that her college friend, clearly suicidal, suffered years ago.

I want to ask her opinion on the clothing that I want to order, but we've never done that before. I think: I really like Sarah's clothes, that is something I value about her, taking after a suggestion from an article I read online about how to get along with people. Focus on their strengths. Sarah pauses to take a drink and say, 'Ugh, anyway.'

I take my opportunity.

'So I think I'm going to get some new work clothes – and maybe just some new clothes in general.'

'Oh,' she says. Incurious, flat.

'Yeah, I was thinking that if I'm going to be committing to a new job that I'm not really that hot on, I should at least enjoy some of the perks.'

'They offered you the job?'

'Not yet, but I thought it would be a good idea to get myself in the right headspace to accept the offer when it comes.' This sounds reasonable to me. Almost true.

'I can't really afford clothes right now,' she says. 'I bought these socks a few months ago, they're really expensive, but I wear them like three times a week.'

I look at her socks and tell her she's mentioned them before.

'But whatever,' I say, 'I'm not rolling in money now or anything, but all of my clothes are too tight and have holes and stains.' This she knows, so I don't know why she's looking at me like I'm the fucking king of France. 'And I want to get a few new things. I don't know, I feel like it might help.'

'Sure, why not, if you have the money and you don't have any student debt or bills, why not?'

I stare at her.

'Can I show you what I'm thinking of getting?'

I recognize that she can't actually say no, even if that's what she wants. Even if all parts of her are screaming no, she can't actually say no.

She makes a face close enough to a nod and doesn't verbally object, so I get my laptop. I wanted her to say yes. I wanted her to want to help me with this. This should be fun. I would be more than willing to help her cultivate a more professional appearance, if that's what she wanted. Working on a project or a problem is something friends do together, to help them bond.

I show her a plaid smock, thick tights, a cardigan, an oversized turtleneck sweater, a button-up shirt, fake suede gloves. She manages an 'Oh, that's cute' to the button-up. 'I'm horrible with clothes,' I say. 'I really need a new coat, too, but I'm at such a loss.'

She says the clothes are fine, and then goes on to tell me that I shouldn't worry about it. She mentions maybe waiting until I get the job offer to buy the clothes, and I say, 'But you think I should get these?' She says, 'Yeah, they're fine. I mean, if you can afford them.'

The night is not going as planned. We drink all of the beers, and switch to a bottle of cooking sherry that I keep in a cabinet by my spices. I'm not sure if it's even alcoholic, but it tastes alcoholic, especially in my mouth the next morning. She still wants to talk about whatever friend or family member with whatever drug problem, and I lean forward and say, 'So you guys were pretty close, so that's why you're taking this so hard.' I put my hand on my chin and furrow my brow. 'This is really affecting you on a day-to-day level.'

'Well, I mean, no, we weren't that close, it's just on my mind.'

'Is it on your mind because you feel that Chris isn't taking your criticisms of his management style the right way? And you feel some connection there, between your cousin's frustrations and your own?'

'I mean, now that you mention it.'

'I think the best thing to do in these situations is to just take things as they come. Take it more in stride. You're going to be fine, none of this is a big deal, you can't control other people – you could adopt that as a mantra.'

She launches back into the same old story from the top, and I catch a glint of my laptop on the kitchen counter, calling to me. I should pull the trigger on those dresses. The last thing I remember doing with a clear head is thinking about pulling the trigger.

In the morning, in bed with only my pants on, fragments come back. Sarah talking about how some event came right before her 'promotion'; how some argument between her and her other friend was when they both got their 'promotions'; the slug in my gut swirling around, gurgling things to me about 'promotions' and a secret voice whispering to me that I am not going to get a promotion, that my promotion is the one that should be in quotation marks.

Sarah talking about her fabled student loans again while I pulled the trigger on some new dresses for my new lifestyle.

Some garbage stories about people I don't know, flaccid pickings at gossip, rote monologue, hollow martyrdom. Little digs. Everyone taking little digs.

A pounding in my head like something wants out. A memory of how I wanted today to feel, that memory transposed on top of what's really happening: not getting calm pancakes with Sarah, but hating her deeply, blindly, a barfy feeling as I'm still trying to make the dream possible: still might finish my cleaning project, still might sign up for that yoga class, still might, still might. I step into the shower and almost faint, an image of taking the day by the throat and bashing its head against the wall floating in my mind.

Some hours pass. I put on a coat and other necessary winter gear and leave my apartment. The sun is shining even though it's incredibly cold. I go to the park across the street where the high school has its gym classes. I walk the concrete path around the park, lined with trees, circling a small baseball field, a basketball court, a defunct community garden. As I walk I feel like the scenery is coming at me, rather than me walking through it. I can barely feel my body moving, trees coming at me, feeling the 3D space, a gray stumpy tree shifting and gliding past me, movie-theater roller coaster, rounding the corner of the track, watching the garages, back porches, dumpsters, wires shift in and out of view. Almost transcendent. Feeling myself finally calming down. Feeling my face relax to the point where I can't even feel my face.

I see a dog in the park. I see kids playing on the playground in their puffy coats, parents or maybe nannies on the benches watching, talking.

I walk the track over and over, thinking about my situation. Assessing my life. Where will I go and what will I do?

I almost feel like I'm flying, light and easy.

I walk for maybe forty minutes in this circle, until a woman in a polo shirt with a whistle approaches me, smiling.

'How we doing today?' she asks, and I wonder if it's really that easy to get people to engage with you, if relaxing really is the key to socialization.

'I'm doing well,' I say, not wanting to stop, feeling myself almost try to walk past her, but her stepping in the way of my path, me pivoting, slowing, reluctant.

'So we're doing okay today?' she asks, again, the tone in her voice has force, I recognize it as malevolent almost immediately. I start to get nervous.

'Yeah, we're doing fine today.' Haha.

'Been doing a little bit of drinking today, maybe?' she asks.

'Drinking? Oh, no, for sure not. I'm just clearing my head, going on a walk in the park,' I say. Then, like maybe it will make a difference, I point over my shoulder and say, 'I live right there.'

'Seems like you've been walking around in circles and stumbling a bit for almost the past hour,' she says. I notice a family in the playground behind her. The son throwing a lackluster snowball, his puffed suit moving unnaturally, his mother watching with tight lips. I know she did this to me. Fuck you, I think. Fuck you.

'Stumbling, I'm not sure,' I say. 'I had a long, stressful week at work, and I'm just getting some exercise.' It sounds completely reasonable to me, as it comes out. The intonation is perfect. If we were on the phone, with this kind of intonation, this kind of diction, I could get her to give me her checking account number, maybe some health details, depending on context.

But we're not on the phone, and the context here is clear: she, in a white thermal under a baby-blue Chicago Parks District polo, a whistle and keycard lanyard, and those noisy kinds of jogging pants, fogged breath coming out of her, a tight, unforgiving braid almost at the crown of her head, and me in my brown men's overcoat with the lining hanging out the bottom, sweatpants and cheap snow boots – though I would think she might respond to the sweats, find some affinity there – and my hair still clearly uncombed and freezing in parts from my shower even though it's mostly underneath my dollar-store stocking cap. The context is clear. If only I still had my glasses. It's amazing what a person can get away with when wearing glasses.

I imagine her getting a walkie-talkie call about me – the creepy stumbling man/woman – and looking down at me from her window in the field house, and deciding that she was going to just nip it, just come down here and take me out, get 'er done, as they say, and then her hustling down the stairs, body in full motion, a little articulation of the elbows, a little pneumatic pump of the arms. Nothing really that my ultra-smooth cadence can do to convince her of my innocence in the matter.

'Well, maybe you want to get your exercise somewhere else, and you can come back to the park when you're feeling better.'

'I'm feeling fine, miss,' I say, 'but I also don't want to cause any trouble'. The feeling of relaxation in my body is so profound as I say this that I almost start laughing. I feel light. I feel that it would not be completely out of the realm of possibility for me to daintily raise my hand and give this park ranger a cupped and not too hard slow-motioned slap across her face.

I find it odd that neither of us is leaving and neither of us is talking, and it makes me smile.

'Oh, yes, right,' I say, remembering that I'm the one who is supposed to leave. She works here. I think toodle-oo, but don't say it, and I walk off towards Augusta, the opposite direction of my apartment. Possibly she thinks I was lying about living nearby, but this is one of those small things that everyone is always encouraging everyone else not to worry about too much – who cares what she thinks of my apartment? Her mention of alcohol does make me want to stop by the local winery for a bottle of their finest, but maybe I should take a hawt bawth instead, what do you think, Chancellor? Oh, Madame, a hawt bawth would be lovely, but I do on occasion wonder if you'll be lonely tending to your own bawth. Will you not be there with me to draw it, sir? Ah, Madame, I would be if it were now, but so many things can happen between the promenade and m'lady's bawth, that promises cannot be made, and wishes might be left unfulfilled.

A light snow begins to fall, little pieces of it kissing my cheeks, my lips, sweet lover, in my hair, cooling my anxiety sweat, making the wetness of my socks in these boots with the hole a little more festive. I take a deep breath, imagining it filling up my brain, then chest, then stomach, and I let it out through my mouth.

The liquor store isn't open yet. I walk aimlessly a while longer, between that space where it would be a gift from the sweet Lord Jesus to run into someone I knew and get some spiced hot cider, and it being the worst because I'm not wearing underwear and didn't brush my teeth because I was afraid of the taste of the water. Aimless, giddy dread fills me. I could swoon. I remember that my new clothes arrive on Thursday, and I say, 'Oh, well that's nice,' out loud, to no one. ■

Courtesy of the author

EMMA CLINE

1989

Emma Cline is the author of *The Girls*, shortlisted for the 2016 Center for Fiction First Novel Prize, the 2016 John Leonard Prize from the National Book Critics Circle and the 2016 *LA Times* Book Prize. She was awarded the 2014 *Paris Review* Plimpton Prize for her story 'Marion'.

LOS ANGELES

Emma Cline

It was only November but holiday decorations were already starting to creep into the store displays: cutouts of Santa wearing sunglasses, windows poxed with fake snow, as if cold was just another joke. It hadn't even rained since Alice moved here, the good weather holding. Back in her hometown, it was already grim and snowy, the sun behind her mother's house setting by 5 p.m. This new city seemed like a fine alternative, the ceaseless blue sky and bare arms, the days passing frictionless and lovely. Of course, in a few years, when the reservoirs were empty and the lawns turned brown, she'd realize that there was no such thing as unending sunshine.

The employee entrance was around the back of the store, in an alley. This was before the lawsuits, when the brand was still popular and opening new stores. They sold cheap, slutty clothes in primary colors, clothes invoking a low-level athleticism – tube socks, track shorts – as if sex was an alternative sport. Alice worked at a flagship store, which meant it was bigger and busier, on a high-visibility corner near the ocean. People tracked in sand and sometimes beach tar that the cleaners had to scrub off the floors at the end of the night.

Employees were only allowed to wear the brand's clothes, so Alice had gotten some for free when she started. Emptying the bag on her bed, she had been stirred by the pure abundance, but there was an awful caveat: her manager had picked them out, and everything was a little too tight, a size too small. The pants cut into her crotch and left red marks on her stomach in the exact outline of the zipper, the shirts creasing tight in her underarms. She left her pants undone on the drive to work, waiting until the last minute to suck in her stomach and button them up.

Inside, the store was bright white and shiny, a low-level hum in the background from the neon signs. It was like being inside a computer. She got there at 10 a.m. but already the lights and the music conjured a perpetual afternoon. On every wall were blown-up photographs in grainy black and white of women in the famous underpants, girls with knobby knees making eye contact with the camera, covering their small breasts with their hands. All the models' hair looked a little greasy, their faces a little shiny. Alice supposed that was to make sex with them seem more likely.

Only young women worked the floor – the guys stayed in the back room, folding, unpacking and tagging shipments from the warehouse, managing stock. They had nothing to offer beyond their plain labor. It was the girls that management wanted out in front, girls who acted as shorthand to the entire brand. They roamed the floor in quadrants, wedging fingers between hangers to make sure items were hung at an equal distance, kicking dropped shirts out from under the partitions, hiding a leotard smeared with lipstick.

Before they put the clothes on the racks, they had to steam them, trying to reanimate the sheen of value. The first time Alice had opened a box of T-shirts from the warehouse, seeing the clothes there, all stuffed and flattened together in a cube without tags or prices, made their real worth suddenly clear – this was junk, all of it.

At her interview, Alice had brought a résumé, which she'd made some effort to print out at a copy store. She had also purchased a folder to transport the résumé intact but no one ever asked to see it. John, the manager, had barely asked about her employment history. At the end of their five-minute conversation, he instructed her to stand against a blank wall and took her picture with a digital camera.

'If you could just smile a little,' John said, and she did.

They sent the pictures to corporate for approval, Alice later discovered. If you made the cut, whoever did your interview got a $200 bonus.

Alice fell into an easy rhythm at her post. Feeding hanger after hanger onto the racks. Taking clothes from the hands of strangers, directing them to a fitting room that she had to open with a key on a lanyard around her wrist, the mildest of authorities. Her mind was glazing over, not unpleasantly, thoughts swimmy and hushed. She'd get paid tomorrow, which was good – rent was due in a week, plus a payment on her loans. Her room was cheap, at least, though the apartment, shared with four housemates, was disgusting. Alice's room wasn't so bad only because there was nothing in it – her mattress still on the floor, though she'd lived there for three months.

The store was empty for a while, one of the strange lulls that followed no logical pattern, until a father came in, pulled by his teenage daughter. He hovered at a wary distance while his daughter snatched up garment after garment. She handed him a sweatshirt, and the man read the price aloud, looking to Alice like it was her fault.

'It's just a plain sweatshirt,' he said.

The daughter was embarrassed, Alice could tell, and she smiled at the father, bland but also forgiving, trying to communicate the sense that some things in this world were intractable. It was true that the clothes were overpriced. Alice could never have bought them herself. And the daughter's expression was recognizable from her own adolescence, her mother's constant commentary on the price of everything. The time they went to a restaurant for her brother's eighth-grade graduation, a restaurant with a menu illuminated with some kind of LED lights, and her mother couldn't help murmuring the prices aloud, trying to guess what the bill might be. Nothing could pass without being parsed and commented upon.

When the father relented and bought two pairs of leggings, the sweatshirt, and a metallic dress, Alice understood he had only been pretending to be put off by the prices. The daughter had never considered the possibility that she might not get what she wanted, and whatever solidarity Alice felt with the father dissipated as she watched the numbers add up on the register, the man handing her his credit card without even waiting to hear the total.

Oona worked Saturdays, too. She was seventeen, only a little younger than Alice's brother, but Henry seemed like he was from a different species. He was ruddy-cheeked, his beard trimmed to a skinny strap along his chin. A strange mix of perversity – the background on his phone a big-titted porn star – alongside a real boyishness. He made popcorn on the stove most nights, adored and replayed a song whose lyrics he happily chanted, 'Build Me Up Buttercup', his face young and sweet.

Oona would eat Henry alive, Oona with her black chokers and lawyer parents, her private school where she played lacrosse and took a class in Islamic art. She was easy and confident, already well versed in her own beauty. It was strange how good-looking teenagers were these days, so much more attractive than the teenagers Alice and her friends had been. Somehow these new teenagers all knew how to groom their eyebrows. The pervs loved Oona – the men who came in alone, lured by the advertisements, the young women who worked the floor dressed in the promised leotards and skirts. The men lingered too long, performing a dramatic contemplation of a white T-shirt, carrying on loud phone calls. They wanted to be noticed.

The first time it seemed like one of those men had cornered Oona, Alice pulled her away for an imaginary task in the back. But Oona just laughed at Alice – she didn't mind the men, and they often bought armfuls of the clothes, Oona marching them to the cash register like a cheerful candy-striper. They got commission on everything.

Oona had been asked by corporate to shoot some ads, for which she would receive no money, only more free clothes. She really wanted to do it, she told Alice, but her mom wouldn't sign the release form. Oona wanted to be an actress. The sad fact of this city: the thousands of actresses with their thousands of efficiency apartments and teeth-whitening strips, the energy generated by thousands of treadmill hours and beach runs, energy dissipating into nothingness. Maybe Oona wanted to be an actress for the same reason Alice did: because other people told them they should be. It was one of the traditional possibilities for a pretty girl, everyone urging the pretty girl not to waste her prettiness, to put it to good use. As if prettiness was a natural resource, a responsibility you had to see all the way through.

Acting classes were the only thing Alice's mother had agreed to help pay for. Maybe it was important to her mother to feel Alice was achieving, moving forward, and completing classes had the sheen of building blocks, tokens being collected, no matter if they had no visible use. Her mother sent a check every month, and sometimes there was a cartoon from the Sunday paper she'd torn out and enclosed, though never any note.

Alice's teacher was a former actor now in his well-preserved fifties. Tony was blond and tan and required a brand of personal devotion Alice found aggressive. The class was held in a big room with hardwood floors, folding chairs stacked against the wall. The students padded around in their socks, their feet giving off a humid, private smell. Tony set out different kinds of tea and the students studied the boxes, choosing one with great ceremony. Get Calm, Nighty Night, Power Aid, teas whose very names implied effort and virtue. They held their mugs with both hands, inhaling in an obvious way; everyone wanted to enjoy their tea more than anyone else enjoyed theirs. While they took turns acting out various scenes and engaging in various exercises, repeating nonsense back and forth, Tony watched from a folding chair and ate his lunch: stabbing at wet lettuce leaves in a plastic bowl, chasing an edamame with his fork.

Every morning in Alice's email, an inspirational quote from Tony popped up:

DO OR DO NOT. THERE IS NO TRY.

FRIENDS ARE GIFTS WE GIVE OURSELVES.

Alice had tried, multiple times, to get off the email list. Emailing the studio manager, and finally Tony himself, but still the quotes came. That morning's quote:

> REACH FOR THE MOON. IF YOU FALL SHORT, YOU MAY JUST LAND ON A STAR!

It seemed shameful that Alice recognized celebrities, but she did. A stutter in her glance, a second look – she could identify them almost right away as famous, even if she didn't know their names. There was some familiarity in the way their features were put together, a gravitational pull. Alice could identify even the C-list actors, their faces taking up space in her brain without any effort on her part.

A woman came into the store that afternoon who wasn't an actor, but was married to one: an actor who was very famous, beloved even though he was milk-faced and not attractive. The wife was plain, too. A jewelry designer. This fact came to Alice in the same sourceless way as the woman's name. She wore rings on most fingers, a silver chain with a slip of metal dangling between her breasts. Alice figured the jewelry was of her own design, and imagined this woman, this jewelry designer, driving in the afternoon sunshine, deciding to come into the store, the day just another asset available to her.

Alice moved towards the woman, even though she was technically in Oona's quadrant.

'Let me know if I can help you find anything,' Alice said.

The woman looked up, her plain face searching Alice's. She seemed to understand that Alice recognized her, and that Alice's offer of help, already false, was doubly false. The woman said nothing. She just went back to idly flipping through the swimsuit separates. And Alice, still smiling, made a swift and unkind catalog of every unattractive thing about the woman – the dry skin around her nostrils, her weak chin, her sturdy legs in their expensive jeans.

Alice ate an apple for lunch, tilting her face up to feel the thin sun on her forehead and cheeks. She couldn't see the ocean, but she could see where the buildings started to dissipate along the coast, the spindly tops of the palms that lined the boardwalk. The apple was okay, bright and clean-fleshed, slightly sour. She threw the core into the hydrangea bushes below the deck. It was her whole lunch: there was something nice about the way her stomach would tighten around its own emptiness afterwards, how it made the day slightly sharper.

Oona came out on the back porch for her break, smoking one of John's cigarettes. She had cadged one for Alice, too. Alice knew she was a little old to take this much pleasure in Oona, but she didn't care. There was an easy, mild rapport between them, a sense of resigned camaraderie, the shared limits of the job alleviating any larger concerns about where Alice's life was going. High school was probably the last time Alice had smoked cigarettes with any regularity. She didn't talk to any of those people anymore, beyond tracking the engagement photos that surfaced online, photos taken on the railroad tracks during the golden hour. Worse: the ones taken on the shores of a lake or in front of sunsets, photos name-dropping the natural world, the plain, dull beauty of the shore. Children followed soon after, babies curled like shrimp on fur rugs.

'It was the guy,' Oona was telling her. 'With the black hair.'

Alice tried to remember if she'd noticed any particular man. None stood out.

He'd come in that afternoon, Oona said. Had tried to buy her underwear. Oona laughed when she saw Alice's face.

'It's hilarious,' Oona said, dreamily combing her long bangs out of her eyes with her fingers. 'You should look online, it's a whole thing.'

'He asked you to email him or something?'

'Uh, no,' Oona said. 'More like, he said, "I'll give you fifty bucks to go into the bathroom right now and take off your underwear and give them to me." '

The upset that Alice expected to find in Oona's face wasn't there –

not even a trace. If anything, she was giddy, and that's when Alice understood.

'You didn't do it?'

Oona smiled, darting a look at Alice, and Alice's stomach dropped with an odd mix of worry and jealousy, an uncertainty about who exactly had been tricked. Alice started to say something, then stopped. She moved a silver ring around her finger, the cigarette burning itself out.

'Why?' Alice said.

Oona laughed. 'Come on, you've done these things. You know.'

Alice settled back against the railing. 'Aren't you worried he might do something weird? Follow you home or something?'

Oona seemed disappointed. 'Oh, please,' she said, and started doing a leg exercise, going briskly up on her toes. 'I wish someone would stalk me.'

Alice's mother didn't want to pay for acting classes anymore. 'But I'm getting better,' Alice said to her mother over the phone.

Was she? She didn't know. Tony made them throw a ball back and forth as they said their lines. He made them walk around the room leading from their sternum, then from their pelvis. Alice had finished Level One, and Level Two was more expensive but it met twice a week plus a once-monthly private session with Tony.

'I don't see how this class is different than the one you just took.'

'It's more advanced,' Alice said. 'It's more intensive.'

'Maybe it's okay to take a break for a while,' her mother said. 'See how much you really want this.'

How to explain – if Alice wasn't taking a class, if she wasn't otherwise engaged, that meant her terrible job, her terrible apartment, suddenly carried more weight, maybe started to matter. The thought was too much to consider squarely.

'I'm pulling into the driveway,' her mother said. 'Miss you.'

'You too.'

There was only a moment when all the confused, thwarted love locked up her throat. And then the moment passed, and Alice was alone again on her bed. Better to hurtle along, to quickly occupy her brain with something else. She went to the kitchen, opening a bag of frozen berries that she ate with steady effort until her fingers were numb, until a chill had penetrated deeply into her stomach and she had to get up and put on her winter coat. She moved to catch the sunshine where it warmed the kitchen chair.

There were countless ads online, Oona had been right, and that night Alice lost an hour clicking through them, thinking how ludicrous people were. You pressed slightly on the world and it showed its odd corners, revealed its dim and helpless desires. It seemed insane at first. And then, like other jokes, it became curiously possible the more she referred to it in her own mind, the uncomfortable edges softening into something innocuous.

The underwear was cotton and black and poorly made. Alice took them from work – easy enough to secrete away a stack from the warehouse shipment before it got entered into inventory or had any tags on. John was supposed to check everyone's bags on the way out, the whole line of employees shuffling past him with their purses gaping, but he usually just waved them through. Like most things, it was frightening the first time and then became rote.

It didn't happen all that often, maybe twice a week. The meetings were always in public places: a chain coffee shop, the parking lot of a gym. There was a young guy who bragged about having some kind of security clearance and wrote to her from multiple email accounts. A fat hippie with tinted glasses who brought her a copy of his self-published novel. A man in his sixties who shorted Alice ten bucks. She didn't have any interaction beyond handing them the underwear, sealed in a Ziploc and then stuffed in a paper bag, like someone's forgotten lunch. A few of the men lingered, but no one ever pushed. It wasn't so bad. It was that time of life when anytime something bad or strange or sordid happened, she could soothe herself with that forgiving promise: it's just that time of life. When you thought of it that way, whatever mess she was in seemed already sanctioned.

Oona invited her to the beach on their free Sunday. One of her friends had a house on the water and was having a barbecue. When Alice pushed open the door, the party was already going – music on the speakers and liquor bottles on the table, a girl feeding orange after orange into a whirring juicer. The house was sunny and big, the ocean below segmented by the windows into squares of mute glitter.

She was uncomfortable until she caught sight of Oona, in a one-piece swimsuit and cutoffs. Oona grabbed her by the hand. 'Come meet everyone,' she said, and Alice felt a wave of goodwill for Oona, the sweet girl.

Porter lived in the house, the son of some producer, and was older than everyone else – maybe even older than Alice. It seemed like he and Oona were together, his arm slung around her, Oona burrowing happily into his side. He had lank hair and a pitbull with a pink collar. He bent down to let the dog lick him on the mouth; Alice saw their tongues touch briefly.

When Oona held up her phone to take a picture, the girl who was manning the juicer lifted her shirt to flash one small breast. Alice blanched, and Oona laughed.

'You're embarrassing Alice,' she said to the girl. 'Stop being such a slut.'

'I'm fine,' Alice said, and willed it so.

When Oona handed her a glass of the orange-juice drink, she drained it fast, the acid brightening her mouth and her throat.

The ocean was too cold for swimming but the sun felt nice. Alice had eaten one greasy hamburger from the grill, some kind of fancy cheese on top that she scraped off and threw into an aloe plant. She stretched out on one of the towels from the house. Oona's towel was vacant – she was down by the water, kicking in the frigid waves. Music drifted from the patio. Alice didn't see Porter until he flopped down on Oona's towel. He was balancing a pack of cigarettes on a plastic container of green olives, a beer in his other hand.

'Can I have a cigarette?' she said.

The pack he handed to her had a cartoon character on it, some writing in Spanish.

'Is it even legal to have cartoon characters on cigarettes?' she said, but Porter was already on his stomach, his face pressed into the towel. She palmed the pack back and forth, eyeing Porter's pale back. He wasn't even a little handsome.

Alice adjusted her bikini straps. They were digging into her shoulders, leaving marks. She surveyed the indifferent group back on the patio, Porter's prone body, and decided to take her top off. She chickened her arms behind herself and unhooked her bikini, hunching over so that it fell off her breasts into her lap. She was having fun, wasn't she? She folded the top into her bag as calmly as she could, sinking back onto the towel. The air and heat on her breasts were even and constant, and she let herself feel pleased and languid, happy with the picture she made.

Alice woke with Porter grinning at her.

'European-style, huh?' he said.

How long had he been watching her?

Porter offered her his beer. 'I barely had any, if you want it. I can get another.'

She shook her head.

He shrugged and took a long drink. Oona was walking down by the shoreline, the ocean foaming thin around her ankles. 'I hate those one-pieces she wears,' Porter said.

'She looks great.'

'She's embarrassed about her tits,' Porter said.

Alice gave him a sickly smile, and pushed her sunglasses back up her nose, crossing her arms over her chest in the least obvious way she could manage. They both turned at a commotion further down the sand – some stranger had made his way to this private beach. The man seemed a little crazy, gray-haired, wearing a suit jacket. Probably homeless. She squinted: there was an iguana on his shoulder.

'What the fuck?' Porter said, laughing.

The man stopped one of Oona's friends and then moved on to another one.

Porter brushed sand from his palms. 'I'm going inside.'

The man was now approaching Oona.

Alice looked toward Porter but he was already heading back, unconcerned.

The man was saying something to Oona, something detailed. Alice didn't know if she was supposed to do something. But soon enough the man moved away from Oona and was now heading toward Alice. She hurried her bikini top back on.

'Want to take a picture?' the man asked. 'One dollar.' The iguana was ridged and ancient-looking and when the man shook his shoulder in a practiced way, the iguana bobbed up and down, its jowls beating like a heart.

The last time she ever did it, the man wanted to meet at 4 p.m. in the parking lot of the big grocery store in Alice's neighborhood. It was a peculiar time of day, that sad hour when the dark seems to rise up from the ground but the sky is still bright and blue. The shadows of the bushes against the houses were getting deeper and starting to merge with the shadows of the trees. She wore cotton shorts and a plain sweatshirt from work, not even bothering to look nice. Her eyes were a little pink from her contacts, a rosy wash on the whites that made it look like she'd been crying.

She walked the ten blocks to the parking lot, the light hovering in the tangle of blackberry vines that crawled up the alleyways. Even the cheapo apartment buildings were lovely at that hour, their faded colors subtle and European. She passed the nicer homes, catching slivers of their lush backyards through the slats of the high fences, the koi ponds swishy with fish. Some nights she walked around the neighborhood, near the humid rim of the reservoir. It was a pleasure to see inside those nighttime houses. Each one like a primer on being human, on what choices you might make. As if life might follow the course of your wishes. A piano lesson she had once watched, the repeated scales, a girl with a meaty braid down her back. The houses where TVs spooked the windows.

Alice checked her phone – she was a few minutes early. Other shoppers were pushing carts back into jangled place, the automatic doors sliding open and open. She lingered on an island in the lot, watching the cars. She checked her phone again. Her little brother had texted: a smiley face. He had never left their home state, which made her obliquely sad.

When a tan sedan pulled into the lot, she could tell by the way the car slowed and bypassed an open space that it was the man looking for her.

Alice waved, foolishly, and the man pulled up next to her. The passenger window was down so she could see his face, though she still had to stoop to make eye contact. The man was bland-looking, wearing a fleece half-zip pullover and khakis. Like someone's husband, though Alice noticed no ring. He had signed his emails *Mark* but hadn't realized or maybe didn't care that his email address identified him as Brian.

The car looked immaculate until she caught sight of clothes in the backseat and a mail carton and a few soda bottles tipped on their side. It occurred to her that perhaps this man lived in his car. He seemed impatient, no matter that they had both gotten here early. He sighed, performing his own inconvenience. She had a paper bag with the underwear inside the Ziploc.

'Should I just –' she started to hand the bag to him.

'Get in,' he interrupted, reaching over to pop the passenger door. 'Just for a second.'

Alice hesitated but not as long as she should have. She ducked in, shutting the door behind her. Who would try to kidnap someone at 4 p.m? In a busy parking lot? In the midst of all this unyielding sunshine?

'There,' the man said when Alice was sitting beside him, like now he was satisfied. His hands landed briefly on the steering wheel, then hovered at his chest. He seemed afraid to look at her.

She tried to imagine how she would spin this story to Oona on Saturday. It was easy to predict – she would describe the man as older and uglier than he was, adopting a tone of incredulous contempt. She and Oona were used to telling each other stories like this, to dramatizing incidents so that everything took on an ironic, comical tone, their lives a series of encounters that happened to them but never really affected them, at least in the retelling, their personas unflappable and all-seeing. When she'd had sex with John that one time after work, she heard her future self narrating the whole thing to Oona – how his penis was thin and jumpy and how he couldn't come so he finally rolled out and worked his own dick with efficient, lonely habit. It had been bearable because it would become a story, something condensed and communicable. Even funny.

Alice put the bag on the console between herself and the man. He looked at the bag from the corner of his eye, a look that was maybe purposefully restrained, like he was proving he didn't care too much about its contents. No matter that he had found himself in a parking lot in the unforgiving clarity of mid-afternoon to buy someone's underwear.

The man took the bag but didn't, as she feared, open it in front of her. He tucked it in the pocket of his side door. When he turned back to her, she sensed his disgust – not for himself, but for her. She no longer served a purpose, and every moment she stayed in the car was just another moment that reminded him of his own weakness. It occurred to her that he might do some harm to her. Even here. She looked out the windshield at the cars beyond, the trees. It would be dinner time at her mother's house. Her mother steaming rice in a bag and putting out placemats that easily wiped clean. Asking Henry if he had a good movie in mind for after dinner. Henry loved documentaries about Hitler or particularly exotic animals. It suddenly seemed nice to load the dishwasher and wish for small things.

'Can I have the money?' she said, her voice going too high.

A look of pain fleeted across his face. He took out his wallet with great effort.

'We said sixty?'

'Seventy-five,' she said, 'that's what you said in the email. Seventy-five.'

His hesitation allowed her to hate him, fully, to watch with cold eyes as he counted out the bills. Why hadn't he done this ahead of time? He probably wanted her to witness this, Mark or Brian or whoever he was, believing that he was shaming or punishing her by prolonging the encounter, making sure she fully experienced the transaction, bill by bill. When he had seventy-five dollars, he held the money in her direction, just out of reach so Alice had to make an effort to grab for it. He smiled, like she had confirmed something.

When she told Oona the story on Saturday, Alice would leave this part out: how, when she tried to open the car door, the door was locked.

How the man said, 'Whoops,' his voice swerving high, 'whoops-a-daisy.' He went to press the unlock button, but Alice was still grabbing at the door handle, frantic, her heart clanging in her chest.

'Relax,' he said. 'Stop pulling or it won't unlock.'

Alice was certain, suddenly, that she was trapped, that great violence was coming to her. Who would feel bad for her? She had done this to herself.

'Just stop,' the man said. 'You're only making it worse.' ■

Courtesy of the author

JOSHUA COHEN

1980

Joshua Cohen was born in Atlantic City and now lives in New York. His books include the novels *Book of Numbers*, *Witz*, *A Heaven of Others*, *Cadenza for the Schneidermann Violin Concerto*, a collection of short fiction, *Four New Messages*, and *Attention! A (Short) History*. *Moving Kings*, from which 'Uri' has been adapted, will be published by Random House in the summer of 2017.

URI

Joshua Cohen

Kivsa Brigade, Akavish Battalion, Tziraah Company, Platoon Bet, Squad Bet – the Death Alley Ewes, the Heroes of Shujaiyeh, the Martyrs of Salah al-Din Road – wasn't a special unit, just a specialish unit, not elite, but elite enough. Nothing about them made sense. Take, for instance, their name, which they'd regarded as a joke – that they were referred to as ewes, or frail female lambs – until they went into combat and the joke, like sheep's milk, went sour. They were infantry, after all, so it was difficult not to feel like sacrificial bleaters, fleecy soldiers who'd been sent off to slaughter.

Kivsa, Akavish, Tziraah.

Ewe, Spider, Wasp.

The source of this, their full unit designation, was to be found in Torah and in other venerably tedious books that were like Torah, whose legends had been introduced to them by an old – but a forty-something-year-old – veteran on the very first day of their training. It's strange, how your only religious training can come from the army . . . how your only religion can be the army . . .

> Once there was a young shepherd boy who, because he understood everything, had been chosen by God to become the next king of Israel. This boy understood

everything except why God had created the spider and why God had created the wasp. The spider weaved webs for itself but nothing for man. The wasp was not a bee and so didn't even make honey.

God counseled the boy to have patience.

And so one day this young shepherd who would be king found himself pursued by the army of the king before him. Desperate to elude capture, he ran into a cave, and just as the army approached, God sent a spider to spin its silks over the mouth of the cave, to conceal him, and so the shepherd was spared.

Later, the shepherd retaliated by raiding the enemy camp, only to be apprehended and dragged to the tent of the general. But just as he was about to be executed, God sent a wasp to sting the general, who hopped around and shrieked like a woman, and so the shepherd who would be king ran away.

To serve in a unit that bore the name of the ewes of the shepherd king, and of his spider and wasp, was supposed to be inspirational.

But the only lesson they ever took from their naming was this: they were creatures created for a single purpose, a woolly clumsy freakish creature with an excess of bristly limbs and just one measly stinger going dull through overuse.

They were useless until they were necessary.

Their unit's insignia, their official patch, was a shepherd's staff, or crook, as if to symbolize how they'd been herded together out of a number of totally unrelated and disorganized flocks. Their unofficial song was 'Dimona Party' by DJ Skazka, featuring Avram Kaplansky. Their motto was: Thou art the men. Though they never used that and instead came up with their own: Useless until necessary.

Or, until they were discharged. Until they were redeployed, or had redeployed themselves, but as civilians.

Because this was what they did, what most of them did: they left.

The moment their stints were up, they left the land they'd defended – the land they'd been conscripted by, and so it was never much of a choice, their defense.

After having served the State of Israel for thirty-six months, or 144 weeks, or 1,008 days, they exchanged their drabs for denims, beat their munitions into passports, and shipped beyond the sea to find their fortunes. To find themselves, or the selves they'd been, and to forget the commands that bound them.

Historically, of course, that had always been the function of exile, or diaspora. Wandering was just an emergency measure: the Jews would dwell in a country until that country expelled them, or tried to destroy them, and then they'd have to flee.

But the soldiers of Kivsa/Akavish/Tziraah/Bet/Bet weren't Jewish, or weren't exclusively Jewish – they were also, primarily, Israeli, which meant they just served their compulsory tours in their nation's armed forces until they were at liberty to book tickets abroad. All the fit, tanned, twenty-one-year-old vets who could afford it, or whose families could afford it, would mark the conclusion of their military service by going on a holiday that ever since First Lebanon – their parents' last war – had come to feel as compulsory as that service itself, as if vacationing were merely war's covert continuation, an undercover mission camouflaged in sportsgear.

And though backpacking between the better hostels of East Asia will never be as dangerous as bulldozing hovels in the West Bank, there was still the chance of not coming back, or not coming back alive.

They were in Kathmandu and drunk on rice, stumbling through the earthquake rubble.

They were in Patan, where they bought this stinky local leaf that didn't fuck them up the way they'd been promised that it would fuck them up, and when they brought what was left of it back to the old non-combatant man who'd sold it to them, he put up his hands and showed with a smack of his toothless mouth: don't smoke, chew.

They were in Pokhara, where they bumped into a bivouac of guys from border patrol, who despite being border patrol knew their way around, and took them to visit whores who knew how to say all the nasty shit that can't be said in Hebrew and how to do all the nasty shit that can't be done by Jews, and two of the guys – not their guys, the other guys – told the girls that they were virgins, but the truth was that four of them were virgins, and for an extra 5,000 rupees, roughly 180 shekels, condoms weren't required.

The girls had a misguided trust in the circumcised.

They were up in the Himalayas and marching, they were hiking, and the flatness steepened, and the steepness flattened, and they settled into a count. Everything had been planned like it used to be, except that now they'd planned it for themselves: they'd mapped everything out, set their own mealtimes and rest times, the kilometers to cover, decided the alternate routes, deferring to one another by specialty and rank, but then the elevation and landscape changed so that no specialties applied and the ranks fell away like a boulder. The mountains seemed no closer. The mountains seemed cut out of the sky. They went ahead in formation, single file in the narrows, becoming partnered again as the ways went wide, vigilant for the slightest disturbance, a hostile blur or rustle. Thorong La would be theirs by Shabbat, the Annapurna Massif would be in their hands, and they'd plant their flag at the peak of the pass, claiming everything unto the Tibetan plateau in the name of Pvt Shlomo 'Shlo' Regev, who'd been hit in the face by a mortar near the Erez border crossing – in Gaza.

After their discharge, some of Kivsa/Akavish/Tziraah/Bet/Bet stuck together, some struck out on their own:

Avi went to Mexico, to export electronics. Binyamin went to Canada, to import electronics. Yaniv was trekking the Amazon. Chaim was living with a paddleboard in Thailand, or with a sailboard in Cambodia, or dwelling homeless and shoeless like a monk in Vietnam, weaving baskets out of bamboo just for the therapy – he was like a loose reed himself, blown along the coast between Hanoi and Ho Chi Minh.

And Micki's conquering Paris, Amir's laying siege to Berlin. Moti and Dani are storming Warsaw, having left Cracow in smoldering ruins.

Uri, meanwhile, was sitting around in his childhood bedroom in Israel just jerking it.

Rather, he was devoting all of his considerable energies to not jerking it, to keeping his hands off his cock – because at any moment one or two or three of his older sisters might come crashing through the door in storms of wet hair and nails – to check on him, to call him for meals, to ask him about their hair, nails, outfits, and boys as pretexts for checking on him, to nag him about his own romantic prospects now that everything with Batya Neder was in absolute collapse – 'That girl was like a wall,' they liked to say, 'no curves' – giving him advice but no privacy, never any peace . . .

Such were . . . *ha'uvdot b'shetach*, 'the facts on the ground': that Uri was still grounded in Israel, that he was living again with his family and unable to relocate out of a lack of imagination or shekels or both, that he was in the process of cutting himself off from his only friends, his squadmates, out of the shame of being the only one of them to have left the army with no education arranged, no employment set up, and headaches that the miracle rabbi his mother would send him to – that even the Psycholog his sisters would send him to, unbeknownst to their mother, who wouldn't have approved – would dismiss as every bit as psychosomatic as his dreams. Which wouldn't stop the dreams, or make them taper, or deny their legitimacy, their truth.

Even Rotem, who'd lost his legs and was in a wheelchair, would wheel himself to their monthly squad reunions. Even Dror would show, despite his oxygen tank, for which he'd quit smoking, for which he'd quit drinking.

Uri was the only one missing, the only one who'd skip. He was too busy not returning their emails, having anger issues, putting fists through walls, mortaring closet doors, bare-knuckled. His parents had been whispering together so he wouldn't understand. Arabic, but a sophisticated dated Arabic, was becoming – as it'd been under the reign of his Moroccan grandparents – the higher language of the house.

His mother had gotten Uncle Peretz, a senior warder in the Israel Prison Service, to get him an interview for the guard program, but he'd missed the deadline to register, and then he'd missed the extended deadline, and since then, his mother's crying. His father had brought him along on a roofing job, but by week's end his dizziness was such that he'd had to step down the ladder and leave, and since then, his father's howling.

Crying and howling were Arabics too, which were still happier than the chastening he got from Batya Neder.

Uri had grown up with Batya and loved her and made the motions of love to her in a field. But because the army requires all men to serve for three years and women for two, she'd already been out for one, and in just that one had managed to leave pitiful Nika for Tel Aviv, enroll in a computer academy on a scholarship, get recruited by a man to join his firm, which developed or just adapted apps, and – don't think about it – to share the man's apartment, his duplex.

The Batya Uri had known had been a pretty athletic Teimaniyah (Yemenite), not a sedentary coder. She must've picked up that computing interest in the army (in Intelligence), and yet she'd never mentioned it in all the txts she'd sent, the fewer and fewer txts, or on any of the brief occasions their leaves coincided. He'd also never known her to hang up on him. Their last conversation he'd tried to stay on non-erotic terms, which she'd initiated. She'd been filling him in on her life, but that single word, or the fact that he hadn't recognized that word and had asked her to repeat it, and then had asked her to explain it, and she'd laughed, had set him off into a rage. It wasn't even Hebrew, or it hadn't been until Batya and others like her had made it Hebrew: duplex.

'What do you mean – others like me?' she'd said.

Others like people who go to co-ed computer academies. Or people who cohabitate with their instructors and speak fancy languages and make fancy salaries and have copious oral sex at artistic parties in Tel Aviv.

'You'd better get out of Nika,' she'd said.

Nika was a dusty moshav halfway between Kiryat Gat and Beer-Sheva and so halfway between nowhere and not quite somewhere. The place barely existed and yet was impossible to leave. This was because it was laid out in a concentric circling, like a target's roundel or the cross-haired reticle of a telescopic sight, with roads that compassed around and around and around and never intersected. To get to the bullseye, which was just a runty stucco administrative office that also held pesticides, you had to walk through people's orchards, through people's gardens. Past the outer rim road were the communal fields: the fields that were in every way identical because all-encompassing, or in every way identical because always changing, with crops and clearings appearing and disappearing seasonally, so that to get Batya alone Uri had always had to do some reconnaissance, some fieldwork, and remember the location of a certain cleared space, and hope that it would remain clear for however long it would take him to check the school, or the silos, or the aquifers, for her – for however long it would take him to coax her. He recalled that spring patch where he'd laid Batya down for the first and she'd run away, leaving him to grind into the soil and spew himself, panting. He recalled that autumn patch to which he'd dragged her, a harvest and two acne regimens later, and to which he'd dragged along a blanket and spread it out and spread her out atop it. The blanket was from his bed – he'd rolled her in it, rolled her wrapped in her clothes and then just in her hair. She had tiny hairs on her ass like browned grass. Tiny brown anthill tits but nipples like carob pods. An ant had crawled up from an ear and across a closed eyelid and she'd felt the crawl and wouldn't open up. That blanket they'd used, the same child's blanket that still covered his bed, had remained blue even when the sky itself hadn't and the only indications of all the sweat and time that'd elapsed since then was that the white of its cloud pattern was pilling and her bloodspot had yellowed.

Now he'd just sit with legs wedged under the bed, window shut, curtains drawn, lights off, naked so as to deter any entering sorority, naked except for his stubble (buzzcut growing out, unibrow grown out), aviator sunglasses tangling with his unibrow – and there in that stifling darkness he'd do sit-ups (crunches, bicycle and butterfly and regular). He'd lie, with his feet wedged under the dresser, his feet lifting the dresser to just before the point at which it'd tip and fall atop and crush him. Candidates for guard in the Israel Prison Service had to be able to complete at least fifty regular crunches in a minute or less. Candidates for guard in the Israel Military Prison Service had to complete seventy. Uri was averaging one hundred, and thirty pull-ups (hands in), thirty chin-ups (hands out), sixty-five each of push-ups and crossed-leg push-ups and knuckle push-ups.

Uri would work out until his sisters burst in or he was defeated by sleep. He dreamt of cities and burn wards, of his middle sister Orly sneaking into his room and spraying this rancid green aerosol in his eyes to give him night vision and in his ears to give him night hearing and all over his body to armor it and give him night touch. The way he exercised, it was like he was planning something. He squatted like he dreamt, like a man pursued.

What he was proudest of was that his arm muscles and leg muscles were equally developed and that, when it came to his arms, his biceps and triceps were equally impressive. He hadn't made that common amateur's mistake of neglecting one set of fibers in favor of another and, when adrift in refractory moments, had the tendency to keep a hand on one or the other, left arm or right, biceps or tri, gripping it, pumping it like a flotation device, packing it like a parachute, kneading it like bread.

This was the same process, it turned out, required to stuff and button all his newish bulk into his shirts and pants from before the army. To cram himself into shoes, the type of shoes where you have to wear socks – you have to polish.

Uri had been granted an audience with the Baba Batra, that most famous of diminutive rabbis, or that most diminutive of famous rabbis, depending on whom you asked. It was a privilege you had to dress up for, you had to make a donation. Uri was dreading it, but his mother gave him no choice: she swore by this wonder-working sage who'd brought babies to barren friends, banished a cousin's Armenian fever, and eradicated Tay-Sachs from the family genes. Uri's sisters wished him luck, but tartly, and darted off to class, which meant something different to each of them: cosmetology class, merchandising class, the mall.

Uri's father – a tolerant skeptic who always drove Uri's mother to work, dropping her off first even if his current construction site was closer to home than her tailoring job at a bridal emporium – dropped Uri off at a modernist, but ancient modernist, faith complex in Netivot of six stone tents resembling a vivisected star.

Bustling men in white – asylum orderly but also piously white – passed his cash, his name, and his person down halls, left him sitting, to wait.

There was no one ahead of him, there was no one behind, but still: there was waiting. A condition so chronic, so Messianically anticipant, that its trappings didn't matter. Sometimes you waited at home in your room so demobilized into quiet that you could just about feel the masking tape losing its stick and your mortifying teenaged posters of American movie stars who were 50 percent Jewish and Argentinian-German models who were 100 percent hot, Uri Malmilian (the football striker), Uri Geller (the mentalist), and Ha'Tzanchanim (the Paratroopers), peeling slowly from the walls, and sometimes you waited away from home in a room cluttered up with pews and vociferous copies of *Yom Le'Yom*, *Maariv*, and *National Geographic*, which mocked with all the exotic destinations in which your friends were becoming themselves, or themselves as other people, as bicycle messengers, yoga instructors, contractors in Sudan, pure – and sometimes you waited in no rooms at all, just out in the cold sun, blanking.

He'd waited in yards, in tents, in trailers converted to offices: in line. At the Lishkat Ha'Giyus, the Recruitment Bureau, he'd stood for his physical, a stethoscope cupping his back just below its sole tuft of hair. His face was photographed (no smiling), his teeth were photographed (in case his face got mangled). His fingerprints were taken and then two young Persian women took his damp hands into theirs and one told him to turn to her and he did and the other woman stabbed him and so he turned around to her and the woman who'd spoken stabbed him too, inoculating him against tetanus, meningitis, hepatitis, flu, and trust.

He sat waiting for his haircut, as curls tumbled like desert weeds across the floor and earrings were removed from the people around him, and because the guys doing the shaving and earring removal were fans of a rival team, Hapoel Jerusalem, they joked about eliminating this other guy's Beitar Jerusalem tattoo by skinning him with their razors.

He filled in the bubbles of the psychometric exams, grasping for analogies, grasping at the math. Among mankind's greatest faults is his a) kindness b) generosity c) fortitude d) contentment e) vanity. That was debatable. But the Pythagorean theorem was not, and if the civilian Uri was one side and the soldier Uri was the other, the true him was the hypotenuse, slanted opposite, the squared sum of both.

He waited for his ride to the Bakum, the Induction Base, and waited out the ride, counting the kilometers on his way to playing other games with puzzles, blocks, and balls, which he would've enjoyed except that they kept him away from the sweltry hut he shared with a gang of rowdy arsim – swaggering Mizrahim descended from families like his that'd fled Casablanca, or been tossed out of Algiers, Tunis, Benghazi, and Baghdad and so who hated the Arabs, but in that special covetous way only a brother hates a brother. They fought over who was the most Arab, meaning the most cruel, but also the coolest, the best, and never kept their shirts on, or their pants on, stroked semen into one another's boots, and reveled in the license of their youth and the exacting lunacy of their circumstances by beating one another to the ground.

One noon, Uri was called away from that roughhousing and brought to a climatized shed for an interview. Officers asked him what placements he wanted, which is to say they were asking who he wanted to be, and so he answered them: either Duvdevan or Sayeret

Matkal, the dark stuff, the hushed stuff, counterterrorism ops, or, above all, he wanted to be a Tzanchan, he wanted to jump out of a plane – only to be told that his answers were useless, rather that if they were useful in any way it was only insofar as they provided ancillary snippets of psychological data for his profile.

That would be the last blast of full information he'd get in the army – the rest would be need-to-know, guesswork, divining: why he'd been placed in the unit he'd been placed in, why the others who'd gotten the same placement had gotten it, and what if anything that might say about him. Because the army never made mistakes. It never failed or lapsed. Each soldier got the assignment he deserved, rather each assignment got the soldier, and if your M16, M4, Galil, or Tavor overheated or jammed, even that was merited too, the malfunctions were intended: to prevent friendly fire or a wrongful slaughter. If your chute didn't open, or your engine stalled, or your wings fell off, it was better that way: there were reasons. Nothing ever happened out of whim or caprice. Everything was logical, logistical, systematic, each mission backed by a sacrosanct wisdom to which the average grunting soldier would never be privy. The army was a family, the officers were parents, the soldiers their kids: they received instructions, not explanations, the tactics, not the strategies, and the only way to ever survive this regime was to stop seeking its meanings and just submit, subordinate – surrender.

Imagine this vast staff of shadowy relations that keeps claiming to know what's best for you, or to know what you'd be best at, through the practice of an official magic, an authoritative mysticism involving myriad complex batteries of mental and physical tests, interviews, background checks, and just standard full-time surveillance, whose sole objective was to uncover from within the body, mind, and soul of an eighteen-year-old virgin his deepest essential competencies, native ingenuities, and capacities for development – the trail or path for which he'd always been intended. If a soldier was happy with the match that was made for him, then all the magic was true, the mysticism was science, and the organization responsible was close to divine, but if a soldier was unhappy, then the entire system was bankrupt, debunked, and he'd feel like he was losing his religion. This was the first lesson of the army, then, or the first that Uri retained, in the lull before his assignment: that were his wishes ever to be taken into account, the whole edifice would crumble. It was only by ignoring preferences that the theology endured.

Let the weak be disappointed – Uri was strong and would grow into any situation, like that invasive species of cactus, the prickly pear, which had been imported from South America to flourish in the desert at the fringes of the base: the sabra, it was called.

Let his fake gangster hutmates flex their pecs that were like the pads of the sabra and grumble about not becoming paratroopers or pilots – let them weep over not being, over officially not being, what they'd been convinced they were at core: paratrooper or pilot material. That was an ugly delusion, though not uncommon among such overconfident prickly youths who came out of the rougher poorer neighborhoods afflicted with bad eyesight, bad hearing, and mild scoliosis. Who, in a country you can't drive out of, doesn't want to fly? Or at least want to take a submarine and surface near Ibiza?

A week later, though it'd felt like a month, Uri had his qualification: his suspicions about himself, his incipient uniqueness, had been confirmed, and he'd been granted a gibush – a next-level try-out for the special forces, the eliter commandos.

He was bussed to another facility, spent a sleepless indeterminacy he regarded as a week getting shrieked at and walloped, bushwhacking up hills, up scrabbly mountains, wading through bramble and thorn with a rock-filled pack. Each day, a handful of guys would drop out. Or be drummed out. Because of broken hands or feet, broken minds.

Uri's story was this: once, after they'd rappelled themselves from a particularly strenuous free-climb ascension, everyone was groveling sloppy with their uniforms untucked, and the drill instructor decided to make an example, he decided to make Uri an example, and so gathered a fistful of his shirt tails and jammed the fabric below his belt into his pants, until the faggot was gripping Uri's dick, he was twisting. Uri keeled. And then got up. And punched the faggot and kept punching, at all his fellow candidates, at every drill instructor at the facility, every officer in the country – the Defense Minister, the Prime Minister, the President, every living member of the Knesset: it took all of them to take him down.

That, at least, was the indignant yet aggrandizing tale he told the squad to which he was remanded the following month: Kivsa/Akavish/Tziraah/Bet/Bet.

He'd shown up, toward the conclusion of its basic training, horridly scraped at neck and knees. His cheeks were still puffy and tender. The clinic had been an incarceration, so sterile and tranquilized that even the infantry was preferable. He was in the infantry now.

He was in Kivsa/Akavish/Tziraah/Bet/Bet, specifically, because it was short a member: this Shimshon the others had barely known – because they hadn't been together long enough to know him as anything other than a chunky South African – had been climbing a ladder during an obstacle, fallen off, and shattered his pelvis. The ladder had been positioned by his training partner and squad opinion was still split as to whether it was all the partner's fault.

Even if it wasn't his fault, Yoav, the partner who now became partners with Uri, was the worst soldier in the squad. Uri, to compensate, became the best soldier, meaning he never directly questioned whether their pairing was a punishment or compliment.

If during their initial Krav Maga scrimmages he fought as normal and choked Yoav out fast, immediately fast, during subsequent matches he let up and let Yoav thrash all his glib lanky body for each round's full duration.

Uri had realized that by hurting his opponent, he'd only hurt himself – they still had years to go together and there was no way to rush the time.

But then there was no impatience like that of a graduating recruit standing at attention to be sworn in at the Kotel, while the chief rabbi, this squinting screeching Ashkenaz, went on amplifying his remarks with misquotations of the vicious minor prophets.

After the swearing, saluting, and flag worship, they were finally soldiers, and they flung their berets into the air and then scrambled to scoop them up and put them back on: you can't stand at the Kotel without keeping your head covered.

The field days followed in procession: indomitably hot stretches of sentry duty spent just clenching bowel and bladder and greasing your gun, the perspiration coursing, as you stooped, drooped, and melted – the country was melting. The borders shrunk, expanded, kept being moved, until you found yourself trapped between where yesterdays had been and tomorrows would be – until you, yourself, had become the border, dug into sand along roads rived by rebar and garbled with barbed wire. This was a checkpoint, between Israel and a land Palestinians called Palestine and Israelis called Judea and Samaria, because Jews can't agree on anything, they can't even agree with themselves and so both names were used. Formerly called the West Bank, though it's located just east of the country, about 40 billion of the old Canaanite cubits in psychological distance but also only forty kilometers as the rockets fly, from where the rockets were flying from Gaza. But here you saw none, here you heard none. You just were. Put here, like you'd been put here on earth, to reinforce the patrols. Given all the recent unrest and skirmishing.

The border felt, from the outset, like a demotion. A disparagement. A squandering. The lines were endless. The days were endless lines. A checkpoint just marks the middle, the sandbagged roadblocked middle, of endless vallar lines. Palestinian workers going to, coming from, the factories in the Israeli industrial zones. Palestinian shepherds coming and going, to graze and water their flocks. Maids heading from Bethlehem to clean the factories when what they should've been cleaning weren't the factories but Bethlehem. A woman who wasn't a maid trying to cross using the ID of her sister who was a maid but had a tumor that was preventing her from working and the family couldn't afford to lose the job. From dawn to dusk checking IDs. Checking permits. Car papers. Fucking sheep papers, as the sheep just shat and pissed. Some days the orders were to let only a certain number through, or a certain designation through, or not to let any through, at certain times. Some days you just invented the orders. You had to act as if your presence here was permanent and your authority just another element of the surrounding inarable wastes. If you convinced yourself, then you convinced the people crossing, and if you convinced the people crossing, then you convinced the wastes. That you were as rooted as the olive trees. As elemental as the clays.

There were Palestinian police, on the Palestinian side. And Israeli police, on the Israeli side. Your role, as army, was to police the police. To relay the irreconcilability of all their orders. To scan the plates. Get the driver and all passengers out of the car, their arms and legs spread and hijabs off. Put the mirror under the car like you're checking it for breath. Check the trunk and under the hood, the interior. Check the fluids. You had to be, at once, a soldier, a grease monkey, and the angel of death. You had to be a brother and a son, even after you were relieved and took your turn in the booth using a contraband cell phone to call your parents, who were slumped in a bunker underground, eating Bissli, drinking Coke, and squabbling – toggling the TV between Sport 5 carrying Maccabi Tel Aviv vs. FC Basel and Channel 1 with its screen-blue sky and the smoke of Qassam rockets crazing through like static.

Occasionally there'd be some Hasidic rabbinic or rabbi-esque figure bearing down the settlement road in his dove-gray Mercedes-Benz 190 between the industrial zone and the settlement on the ridge above the shepherd village and his windows would be downed and with a shake of his payos he'd be screaming at you for making him late and the funny thing would be that every once in a while the guy, because he was a Jewish transplant from America, would be doing all that screaming in English, which Uri wouldn't understand, or would only half-understand, and he'd speak to the guy in Hebrew, which the guy wouldn't understand, or would only half-understand, and the guy would just keep shouting something in English so that Uri would have to get Yoav to moderate the languages, if only to keep from just slapping the guy, which was never advisable, not because the guy was a Jew, or an American, or possibly an Israeli citizen, or a Hasid who resembled a rabbi, or possibly even a bona fide rabbi ordained, but because he was a settler, and as a soldier Uri was basically his employee – basically his bodyguard.

Occasionally there'd be a protest to break up, to break up the monotony: Palestinian and even Israeli, but then occasionally there'd be a few Israelis out at the Palestinian protests and everything would get confusing.

Then maybe there'd be some kid at some protest who'd maybe hurled a rock and you'd try not to shoot him, even though your gun only had rubber bullets, even though you'd been so bored you'd spent all your day crushing the rubber bullets up into small sharp pebbles so that while the rules would be respected and no laws would be broken, the skin would be, the skin would be pierced.

In general, you tried not to hit kids and women – anyone who made a fuss if they were hit: journalists.

Every once in a while there'd be a midnight run through a village just to light it up. Searching for someone. Or for no one. Finding someone else. Or no one. Going into a house, to surprise the house behind it, to surprise the neighbors next door. Taking the doors off and going room to room. Herding a family into the kitchen and then heading upstairs to ransack the closets and unscrew all the beds nut by bolt. Slashing up the divan in the den and then sitting down on the framed remains to cruise the news on Al Jazeera. Or playing PlayStation. Or Wii. Awaiting further instruction, awaiting Intelligence. Babysitting a son or brother bound to the divan with plasticuffs draining him white and a drenched towel over his face keeping him cool, until the interrogators came. On your way out, confiscating bangles for your sisters, candlesticks and goblets, checkered boards for every game involving kings. A woman keening in the kitchen to the pitch of boiling water, you shut her up with the butt of your gun. You butted a jug and it sharded apart into archaeology even before it hit the floor.

The time after action was different from the time before – you couldn't wait to be sent into Gaza, but then once you got out, you could wait again forever.

The wait to be discharged – should you be feeling so impatient? The wait to get on with the rest of your spared life – why be in such a hurry to get hustled and now have to pay for your own lodging, meals, and clothes?

But still the army dragged on. With debriefings, memorial services. Notching the days with a pocketknife on the shank bone of a lamb, which you were trying to carve into a dagger. Dribbling your shadow like a football across the half-line, leaving your dead in the dust running wretched behind you, running out the clock, fouling toward the goal.

The very last days, the split begins: from thinking about the unit, to thinking about the self, about yourself. About the resources available to you after the army. The scope of the imagination, being circumscribed by family, would reveal your family: would reveal your finances, culture, class. Menachem started flipping through Harley-Davidson brochures, wondering which bike to buy with the reward his parents were giving him just for finishing his stint. Gad started drifting off to lounge under a palm and reacquaint himself with the state of international poetry. Everyone was becoming de-equalized, each groping toward his individuality in a great dismemberment of a corpse – the amputation of shredded legs (Rotem's), the removal of ruptured spleens (Dror's) – and the pain Uri would come to feel would be like a phantom pain, as the spare parts of what had also been him went out stumping across the earth, or were buried alone below it.

Finally, there was another ceremony, this at the base in Eliakim, when you were reminded of what you'd been forced, or had forced yourself, to forget. When the same parents who'd said the shalom that meant goodbye to their boys at the Kotel now caravanned out to the grassy vale of the Galilee to say the shalom that meant hello, to pick their boys up and bring them home again as men – the parents too had aged in the interim.

You were reminded, by the fathers' flashy phones and the mothers' flashy jewels and especially by all the flashy Chevy Malibus they drove, of how divided everyone was, of how disparate your own brooded circumstances.

Because Uri's parents didn't make it: they couldn't. The family Dugri hadn't been present at either occasion: neither the induction nor the farewell. They never took off work. Or they'd only have taken off work for a funeral.

He went out, thumb out, hitchhiking. He was picked up by an assistant to a Rosh Yeshivah and then by a dump truck, which dumped him in Tel Aviv from which he took a sherut – charity be damned.

Because he was damned. In that the army, which had always purported to be so boundlessly concerned for him that he'd barely conceived ever having to outgrow it, now appeared to him spiteful, resentful, and conjugally cruel – as limiting as the dates on Shlomo 'Shlo' Regev's gravemarker: (5754–5774)/(1994–2014) – a time parenthetically tragic, whose sole legacy was an evasion, and a skill set inapplicable, even inimical, to adulthood. He'd been discharged as an expert in stealth who now to succeed had to make himself heard and seen. An expert in orienteering who now had to navigate the nettles of the Occident. He was a man with a single citizenship and, discounting his Arabic, a single language, both of which were welcomed only in lands as distant from one another as the black pentagons on a white football. He was a single man who'd become single-minded about calibers and ranges, after all his juvenile interests in metal guitar and manga and capoeira and scorpions – after all the interests he'd had before his service that weren't Batya – had been decimated by the protocols and facts.

Like, the Al Ghoul is a 14.5mm rifle so accurate that if fired from Gaza can mow the lawn in Sderot, up to two kilometers away.

Like, the M113 APC Zelda has insufficient armoring against IEDs and Hashim RPGs and is, in general, an inappropriate vehicle for urban conflicts.

Don't confirm insurgent identity by uniform, confirm by gun. The enemy might copy your vest but they're carrying Kalashnikovs.

Just because you're not in a tunnel doesn't mean you're not above a tunnel, which might collapse. No tunnel's cleared until it's collapsed.

If one of the cows of the Arabushim wanders out from its pen and falls into a pit, it's better not to attempt a rescue, it's better just to shoot it.

The most dangerous spiders are the brownies and the most dangerous brownies have red or orange hourglasses on their abdomens. The yellow-patched wasp or hornet nests underground and feeds sweetly on bees. Also the human body, left alone, with no other persons, materials, or objects around – no dumb-bells or door handles and no weapons, of course – is incapable of self-destruction.

Sure, the body can always wait itself out, by dehydration or starvation, no doubt, but assuming a certain time frame – between a day or three, say – no human can do enough damage to himself with his own hands, with his own lonesome somatic contortions, to die. Try and hold your breath, you'll eventually, reflexively, gasp. Try and strangle yourself, just fingers choking your throat, and while you might pass out, you'll come to soon enough. There's just no way, unassisted, to commit suicide.

But then there's no way to be just a human, isolated, stripped or just stripped of contexts – because even a cell must have a floor, a ceiling, walls.

And God, don't forget God.

That Creator of all, Who's everywhere: He's everywhere at all times and even nowhere, or especially there, numinous in void. Uri had known a lot of people who'd believed that. Who'd believed that and used Him, both in and out of the army. He'd known a lot of people who'd committed suicide with God.

This was what he'd intended to bring up with the Baba Batra, the Master of the Last Gate, the Light of Porat Yosef. But once he'd finally been admitted to the rabbi's inky cramped chambers, he'd been sapped of nerve.

He was being called to account for his piety, his habits hygienic, dietary, doxological – 'You pray the Shema?'

'I do,' Uri said, 'yes.'

'Every day?'

'Every day, rabbi.'

'When you go to sleep and when you wake up?'

'Yes, rabbi.'

'With your strong hand covering your eyes like you're cupping a flame?'

'Covering, yes, absolutely.'

'And you say it aloud so that anyone who passes your door can listen in and share in the deed, but the blessing that follows you say to yourself in a whisper?'

'In a whisper.'

The rabbi growled, 'Then I will tell you why you have the headaches.'

'Why?'

'Because you lie to me. The headaches you have are all in your head. Tell me, where else should they be? In Tafilalt or Antwerp or Los Angeles, where? Should they be in this lamp? Or doing the Mimuna dance inside this computer? It's the truth, this pain of yours. It's the truth in pain because confined.'

'Honestly, rabbi, I do pray.'

'Not the Shema?'

'No.'

'That's not enough for you?'

'The Shema? All it says is that God is One – it doesn't even ask for anything.'

'So what then?'

'Please God don't let me die. Or do let me die. Please God for Batya Neder. I pray that I always have enough water or enough of the tablets that purify water. That I have no more freeze-dried goulash or freeze-dried schnitzel or loof. Hashem, I pray, no more dreams.'

'Amen.'

'But, rabbi, what do they mean?'

'The dreams? What don't they mean? Like every election has its scandal, every dream has its nonsense. This is why no dream is ever completely fulfilled.'

'So trying to explain them is futile?'

'Like dreaming that your dream is being interpreted. My beard is the interpretation.'

Uri fidgeted, the rabbi picked at his beard. 'Consider the difference,' he said, 'between trials and tests – what's your name again?'

'Uri.'

'The warrior, kindled by God – it's up to you, Uri, to distinguish between them.'

'Between what?'

'There are trials of faith, given directly by God. Like how God told Abraham to leave his land and kill his own son and how because Abraham set out to do what he was told, we became the chosen and an angel was sent at the last moment to grab the blade away.'

'And what's the other kind?'

'Tests that are temptations, tricks, deceptions. Which are the work of women, serpents, and brothers.'

'All of them together?'

'Who offered Adam the fruit? A woman, Eve. And who offered the fruit to Eve? The serpent, Satan. Cain murders Abel and then, given the chance to admit his guilt, decides to lie, like you've lied. And this is just one family.'

'You're saying it's like my family?'

'I'm saying that in life, it's most important to understand what is being judged. And what is the intention.'

'I don't understand.'

'Your loyalty is being judged.'

'How? Because I'm so – ' and hesitated, and then said it – 'fucked up?'

'No,' the rabbi said, 'nothing to do with fucked up.'

'Then why?'

'Because the army might not be over. Because the army might never be over. You're being challenged, as to whether you believe that.

Or else it's all just a ploy and you're being tricked into believing you were discharged.'

'It is? I wasn't?'

'No, Uri – because you can't stop being a soldier, just like you can't stop being a Jew. They're both permanent conditions, for life. This is the position of the State of Israel. You were born a soldier, because you were born a Jew, and if you weren't given an Uzi at your bris it was only because the government won't issue them to anyone not old enough to handle the commitment. To handle the burden. To join the army is to accept who you are. To formally accept it. And the age requirements and set period of service are just traditions – bureaucracy.'

'So I'm still serving – that's what you mean? And you don't mean like in the reserves?'

'At age thirteen, you were called to the Torah to become a bar mitzvah – a son of the commandments?'

'Of course.'

'Of course – you know this, you remember. But did you know that at age eighteen, you were called to become another thing, a bar pekudah – a son of the commands?'

'I didn't.'

'Tell me, bar pekudah, after you became a bar mitzvah and read from the Torah – maybe had a little party, maybe had a little cake – did you stop being a Jew?'

'Of course not.'

'Of course not. So then why, after the army asks you to leave, do you stop being a soldier?'

'I'm not sure.'

'It's only after the army asks you to leave that you start – because it's only after that you're prepared, with a feeling for the graveness of the duty.'

The Baba Batra's phone illumined and vibrated across his desk to a trance-hop ringtone and he leaned to mute it, put a palm to Uri's forehead, blessed him.

White-clad flunkies ushered Uri out and down the halls past the expectant infertile and abiding cancered and all the crutches and casts of the waylaid maimed, who reached out to touch the hem of his garment. ■

Courtesy of the author

MARK DOTEN

1978

Mark Doten was born in Minnesota. His debut novel, *The Infernal*, was published by Graywolf Press in 2015. He is the literary fiction editor at Soho Press and teaches at Columbia University, in the graduate writing program.

TRUMP SKY ALPHA

Mark Doten

Trump Sky Alpha, the rigid airship that docked on the roof of the White House and the roof of Trump Tower, a thousand-foot vessel from the bridge of which Trump delivered streaming YouTube addresses every Wednesday, DC to New York, and every Sunday, New York to DC, the ultra-luxury Zeppelin – 'Crystal Palace of the Sky' – on which the 224 seats ('Luxury berths in an Open Loge Style') went for a starting price of $50,000, a figure that jumped with the addition of various ultra-deluxe packages and enhancements, 'Diamond' and 'Diamond Troika Elite' tiers, four figures for the 'Ten-Star Double Platinum Seafood', 'certified eight-pound' lobsters with TRUMP embossed on tail fin and right claw, wine pairings offered by the animated 'Founding Foodie' Ben Franklin on touchscreen, Franklin adjusting spectacles and cataloging flights of Trump Wine ('An Exquisite Taste of Trump'), the *Feu de Cheminée* and the *Blanc de Blanc de la plus Blanc*, the final bill after disembarkment running to twenty pages or more of often obscure fees and surcharges, bag fees and negative weather clemency credits and per-use charges on the ergonomic loge controls – every seat adjustment noted by the system and itemized – the seats arranged in an oblong spiral that looped the transparent floor six times, the entire body of the aircraft constructed from a revolutionary transparent membrane stretched over a skeleton of moth-white aluminum, seats facing inward, amphitheater-style, and at the center a circular bridge of bulletproof glass, the views from all 224 seats opening vertiginously onto the National Mall or Central Park and Midtown as the craft lifted off, offering a 'pristine God's-eye view of our Great Nation', seats sliding backward on mobile tracks, while a system of giant claws and pulleys yanked other seats up overhead and moved them forward, closer to Trump, the price of your enhancement package determining how far up you went, a leapfrog of one or ten seats, the 'Troika' or 'Triple-Star Emerald Troika' or 'Deca-Diamond Troika Extreme', the last of which, for a modulating price somewhere in the seven figures, placing you at Position #1, which you would then enjoy for a minute or an hour until someone else ordered it, everyone knocked back one position, chairs almost continuously moving backward on a track on the floor, clacking against each other, so Trump's words were overlaid with big echoing vibrations like huge skee balls loading and sharp but stifled human gasps as giant claws snatched the next upgrader, seats whooshing overhead, at any given moment eight or ten or twelve seats zipping around unpredictably above, the transparent floor provoking a certain amount of nervous loge-adjustment as Trump spoke (each adjustment itemized), big spenders with corporate or government sponsors taking their turn up front as Trump gives his twice-weekly address at the helm of the Zeppelin, or if not the big spenders themselves then stand-ins the sponsors had hired, attractive actors filling in for company executives after earlier accidents and threats and attacks, Monsanto or McKesson or Chevron stitched prominently but tastefully on their suits or dresses, Trump's hands on and then off the wheel as he gestures during his live-streamed address, seeming to float at the center of the craft, unleashing all the old familiar gestures, the little pointy duck bill, the poke, the palms-out 'stop' that would flow into a second gesture, fingers still fanned but palms turning in to face each other and then squeezing in and out as though meeting a resistant force, a crazy horizontal spring, Trump grimacing with the effort, elbows pinching into his waist, whole body contorting at the sheer ridiculousness of whatever enemy he was describing, Trump putting his rubberized face – by turns frog-lipped and hemorrhoidal, pig- and pop-eyed – through its paces, an array of comical disapprovals, hands resting now and then on the big gold-spoked wheel that at times seemed in his power and at others appeared to turn of its own accord, Trump almost floating there in the sky, drawing no salary, wholly removed from the business side of the Trump Organization and Trump Sky Alpha for the duration of his presidency – but he could still *fly* in it, couldn't he? you're not saying *that's* illegal? – the whole bridge rotating behind its circular glass wall, making 360-degree rotations every four minutes, Trump turning and turning as Trump Sky Alpha twice a week made stately progress, warping the clouds and sky behind, above it a massive American flag with Trump's face superimposed, squinting and grinning, the flag itself animated LED-enabled fabric, mirroring Trump's expressions via real-time video capture, the highways and port cities of the eastern seaboard spread out below, Trump rotating and raising a fist, his voice filling the craft, Trump interrupting his own extemporaneous thoughts on the events of the past week to point or wink at a chair that had moved to the front ('We've got Walmart coming up, looks like Ford right behind, try the surf and turf, it's really fabulous!') while several copilots and a whole team of staffers and security personnel and military folks worked in a concealed bay in the aft, a white opaque bay that was markedly empty tonight, no copilot, no staff, no passengers, Trump Sky Alpha tonight tearing its moorings from the White House roof, shocking the military and Secret Service and the White House staffers who milled about on the ground (even Trump's private security caught flat-footed), staffers and military and members of the deep state who had told the president again and again that day, all day long, that under the extraordinary circumstances unfolding around the world, the nuclear attacks, the hundreds or thousands of ongoing conflicts, the millions or tens of millions already dead, Trump would absolutely not be permitted to fly Trump Sky Alpha, *Mr President, we can get you into a bunker with full communication equipment and you can give your address there, you just can't do it in a goddamn plastic blimp at the start of World War III.*

In the afternoon Trump stopped arguing with them, got quiet, it was after Ivanka went on TV, after she said it was a mistake, the first nuclear launch, and after that Trump wouldn't speak, which they realized later was a warning of things to come – there was Trump sitting catatonic in his big chair in the White House situation room for hours, papers piling up before him, he had authorized a plan the previous evening, a limited nuclear option, and this had been carried out, and Ivanka had gone on TV, weeping, to say it was a mistake, and ever since he had just sat in his big chair, all night and through the day, Trump in the situation room with the joint chiefs, options set down in black binders in front of him, options whose windows were passing rapidly, gone and replaced with new binders, Trump's only real movement when Pence mentioned a possible transfer of power, just for the day, just for an hour, just so a few key decisions could be made, and Trump turned and half-stood, slow and bear-like and implacable, and open-palm smacked Pence's face, knocked him down with a crack that silenced the dozen murmured conversations happening across the room, and there was a tense moment among the Secret Service and Trump's private security, but Pence sat up and rubbed his head and said, *I'm fine, it's fine*, and then all at once people were speaking, *Mr President there are a range of options, here's the big one, these are more measured, we advise an immediate response, it's a dynamic and unfolding situation, we advise something limited but decisive, let me walk you through the details* . . . Trump again silent, slouched in his chair, vacantly staring through a deep squint, eyes for long periods the narrowest slits, possibly closed altogether, it was his favorite day, the day he got to fly Trump Sky Alpha and do his live-streaming, twice a week it was his favorite day, but something had happened, today something had happened to his favorite day, and there was Pence, hovering again like a maître d', moving between Trump and the other end of the room, where a certain humming awareness was coming into being, a panic that they, the generals, were watching, just watching, the world end, and there were plans, they had been drawn up very early, even before the inauguration, plans for the Twenty-

Fifth Amendment, his mental illness, his – it had been decided – his dementia, these whispers going back and forth at the generals' end of the room, yes, clear signs of age-related dementia, changes of mood, confusion, difficulty following conversations, and now was the moment to deploy it, the Twenty-Fifth Amendment, compounded by the shock of what had happened to his family, not to Ivanka but most of the rest of the family who had been in New York, the series of attacks in New York among the precipitating events of the crisis, though now since the first 'limited' US nuclear response protestors had filled the streets, demanding peace, demanding no more of this, it was Lewy Body Dementia, that was the emerging consensus, somehow they had landed on Lewy Body Dementia, it seemed better than plain-old dementia, and they couldn't just watch the world end, not when there was something they could do, Trump's private security at the other end of the room sensing the threat taking shape, casually falling into positions around and behind the president, the generals and advisors and deep state, they had to do something, and so at last Pence gave the nod, and the chairman of the joint chiefs cleared his throat, and there was an almost slow-motion interplay of dozens of gazes and hands, hands on all sides of the room moving to the guns holstered under fine-tailored suits, it was all about to be resolved, one way or another, when suddenly Trump was lumbering very fast through the White House and up the stairs, in every hallway and stairwell strong-arming Secret Service out of his way, all the way to the roof access, Secret Service and military personnel asking each other at first jokingly and then not so much if they should just tackle him, but it happened so fast, he was already on the roof and then half-running up the gangway – it was time, the scheduled takeoff time for Trump Sky Alpha, though Trump had been told there would be no takeoff today, not at the start of World War III, didn't he understand? –Trump's feet landing with concussive thuds, and two Secret Service agents tried to take him by the arm (right there on the gangway stairs – it's very dangerous to grab people on stairs, everyone knows that, especially on these flimsy gangway stairs that just go up and up, absolutely terrible!) and with shocking strength for an elderly overweight man, Trump hurled both agents off the gangway and pressed the button that closed it up behind him, three more agents actually grabbing onto mooring cables as the Zeppelin lifted off, struggling up their respective cables for a few seconds before plummeting to their deaths like losers – and that's what they were, *total losers* – Trump in his glassed-in enclosure firing off a few quick tweets ('Happy to be flying back to NYC! Beautiful night! Fake News Media WRONG as usual!!!') as the bridge began to rotate, Trump Sky Alpha rising above the National Mall, which was wholly given over now to military operations, dozens of helicopters and tanks and armored personnel carriers on the green ('Generals doing great job! Say they're glad it's me, not Hillary! Don't listen to lying media. We Keep America SAFE!!!'), Trump activating the livestream, an array of cameras that cut automatically between Trump and the amphitheater-style seats with genuine leather accents, now empty, on what had been until this day a perpetually sold-out flight, two times a week, Trump Sky Alpha heading north, Trump beginning his address, the latest in his series of twice-weekly monologues, while behind him across the Potomac the Pentagon still smoldered, huge clouds of black smoke visible from several of the camera angles the livestream was cycling through, the sunset a lavender and black-and-orange melange that added painterly highlights to Trump's coiffure, Trump turning the gold-plated wheel and touching levers and buttons that controlled the stabilizers and the rotor speed, and across the world the other Zeppelins in the fleet rose from their moorings, all of them linked together, all of them 'Piloted by Trump™', it wasn't a single aircraft, it was several dozen Trump Zeppelins across the globe, a sort of global interconnected organism, so that when Trump Sky Alpha turned right, the Zeppelins all turned right, when he turned left, they turned left, when he accelerated, they did the same, Trump's hologram projected in real time onto the glass bridges of several dozen other Zeppelins, the Zeppelins all linked to his as in a pantograph, as connected pens that reproduce a single image at various scales ('Based on Benjamin Franklin's "Pantograph" Invention, the Ultimate in Luxury Travel'), Trump Sky Zeppelins in Taiwan, the UAE, Kuwait, the Netherlands, South Korea, Russia, Malaysia, the Philippines, and dozens of other locales, took off and followed the same paths, or had, until this night, when worldwide devastation had already rendered half the fleet inoperable, but against the backdrop of blackouts or massive fires the crafts that remained lifted off with Trump, in Kazakhstan tracer bullets sliced up the Trump Sky craft's cabin, sliced up the people in the cabin, it took off as the floor of it broke free and all inside tumbled down except those who were already in the claws, and who burned to death watching a Trump hologram chatter and gesticulate ('You wouldn't know it from the press, just how beautifully it's going, the media has been really terrible, there are a couple people – and I'm not going to name names – but there are a couple people who are just so disgusting, CNN and the failing *New York Times*'), and Trump passed over the Patapsco River and hit the button to click off the really tasteless just *nasty* Kazakh live feed, those people in the claws shrieking and engulfed in flames, but the button he pressed turned out to be the rear rotor reverse switch, and the nose of the craft went up sharply – noses all across the fleet did – and the 2,000-gallon wheeled lobster tanks crashed against the Mount Rushmore-style sculptures that separated the galley from the main cabin, and 2,000-gallon plate-glass tanks all around the world likewise shattered against sculptures of Trump and Eric and Trump Jr and Ivanka, sending huge crustaceans flying everywhere as passengers worldwide screamed in one voice.

The initial plans had been to replicate the flight path of Trump Sky Alpha at a 1:1 scale, and in the same compass bearings, though ultimately Trump had been convinced that the Zeppelins could be oriented in various directions depending on local need, but since the local need was in many cases nil, it still resulted in Zeppelin landing stations in the middle of the desert, or way out in some Hebei province backwater, where there were mountains and big ancient pagodas and other obstructions, so that at last a further compromise of sorts was made, the 221 miles from the White House to Trump Tower could be scaled up or down, and in Yemen, for reasons of security, after the first two were downed mid-flight by shoulder-fired missiles, the Zeppelin now lifted up and went 'in place', whereas the route from Brussels to Frankfurt was a near match, and the longest route in the fleet, from Moscow to Minsk, 446.7 miles, required the Zeppelin to travel at nearly double the speed of Trump Sky Alpha, which had led to the August disaster, but the craft had quickly been replaced and the route recertified, and passengers were leery, to say the least, after all the attacks and accidents, but it had been made clear that Trump wanted full flights, all of them full, it would not do to simply buy them out and send them up empty, Trump watched the crafts from video screens on the bridge of Trump Sky Alpha, and though there weren't enough commercial passengers to fill them (and indeed, given the routes they took, and the times, there was very little utility to the flights, the flights from Brussels for instance left at three in the morning), but nevertheless, the flights were almost always full, booked far in advance, bought out by the sovereign wealth funds of Kuwait, Saudi Arabia, China, and Hong Kong, as well as by corporate partners, the latter tricky at first, many corporations at first resisted – they had stockholders they were accountable to, they couldn't be spending tens of millions on luxury travel – but soon it became clear that certain favors were being granted, playing fields tipped, regulations loosened or disappeared, sabers rattled more or less vigorously, so that in numerous ways, plausibly deniable and otherwise, those in the Zeppelins were accruing certain advantages: money that had previously been allocated to study peatland fires in Indonesia, fires which some individuals had claimed were major sources of carbon emission and global pollution, had been zeroed out; and State reversed its opposition to certain uses of lèse-majesté in Thailand, after all these people had their own ways and traditions and who were we to interfere; and Trump himself gave a big thumbs up in a Fox News interview to Azerbaijan's overrun of Nagorno-Karabakh, as part of a larger package of policy initiatives geared to combat terrorism in the region; and in Zimbabwe, human rights restrictions were lifted following the death of Robert Mugabe, and the Zim diamond mines were in full swing, despite the fact that in the first months of his successor's presidency over 200 students had been killed by police; and in Taiwan, we temporarily halted follow-on support to certain Tactical Information Distribution Systems that we had sold them; and sanctions were lifted in Yemen and Burundi and Belarus; and the Magnitsky Sanctions were swiftly and quietly scrapped; and those who were not buying into the fleet watched all this from the sidelines until at last they did not, it was the new world system and it seemed more and more that you could not avoid it, but the money that got you advantages a month ago was now not enough, it was always more, and corporations of various sizes, including the very largest multinationals, made extraordinary efforts, each according to their means, buying out the whole ship, for instance, or, on International British Petroleum Trump Sky Day, buying out the entire *fleet*, which was temporarily rebranded, a BP logo added to the rear stabilizers and onto the US flag itself, BP's logo resting tastefully on the canton, while Trump's face mugged and grimaced and gaped (within three months, offshore drilling rights were granted to BP all up and down the coast of California), and as nice as some of the seeming advantages were, those who still purchased seats but didn't keep up with the rising prices of the ultra-luxe enhancements found their interests actively impeded, a less profitable week for a given aircraft could send mysterious vibrations throughout that country, a rash of bad fortune and destabilizing influences, said country scrambling to increase its purchases, to spend more, and where would it end, many wondered, where could it all end? so that when the first European Zeppelin was taken down by terrorists there were those who sighed a bit in relief, only to find the Trump Organization suing the European Union, threatening sanctions if the EU didn't assume responsibility for rebuilding the Zeppelin and settling the lawsuits of the dead and massively compensating for the pain and suffering of the Trump Organization itself, two crafts built in its place, twice the demands from the Trump Organization, and the flights had to be full all of the time, but not only full, the passengers had to play perfectly the roles of enthusiastic supporters, smiling as they listened, and frequently applauding or cheering, they were good-looking, they were attentive and well groomed, not long after the fleet had launched there was a move to mix passengers with 'modern dress' and 'traditional garb', this custom had started with the flight in the Middle East, Trump cheerfully complimenting the mix of *modern dress* and *traditional garb*, then wondering out loud the next week why more countries didn't do that, both modern dress *and* traditional garb, it really gave him a kick, and in India women in saris received the same compliments the next flight, and so the following week the proverbial dam broke, there were kimonos and kilts and dashikis and Brazilian carnival costumes and Maasai beadwork and Balinese temple dress and Filipino barong tagalogs in Zeppelins around the world, audiences serving up rapt and approving expressions as Trump played on their screens, Trump giving more thumbs up than ever, though on this night, the night following the first nuclear detonations, the fleet was half-empty, or the half of the half that had not already been annihilated was half-empty, and on the flights that weren't ghost ships there was an air of disassociated panic, white knuckles, weeping faces, occasional screams, headdresses askew or clutched nervously in laps, two women on the Italian Zeppelin in dresses and hats out of *La Dolce Vita* rose in hysterical panic as huge lobsters caught in gearworks above popped and sprayed them with viscera, the women quickly gunned down by the twitchy Italian security, blood spraying the white loges as the Leaning Tower of Pisa silently slid by beneath, lobsters elsewhere causing big problems as they were ground into the pulley and claw systems, gumming up the works, chairs dropped in the wrong places, cracking, and in Rio actually shattering the transparent floor, the passengers plunging into Guanabara Bay, giant lobsters with branded TRUMP claws and tails splashing down with them and then drifting contentedly to the seabed, Trump still talking, still calm ('People have called me up crying and thanked me for saving their families, so many calls, now we wanted to keep that private, because I don't think it's anybody's business if people are crying and saying *Thank you, Thank you, Mr President*, but you look at the people and families I've saved, we are talking about millions and millions'), though he did click off the Italian and Brazilian feeds.

But now Trump Sky Alpha was under attack, they had been tracking him, apparently, through his livestream, foreign fighter jets screaming in from God knows where, Trump couldn't get the nose up, and he crashed with a cascade of sparks into some high-tension power lines that bounced him, sent him sailing back the other way, then a few dozen yards and the next bounced him back in the other direction on the central axis, it appears that the Zeppelin's velocity, and the tensile strength and elasticity of the lines, and the distance between the towers, were all so perfectly calibrated that even though twenty or thirty lines were dangling from the Zeppelin's snout, Trump Sky Alpha was still flying, its zigzag path actually helping Trump evade the enemy fighters, giving US planes the chance to shoot them down, Trump still talking, gestures more and more emphatic, conveying in general a look of confidence and ease, speaking the whole time ('We're going to rebuild much better anything that was lost to these animals, and that has been greatly, greatly exaggerated, we're doing very, very well, I know how to build and if it was lost it is not really lost, it is going back better, just fabulous, you know I started off in Queens, my father gave me a small loan, and I made so much more, so much money') while all across the world the linked Zeppelins following his movements without the power lines to bounce them back, and it was a slaughter, Abuja down, Abu Dhabi down, and in capitals and military encampments and shantytowns and suburbs throughout the world it was being reckoned, how this might affect the future, how Trump's reaction to the failure of his fleet might affect the future of the world, as Trump lost control, as enemy planes flew at him and a fleet of US fighter jets and helicopters swarmed around Trump Sky Alpha, jets and helicopters defending Trump Sky Alpha, crashing when necessary into enemy aircraft, slicing through the power lines, and Trump Sky Alpha finally righted itself, rose up above the lines to a safer altitude, there in North Jersey, not far from his destination, but then an enemy fighter appeared, dozens had been shot down or *crashed* down in suicide runs by US aircraft, but this one came roaring in, hugging the ground and then pulling up sharply, huge suddenly at Trump's feet, guns and missiles roaring, and slammed into Trump Sky Alpha, and it all blew up, Trump's Zeppelin, with Trump on board, it massively exploded, taking out a half-dozen helicopters in its escort, the livestream now nothing but noise and fire, and around the world, millions held their breath, everyone watching an instant that seemed to float, the whole world floating in that suspended moment, and then the fireball dissipated, and there he was, Trump, still there, still going, no longer a full Zeppelin, envelope and metal frame burned or fallen away, it was just the glass amphitheater and the bulletproof glass bridge, all the empty seats in their oblong spiral, emergency safety rotors extending out over what is now a much smaller oblong shape with Trump at the center, a dozen moth-white rotors of various sizes keeping the craft afloat, flag still flying, a burned black collection of tendrils writhing like a tub of snakes, and a pale gaping skull-like thing where Trump's face had been stamped, the rest of the fleet unlinked now and crashing, Trump seeming to float, hands at the gold wheel, still speaking, still smiling, 'It's New York now, it's Midtown, there's Trump Tower, Central Park, the best views, the best apartments. I have talked to the generals and the generals who are with us have given me some really, really wonderful codes to work with, and the codes are beautiful, just beautiful,' he said, and right there he authorized it, there aboard Trump Sky Alpha, on the YouTube livestream, he authorized the big one, the biggest possible response, lobsters in Bermuda and Turkey and Paris raising branded claws in silent salute as the flames engulfed them, the last remaining cameras going dark, helicopters and fighter jets crisscrossing the airspace around and in front of the big transparent capsule surrounded by whirling rotors, US President Donald J. Trump floating at the center of it all, he pressed the automated descent button, and the livestream cut out for a final pitch for boutique shopping experiences (Ivanka on video offering bangles and Donald J. Trump signature neckwear and vacation ownership opportunities) and then back to Trump, full frame, at the wheel of the Trump Sky Alpha, another thumbs up to the YouTube livestream audience, to all those watching, those who still had internet, those still alive, and in the situation room, among and between all the generals and the members of the deep state and now even Trump's private security apparatus, a certain humming awareness, a panic that they were watching, just watching, the world end, and wasn't there something they could do, but there were too many, too many different strategies, they were each locked into their own roles, and Trump had already announced it, the big option, right there on the livestream, to the whole world, to all our allies and enemies, and around the world protocols and contingency plans were going into effect, there just wasn't any time, just no way to wiggle out of the moment, to say sorry, to say stop, to say we fucked up, nothing to be done, or rather, they could do the big one, or just nothing, sit passively, hemmed in by life and by all the possibilities they couldn't quite dream into the real, and they understood that to play was to lose, but not to play was something worse, and so it was the football, the gold codes, it was all initiated, it would start very soon, it was all just minutes away, the big event, the one we'd been waiting for for the better part of a century, the button got pushed, it was easy, sure, it really was, now that it had happened, across the Midwest and elsewhere the missiles took to the sky as President Trump landed softly on the roof of Trump Tower, not listening for but hearing nonetheless, somewhere far below, faint and inescapable as his own heartbeat, the oceanic roar of protestors flooding the streets of Manhattan. ■

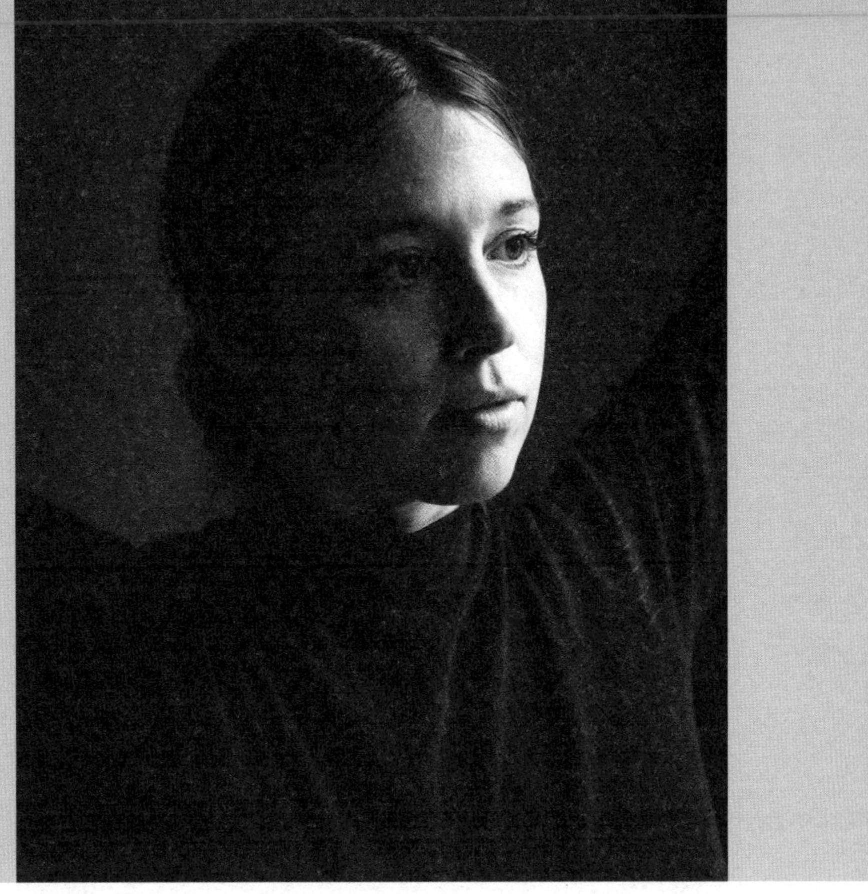

JEN GEORGE

1980

Jen George was born and raised in Southern California. She is the author of the story collection *The Babysitter at Rest*, out with Dorothy, a publishing project. Her writing has appeared in *BOMB*, *Harper's*, the *Los Angeles Review of Books*, *n+1* and the *Paris Review Daily*, among other places. She lives in New York, where she is currently at work on a novel.

REVOLUTIONS

Jen George

Agreements

I was unsure of our understanding or the way things are between most people, how they come to agreements such as sleepovers, eating meals together, being the same person daily. Maybe the man had said something and I had said yes. Or we had said nothing.

'It's kind of funny?' I say.

'What is?' he says.

'That there has been any agreement and that we cannot name what it is,' I say.

'I wouldn't say that at all,' he says. His disease can make him contrary.

Notice of severance-of-relations

When we are informed via a severance-of-relations notice brought by courier that our relationship is to be terminated, the man and

I think that before we part ways it is possible to try for a child. Our relationship had developed in this room, often mid-coitus, for the past two weeks. We'd shunned party duties and meetings and actions, thus bringing our increasingly exclusive arrangement to the attention of the party, resulting in the notice. The party usually broke things up before they reached this point, but there it was, the idea, gestating as it were.

History

Because of this man's large eyes and enormous chest I had noticed him when, at party meetings, while drinking burnt coffee poured from the large percolator, he'd bring up spiritual matters and personal statements along the lines of 'I often forget that the work is limited to life span', or 'So much to do, so little time!' His statements were often struck from official party records because blanket statements masquerading as collective statements when they were, in fact, individualistic statements were considered not only narcissistic but also imitative of the language that the ruling class had adopted and mimicked to masquerade as party-like after the party had initially secured the eastern sector of the city (following many deaths). Things were, at that moment in our history, looking good for us (the party) and we were told it was no time to get soft.

Simple action

If the party belief was true, that the reality of any relationship was simple action that occurred such as greeting, parting, eating and taking up arms together, rather than complex action that occurred, like the enjoyment of one particular person's company, sweet things said or time passed side by side – a party device, a sort of psychoanalytic perception exercise, meant to illuminate the crutches of comfort, loyalty and the illusion of partnership between any two people thereby mitigating exclusivity in terms of personal connection – then the real relationship between the man and me, in the simple action sense, was possibly sex and eating drugstore bread, though I couldn't be sure.

Déjà vu I & Horse height

It occurred to me that this had occurred before and that it would probably occur again. Prior to my commitment to the party, prior to the oaths I'd taken that banned my specific brand of intuition (including déjà vu), I'd been something of a spiritualist, though always with a political edge. For instance, I'd drunkenly invited ruling-class energies in via Ouija board and planchette. The spirits, as they were, came with the express purpose of gaining back lost monies from the banks then under siege and using their monies to purchase new belongings – gilded sofas, legs of ham, cars – to take back to their tombs. At the bank, with the passwords they'd given me, I withdrew everything from their accounts and donated all of the monies to the party, who were making strides by occupying some smaller banks and midsize hotels in the city center. The amount, a sum I thought large, turned out to be nothing remarkable. Not aware I was on any horse, I was told by an established comrade to get off my high one about the donations that got me in the party door. Long-established comrades had called me petite princess. I was hurt by the insult, and I came up with many reasons I was not. At meetings I was either told not to whine or ignored altogether.

I'd cried for some time over the name, over the established comrades' indifference toward me, and I'd come out the other side performing, almost like a tap dance, certain high-risk tactical operations to win favor.

I'd said: Do you like me now?

Long-established comrades had answered: What?

It was then I truly fell in love with the party.

Déjà vu II

This wasn't the first time I'd witnessed such events – a notarized and delivered severance of intra-party love affairs – my own, even – though the saying about stepping in the same river applies; *don't get swept along this time!* The question of a child, in our case, as in most, was one born of feelings of affection and dreams of domesticity (and possibly this man's particular disease, which created in him a strong feeling that he had to leave something of himself behind), and was therefore forbidden.

Why him

The idea was possible because I was susceptible to dissident ideas within dissidence and the man, though raised within the party, went against certain things the party preferred in that he was diseased and somewhat pliable. It was possible we were both flimsy regarding vows.

Not leprosy

His disease was without a name, or was sometimes (insensitively) referred to as *without merit*, or *not leprosy*, or it was otherwise referred to as an umbrella condition for any hang-ups concerning death (also insensitive). It housed many symptoms and was described in local medical journals as something like being on a deathbed during flare-ups – loss of senses, release of bowels and fluids, fake-out death rattles, despair, hope, grand speeches. The disease gave the man a sense of urgency in many areas, but also a sense of resignation in many other areas. Even so, he agreed to the baby quite easily.

Mid-coitus

The news of impending severance surprised neither of us.

'It's not so much about endings as new beginnings,' I say, mid-coitus, though the erection enhancers he'd ordered from the drugstore that promised help with deathbed-like symptom flare-ups, such as half-erections, had not lived up to promises, so it was more half-coitus than full mid-coitus.

We'd been warned

There had been notes left at his street-level window more or less telling us to knock it off; invitations for only one of us at party meetings, another woman – a newer comrade – sent to the door in an oatmeal-colored body stocking, a long knife through the door. Most of the warnings were on the polite side, considering.

Developments

'Oh, it's a little up,' I say, as encouragement. Small praise was like a drug for party members, though we used real drugs too, hard ones, drugs that imbued one with the facility for ruthless violence and multiple orgasms. In effect, he got a little harder. A half-erection.

Beating the dead horse of time

'There isn't much time,' he says (quietly, hoarsely), not as one of his blanket statements, but in reference to conception and the time between now and morning when party officials will come to collect me and take me to a new studio within the eastern sector.

Because the time is short I get carried away, though my arousal is not quite genuine.

'In my dying moment, please go slower,' he says (softly, dramatically).

'It's your disease talking – there will be no dying moment,' I remind him.

Genetics

I cannot forget the genetic line of my blood relatives, the inflated tales of good stock and boasts of managerial positions that my family ate and regurgitated on a loop for hundreds of years in order to feel a sense of pride in and order to their existence, though they were all fantasists with bad teeth who worshipped lottery numbers and coveted wealth and wished for top-of-the-line dentures – clear red flags of personality disorders that may affect our future child.

'Is there mental illness in your original family?' I ask.

'Yes,' he says (almost not saying it).

'A lot?'

'Rife,' he says, 'littered across both sides,' (this takes maybe five full minutes for him to say).

'My side is lousy with it as well. Taboos and stigmas are changing, or easing?' I say.

He makes a face.

What was I even doing?

'What were we even doing when we met?' I ask.

'Drunk,' he says (prolonged u).

'Yes, but –'

'Very drunk. You were dancing in a foolish way,'(stuttered).

'Oh.'

'With the janitor,' (mouthed), 'Your. Legs. Around. His. Torso,' (each word spat out in two-minute intervals). 'Your. Tights. Ripped. Skirt. Up. Around. Your. Waist.'

'What a good memory you have,' I say.

'It was a short time ago, in some regards,' he says (this a mix of sputter, croak and whisper). 'Your face was reddened, your eyes both yellowed and reddened, your hair greasy, your outfit unmemorable. As if . . .' he communicates this mostly with his eyes, then trails off at the end.

'As if –' I say, in effort to get some information about myself from that time in my life, two weeks prior to this moment, but he is not with me. Not dead, just somewhere else.

Acceptance

'And you saw me dancing and . . .' I say, again in coitus, though his half-erection is claylike in temperature and consistency inside of me.

'Doing a whipping thing with your arm . . . lasso?' he says.

'Helicoptering,' I say.

This is an example of him being accepting, seeing me like that. I'd not exactly blacked out, but larger details of the night are lost.

'Was it a country bar?' I used to like line dancing – there was a time, almost like it was yesterday, where people did it for fun, like karaoke.

'No,' he says, but the o's far more protracted, some of his life force leaving him.

'A dive in the deep eastern sector?' I ask, thinking how wild I was, how of-the-people I was. He answers no, again with his eyes.

'A hotel bar?' I ask. He says yes (eyes) and I am relieved because there is something purposeful and obedient in that, even elegant; hotel visits were party assignments, the young sent out to recruit and sew seeds of dissatisfaction amongst otherwise contented-seeming guests and workers. We were to break up marriages, talk shit about higher-ups to lower staff, we were to clog toilets or at least miss the mark in droves. The assignments were a secret favorite of mine because I had always wanted to stay in a hotel.

Affection

I recall brief moments of the night, just not the lead-up to our meeting, or my actions before. He'd half-smiled at me, sideways, his occasional face palsy having flared up, though I'd read the smile as knowing. He'd said 'Whoa!' regarding me, in a way that suggested he saw me. Of him I'd thought, I kind of like him. I'd said, 'I like you.'

I was several sheets to the wind and both our clarity and affection in seeing each other in that moment may be the thing that people hope for in bars, their legs around torsos, lassoing or (more likely) helicoptering. At the hotel bar I'd like to think we'd nodded, or maybe shrugged, possibly made an expression (though because of his face palsy I doubted that possibility), and both come to a similar feeling or idea about one another.

Choreography

The first night, by the light of his studio hurricane lamp we had taken off our clothes. He held my face. I kissed his chest, which was very wide. 'Brutus,' I'd said, because of his chest.

And then in the morning, after our first meeting, after the long night, as he'd been reading aloud from the charred newspaper, I'd said, 'Why am I still here?' We ate bread from the drugstore. He'd shrugged. I imitated him pouring coffee, shaky because of his disease. He imitated me looking out the window, waiting for something else. For a short time his symptoms had not flared up and in those days there was come all over the bed and in my hair and on the old drugstore bread. There was come on his street-level window, on the floor, on his little radiator where it dried and crusted. I'd swallowed so much of his come I was scarcely hungry for drugstore bread. When I talked of my childhood, he'd rolled his eyes. When he'd spoken of his, I'd said, 'So cute and so important.'

When I'd read aloud from an old diary I carried with me from my spiritualist days, he'd said, 'I don't understand the point.' I'd kissed him upon his huge chest for not caring.

By the afternoon, I was in tears.

'You really went to town last night,' he'd said. 'It's just your body dealing with all the alcohol leaving your system.'

It'd given me perspective.

Looking out his street-level window and watching people walking in and out of the drugstore, taking up lead pipes with which to rally and riot, shouting through the community loudspeaker, I'd said, 'Why do we keep doing it?'

'It's what's in front of us,' he'd said, delivering the party line with real conviction. 'There is work yet to do.' It'd made me remember my love of the party.

No door impassable

'I want to tell our child of the meeting,' I say.

'The stories of special romantic meetings are treated with significance by those wanting to believe that their lives can change, that new things are possible, that love will find you,' he says (an eternity).

'Maybe the child will be one of those people and in that case I'll want this story for her,' I say.

'All we did was walk through that door, so to speak,' he says.

'What door?'

'The one that presented itself.'

'What?'

Body stocking

I put on a body stocking made of especially thin pantyhose nylon in a dark blue color. I'd ordered it from the drugstore when we were wild.

'Is it like my body's a special fruit, wrapped in tissue?' I ask him, about the stocking. He doesn't answer and I admire his energy conservation. 'My pubes stick outside of the crotch opening though,' I explain, since his vision is compromised regarding details like pubes and since I think he'd appreciate that particular detail.

I move to the chair at his window, hoping his vision is good enough to see, hoping he can hear the shouts and screams and breaking glass, the bats, the thuds, the clothes ripping, the crying, the loudspeaker messages, the music. It's the work of our people. It's our action, even if we have been non-participatory for weeks.

Re-enactments

Motivated by the body stocking, which is far different in feeling than just wearing nothing, I go through the stages of my life in a performative manner: for baby I just lie there. For girl I do some re-enactments: jumping in a puddle, throwing a large rock at the man's head. His eyes glaze over. I move straight to teen, though with one hand on (an imaginary) Ouija planchette, it's more conceptual. The concept turns him on and I see his erection half-rise, so we return to intercourse. I'm disappointed I didn't get into all of my phases. But, I focus; this is bigger than us, or the moment, or performances. *The future is dependent upon this very moment*, a party line that I never quite understood because there were always moments.

We've always been here

'It seems we've always been here,' I say, since we had not left the room. 'But I'd like to escape this particular moment, which is possibly ongoing, you know, if we've always been in the moment of revolution, as the party tells us.'

He moans.

'And then,' I say, 'how'd I come to spend consecutive nights at your studio?'

'You just fell asleep and woke up each day,' he says (mouth white, no lubrication, crust formed, tongue dry like a stick in sand).

'Did you ask me to?'

'No,' (quite clear).

'It'd have been romantic of you to ask me,' I say.

'Sorry,' he mouths. 'I was brought up in the party and that isn't our way. But I did want you here.'

'I would have liked it if you'd made me a nice dinner,' I say, though not only was there no food for a nice dinner but to say this is a regression to my ruling-class upbringing – a time when, as a very young child, my only desire was for nice dinners or romantic dinners or dinners at restaurants, as well as dentures and monies. 'You could've told me – please stay here with me because you're what I've been looking for this whole time,' I say.

'I did, I do, sort of, as much as the next anyway. The proprietary premise of your desire is against everything we're fighting for,' (slack-jawed, mouth movements like a large fish and gasping for air like one).

'You should've said – I want to marry you, even though it's illegal within the party and I'm too unconventional for marriage. I would've liked someone who I actually wanted to ask me. I'd been asked before, but only by fans.'

'Fans,' he says (eyes crossing).

'I had them when I was somewhat younger,' I explain, 'men who loved my youth and carelessness and sadness. They all asked me to marry them –'

'Suitors – maybe that's a more accurate name. Admirers, even.'

'Fans is the accurate word,' I say.

'We should continue,' he reminds me.

Visuals

Regarding orgasms, his are based on visuals of ownership and control of possessions – he can't help it since they are forbidden and therefore highly desirable. Mine are based on foggy visions (sometimes silhouettes of sex acts in actual fog), strangers' faces, dreams, words, thoughts and with every sexual act it's like pulling the lever on a slot machine to see what combination will pop up. Oftentimes nothing does, and orgasm occurs in a sort of black hole without narrative or imagery or even fog.

Sentiments I

'You never hurt me,' he says after I threaten then fail to leave prior to established comrades coming to take me away.

'I sort of tried,' I say.

'That's why it didn't hurt – your attempts so clearly showed your ruling-class roots in trying to get attention and arouse desire through rejection or some charade of unattainability.'

'I hated you at times. I saw all of your weaknesses, like your disease or your come face and, and at moments, I believed that's all you were,' I say.

'Likewise,' he says, very sweetly.

'What are my weaknesses?' I ask.

'We shouldn't.'

'Please,' I say, 'Tell me the bad things you saw in me – it can't hurt at this point.'

'You can be unloving,' he says, rather easily. 'Almost like you never knew physical affection in any way other than sex, and even with sex, for you, it's not affection – it's desire met with violence plus the hope the other attaches to you. It's how you've survived, though it makes no sense and it's clearly a failed and outdated personal system that you keep repeating.'

Sentiments II

'You'll be a handsome old man if you make it that far,' I say, looking at his yellowed teeth that already resemble fine-looking dentures.

'There were times where I thought I did not want to be around you ever again,' he says (age spots blossom on his face and hands).

'Why are we still talking about this?' I say,

'No one else will want you the way I want you,' he tells me.

'That's my worst fear,' I say. 'You know all I want is for a lot of people to want me.'

He winks. Or one eye is no longer opening.

'There were times I caught glimpses of you as you aged, and the glimpses were grotesque,' he says.

'We're getting off-topic,' I say, not wanting to hear about future visions of myself.

Diversions

To stop his visions, I stand up on the bed and practice my walking-down-the-stairs mime, ending in a heap on the bed.

'It's good!' he says (gagging on fluid).

'Thanks – I haven't practiced for some time,' I say.

'You were doing that, repeatedly, at the bar, the night we –'

'Shh,' I say. I will not be including that in the story of our meeting – that is if I ever tell it.

'I just remembered another thing with you and the janitor,' he says. 'When dancing, you had your ass kind of shaking close to his face.'

I'll not be including that either.

'There are many ways to disrupt and recruit,' I say, knowing that had not been my intention with the janitor. Knowing I had none.

Birthday/Speech speech speech

'It's almost your birthday and I'm going to miss it.'

'Too bad,' he says.

I make a cake out of charred newspaper, nail clippings, cornmeal, shrimp powder, and boxed gelatin.

'Happy birthday to you,' I sing, a candlestick from the drugstore intended for an emergency brightly lit. I say, 'Thank the people you were born and we met and I know you and what are the chances and if we'd not been in that hotel bar together and me all over the janitor that got your attention, and had we not nodded or come to any agreement or whatever it was, and had these two weeks not passed – who knows!'

'Yes!' he says, 'How fortunate,' (happy).

'Who knows . . . maybe we'd be in different studios within the sector mid-coitus with different people, eating different bread, wearing different body stockings.'

'Yes, funny,' (not paying attention).

'Hello?' I say.

'I'm preparing a birthday speech,' (whispered). Speeches are one of his less tolerable symptoms.

'I never knew what I was looking for,' he says. 'I have always had bad vision, literally and figuratively – now more than ever,' (eyes steadily crossed). 'When I saw you, I thought – what is that ruckus-ass doing? Looked like wrestling or lassoing –'

'I was helicoptering, more likely – we've established it's a sort of dance and that it shouldn't be mentioned again.'

'I thought you looked like an urchin, but sexy – I'm saying that only upon reflection – I didn't consciously think that when I saw you – it's only now, in remembering, that I'm trying to provide narrative for what was going on in my head, and it may be false at that, an attempt to give our relationship importance, an attempt at romance, an attempt at giving memory meaning.'

'That's sweet,' I say. 'I love that,' I say.

'At some point, I suppose something would have happened, either we would have continued together because we both would grow similarly, or lack growth similarly, and either way still be in agreement. Or, I would've figured out at some point what I wanted – the way men of the west figure out in middle age what they want is a young, nice sex nurse that they can take to parties, and I'd pursue that at the cost of any quiet integrity I'd built to that point, and eventually people would just say, about my young lover – what is age anyway, or, let him do what he wants.'

'We'd all just get used to it,' I say.

'Please, don't interrupt –' (wheezing, seizures). 'What I mean to say is, I accepted what was in front of me and I didn't question it and you were what was there with the same energy and so drunk, and hungry in the same way and alone in the same way and desperate in the same way and horny in the same way.'

He blows the candle out with a wet cough that produces both a lot of phlegm and a lot of fluid.

The fake-death symptom of his disease flares. His fake-out death rattle is distinct. Since I won't be with him for his actual death, I say, 'I am going to miss you.' Like a widow, I say, 'What will I do now?' Knowing I won't speak at the mass cremation that his body (along with hundreds of others) will be burned in, I say, 'Thank the people we cannot grasp the concept of finality in moments such as these!' Then, 'This life is so fleeting!' He smiles a little. I drag his actually limp body into the large washbasin. I fake-bathe him since water is very, very limited, him naked, me in my body stocking, blood and come crusted in my pubic hair and all over the stocking. 'Your child will be nostalgic for the memory of you,' I say. He has no expression, his breathing has become so shallow it's really like he's died.

The morning has come. The man coughs inside the large washbasin as two established comrades enter the studio. I collect my ripped tights and come-stained clothing – the tactical operation costume that I'd been wearing the night of our meeting. I leave the body stocking. It will be burned in the big fire.

Wheel of fortune

The new studio housing is in the same Eastern bloc style. There are fewer freedoms now, but it was necessary to shed old affections. I'd stumbled – a child! What would I have done with her? My assignments became hotels entirely; I was very good at it. My only skills were well used.

The passage of time

There is some time. I remember – the man and his time, his statements about time, the shortness of time, the way he thought talking about time meant anything. I'd had to remind myself of vows, convictions, and beliefs. I told myself *the revolution!* frequently in order to stay, and I read and reread and memorized our books and pamphlets – righteous things of equality and the nonstop struggle, how to stay pissed and attack people who were wearing looks of contentment and in possession of many items or goods, which I did happily.

My people, the ones I'd come from, the ones whose physicality and behaviors had driven me into party arms all those years ago, wrote letters: *we will pay for you to get out of there*, they said, as though they had monies for bus tickets. The party and I would laugh at my old family, entrenched in their system, opiated by dreams of monies and dentures and tall horses, and we'd burn their letters. My old family persisted, they sent envelopes stuffed with their approved credit card applications to show they had possible lines of credit in sums upwards of hundreds of thousands, along with catalogs promising new spring goods like floral dresses and sandals, and some pictures from before I fled. They sent magazine pictures of men riding big horses and wearing cowboy hats. They sent grocery receipts from purchases bought on credit: several item tickets boasting fresh produce and ice cream cakes. They sent menus from restaurants near the ocean with meals they'd eaten lightly circled in blue ballpoint pen. They'd say: *the ocean is nice and we love the restaurants.* They remained single-mindedly against the party's beliefs and actions that will inevitably encroach upon and then engulf their world.

Revolutions

The fires are enormous. I can see to the west side of town. I see bottles going into their windows. I throw them myself, and often far worse things. I shoot water balloons filled with bleach so as to ruin their clothing. Those in the western sector don't see our gains though our actions do end in deaths – the deaths of their people – but since they are not united and lives are not purchasable, they do not see the deaths as theirs. They buy new panes and clothing and attempt to ignore us. They think all actions are largely inconsequential or that order is the objective and reciprocal state, though their houses and monies are burning and we now occupy three hotels in the city center.

When I pass the big fire I ask, 'What's in there?' The answers come from all sides: phone books, photographs, body stockings, trash, costumes, journals, plastics. I find myself at night thinking, *this is the right way!* Or, *these actions are not choice but necessity!*

Reception of notice

I receive, via courier, an intra-party notice sent by the old man. It's written as a sort of speech: 'Time has sped up evermore.' I take note of his new language, which suggests both a distance from our past and a promotion within the party. 'Time releases us from closeness and even the memory, eventually. I pray to forgetting, the act of abandonment and erasure, it has taken the place of feeling and longing. It is like a child, or at least something familiar. The struggle is the true child. Or maybe there just isn't one – a child that is. The struggle remains real and total. Anyhoo – let's forget about the *child* child. Enclosed is a small lasso. Ever yours in the struggle, as I am ever everyone's in the struggle.' I take the small lasso to the big fire. Afterward I catch myself at night, in the studio of another man, thinking old things. ■

Courtesy of the author

RACHEL B. GLASER

1982

Rachel B. Glaser is the author of *Paulina & Fran*, the story collection *Pee on Water* and the poetry books *MOODS* and *HAIRDO*. She studied painting and animation at Rhode Island School of Design, and poetry and fiction at UMass-Amherst. In 2013, she received the *McSweeney's* Amanda Davis Highwire Fiction Award. She lives in Northampton, Massachusetts. She tweets as @candle_face.

DAY 4

Rachel B. Glaser

Her hair hung around her knees as she pulled up her socks. Loretta dug through dusty boxes until she found the yellow sweatshirt with the faded image of a moose on skis. It still fit. She squeezed into a pair of old leggings and heard the elastic give out. She went through the boxes remembering each thing – where she'd gotten it and what it had meant – until this became torturous and she lay on the floor wanting to die. If the funeral hadn't made her cry, and sleeping in this house didn't make her cry, then it was settled, she was not human.

There was a knock at the front door, probably the landlord. Loretta didn't move. The knocking continued. The doorbell had broken long ago and had never been repaired. When she was sure he was gone, she got up and dumped all the boxes into trash bags. She had until midnight to clear everything out. If she worked hard all day, she could do it. She'd have to fill up the small rental car and make multiple trips to the Salvation Army, or the dump, or some abandoned place where no one would care what she left.

Again she tried to walk into her mother's room, but it was too terrible. It smelled like a bog. The cat was hiding in there somewhere, Loretta suspected. She left the door open and dragged the bags down the creaky stairs. She drank from the kitchen faucet. There was no food in the house and she decided she wasn't hungry.

She lugged the bags out the front door. It was much too hot to be dressed the way she was. She threw the bags into the trash bin and wheeled it to the curb. Across the street, two boys punched each other. The younger one was crying. The older boy held an ice-cream cone in one hand while he punched with the other. Neither boy was wearing a shirt. Maybe they would help her load up the car if she made it seem like a game. 'Hey,' she yelled. She hadn't said anything for days.

The older one looked at her in disgust, as if he knew how she'd been living. Loretta gave them the finger. The crying one stopped crying. He had green and purple Magic Marker scribbled on his chest. 'Got a fucking cigarette?' the older one yelled. He had to have been about eleven, she thought, sizing up his untied Nikes and the thin gold chain around his neck.

She crossed the street without thinking. 'I used to babysit you,' she lied.

'You don't look familiar,' the kid said, digging his tongue into the peak of the cone.

'You were too young to remember. He was just a baby.' She pointed to the younger one, who was jamming a twig into a red gummy bear in the grass. 'You didn't smoke back then,' Loretta told the kid. 'And you had this little dolly named Popcorn.' Now that she was talking she couldn't shut up.

'I didn't have any doll,' the kid said, throwing the rest of his cone into the street.

'It had these ears,' she said, putting her hands to her head. A curtain shook in the window of her mother's apartment. The cat pressed its face against the glass.

'Can you drive us somewhere?' the younger one asked, squinting. He was sort of adorable. It looked like you could tell him anything and he'd believe you.

The kid sat in the passenger seat. 'How old are you?' he asked.

'Thirty-six.'

'You married?' he asked dubiously. Loretta glanced at the younger one in the back, absentmindedly rolling his window up and down.

'People don't get married anymore,' she said. The kid leaned his head against his seat belt. 'Turn here?' She could tell he didn't know where they were. He nodded, staring at her sweatshirt. The moose lay on its back in a puff-paint snowdrift, its four pink skis tangled in the air.

'Is that blood?' he asked, pointing to the stain on her sleeve.

'Old blood,' she said.

'I'm hungry,' said the younger one.

She pulled the white Nissan into a narrow spot between two black cars. The boys were out before she turned off the engine. She opened the trunk and dug around for her wallet.

The boys ran to the pinball machine at the back of Sal's. Loretta watched them gleefully pound away at the buttons and launch imaginary ball after imaginary ball. The floor had been retiled, but she was relieved to find the ugly mural still alive. Though parts had been retouched, Loretta could see the ghost of old graffiti under the phony Sicilian sunset. She ordered a pizza, two sodas and a beer from a teenager slouched behind the register. She felt a thrill that she still didn't know the boys' names.

'Loretta?' Giovanni called from the walk-in. He put down a sack of something and jogged towards her. 'It's Gio.' His white T-shirt was splattered with sauce and tucked into black sweatpants. He wore socks and flip-flops and a gold cross in his ear. 'Giovanni,' he said. 'You know, The Vanni?'

His face had grown puffy. He hadn't been particularly interesting in high school. Kind of nice, but his friends had been jerks. Gio shifted his weight. Back in the day he had worn silk shirts and black jeans. He'd had a ponytail. Loretta remembered dissecting the fetal pig – how some of the boys had gotten too into it, and how some of the girls had refused to even watch.

'I heard about what happened,' Gio said. Loretta's face burned. The town was too small! She looked down and stared into her wallet. 'Please, Lor, it's on the house.'

The teenager closed the register. 'How long you been back?' Gio asked. It wasn't that she died – people died every day. It was how she died, and that everyone knew. More people came to the funeral than should have. People she hadn't seen in decades, people she wasn't close to. They whispered during it. They wanted to see, but there wasn't anything left you could put in a casket. Loretta turned slowly, then walked outside.

She sat sweating on the curb as her mother's narrow face hovered over the parking lot like a hologram. Its pearly eyes bore down on her. It was sucking up all her power! Loretta quickly got up and felt woozy. She staggered into her car and started the engine. She couldn't catch her breath. The song on the radio was an old one she knew. She turned it way up. As she pulled away from the curb, she could see the boys running to the door. She felt like a claw rising out of the earth. She sped off.

The light was yellow and she plowed through it. The next one turned red, but she couldn't stop. Panic and delight danced in her blood. The boys! She missed them. The boys! She had taught them a lesson.

Loretta saw the sign for the highway and thought of all her mother's belongings waiting to be seen and held by her. Legions of porcelain figurines, covered in mouse poop, awaiting their fates. She took the turn without signaling, careening onto the highway, and maneuvered into the fast lane. She let out a whoop that sounded like a dying animal. No one could stop her.

She drove much too fast, as if she had somewhere to be. She imagined the landlord cursing her as he stripped Mother's bed. He'd have to saw apart the sofa if he wanted it out. She'd gotten halfway through before giving up. She swerved around a dead deer. She passed a futon flopped over the median. I should turn around, she thought every now and then, knowing she wouldn't. Part of her mind shut off and she drove in a trance. It grew dark and she was very far from any city. After repeatedly daring herself to, but not actually doing it, she suddenly pulled her car off the road into a field and skidded to a stop.

Loretta opened her door, unfastened her seat belt, then crawled out of the car into the wet grass. She was an orphan! The word sounded beautiful to her. She could do anything she wanted. She took off her shoes and socks. She pulled off the leggings, balled them up, and threw them a few feet away. She was naked except for the sweatshirt and pressed the moose to her chest. She was thirsty. Her mouth and eyes scrunched closer together. Finally, she would cry! But she didn't. She curled into a ball and tucked her knees into the sweatshirt.

She awoke to what sounded like stampeding hooves. Her mind stumbled, remembering where she was. A brown cloud billowed up the black sky. Loretta coughed and shivered, peering through her fists at machines plowing across the barren field. Their motors groaned inside her skull. Loretta reached for her leggings, but the wind caught them. She watched as they flipped through the air then got sucked into the grinding tread of a tractor. She scrambled into the car, turned the ignition, and stomped the gas pedal with her bare foot. Her car lurched and bumped as she steered back onto the shoulder. A white delivery truck blared its horn. Loretta laughed. The radio played a love song and she pressed a button to get something else.

People stared while she pumped gas. Some teenagers whistled. She tugged the sweatshirt to cover her butt. Her mother watched from someplace. Loretta examined the dirty bottoms of her feet until the pump clicked. She put it away and screwed on the gas cap. A bell rang out as Loretta walked into the minimart.

Loretta sat on her car's trunk, wearing neon-green men's swim trunks and eating a hot dog. On the other side of the highway was Kentucky. She wanted to hear someone talk. She pictured the boys in a police station arguing about whether her hair was dark or light, as a sketch artist drew his own version of the moose. Her hair was dark and straight. She hurled a piece of bun at Kentucky.

Decades ago, when they were still a family, her parents dragged her to Leitchfield to see an albino cow with green eyes. When they finally got there, the cow was sleeping. They left and went for lunch and when they returned the cow had fallen into a coma. 'But I need to see its eyes!' Loretta had wailed.

Her father asked a farmhand if he could pry the cow's eyes open. The farmhand hesitated. It was only the four of them under the tent. He approached the cow and took off his leather gloves, looking over his shoulder to make sure no one was watching. He delicately put two fingers on its eyelid and pulled, but it held together like a clamshell. On their way out, Loretta's parents bought a bottle of the cow's milk for twenty dollars and said they'd serve it in champagne glasses that night with dessert, but never did.

Loretta's car lifted slowly off the earth as she drove across the border into Kentucky. It was a moonless night. She wasn't human. Sometimes she was better, sometimes she was worse. Her mind started to combine things. She found herself forgetting she was driving. Her father had died driving. It wasn't the worst way to go. It was better than her mother's way. Loretta slowed until the car was going five miles an hour. A motorcycle flew by. Its headlight left a trail in her sight.

She saw a half-lit sign for a motel and took the exit. She jammed her car into a crooked space in the parking lot and sat there for a while, paralyzed. By noon tomorrow she was supposed to return the car, full of gas, to a Hertz in Pittsburgh, then fly back to Missoula. But she knew she wouldn't make it.

Loretta slid the remaining bills out of her wallet and onto the counter. The clerk handed her a key that had an 8 drawn on it in sharpie. A man walked in humming loudly. Loretta shot him a wild look. He wore jeans and a button-down shirt. She stared at his goatee and let her eyes glaze over. In another time and place he might've been considered handsome. She'd been looking at him too long. He winked. 'Where're your shoes at?' he asked, laughing to himself as she walked out past him.

She closed the door behind her and looked over the room. A water-damaged print of a tree hung crooked in a plastic frame. A red light blinked every few seconds from a smoke alarm on the ceiling. On the cheap dresser sat a small flat-screen TV. Loretta found the remote and pressed a button. It took a long time to turn on, then played a looped news clip of a foreign city under siege. She muted it. She eyed the telephone on the desk, unable to think of a single person she could call.

She sat on the double bed. Mother wouldn't have liked the funeral, except when the *Amazing Grace* CD had skipped. She would have liked that, how the crowd murmured. Loretta stretched. Only one of her legs was shaved. The water at her mother's hadn't stayed hot for long.

She could hear the humming man outside. She pulled the curtain back to look at him, but he saw her. She let go of the curtain. She let him in before he knocked. The man studied her sweatshirt, then scanned the room. She felt a sense of disappointment. 'Am I interrupting something?' he asked, settling into the armchair by the window.

'I've got a couple hours,' she said, still standing by the door.

'You drink?'

'When there's nothing else to do.'

He slid sunglasses over his eyes and handed her a flask. Loretta took a long pull. Her throat burned. 'It's only milk,' he said. He waited for her to laugh, but she didn't. She felt like in real life they'd be enemies. There was only one chair so she sat on the bed. Children cried on the television. Loretta wanted him to sing to her, but assumed that wasn't what he had in mind.

'Close the door,' she said. The man kicked the door shut with his heel and settled back in the chair. They listened to someone wheel luggage past.

'How's it goin'?' he asked, taking off his sunglasses. She looked at his eyes and decided he was older than her. She looked away. 'Talk much?' he said. She smirked. 'You don't care what happens, do you?' He unbuttoned his sleeve and rolled it up. He traced his finger down the tattoos on his forearm, stopping on one that looked like rope.

Loretta watched as he stood up and limped past her bed into the bathroom. She listened as his pee hit the water. Her heart began to thump. She reached for the flask and emptied it into her mouth. She crawled into bed.

'I'm Lyle,' the man said as he came out of the bathroom. He picked up the empty flask and frowned. 'I'll be back,' he said, and left with the flask. Loretta burrowed deeper in the covers and thought some more about the boys. They could have taken care of her. She could have pulled them out of school and taken them on a trip.

Lyle came back clutching a paper bag. He closed the door behind him. He pulled out a fifth of Wild Turkey and passed it to her. She opened it and drank.

'What'd I miss?' he said.

'I started missing these kids I could have had.'

'What's your name?' She tried, but felt unable to form the word. 'You don't have to say,' he said. He looked around the room. 'Mine's just like this, if you wanna see it.' She passed him the bottle and he took a long drink. 'I'm staying here while they fumigate my house.' He rolled up his other sleeve. 'Wife got fed up and left. Now the house is too damn big.' He sighed. She watched the red light blink while he talked.

He cocked his head and leaned in. 'You like men?' he asked. Loretta felt like laughing, but didn't want him to think she was listening. He snorted. 'Feel like I'm talkin' to myself.'

'Fuck it.' He got up and she turned her head away. He took a few steps toward the door and stopped. He walked out and Loretta felt a marvelous pain.

'Lyle,' she said under her breath. She waited. 'Lyle,' she said a little louder. She pushed the covers aside and sat up. 'Lyle?' She rushed to the door.

He walked back in the room. 'People think men don't have feelings,' he said. He looked at his boots. 'I may not look it, but I read a lot of books.' She nodded. She hadn't had sex in years, but didn't think this was how it started. She closed the door and climbed back into bed. He sat in the chair. 'I'm the only one of my brothers that never went to jail. Not even close.'

'I used to keep ferrets,' she said.

He beamed at her. 'Really?' He stroked his goatee and leaned back in the chair. 'I always dreamed of owning a horse,' he said. 'But what's the point of owning a horse if you got no plans to ride it?' Loretta nodded.

'Ever been on a boat? Not a dinghy, one of those big ocean liners you live on for a week?' he asked.

'No.'

'Me either,' he said and looked at her face for a long time. 'Sorry I stormed out like that.'

'Can you sing?' she said.

He blushed. 'I can yodel.'

Lyle drank, then wiped his lips. He looked at her, unsure. His first note rang out of a mountain. Her eyes welled up. He stopped, 'Guess that's not real singing.' She reached out and put her hand on his knee and he began again. Lyle rose to his feet. Loretta watched transfixed as he rocked on the soles of his boots. He tapped his knees with his hands. She wasn't separate from the world, she was woven into it. The phone rang. Loretta stared at it and it fell off the desk. Lyle raised his eyebrows, but continued. He beat out a rhythm on his chest and howled. Finally, his voice broke, and he collapsed onto the bed. Loretta shook his shoulder, but he didn't respond. There was no way to revive him. His eyes were shut. Loretta pulled at his eyelids. He batted her hands away.

'Let me sleep,' he said as he rolled onto his stomach and kicked off his boots.

'Loretta,' she said. She hit the lights and wiped tears from her face, basking in the flickering darkness.

'Let me sleep, Loretta,' he said. ■

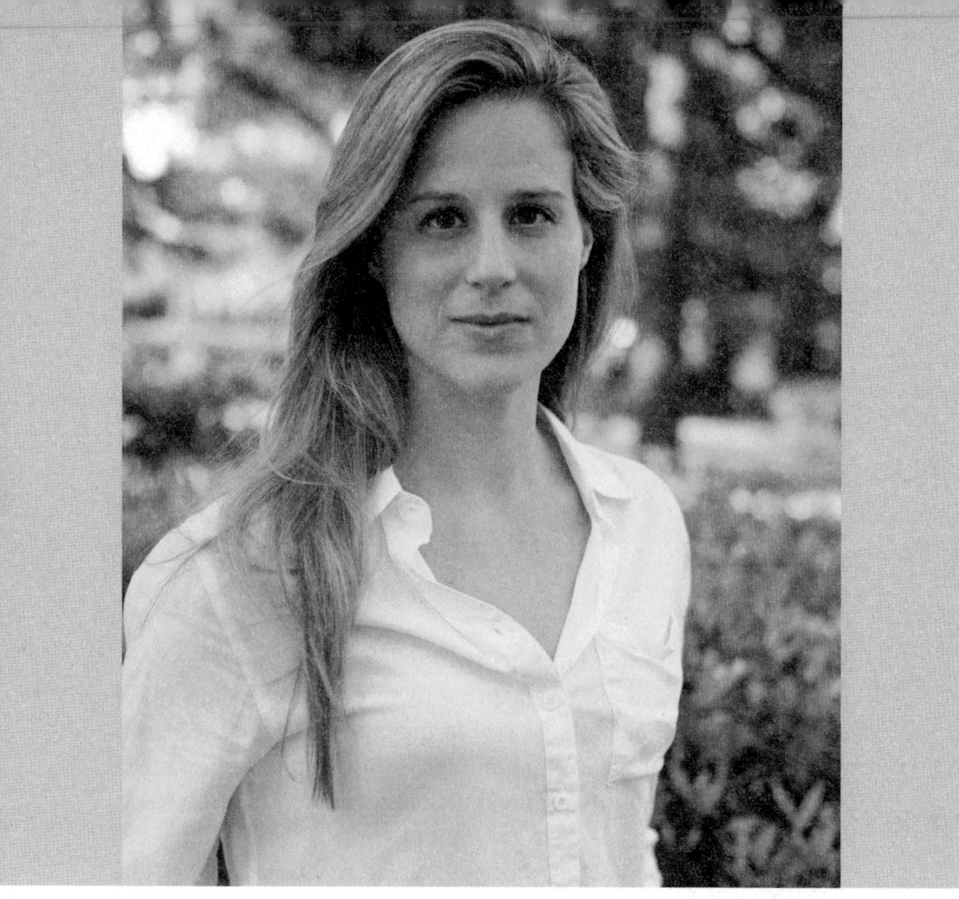

Courtesy of the author

LAUREN GROFF

1978

Lauren Groff is the author of four books, most recently the novel *Fates and Furies*, a finalist for the 2016 National Book Award and the 2015 National Book Critics Circle Award. She lives in Florida with her husband and sons.

YPORT

Lauren Groff

In August, the mother takes her two small sons to France.

She has been ambushed all spring by quick fits like slaps to the heart. She is tired of keeling over on the elliptical or in the streets where she walks her dread at night. Also, summer in Florida is a slow drowning. The humidity grows spots on her skin, pink in the pale, pale in the tan.

She tells her husband that she has to research Guy de Maupassant.

It's not untrue. For ten years, she has been stuck on a project about the writer. Or maybe he has been stuck in her, a fish bone lodged in her throat.

She no longer loves Guy, though she had loved him once, when she was seventeen and an exchange student in Nantes. She was so miserable that she kept having visions of herself leaping off the top of the Cathedral. Guy had come to her at the right time. His short stories had taught her French; also how to hang on.

The mother and her boys spend the first week in Paris.

Her older son is six and muscular, with an elegant large-eyed face like a fawn's, though his beauty is mitigated by extreme sensitivity.

He's like a windless pond, her husband once said. You throw

something in to watch it sink, and you're going to see it staring back at you for the rest of your life.

The four-year-old is sunny, golden. He sucks his thumb and carries around a cat puppet called Whoopie Pie. He makes friends everywhere. On the train from de Gaulle to their rental he shows a German tourist his tiny red backpack. She'd been crying, but when he climbs into her lap, she hides her eyes in his hair.

It disconcerts the mother to find that Paris has become Floridian, all humidity and stucco and cellulite rippling under shorts. They speak with her husband over Skype at lunch, but August is when he works eighteen-hour days, and the boys sense his impatience. When she speaks to adults it is to order things, her French gluey in her head. At night they sleep ten hours in the same cramped room, and in order to have some time alone, she drinks wine and watches French sitcoms on her computer with earphones until dawn.

On the seventh day, they take a train to Rouen. At the station, they rent an automatic Mercedes for the drive to the Alabaster coast in Normandy, where Maupassant was born. She feels wasteful, she has never understood luxury cars, but she couldn't drive stick on the cliffside roads or she'd kill them all.

The drive should take an hour but they get lost in the twisty villages. The four-year-old pukes on Whoopie Pie then falls asleep. The six-year-old cries about the smell. She has to crack the window to settle her own stomach and the drizzle whips into her eyes. She pauses in Fécamp to ask directions of a man who pretends not to understand her French, when she knows, irritated, that her French is fine.

At last they swing down a steep hillside into Yport. It is a fisherman's village, silex and brick. There is a curve of beach covered in stones, bracketed by cliffs of creamy limestone with horizontal veins of flint. She parks at the Casino lot to await a man named Jean-Paul, who will show them the house at three. It is only eleven.

When she steps out, the wind is chilly, the gulls scream, but there's a lift in her. Yport is so small. Surely, her dread would never look for her in such a place as this.

The boys chuck rocks into the boiling waves, loving the rattles the stones make in the troughs, the gulps in the crests. They climb into a cave in the cliff, but get spooked. She doesn't notice when the little one strips to his underoos and runs into the waves. She sees only a flash of gold going under, then wades in and drags him out. His skin is blue and his face is startled but when the older brother laughs at him, he laughs too.

It is so cold. The little boy is shuddering but she is too tired to go back to the car to change his clothes. There is a set of tin shacks on the beach for souvenirs, fried seafood, gelato. There, protected by a luffing sheet of plastic, she orders three buckwheat galettes with cheese, and one caramel crêpe for dessert. At home they eat no sugar, it is a poison, it can make you fat and crazy, but she wants her boys to love France and she isn't above bribery. She holds the little boy under her cardigan to warm him but the bigger one says that he is cold, too, and she lets him in. She isn't hungry. She drinks her local cider. Its notes of manure and grass nauseate her less when she thinks of it as terroir. Guy de Maupassant tasted the same thing long ago.

She sees, at the top of the cliffs, emerald meadows blown back by the wind like pompadours, dotted with white specks. Cows or sheep? she asks the boys. They make fun of her terrible eyesight and finally say, Oh, Mommy, sheep.

She imagines one iconoclastic sheep, after a life of envying the birds in their graceful hovers, coming to a sudden decision. He'd take a step. He'd become bird for a glorious flight; he'd meet the ocean, become jellyfish.

The boys jump off a stone wall in front of the Casino into a bed of lavender fat with bees. She lets her children make their own mistakes. There are worse lessons than bee stings.

A stocky man is coming down the hill, hallooing. Jean-Paul. His face is wind-battered. If he has eyes, they are so deep she can't see them. His odor shakes her hand before he does: unwashed clothes, body, salt.

He says the house is ready. He is surprised at her French. Not bad! He has a gift for her, he was told that she was researching Guy de Maupassant, and . . . He pulls out a wad of paper from the back pocket of his jeans.

She looks at it. He'd printed out the French Wikipedia page for Guy de Maupassant. She swallows her laugh, says that he shouldn't have, thanks very much. This is apparently insufficient. He frowns and squints then takes the little boy's hand. They chat, despite mutual incomprehension, and start up a long flight of stairs, seventy-four steps she'll count later, carved into the hillside. The mother carries all the heavy bags.

The older boy hangs back and whispers that he doesn't like that man.

At the top, Jean-Paul and the little boy have turned around and are watching her power upward, step by step. Jean-Paul calls out that she reminds him of a she-goat.

She says, I don't like him either, Monkey.

Atop the hill, the streets are haphazard, jogs and alleys, spills of red geraniums.

In the sun, out of the wind, it is warm.

At last, Jean-Paul pulls out a key, opens a door in a wall, steps in. The house is sparse, which suits her, rock, wood and plaster, three stacked rooms connected by a spiral staircase. There is a fatty, rotting smell that she recognizes from a long-ago apartment, after a rat died in the walls. There is dirt on the windowsills, hairs and sand in the drains.

The two skylights in her room at the top are open. She sticks her head through. On one side, she sees the sheep, the cliffs. The other is all slate rooftops, shining like damp skin. Everything from up here is striped: red-and-tan clock tower, blue-and-white tin cabanas on the beach, creamy cliffs with their flint veins, oceans navy with whitecaps, tiny people walking in mariner shirts. The wind is raw on her cheeks.

She brings her head in. Jean-Paul is standing close. His scent combines with the dead-animal smell from the kitchen to become an unpleasant taste in her mouth.

He wants to show her how to use the television, the Wi-Fi, the stovetop, but she goes down the stairs, opens the door. He hangs back. She says goodbye three different ways. He slinks out. She opens all the windows and waits as the wind blows the last of him out, then when she is sure he is gone, she makes the boys put their sandals on again.

The woman at the town's only épicerie laughs at the mother when she tries to fit the groceries into her reusable bag. The mother found an excellent burgundy at an astonishing price, one-fifteenth of what it would have cost at home, and bought all four bottles on the shelf. The woman gives her a cardboard box, and the bottles make it heavy. The boys pass the bakery slowly, speed by the butcher shop's window, gruesome with flesh. They don't eat creatures with faces.

It had been simple to get to the center of town, but now the mother has lost her way back. People throng the streets that had been silent and drizzling before. She asks someone where their street is, but he responds in a way that makes her fear she has lost her French entirely. Yportais is its own dialect, knotty as rope, she'd learn later.

At last she puts down the groceries, and rubs her arms. Don't cry, she orders herself.

The oldest boy comes over and stands on her feet, pressing his head into her sternum. He looks up at her. Isn't that it? he says, pointing to a cracked terracotta pot with red geraniums, beside the gap in the houses that leads into their narrow street. Sweet child; he'd known where he was all along.

She scrubs the house while the boys play, though it was supposed to have been cleaned. She can do nothing about the smell but keep the windows open and hope for a quick decay. They eat dinner. The boys go to sleep.

Downstairs, people pass the window, their voices loud. She closes it. The Wi-Fi won't work, though she turns the router on and off many times and follows the instructions in the binder. She opens her notebook. She opens a bottle of the great cheap burgundy and is startled to find the bottle empty so soon. The page before her is still blank. Fuck it, she thinks, it is the strain of travel, the stink in the house. With effort she climbs the staircase up into her cold windy room.

But the sun still blazes, even so late. She pokes her head through the skylights and sees the tide far out, the exposed seabed sinister as the surface of the moon. Tiny people pick their way across.

There is a line of seagulls on the next rooftop. They are still, facing away from her, toward the sea. This is a species that is never quiet, they are three-fourths scream, birds of rage, all of them mothers, even the male gulls are mothers. Their silence makes her anxious.

Navy spreads across the sky; the sun blazes then blows out. The biggest seagull opens its wings. At once the birds break into shrieks, laughter, wild flapping, deafeningly loud. She is so startled she hits her head on the skylight. The seagulls lift up in the wind, peel off, carry backward over her head, their tongues like pink worms darting out of their mouths.

In the morning, a tiny freezing body climbs under her duvet, then another. The boys fidget but are quiet. Together, they watch the sky lighten overhead. She hadn't shut the skylights and the room is frigid.

At the bakery, she makes the boys order what they want in French. The baker hands over the paper twists of pastries, and holds the mother's hand for a moment, in blessing.

Yport is mostly asleep. A man bullies his spaniel down the street.

The fishermen winch their boats with long chains over the rocks and through the channel.

The mother drives the road to the top of cliffs, bright in the early sun. Tiny forests, meadows, signs pointing to Étretat.

Guy de Maupassant loved Étretat. He built a house there when he made money. Perhaps the place he loved would reveal him to her.

The Mercedes purrs into town. On the boardwalk, the red flags are up, as if anyone would brave such waves. The beach is like Yport's, but supersized. Here, the cliffs take her breath away.

When they grow too cold in the wind, they walk the town, but something about the place feels mean. The houses have brown timbers and third stories that lean far off their foundations into the street. The style seems airless; the effect is disdainful, the leaning buildings like women watching her and whispering. They go up the long climb to the church atop the cliff, and she carries the little one when he grows too tired. There is nothing else to do when they walk down, so they climb to the top of the other cliff, where there is a staircase carved into the rock and a winding pathway with no guardrail to keep people from tripping and falling three hundred feet into evil.

Ow, says the older boy, trying to rip his hand away from hers, but she won't let go. Keep me safe, she says, pretending to be afraid. Both boys then hold her hands and steer her around rocks and talk to her in gentle voices. They are good boys. She hopes they will be good men. When they cross a bridge over a vast drop, the wind nearly blows the sunglasses off her face, and she becomes genuinely frightened. She has visions of the boys' shirts filling with wind, pushing them up and into the air like kites. She will tether them here, to the earth, with her body.

I'm not scared, the small boy says, pressing close. Though Mommy is.

Mommy's scared of everything, the older one says.

From here, the other cliff they'd climbed to shows itself to be perilous, the church ready to fall off in a gust of wind. Nausea rises in her throat.

Sunset is still three hours away but the quickest way to happiness is sugar, so she buys them ice creams. They sit in an upturned fishing boat to eat.

The boys vibrate until they fall asleep, and she carries one on her back, the other on her front, huffing all the way home.

She puts them to bed and doesn't bother to turn on the lights. She likes the gloomy dim. She looks at her empty notebook until its emptiness is seared into her brain and then she opens one bottle of burgundy and drinks it, opens the second. She tries the Wi-Fi again but nothing works. She can't figure out the television. The books she'd brought are full of Guy, and she's in no mood for his bullshit after dealing with Étretat today.

She stands; she'll go to bed. Her eye falls on the door and she sees the silhouette of a man there, arm moving.

She can't remember if she locked it. There is a single soft knock. She stares at the knob, a curled lever, but it stays where it is.

After a while, the man moves away, elaborate whistling, footsteps.

She locks the door and puts one of the kitchen chairs under the handle. She shuts every window and crawls up the spiral to her bedroom, where there is still light in the skylight. In the night, she wakes to see an outline in the middle of the floor. When she fumbles her glasses onto her face, it turns out to be her own dress drying on the back of a chair.

After three days they brave the water. The cold is not terrible, at least as soon as breath returns. After every dip, they huddle together under the towels and wait to stop shivering.

The older boy, who reads *Astérix* in the tin shack library, makes a menhir of beach stones, which are called *galets*. She likes the chalk ones, like bone cracked open to reveal gray flint marrow inside.

The little boy wanders over to a girl his age, making friends. The mother lets the sun shine on her spotted skin. But when she checks on the little boy, he has moved away from the girl in her ruffled suit and is talking to the parents.

She goes to fetch him. The other parents are British; the woman is dark-haired, gamine, and the father is charming. The mother hasn't spoken more than a few sentences to an adult in so long that she is having trouble coming up with anything to say.

Hullo, the father says. Sweet boy.

He is, she says.

The dark-haired woman says, He asked us an interesting question. When the universe stops expanding, will time stop?

The mother thinks. Will it? she says.

We said children needn't worry about it! the dark-haired woman says.

The mother searches for something to say, gives up, calls the little boy's name, says it is time to go up to the house for lunch.

But the woman isn't done. Your son seems a bit anxious, she says.

The mother laughs. Not this one, she says. She gestures at her other boy, scowling in concentration at his sculpture. That one, maybe. This little guy's made of light.

Oh? the father says. Well, you'd know. Only, he asked us what would happen if a tsunami came in the night.

We said a tsunami would never come! the woman says.

We explained that most of the houses are well above surge level, so nobody would be hurt.

The children would wake up in the morning to starfish on their front steps! the woman says.

Such liars. The mother picks her smaller son up and he wraps himself around her. The bad feeling lingers in her until they reach the house, where the garbage had been taken from the cans, all the wine bottles left on the step. The mother's face burns. Once they are inside, she starts a movie on the iPad, and puts all of the glass in plastic sacks, and hides them behind the bookshelf near the front door.

She is drinking champagne from the bottle. It is colder that way; she wants the burn all the way to her bones.

The seagulls line up on the opposite peak. The giant seagull flaps to a stop on the chimney, basks there. In the center of the long row is a tiny bird that struggles its shoulders against its neighbors, too skinny to be at ease.

They've gone quiet. She doesn't know what she is watching at first when the seagull to the left of the mangy one bows its head. Then the one to the right bows. Perhaps, she thinks, the little bird is some kind of prince. Perhaps they are paying their respects. The other seagulls move in, and now she knows that they aren't bowing, they are pecking the skinny one to death.

If she hurls the bottle at them they'd stop. But she has frozen. It is over quickly, a heap that slides out of view.

The little seagull hadn't even screamed. Surely it had a right to scream, the moral luxury of protest.

She winches the skylights shut, puts plugs in her ears, tries to press the pillows against the very center of her brain, where all the heat lives.

In the morning, the bottles are again on the steps, ghosts of her nights. Someone is trying to tell her something. She heaps them inside. The pile makes her desperate. There is too much fog in her head to leave the house. She lets the boys stay in their pajamas and watch *Tintin*.

The little boy farts, says, *Un pistolet!*

When they go to the beach, they find the tide withdrawn. The older boy says in Captain Haddock's voice, *Mille milliards de mille sabords*.

They sit out of the wind at the library. From time to time she looks up from her book at the tiny figures picking at the edges of the tide plain.

There is in her something beating behind her thoughts, that same old dread from home, but she can't look at it; if she does, it will come closer, rub up against her. She can't let it, all alone in this cold place with her boys.

Her big son leans his dark head against her knees. The little boy says, My friend!

She sees the galoshes, the jeans, the belly jutting over the belt. Jean-Paul. He is grinning, teeth thick with tartar. The little boy waves Whoopie Pie at him.

Jean-Paul had seen them from way out, he'd come in to see how the house was.

She says fine. She thinks of the broken Wi-Fi, of her hunger to talk to her husband, but doesn't want Jean-Paul in the house.

He stares at her, then shows the boys his bucket. There are shells moving slowly in it. *Les bulots*, he says, whelks. Sea snails.

The little one dandles his hand in the bucket, but the older one makes a polite noise and leans away.

There is not much to say. Jean-Paul offers them some and she says no thanks! and then he makes jokes with the boys that they don't understand and then when the silence goes on too long, he crunches away.

She is asleep when something falls into her dream.

It is the biggest seagull. It is looking at her. She stills her body. The bird stands in the silvery light. She wonders if it is about to speak because that's what birds do in stories. It doesn't.

In the morning the boys come in. They are quiet. She unpeels her eyelids. I had a dream, she says. An enormous bird fell into my room.

Your breath stinks, the older boy says.

Can we watch *Tintin*? the little one says.

When she can gather her body to move, she finds a giant bird dropping in the middle of the floor, bloodshot as an eye.

The mother has never seen a city as ugly as Fécamp. The day is tannic. The beach's curve between the cliffs is larger here, dwarfing the cliffs so they seem an afterthought. Off the boardwalk, there is a carnival covered in tarps. The carnies smoke moodily in plastic chairs. The boys beg to see the rides, but the carnival won't open until afternoon, and the mother would die of sadness if she stayed in this town that long. She drags her boys into a restaurant.

She capitulates and lets them eat pistachio ice cream for lunch. Each bowl comes with tiny lit sparklers. She drinks a pitcher of cider and picks at her scorched omelet. On the boardwalk the flags snap in the dirty sky. The tourists seem morose, hurry into the restaurants, warm their hands on copper pots full of mussels in creamy sauces.

Every hundred feet down the boardwalk are tiny playgrounds. She decides to turn the day into a workout. The other parents watch her from the corners of their eyes as she does crunches and pull-ups while the boys scream and climb the equipment. They leapfrog down the string of playgrounds. They arrive at a lighthouse at the end of a channel. Ships, rusty and gray, are drawn into the safety of the town to rest. The armpit where the pier extends into the sea is host to deadly waves. The *galets* leap like salmon; a wader would be brained. They stand watching the leaping stones for a long time, and then she looks at the map on her phone and crows. Look! she gestures up the harbor at a cluster of nineteeth-century houses on the other side of the channel. That is where some people say that Guy de Maupassant was born, and others say the Château de Miromesnil, where we'll stay when we're done with Yport–

I'm done with Yport, the older boy says.

Me too, the little one says, I don't know who Guy de Whatwhat is, but I *hate* him.

I hate him too, the mother says. She does. When she returned to Guy as an adult, he disappointed her with his hatred of women, with his syphilitic brain. She'd thought there was a moral center to him, but there wasn't. He was rotten to the quick.

The boys are surprised. *Hate* is the worst swear they know.

Why are we here, then? says the older boy.

To get away from Florida in the summer. The heat makes me want to die, she says.

She doesn't say, Also, dread.

Cold makes *me* want to die, says the older boy. I *hate* France.

I want Daddy, the little one says. I want my summer camp. It's pirate week!

The older boy hugs his brother. It's always pirate week at summer camp, he says sadly.

They've been in Yport for ten days when she notices the placard announcing free Wi-Fi in the church square. She takes the boys. She has thousands of emails. There are ten messages from her husband, breeding exclamation points. She tries Skype, but he doesn't answer. In retaliation she won't answer his emails. Let him dangle.

There are five emails from different people, all with the same friend's name in the subject line. The friend is slender, humble, vegan. He has tattoos from his punk-rock youth. He is now a librarian, a writer. He is too kind to be a great writer, but perhaps that will change; most people get meaner as they age.

Once, he stopped to chat when he saw her and she confessed her sadness, and he hugged her and that night he left an entire vegan chocolate cake on her porch.

A year ago, she'd gone to his wedding. He and his wife had moved from Florida to Philadelphia and had a baby. They'd given the baby the name of the best character from the mother's last book. She thinks that it was probably a coincidence.

Every email says that this good man had killed himself.

When she looks up, the square has blurred.

Why are you crying? says the littlest boy.

Because, she does not say, she has a bright flash in her gut, and it feels like relief.

Her boys let her hold them. They could do with a bath. She should toss these rotten shoes. But, God, she thinks. Let them stink.

At last, they pack up the Yport house and drive inland to the Château de Miromesnil. They stay in a fragrant tower room. After the constant noise of the sea, the place is eerily silent.

The birds sing, but songs. The gardens are dreamy. Espaliered pears, a miniature apple trained on a knee-high vine. Black dahlias, glossy eggplants. She has the sense of looking for something but not finding it.

The boys swing the bell in the chapel. She takes pictures of them with a mossy bust of Guy de Maupassant. In every picture, her older son scowls.

A storm rises in the night, the trees lashing the garden. She watches the boys on the floor in their sleeping bags. They belong in their own beds; she doesn't belong in France. How dispiriting, to learn of herself that Florida is home.

Still, it is this image that will stay with her forever: she is crouching beside her small son in the exposed seabed. The tide pool is a tiny ocean. A snail retreats his horns, a red anemone pulses. The older boy picks across the rocks, toward the cliffs. He is the size of her palm.

If a meteor came right now, would we die? the little boy says.

The truth might be moral, but it isn't always right. Yes, she says. But it'd be like falling asleep.

The older boy is the size of a thumb. Too far to save him in a calamity: rogue wave, kidnapper. The mother doesn't call for him. There is something resolute in the set of his shoulders. He isn't going anywhere, just away. She understands him.

When she looks back at her younger son, he is holding a rock over his head. He is aiming at the snail. Boom, he whispers. But he keeps his arm in the air. He holds his fingers closed. ■

© Cody Pickens

YAA GYASI

1989

Yaa Gyasi was born in Ghana and raised in Huntsville, Alabama. She received a BA in English from Stanford University and an MFA from the Iowa Writers' Workshop, where she held a Dean's Graduate Research Fellowship. She lives in New York. Her first novel is *Homegoing*.

LEAVING GOTHAM CITY

Yaa Gyasi

It's true. I was in jail when my brother called, but things didn't go down the way Sassy says they did. Her girls over at the hair-braiding salon get to talking in her ear and all of a sudden something that was supposed to be just a private conversation between on-again, off-again lovers turns into some trumped-up assault charge. It's my fault. I should have known better than to fuck with a Jamaican.

Edwin picks me up the next morning in a rented silver Prius. 'I'm in town on business,' he says as I get in. I slam the door just so I can watch him wince. 'When's the arraignment?' he asks.

'There won't be one.'

He smirks. 'Oh yeah, how do you figure?'

'Sassy'll drop the charges,' I say.

'Sounds like you're speaking from experience.'

He pulls out of the parking lot onto the road. We pass the steely gray of the jail, the overgrown weeds and brush that line the gravel pass. Looking out of the window, I see a dreadlocked man in bright orange walking out into the sun.

My brother, he doesn't come like clockwork, but he comes. Every once in a while, his New York-based consulting firm will send a couple of people out to Columbus. Edwin can fulfill his brotherly duties on the company's dime. He used to take me to dinner at the Kahiki on

East Broad until it became a Walgreens. Now, anything will do.

We end up in the back booth of some cheap restaurant. 'You drinking?' Edwin asks.

'Better not.'

He nods and pores over the menu. We wait. When the waitress comes, she's smacking gum, her hip cocked. She wants to make sure we know how much our presence bores her, and I want to say, *Honey, you're nothing special either*. It's what I'd say if Edwin weren't here.

'You ever gonna marry that girl?' Edwin asks once the waitress is gone. He has this habit of wiping his forehead with the back of his hand like the old ladies at church when they're about to catch tongues. He probably learned it from them, back when Auntie Rose used to drag us to the African Christian on Cleveland.

'Why?'

'I'm not accusing you,' Edwin says. The waitress plops a basket of rolls down on the table and one jumps out. She does it quick and keeps moving, like a drive-by. I grab the stray roll and start laying butter into it while Edwin watches me. 'Nana,' he says, 'I'm not accusing you. I was just asking. Who am I to give relationship advice, right?'

He's referring to his divorce from Emily, this tight-assed white girl he met in college. Edwin would never admit it, but she couldn't stand me. She only came to Columbus once. Auntie Rose and all the other Ghanaian women from our hood spent a whole week preparing food for this bitch's arrival, and all she ate was a salad. When she met me, she smiled, but it was one of those smiles that rich people volunteering at soup kitchens give to the homeless: pitying and false, filled with the comfort of knowing they never have to see them again if they don't want to.

The night the divorce went through, Edwin was in Columbus. I got him pissy drunk in a Motown-themed bar, and he let it slip that Emily used to call me his thug brother to her friends at parties. Like, 'Edwin's thug brother works at a gas station,' or, 'Edwin's thug brother was picked up for possession.' When he told me, he'd started crying, and I had to prop him against my body just to get him out of there. And when I put him on the couch in my apartment he was still crying and whispering how sorry he was, but when he woke up he couldn't remember anything.

'Sassy doesn't want to get married,' I say. It's only kind of true. Sassy doesn't want to get married *anymore.* She did once. When we were high-school sweethearts. Before she found out I was sleeping with other people or that I was using or that every time I said I was going to get her out of Columbus I knew that I wasn't. That I couldn't. We've been fucking with each other so long it feels like we're married. She even looks at me that married way sometimes, like the joy and sorrow of all of our years together is hitting her just behind the eyes. But then the joy leaves.

'Is it cool if I stay with you?' Edwin asks. Our food has come, and it's nothing to sing about, but I'm so hungry I could eat a horse eye. I look up, nod.

When we get to my apartment, I make Edwin stand outside so I can do a quick sweep. I've been mostly clean, but I keep some shit around, in case of emergencies. I let him into the apartment and show him how the couch folds out, and he listens. I pour us a couple of whiskeys and turn the TV on while I go listen to my messages. The first one's from Sassy saying she's sorry, and the second one is from my lawyer saying Sassy dropped the charges.

I come back into the living room, and Edwin's made himself at home. He's got his feet on the coffee table and his shirt off, and he's nursing the whiskey bottle, his empty glass beside him. I start to laugh.

'What's funny?' he asks.

'You look ridiculous,' I say, and he laughs too.

'Ah fuck, I haven't been back in a minute, huh?' He stretches out. He's got feet like mine. The toes all spread out like they can't stand to be next to each other. We're seven years apart, we've got different fathers, and we don't look anything alike, but every time I see those duck feet, I know he's got to claim me.

It's been five years since Edwin was here. I know because I've been counting. I get on the couch beside him and start flipping channels.

He cuffs a hand over his bald head and sighs. 'Who do I need to see?' he asks. 'Who's still here?'

I run through all of them in my mind: Kojo, Kwesi, Akosua who was Edwin's girl back in the day, Tatu and NaKwame, the twins Panyin and Kakra. Everyone's here really. Edwin's the one who left.

'Folks are around,' I say.

He nods. *America's Most Wanted* is on Channel 6, and I leave it there. I can feel Edwin looking at me, but he doesn't say what I know he's thinking. Auntie Rose used to watch this show. Every Saturday night. We used to joke that the best gift we could ever give her would be to plant one of those crooks somewhere she could spot him and call in. We'd go up to the criminal and be like, *Yo, can you meet us by the plantains at the Asia Market on Cleveland? And don't leave until you see this wrinkly, old black woman in a headscarf calling the police on you, okay?*

'You still watch this shit?' Edwin asks. He's coughing from the whiskey and his eyes are getting heavy and liquid, but he hasn't put the bottle down.

I shrug. 'Nothing else on.'

He starts to nod off after they show the second criminal sketch. I move him over, take the slipping whiskey bottle from his hand, and put a blanket over him.

I go to my room, smoke a cigarette out the window, and try to fight the urge to call Sassy. When I lose, I watch my fingers dial her number. She answers with sleep in her voice, but it's only nine o'clock.

'Nana,' she says. Her accent was the first thing I ever loved about her. The way she didn't sound like the Ghana girls or the akata girls I was used to running with. Even when she's angry, she sounds like she could burst into song at any minute.

'Yeah.'

'You want to come over?' she asks. 'Talk?'

I picture her. She turned twenty-eight a few weeks after I turned twenty-nine. Everything on her body's gotten softer. Her breasts, her skin, her smile. When we were younger, when her body was high and hard-edged, I couldn't wait to fuck her. Couldn't wait to tell my friends I was fucking her. Now, I mostly think of what all that softness feels like.

'I can't,' I say. 'Edwin's here.'

I hear her smile through the phone. 'Edwin come back finally? Well Auntie Rose must be shouting in her grave.'

'Yeah,' I say softly. A breathy silence follows before the click. I can't remember the last time we said I love you before hanging up the phone. I can't even remember the last time we said goodbye.

In the morning, I come out to find Edwin in the kitchen frying eggs. 'Yo, when was the last time you used these pans? I had to run to the store to buy a fucking spatula. And food.'

'I don't cook.'

'What do you eat?'

I pull out a box of cereal from the cupboard and shake it at him. I grab a bowl near the stove.

'What's on the agenda today?' Edwin asks.

'I have to work,' I say. 'Three to nine, but if you want to go see folks in the old neighborhood I can meet up with you after. I bet Mama Phyllis'll cook something up for you if you tell her you're here.'

'I don't want anybody to go to any trouble,' Edwin says, but we both know that once word gets out there will be at least one house party with no less than ten Ghanaian women trying to prove that they're the best cook in all of Columbus, even though Mama Phyllis has always held the title.

Edwin was eight when we left Ghana. I was just a baby. We came to Columbus with Auntie Rose. She told immigration that we were her kids. Our mother was supposed to follow after somehow, but she never found a way, and we never got to know her. At the time, all the Ghanaians coming in were either going to Columbus or the Bronx. It just depended on who you knew. Auntie Rose knew a woman from boarding school whose brother was getting his PhD in linguistics at Ohio State. He took us in.

Our whole childhood was Little Ghana. Parties at the lodge, outdooring ceremonies and wakes. The African Christian Church was half-Nigerian, but the other half was us, the men shouting prayers and the women in dukus. You could go into any convenience store and start speaking Twi to somebody behind the counter or in the aisles. Edwin's first kiss was with Akosua Mensah in the steam room of the Red Roof Inn. I walked in on them and they yelled at me. Later, when I asked Edwin how it was, he told me her tongue tasted like crayfish.

Back then all us kids wanted to be like Edwin. He still had the smell of Ghana on him, that authority about him. He had memories of the old country, memories of our mother, the school where she worked in Mampong. He could still speak the language when so many of us had never known anything but English. Edwin even got to play the dondo in church. He'd make the drum live up to its name, flipping it, tapping it, making it talk. We could walk around the playground of Buckeye Village for hours, no adults, just a line of little African ducklings following behind my older brother.

Two weeks after Edwin turned fourteen, he got jumped by some black kids on the east side. Some fucking akatas with nothing better to do than wail on a kid. He told the police they made fun of his accent and told him to go back to Africa, but the police just laughed at him. *You're black too*, they said. *Who are you describing?* They were joking, but Edwin wasn't the same after that. He refused to speak Twi, even with Auntie Rose. He started dating white girl after white girl. He'd sit in the church, stony-eyed and forlorn. One day, three years after Edwin got jumped, I asked if he would take me and NaKwame to the Rec Center for some touch football, and he yelled at me. He said when people looked at us all they were ever going to see was our blackness, not our Africanness. There would be no difference unless we made one. He said we were stuck in a country that would eat us alive if we didn't learn how to live in it. I was ten. I'd already been picked up for stealing from a video-game store. I thought I was living.

I get to work a few minutes late, but it's no big deal. Uncle Eddie owns the gas station. He owed my Auntie Rose more than a couple of favors, so I mostly get to do what I want around here, though I try to do the right thing.

'I hear Edwin's in town,' Uncle Eddie says.

I pick up a broom and start sweeping. 'Where'd you hear that?'

'Some Ghana boys saw you at a restaurant,' he says. 'Tonight we'll party, enh? Mama Phyllis is killing the goat as we speak.' He laughs then rushes out.

The station is quiet. I listen to the clock and try to count each click of the second hand. The slushie machine behind the counter churns red over and over and over. Before long, a group of kids pull up to the pump, rap music blasting. The driver comes in. He's white, blond hair and a polo shirt.

'Hey, whattup? Can I get twenty dollars on number two?' He grins at me and looks out at his car. The top half of a brunette's body is leaning out of the window, her tits barely contained by the top she's wearing. She waves at him, and he flips her off, laughing, turning back towards me with a shrug.

I print the receipt, and pass it to him, and he leans over the counter. 'Hey man, you wouldn't happen to know where to buy some weed around here, would you? We're in town for the football game, and I don't have any Columbus connects, so . . .' His voice trails off. He's still got that daft grin on his face, but he's looking at me like we're old friends.

I do my best Nigerian accent because I never mastered a Ghanaian one. 'Get out of my store-oh!' I shout. 'Get out of my store before I cause you to suffer!'

The boy backs away slowly, confused. His car hits the pavement outside, and I can hear him yelling, 'The dude was crazy!'

I pop open the can of beer I keep behind the counter for days like this. At nine, Edwin picks me up from the store. He throws me a change of clothes. 'Uncle Eddie told you about the party, huh,' I say, trying to wiggle out of my work pants.

'Nope,' he says. 'Kos called.'

The party is at Mama Phyllis's house. She greets us at the door. There isn't a fatter woman on the planet, at least not one still capable of walking, but she knows she looks good, that she cooks good, that she has fed an entire community of people for decades. She pulls Edwin into the folds of her skin, the long line between her breasts splitting open to welcome him.

'Akwaaba!' she sings.

We push into the room, and it's a familiar sight. Little girls with their hair in Afro puffs bossing around the little boys in suits. Bored teenagers, hunched over their cell phones, waiting for the moment when their parents will be too drunk to notice them sneak away. And the adults, the old heads, dressed as if Ghana were just a place in the back of their closets instead of miles, miles away.

Edwin shakes hands with all the uncles as we pass through the hallway. In the kitchen, the aunties are gossiping as the soup simmers.

Akosua is there. She's balancing her son on her hip and with her free hand she holds her daughter.

'Edwin,' she says. 'Good to see you.'

Edwin mumbles something in response and moves closer to her and her kids. I go off to the back porch where Uncle Eddie is busy grilling meat. He has a kente-cloth apron with KISS THE COOK written on it. I grab a Guinness from the blue cooler by the door and stand next to him. He slings an arm over my shoulder.

'Eh Nana, I bet you are happy to see your elder brother!' he says. I nod absently. I can see into the kitchen from the window at the back of the house. Edwin is holding Akosua's baby, and her girl is running around him in circles. Mama Phyllis and Auntie Mensah watch them discreetly from the stove, and I can imagine what they're saying. *Isn't this the way it was supposed to be?*

NaKwame enters from behind the fence. 'What's good, bruh?' he says, slapping my hand. He smells of weed, but if Uncle Eddie notices, he doesn't say anything. 'Where's the Ghanaian prince?' NaKwame asks.

I point to the window. He shakes his head. 'Yo, if your brother gets Akosua hung up again before he bounces, I'll fucking kill him myself. I don't care if he's family.'

Uncle Eddie clips the back of his head with the tongs. 'Watch your mouth!' he shouts.

NaKwame rubs, but doesn't speak. He motions for me to follow him, and we creep into the house. The younger kids are chasing each other in the living room. A can of orange Fanta flies off the table and spills all over the carpet. The kids stop, arrested, but moments later they're back at it.

NaKwame and I go up to the bathroom on the second floor and lock the door behind us. He pulls out a glass pipe, translucent, blue. I crack open the window while he packs a bowl, and below us the music starts at full volume, causing the floor to vibrate. Soon someone will come find us and drag us onto the dance floor.

'What happened with Sassy?' NaKwame asks.

I take a hit and hold it until my chest starts to burn. 'She dropped the charges.'

'Jamaicans, man,' he says, as though that says it all, and I nod. 'You know, we could drive over to Cleveland and see what's up. How long is Edwin in town?'

I shrug. 'He didn't say.'

When Edwin left for Princeton there wasn't a Ghanaian around who didn't know about it. Auntie Rose used to shout from the rooftops. All us younger kids kept hearing what an example he was, but when he didn't come home for Christmas or the summer, they started to worry and clutch their children closer. Who knew what America did to children? Auntie Doreen said at the hospital where she worked a white girl had slapped her own mother. An akata girl with five kids and no husband had come in with bruises on her face and hands. All of this was America's fault. It didn't matter what color you were, if you were American.

I'm high when the yelling starts. NaKwame puts the weed away and flushes the toilet. We wave our hands wildly like we can make the air move faster.

'Open this door!' a voice roars. It's Mama Phyllis, her voice so low I can feel it in my stomach.

I open the door, and take her in. There's panic in her eyes. 'Come, now,' she says. 'Edwin is shouting.'

NaKwame sits on the edge of the tub. He's staring at the ceiling and blinking slowly, the redness of his eyes disappearing behind his lids.

'Stop what you are doing and come,' she says, disapproving.

NaKwame and I go downstairs, then out to the back, where a circle of people watch Edwin and Akosua. I have to push through them to get to the front, and even then Priscilla's giant 'fro blocks my view.

'What do you know?' I hear Edwin shout at Akosua.

'You couldn't even come home for my daughter's outdooring! You've completely lost touch with everyone, even Nana. Do you know what is happening to Nana? He hasn't been sober one week since Auntie Rose died. He's a fucking mess.'

Then, Priscilla steps to the left, and it is like the end of a solar eclipse, the moon of her hair making way for Edwin's eyes to meet mine.

We watch each other for a minute, and then Edwin walks away, silent now, past the uncles and the aunties, into the house, out the front door.

I go up to Akosua, grab her shoulders and stare into her eyes. I want to shake her, but I remember Sassy, remember how I shook her last week when she told me she didn't want to see me anymore. When she told me that we couldn't keep doing this to each other.

Instead, I clutch Akosua so hard my fingers start to hurt. She gulps in a sob and whispers, 'Don't hurt me, Nana. I'm sorry. I'm sorry.'

NaKwame comes through. He seems to have gained control over his face. He lifts my hands from Akosua and moves me aside.

I look around as the crowd hesitantly disperses.

'Can I have your keys?' I ask NaKwame, and he tosses them to me. I run out of the house to the beat of highlife music.

At first, I don't think that this is an emergency, but then I remember the stash between my mattress and box spring, and change my mind, get myself worked up. I've got one tiny, glistening rock left, and I know it won't get me high enough to begin searching for Edwin. I go back to my apartment, smoke it quickly, and try to decide on a course of action.

NaKwame drives a souped-up Cadillac, nice rims, clean. I check his seat cushions, but there's nothing in them. I cruise around Franklinton until I find some boys who I know sell cheap. I smoke until my head is a cloud of calm, and then I drive to Sassy's salon.

Tisha comes to the door. She is a black brick of a woman, a six-foot-tall Bajan with dreadlocks down past her ass and arms that look as though they've been used strictly for the purpose of holding up the world. 'Nuh-uh,' she says.

'This is an emergency, Tish.'

'You're high off your ass, Nana. I'll be damned if I let her go anywhere near you today.'

I do my best impression of a sober man. 'Tisha,' I say, counting my blinks, making sure to space them appropriately. 'My brother is missing. He's been having a hard time, and I don't know if he's in some kind of trouble.'

'*He's* having a hard time? Is he high and harassing his girlfriend too?'

I start to cry, which was not part of the plan. 'I just. I need her, okay? I need Sassy.'

Finally, Sassy comes to the door. Tisha gives her a hard look, but she nods her away. We go out to a bench on the sidewalk.

'I really didn't mean to come here like this,' I say.

Sassy rubs her hand along my forearm, but she's sitting at a distance. You could fit two bodies between us.

'I've never seen Edwin angry like that. Not like that.'

She sighs. 'He's a grown man, Nana. Let him go. This place is Gotham City to him, right?'

Gotham City. Edwin and I used to talk about it all the time. I was seven and obsessed with Batman. Back then, Auntie Rose was working the night shift as an LPN at the nursing home on Clime. We could barely afford food, let alone movies. She used to steal the VHS tapes from the storeroom in the back whenever she could, and one day she managed to get a copy of *Batman Forever*.

I can't remember the details of the movie. I can't even remember who played Batman, but I remember that Edwin watched it with me on the busted television set we'd picked out of the dumpster behind Muskingum Court. Auntie Rose had the night off and she sat at the kitchen table folding clothes for the care packages we used to send back to Ghana every month. On the screen, Gotham City was being ravaged by the villain of the week.

When it ended, Edwin and I saw that Auntie Rose had fallen asleep at the table. I helped him carry her to her bedroom. We slipped her shoes off and placed the comforter over her. Edwin dimmed the light, and we went out into the living room to pack our lunches for the next day: corn beef sandwiches, no chips, no drinks. We washed the dishes, finished folding the clothes for the care packages, swept the floor, and then crept into the tiny bedroom we shared.

'You know what I don't understand?' Edwin asked. The streetlamp outside our window flickered its eerie glow, cutting the darkness. I could make out Edwin's eyes and teeth and sometimes his hands.

'What?'

'I don't understand why anyone would want to stay in Gotham City. It's a stupid place with all these crazy motherfuckers walking around killing people and blowing shit up. Why don't they just leave?'

I laughed when he said it because I was too young to understand that Edwin was serious, that he was beginning to rework an idea our families had latched onto, fought for, years before, when they'd dragged Ghana-must-go bags onto the shores of this strange new land. You shouldn't stay somewhere that isn't working.

Now, I scoot a little closer to Sassy and stroke her face. She lets me kiss her, lets me lean my head down against her breasts, and she holds me to her for a while. At first, I think I'm the one crying, but then I realize it's her. Her chest heaves up and down, little waves that bob my head against their current. She clutches tight. A few minutes later, I leave. I know where Edwin is.

We buried Auntie Rose five years ago at Union Cemetery. That was the last time Edwin was in Columbus. I find him sitting down next to her headstone, marked: LOVING MOTHER, SISTER, AND FRIEND.

I sit beside him.

'You took good care of it,' he says. The grass around the headstone has started to die, but there are flowers at the base and little tea candles from the vigil the deacons from church hold every year on the anniversary of her death.

'I'm sorry,' I say.

'For what?'

'For being such a fuck-up.'

Edwin shrugs then turns back to the headstone. 'We're just fucked up in different ways is all.'

I run my hand down my face. 'Sassy and I broke up,' I say. 'For good this time.'

'When did this happen?'

'Just now.'

Edwin smiles at me and puts an arm around my shoulder. ■

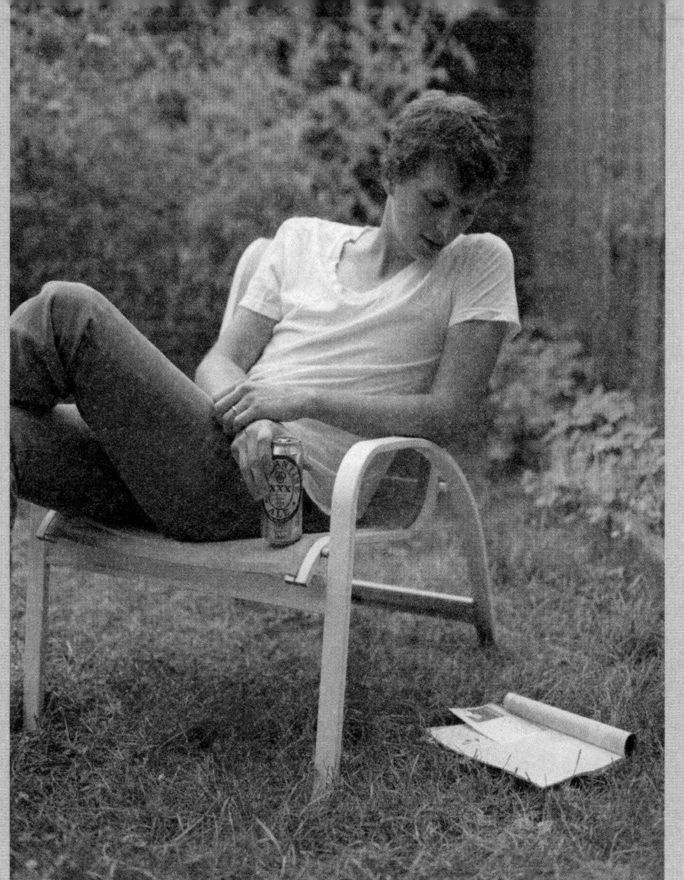

Courtesy of Chris Eichler

GARTH RISK HALLBERG

1978

Garth Risk Hallberg was born in Denham Springs, Louisiana and grew up in North Carolina. His first novel, *City on Fire*, was named one of the best books of 2015 by the *Washington Post*, the *Wall Street Journal*, the *Guardian*, *Vogue* and others. His short fiction and essays have appeared in *Best American New Voices*, *Prairie Schooner* and the *New York Times*. 'The Meat Suit' is taken from something longer.

THE MEAT SUIT

Garth Risk Hallberg

All life is suffering. At the zendo where Jolie went Thursdays after sixth period, not much in the way of portable wisdom got dispensed, but this was, near as she could tell, the through line. It didn't show up in quizzes or drills. Only twice had she even encountered it as a verbal formulation: once among some pamphlets racked in black plastic by the door; once in a piece of supplemental reading – the *Dhammapada*, maybe. Or Wikipedia. But by the time she stumbled into the antechamber for what would turn out to be her final visit, this First Noble Truth no longer seemed like a subtlety. She was five minutes late. She was possibly a little tipsy. She forgot to ditch her backpack before bending to remove her shoes, and it whammed into an end table behind her. And when she turned to keep the delicate alms bowl on top from falling, what struck her about the room beyond was her own sadness, flashing back at her from every surface.

There were the mats, for example, reed mats so thin their only conceivable purpose was to call attention to the cushioning they failed to provide. And there was the roshi, nearly as thin in his penitential sweater. Her mental imagery going into this had been shaped, admittedly, by the statues in Chinese restaurants – smiling and slightly louche Buddhas in 70s vests and love beads, their plump bellies begging to be rubbed – but Roshi Steve could only muster a glower. And then suffusing everything was the light from the picture window that ran the basement's far wall. Something had been done to the glass or to the courtyard outside to lend each object in here a terrible clarity. The hard linoleum. Her clumsy fingers. The kamikaze bowl.

People looked up from their meditations just in time to see the bowl shatter. The usual Open Session crowd was office workers in their twenties, a few fixie dudes with man buns and frockish shirts mixed in, but the light brought out lines in their faces. (Rivers, she used to call them, running a thumb from the corners of her mother's eyes. Mommy, another river.) Mindfulness on such faces could look like anything from fatigue to a sort of pinched constipation, but never like actual enlightenment. Yet when the roshi sighed and used his bamboo thing to indicate a mat – could he smell the booze from there? – Jolie tried to accept his wisdom. The shards at her feet were an illusion, and could wait. Her soul could not. And the desolation she'd spent these last months circling the edges of? That was just what life was. The way a fire was its burning.

Of course, everybody knew that already, right? At least, everybody over the age of about ten. So why had Jolie kept coming here each week to shove a few more dollars of her bat mitzvah money into the now-defunct bowl? One potential thesis, which it had taken several sessions to refine, was that there were different ways of knowing things. Or different kinds of things, aspiring to different kinds of knowledge. Knowing, say, that Juneau was the capital of Alaska wasn't the same as living there. And for Jolie, the impossibility of abiding joyfully in the suffering of the world was matched only by the impossibility of kneeling in place for sixty minutes and not letting the distress signals from the knees reach your ostensible diamond of a brain.

Then again, it was possible she was just wired for this, somehow. Her paternal grandfather had been a priest, she knew, had presided over an Episcopal school in Maine, even if she hardly remembered a time when he was alive. And though her mom's people had been among the non-observant elite of prewar Vienna, you wouldn't want to rule out the possibility of a rabbi somewhere in there. Genetic explanations were a cop-out, obviously, but she couldn't deny the tug she'd always felt toward anything even slightly metaphysical: the smudged foreheads that appeared in the streets on Ash Wednesday; the Sufis she'd once heard belting out their version of 'Happy Birthday' at a vegetarian restaurant downtown; Sufism more broadly; vegetarianism more broadly . . . She'd wasted an entire Sunday in fifth grade following that white Shabbos string around the Upper East Side, not quite trusting Mom's insistence that it was a closed loop. For Jolie, things of the spirit had a taste, almost, the way the air in a Catholic church had a taste even though you weren't eating it – some stone-cool and incensed unreasonableness at the heart of the late-capitalist world. She even loved this faintly churchy phrase, *late capitalism*, which she'd picked up from a clerk in the Bluestockings bookstore on Allen Street and repeated any chance she got.

So perhaps the deeper question was why the zendo, rather than any of these other places? But here, too, there were strings. And they seemed, if she followed them, to join up somewhere in the dreariness of last winter.

That was when Mr Koussoglou, who taught Exploring Cultural Richness, had busted her for drinking at the middle-school dance. Which, to be fair, she'd largely spent behind the locked door of the faculty bathroom with her new friend Precious Ezeobi and half a pint of Precious's sister's gin. Jolie had never had anything stronger than Manischewitz, unless you counted the whiskey her nana had once let her dip a finger in. She seemed to recall Mom saying something cautionary at the time, but a close-quarters hang with the most interesting girl in the eighth grade wasn't the moment to get all scrupulous – and after that first, throat-scorching sip, the liquor seemed to announce some deeper rupture. Out on Second Avenue afterward, when Mr Koussoglou had confronted them with the empty bottle, Precious had told him to make a formal accusation, if he thought he had the evidence (some litigious top notes were more or less unmissable), and then had clomped off on platform shoes into the night. But this left Jolie, a year younger and a head shorter, to convince Mr Koussoglou she was sober enough to take the subway home – that he shouldn't call her mom to come get her. 'I guess you could try email. But she doesn't pick up for unknown numbers.'

'What about your dad?' Mr Koussoglou had asked.

'My parents aren't together anymore,' Jolie said. And though it was hard to tell under the streetlights and with the light drizzle that had begun to fall, a kind of soulfulness seemed to pass over his face – one she wasn't too wasted to spot. 'Come on, Mr K. Give me a few days first to own up to my mom myself. Isn't that the real punishment?'

'Not per the student handbook.'

'The people who wrote the student handbook didn't know my mom,' she said, pushing out her lower lip, but not too far.

The following week was winter break, and her hope was that the time off would be enough that he'd forget, but evidently, she'd been naïve. Some adults were like psychological Mormons this way: you let them in as far as the vestibule and the next thing you knew they were in the middle of your living space, studying the photos on the wall and awaiting offers of refreshment. Then again, if he'd passed by without even knocking, she'd probably have taken it as a rejection. And so that first Monday back, leading her mother past a scrum of staring eighth-graders and into a first-floor classroom, Jolie found herself in the position she'd come to think of as her default, wanting things so many different ways as to pretty much ensure her disappointment.

The room was unoccupied, but up near the whiteboard, three student desks had been dragged into powwow formation. Mom folded her long legs under the writing surface and fiddled with her pledge-drive go-cup. To sit down beside her to wait would have been to invite more of the conversation Jolie had spent the last forty-eight hours avoiding ('How am I supposed to know what he wants, Mom? Didn't he mention anything in the email?'), so she lingered by the bookshelves, taking another inventory of Mr Koussoglou's university-press paperbacks, their umlauted authors and promises of disenchantment. In the fall, when he'd let her linger here during the lunch hour, they'd been the first thing at her new school that felt like home. But now he bustled in with an armful of papers, so chipper she wondered if his sympathy had been a front. 'Sorry to keep you waiting, folks. The photocopier gets traffic jams this hour of the morning. Anyone need coffee before we start?'

'I brought my own,' Mom said, indicating the go-cup. 'I'm Sarah, by the way.'

'Right, forgive me – Brandon. Koussoglou. I keep forgetting email isn't actually a form of introduction. Jolie, you fixed for caffeine there?'

Jolie had been experimenting with the idea of herself as a coffee drinker, but the question was rhetorical. He was already launching into his prologue with Mom: how good of her to come on such short notice, how good to sit down and finally get to know each other. It was the cheerfulness that was the front, Jolie realized. He was nervous – which was probably why he kept punting on any specific charges. '. . . so I gather Jolie's told you why I asked you both in here?' he concluded. But she was thinking now of the fire in Precious's eyes. Of rituals where people symbolically consumed their gods in order to take on their powers.

'To be honest, you might have to spell it out, Mr K. Because neither of us has the faintest clue.'

'Interesting. No clue, Jolie? Really?' He cleared his throat, as if still expecting her to help him, but her habitual indecision had lifted, leaving her strangely reckless. Strangely free.

'Well, why don't we start with the big picture,' he said, finally. 'I took the liberty of glancing back over the permanent record, and I was surprised to discover a certain Jolie Aspern on the honor roll going back to . . . ah, basically back to whenever they start the honor roll. You understand why I say "discover".'

'The report cards this year have been less than stellar, I'll admit,' said Mom. 'But Jolie's still pulling what, a B in here?'

'She'll be lucky to salvage a C minus, now that I've got the midterms graded.' He had a marked copy of the exam ready. Jolie grew a little uneasy as Mom flipped through the pages.

'Brandon, if this is just about the grades, I teach, too –'

'Right. American Studies. At Columbia, Jolie mentioned.'

'Barnard, but same difference. Anyway, I don't want to get hung up on a few stray data points. I've seen how destructive this whole rise of the helicopter parents has been.'

'Again, though, the academic record's just a starting place,' he said, before retreating from the obvious segue. (Why that should deepen the discomfort was hard to say.) 'Look, here's a copy of her final paper from the fall. Choose your own theme: a comparative study of genocide in Cambodia and Rwanda. Or really just an essay on the brutality of human nature – very loose with the citations, I might add, hence the low grade.' This, too, he slid to her mother. 'The nihilism, by itself, is one thing. But looking back, I'm seeing it alongside the recesses Jolie's been sitting out. The lunches eaten alone, if at all. The listlessness, the going around in all black –'

'It's a fucking – !' This was Jolie. 'I mean, pardon my French, but it's a tuxedo jacket, from a thrift store. Jimmy Page, *Hammer of the Gods* tour, hello?'

'Black jeans, black sneakers, black T-shirts on Casual Friday, now shading into various other forms of acting out. Do you really want me to finish the itemized list, Jolie? Or am I allowed to just cut to the chase of what this all starts to look like from where I'm sitting?'

Her face was burning. He hadn't actually used the d-word, depression, but the effect was the same: this was an ambush. An accusation.

'I'm saying, is there something going on at home I should know about?'

Asshole, she thought. With your puppy-dog eyes.

When she didn't answer, Mom spoke up. 'Well, I can't identify anything specific. But I suppose I have noticed some moping around lately.'

And now Jolie's wrath swerved toward Mom, and had to be

brought back under control. 'Maybe I'm bored, has anybody thought of that?'

'Honey, how can you be bored? There was the musical, you've got swimming – not to mention, you live in the least boring city in America.'

'Everything is relative, though, isn't that what you're always saying? Maybe from a relative angle American life is, like, really, really boring.'

'Jolie, it's a more or less objective fact that we're among the most lavishly entertained people in the history of the world. If you're bored, it says something about you.'

'So you've raised a boring person, I guess. But that doesn't mean I need some like *intervention* from the social studies teacher.' She was daring him, almost, to bring this back to the drinking; he couldn't know the first thing about what was going on inside her. 'Or are you going to discount my take on things just because I've started to think for myself?'

For some reason Mr Koussoglou held his peace, and it was Mom who took the bait, turning back to him.

'Well, these are survey classes you're teaching, right? No offense, but is it possible she's been a little under-stimulated at school?'

'I'm not trying to prosecute any particular case here,' said Mr K, 'but I have a duty to speak up when I see behaviors that concern me.' He looked meaningfully at Jolie. 'As an educator, or just as a human being.'

And suddenly she saw her way through: Don't resist. Engage. 'Okay, Mr Koussoglou, yes. But what you're treating as warning signs aren't warning signs, is what I'm saying. What do you need me to do to prove to you this has all been a big overreaction? Or aberration, or whatever – that I'm getting back on track?'

He continued to study her for a minute, as if gauging her sincerity. Then he rose and began searching his shelves. When he returned, it was with a battered paperback, black cutouts dancing on a purple cover. 'This one you know, I bet?'

'Geertz, sure,' Mom said. 'We had to read him for comps.'

'Jolie, your contention is that you're just bored. What I hear your mother saying is that nothing is boring if you look at it closely. Which is essentially the argument of this book. So what if I proposed a little test?'

'This is my punishment. More homework.'

'But remember, it can hardly be a punishment, right, when we can't point to anything you've done wrong.'

She'd never imagined having a secret between them might ultimately work to his advantage, rather than her own.

'It's been suggested that we could be doing more to challenge you here at school, so call this an independent study.' Her mission, he told her, would be to visit a site of Cultural Richness, however she construed the phrase, and to write six to eight pages of thick description, on the model of 'Notes on the Balinese Cockfight'.

'– which you would obviously have to read,' said Mom, eager to be back on the side of progressive education.

'Along with the rest of *The Interpretation of Cultures*, plus let's say three secondary sources of your choosing,' Mr Koussoglou said. 'You and I would meet weekly through the spring for updates. And your mom could be there as a resource throughout. But the real commitment would have to come from you. If you got a credible paper in by the last day of the semester, it would be evidence of a turnaround, your final grade would get a bump, and I'd consider my larger concerns addressed. Meantime, I'd agree to hold them in abeyance.'

It was like a dare of his own – like he was trying to pile on the work until she just threw up her hands and confessed. She was still trying to figure out a winning angle when her mom said, 'Well, that's that, I guess. You know, you have this fear, with middle school, that you're sending them into the jaws of some vast machine.'

'I'm sitting right here, Mom.'

'So even if this is just typical teenage stuff, I'm grateful to know someone's looking out for her.'

'You know how it is, I'm sure,' Mr Koussoglou was saying.

'Sometimes you don't know where the kids are coming from until you get everybody in the room and get a dialogue going. But I'm willing to try taking Jolie at her word here. There's nothing I'd like more than to have misunderstood.'

Her first thought for the fieldwork . . . well, her first thought was not to do it. The way he'd framed things, though, his silence about the drinking now depended on her submission, so she began to look around her own neighborhood. Maybe the African drum circle that met Saturdays in the park? Or the Ukrainian social club by the cathedral? She used to love on warm days to watch men in Ban-Lon sling their dominoes across a folding table. But it was funny: since she'd last looked, a sheet of glass seemed to have descended between her and the Cultural Richness of Morningside Heights. Was this the point of the exercise? For her to face the possibility that there was indeed something wrong with her?

Then, toward the end of March, on one of her dilatory walks from train to school, she passed a certain wisteria'd townhouse with an oblong of wood bolted to the basement level, a word there she'd never seen before. As she stared, the sign broke into syllables, punctuated itself. ZEN: DO. And after school ended, she found herself altering her route home to pass it again.

The floors above looked residential: half a lampshade visible in a second-story window, a sill of leaning DVDs. But the basement blinds hadn't budged, as if a secret were being harbored there. The idea that anything could still be secret in this city, in this century, seemed indisputably non-boring. Even a little daunting. For ten minutes or more, she hung on the nearest corner, ghosting her finger across her phone, preserving the option of retreat. To anyone watching, she'd appear to be just another passerby. But at two minutes to four, seeing nowhere obvious to ring, she seized the knob at the center of the plain wooden door. A buzzer somewhere began to buzz.

For a moment, she pictured a whole audience turning toward her in horror, but inside was only a bare room, aqueously lit; what she'd taken to be pulled shades were in fact sheets of rice paper. Her eyes adjusted to register the alms bowl with its crumpled bills, and then, past the doorframe, a larger room, a rigid grid of mats laid out on the floor. The handful of people already in there looked normal enough from the ankle up, but the fact that they were padding around in stocking feet was almost weirder than if they'd been nude. The odor was weird, too, toasty but also loamy, like fish food.

It was when she turned to flee that the buzzer buzzed again and two men shoved in behind her. Jolie's need to escape was weighed against their bro-ish vibe of possessing the space – only without words, for the strangest thing about the basement, so strange she'd only just noticed it, was that it was clearly verboten to talk. Jolie, being Jolie, was the one to yield. And once the guys were past, she saw them making for a shoe rack, something no more exotic than you might see in the front hall of a family apartment. It occurred to her that she could get through this the way she'd gotten through her first time being panhandled on the subway: study other people and do what they did . . . though it was too late to do anything about the socks hiding under her Vans, other than wait till these guys cleared out and hope no one noticed the individual sheaths at the toe caps, or the peace signs stitched at the end of each. It seemed a neophyte's dead giveaway, somehow, toe socks at the zendo.

Two hours later, she was letting herself into the apartment, her head an exquisite blank. It was the sight of the second key ring on the mail table that brought her hurtling back into meatspace. Her mother must have cancelled office hours and come home early.

'How was practice?'

Jolie put down her bag and headed after the sound.

'It's not practice, Mom, it's voluntary free swim.' Coach Duff wasn't technically supposed to require pool time in the off-season, but it was understood that girls who didn't volunteer weekly for the quote/unquote free swim were forfeiting spots on the team in the fall.

'How was voluntary free swim, then?'

Jolie's hair was dry, her eyes lacking that raccoon look they got after eighty minutes in goggles; she wasn't planning to keep the afternoon's discovery to herself. But if there was a moment to speak up, the sight that greeted her as she entered the living room knocked it into a side pocket. 'I thought that thing was in storage.'

Atop the black arthropod of her futuristic Exercycle, Mom's legs were churning at roughly twice the speed of anyone riding a normal bike. It did something to the handlebars, swept them backward and forward in quarter time. The overall effect was obscurely reminiscent of folk dance. 'I had Vikas bring it up,' Mom said.

'Yeah, but why?'

'Look at you. You're in the pool four hours a week. Me –' She was short of breath. 'Yesterday a kid your age offered me a seat on the subway. Like I was old.'

'He could have thought you were pregnant.'

'That's not funny.'

'Some people join a gym.'

'I have a membership through school. But I never go, so.'

'Well, don't let me get in the way of your rhythm.' Jolie turned to leave.

'Oh, honey, before I forget, though. Your laptop was doing its blurbling thing. That's Skype, right?'

She was instantly on guard; there was only one person in the world she ever Skyped with, and it could be months between attempts. 'This wouldn't have anything to do with that stupid conference at school, would it?' Because that would be just like Mom. If you weren't happy, it was because of some historical decision by human agents – a divorce, say – rather than the hopeless muddle of existence itself.

'Jolie, it's not my habit to go running after your father about things like that, even if I could reliably get ahold of him. But don't you think the two of you could keep in better touch about what you're up to? I know you've been clawing your way back academically, for instance. Or that's what your teacher says, Mr . . .' She snapped her fingers.

'What, Koussoglou's debriefing you now? Oh, forget it.'

That she'd succeeded in getting the pedaling to stop brought no real satisfaction. In the hall, she waited for the flywheel whir that would mean it had resumed. Then she turned toward the kitchen. In the cabinet above the range hood, she recalled, were a few old bottles. She didn't know where they'd come from; they only saw the light of day for her mom's parents, Nana and Albert. But now she took one. Or collectivized it, as the guy at Bluestockings might have said – promoted it to the recesses of her bulgy backpack, pausing only to sniff along the cap for the flutter she got just from the smell.

And now, in April, it had become part of her ritual to seal off the weekly meditation with a drink or two. If there was no one around, she liked to do it right afterward in the little community garden across from the zendo and ride home with her head feeling like a slope cleared by brush fire. Nothing could touch her then. And the secrecy was important, as the ritual was important. The secrecy was how she knew she hadn't totally knuckled under. It was a positive pleasure, for example, to sit talking ethnography with Mr K and to know that at the bottom of her Navy surplus bag not three feet away was the grenade-sized Poland Spring bottle full of vodka. Even when she submitted the required draft in a few weeks and revealed that there was something in the world that actually interested her, she'd be holding more back in the margins. For the time being, she stalled, saying she had several potential subjects and needed to do further research. The last bit was true, in its way. She was researching the body's capacity to empty itself of thought, to detach itself from the shifting pageant all around and burrow down to the ground zero of consciousness.

And perhaps that's why this afternoon, heading north into Kips Bay after school, she'd been so slow to notice Precious Ezeobi stuck on the same street corner, waiting for the light to change. In the two and a half months since the dance, Precious had become just another figure to avoid during lunchtimes and passing periods; they did the chin nod if they had to, but never acknowledged they'd been in the trenches together. Nor was either about to surrender this corner to the other, even as the pedestrians massed around them, even as the year's first blossoms clung to the wet windshields of parked cars and the trees shimmied in their boxes. Had something gone wrong with the signal?

'You didn't have to sell me out like that, you know,' Jolie heard herself blurt. The words had just appeared, as if the intervening months had been erased – except without them she wouldn't have had the nerve to speak.

'Sell you out like what?' And now Jolie understood the reason they told married couples not to go to bed mad. It was like a third presence on the sidewalk between them, restless, motile, prickly.

'You were supposed to spend the night at my house, Precious, and what did you do? You ditched me the minute Mr Koussoglou showed up.'

'What I did was try to drag you away,' Precious said. 'You were the one who stayed behind jawing with him. No one asked you to like *volunteer* you'd been drinking.'

'I'm a terrible liar! And I was trying to take a bullet for you. I said the bottle was mine.'

'Oh, I get it. I do dumb shit, it makes me a bad person, but when you do dumb shit it's because you're so virtuous.' But just as Precious was opening up an edge, she relented. 'You notice I'm admitting I do dumb shit, too.' And here came the old, confiding closeness. 'I see now we should have stuck together, I'm saying. Plus it's probably my fault he stopped us in the first place. That asshole's been after me since last year.'

'He's just doing his job,' Jolie said quietly.

'There you go defending him again. You sound like that heiress, what's-her-name, talking about "My Tiko's such a sweetheart".' Ever since they'd met, Jolie had assumed Precious was the one with the power and herself the one with the need, but perhaps they'd both had something at stake; if she could have just taken the tone here as teasing, the balance might have been restored. But she'd already gone a block past her destination, and either she had to find a quick way to level with Precious or she wasn't going to score a mat before the bell that opened the hour. The solution she came to surprised her.

'You know what?' she said. 'The dumb shit was ever to trust you in the first place.' And turned to double back, though not before she got a look at the sucker-punched contours of Precious's perfect face.

She wished she hadn't; they would stay with her in the unlocked garden, where she sat swilling fake Poland Spring, trying to numb her heart, and then in the shoe room above the million shards of bowl, and even now, forty minutes in, invading the fragile white space that was supposed to open up and render meaningless all the messes she'd made. She tried to attune herself to an ant wobbling its mindless way across the reeds of her mat. To the bead of sweat reposed between her shoulder blades, waiting to drop. She'd always been good at repression. But repression was so effortful, and effort was the opposite of presence . . . not to struggle was such a struggle. Even the booze didn't seem to be helping. And then a car alarm erupted outside, cycling through its insistent jingles and springing free the droplets that were somehow in her eyes, and she'd killed her one chance at understanding – oh, what was she even doing here?

The roshi betrayed no particular surprise as she rose from her mat and blundered past the kneeling bodies, the faces too vacant to flinch. 'Sorry, sorry,' she said, and put a hand on her middle, as if the problem were with her stomach. Which in fact was feeling a little rocky all of a sudden. In the shoe room, unable to stop herself, she plucked up a few of the larger jags of bowl, deposited them in the trash. And the last she would see of the zendo, framed by the inner doorway and the outer, was the roshi's expression, which she'd been wrong about all along. It wasn't disapproval, so much as perfect indifference.

And then it was rush hour on the street and the universal was in full flight behind the particular, the truth of what the world was receding again behind the manifest fucked-upness of the world not being some superior and palpably adjacent way. Someone's medicine-ball handbag was slamming into her arm, and she narrowly avoided the shit some dog owner must have thought too tiny to pick up, and men in helmets had the sidewalk closed for the erection of yet another oligarch's redoubt, and people were flooding up the down side of the subway stairs. Strange how some days the object world conspired against you. Strange how the beauty withdrew. She found a pillar to lean against in the middle of the platform and put her subway face on and her earbuds in and was just about to pull up the Albums menu and lose herself in *Led Zeppelin II* when the phone slipped from her hand. There was a slight, distinct tug at the end of the knotted white cord – a fish striking the end of a line. Then the jack gave out and the phone continued on its downward trajectory, clipping the yellow Braille of the platform edge, spinning off, and clattering to the tracks below.

'Mother*fuck*er,' Jolie said, and checked to see if anyone had noticed, but this was New York, after all. She should have posted herself closer to the mouth of the tunnel, where beyond a risible little gate with a notice too small to read was a ladder leading down to the tracks. On the other hand, the arrival sign was saying three minutes till the next 6 train to Pelham Bay Park – more than enough time to get down there and back to the middle of the station and then do the whole thing in reverse. And the strange thing about being fully in the present is that your choices don't always feel like choices, especially when your $400 phone is at stake and your mom's unlikely to spring for a new one. She wasn't even convinced it was a thing she was doing, really, threading through the crowd, climbing down the demi-ladder, making her way along the sooty track toward the platform's midpoint, keeping a nice wide margin from the third rail. The shoes of the waiting passengers were at eye level. Their heads, in their newspapers or phones or private dramas, should have been a million miles above, but after a couple people called out to her from beyond the opposite track, more people this side began to stir. She pretended not to hear, because fuck you. And when she got up onto the platform again she would walk right back to her spot like butter wouldn't melt in her mouth. Her fingers closed around the phone, whose glass, amazingly, was not cracked. It was such a deviation from her recent run of luck. She should turn and get back before she saw a rat or something. Then, in what order was hard to say, a puff of sour air pushed her hair from her forehead and a small white light appeared beyond the tunnel's mouth, a hundred yards off. No way it had already been three minutes. Not unless she was drunker than she thought.

And at this point whatever string Jolie Aspern had been following these last months ran out, or made a kind of split. Part of her – the body part – began to panic. But her mind was oddly clear, as if a hole had been wiped in a foggy window by some obliging sleeve. *Huh*, she thought. *I did not see this coming.* She could see now the headline in the *Post*, after she proved too short and weak of arm to pull herself up onto the platform. And how this would all look to Mom. To Dad, even. To Mr K. Like some kind of consummation. And was it? A snatch of that Sufi birthday song came back. What they sang, instead of 'Happy Birthday, dear bla-bla' was 'May you realize in this lifetime . . .' It had sounded so opaque: realize *what*? But now she understood that the verb took no object, was simply itself. She had failed to realize, she was realizing, as the light grew bigger and the horn came down the long tunnel and a voice could be heard over the others, a short guy with a shaved head and a boxer's face, an ordinary laborer's face, kneeling at the edge of the platform with his arms out. They were as thick as small trees, but the tattoos made them look somehow fragile. *Don't*, she wanted to say. *I'll only drag you down.* But it was the other part, the body, that was calling the shots. She reached for the hands, which closed around her forearms, like chains. As they pulled, she had a sense of slippage between fabric and skin, of bruises setting in – and then of a blinding, a blackness spreading so quickly over everything, the screaming, the warmth of human contact, that it would be hard for a long time afterward to tell in exactly which way she'd gotten free. ■

©Shelton Walsmith

GREG JACKSON

1983

Greg Jackson is the recipient of a 5 Under 35 award from the National Book Foundation for his first story collection, *Prodigals*. A winner of the Balch and Henfield Prizes and a finalist for the National Magazine Award in fiction, he has been a Fiction Fellow at the Fine Arts Work Center and the MacDowell Colony. His writing has appeared in the *New Yorker*, the *Virginia Quarterly Review* and elsewhere. 'Country & Eastern' is part of a longer work.

COUNTRY & EASTERN

Greg Jackson

Some days, not often, he still believed that revolution might begin with him. The way a bonfire took from one spark. The way, centuries ago, bonfires passed Joss Fritz's revolutionary message from hill to hill through the Rhine valley. His optimism in this direction had to do with the strong black coffee he drank early in the morning on Richard's back porch. He drank his coffee, listened to the birds, and thought that maybe it had not all been in vain.

But thinking, he knew, was only an organized method of self-deception. Topel had no truck with credulity, not at this age. And still, it was very hard to *know*. The delusion and fantasy of the ruling classes kept pace with the wishful thinking of idealists. The edifice of established order practically tesselated cracks. And most of them were cosmetic, sure, but it only took one fatal line of distress. When the structure came down, it would come down in a hurry. History taught as much. It would come down fast and unexpectedly, and later we would say, inevitably, looking back and seeking to restore our faith that behind history sat a governing narrative logic. First though people would need leaders, answers, and a program. They would need the idea of a future to strive into. So strange, wasn't it (marvelously strange, Topel heretically thought) that a world built on stuff, on the gross practicality of the human body, in fact rested on a background webbing of ideas. Ethics, theories, ideals. On a vast immaterial buy-in, our collective faith in an order we never more than half-consciously espoused – its reality, inevitability, and justice. The law deceived us in obscuring this. Civil order endured thanks to police and judges to about the degree that a coat of paint kept a house upright. Nail polish on an idle fist. Nietzsche's superfluous man, who thought himself good simply because his claws weren't sharp – a good description of the modern type, Topel thought, as smug in his self-approval as in the disavowal of his power. The strength of a social fabric derived from people's confidence in it and their acceptance of it, and it followed, then, that the cloth was as strong or weak as the aggregation of individual belief. Courts offered little more than a show of dispassion in the moral sanctioning of slavery and misuse. Like the Church, they obscured the conservative aim – the preservation of authority and wealth – in ceremony and doctrinal arcana. But then the question of why the system had endured so long. This had troubled Lenin a century before. And capitalism had returned from the precipice of its excesses many times since, from the moment in cannibalizing itself when functional return did not seem possible. Topel had gotten into it with that kid reporter the other day.

'Shouldn't we consider,' the kid had said, 'after the big crises – '29, '08 – after the fall of the Soviet Union, the reforms under Deng Xiaoping, after – God – Nazism and the consequences of Versailles, and on the plus side the success of social democracies in Europe – don't we have to consider at least that a market system and representative government might be the most stable model? The most flexible – imperfect, maybe, but able to self-correct just enough?'

Poor kid. They had driven him around for six hours with a blindfold on, checked him for recording devices, made him change clothes. His phone, keys, and wallet were back in some bookstore office in New York. Thin and a bit pale, he struck Topel as overexcited, sprung like a knotted hose. A seasoned journalist would have worked Topel obliquely. Arguing theory like this meant the kid was an idealist himself, a dreamer. No doubt the whole escapade thrilled him. The stupid spy shit. The hint of danger and contact with an extant underground. He probably thought this was the Oakhill Office Building parking garage in '72. Well, Topel didn't need to burst his bubble.

'Silly Putty is very flexible,' Topel had said. 'It doesn't mean I'd ask Michelangelo to sculpt David with it. But perhaps you mean to say we've misunderstood the constitution of human nature – assuming the thing exists. Shaw said that if human nature didn't change, we'd still be swinging around in trees . . . But well, if we're looking to the historical track record for justification, would we have believed in the viability of popular self-governance in, say, 1750? That day's "realists" would have said that what looked good in Montesquieu's hand on paper could never work in practice and showed an absurd faith in individual foresight and temperance. It seems to me that you're also describing, or supposing, a world in which people are more self-serving, narrow-minded, and fearful than I believe they are. And yes, you might say they've become this way, overworked and undereducated and cut off from the forms of association through which we find meaning and common cause. Or you might say the world has changed and new technologies have introduced new degrees of top-down control, distraction, or isolation –'

'Or that things are good enough? People don't want to jeopardize the life they have? Perfect is the enemy of the good, and so on.'

'And you'll find no shortage of people who agree with you,' Topel said. 'And not just conservatives and mainstream liberals, but class collaborationists. Labor leaders, unionists. The descendants of Debs – of Laski and Attlee in Britain . . . But the question is for whom are things good enough? For how many? You assume that a revolutionary movement needs a disaffected bourgeois class. This isn't even a vanguardism Lenin or Trotsky subscribed to. Mao saw the peasantry as the revolutionary wellspring. Maybe history tells a different story so far, but recent history has also written a fairly bleak epilogue to the labor movement. To the whole collaborationist notion that leftist movements can work within democratic and capitalist systems to advance human rights, legal protections, and broadly shared wealth. What I see instead is that we keep drifting to the brink of catastrophe and pulling back. Drifting and pulling back. For many in this world, life is already one long catastrophe. And in this situation one of two things happens, I think. Either we drift too far one day and can't pull back. Or we come to see the insanity of this yo-yoing – which, let us be clear, is by no means natural or inevitable, but simply profitable. For a tiny minority. The misery we see everywhere we look is rooted not in scarcity, but in greed.'

'And you're sure there's no middle ground? Better regulated and more transparent markets. Employee-owned companies. Wealth taxes. Guaranteed minimum incomes . . .'

The kid – how old was he? Twenty-nine, Topel thought. Why had that number come into his head? It was the age, he'd come to think, when you reached the top of the mountain you had been climbing and either started your long descent right then and there or else closed your eyes and kept on climbing, on the stilts and ladders of the imagination, up the mountain not yet risen to the heavens sighted in vision and belief.

Topel sighed. A library book between them showed the county name stamped across the bottom pages. They were supposed to sweep the house for such things: newspapers, area codes on scraps of paper. He turned the book away from the kid, affecting a momentary interest in the cover: Eagleton on the God Debate. Years in hiding left you with a different relationship to information, to the small things we were ever revealing and the endless sloppiness that characterized our encounter with the world.

It was here his mind lingered as he began unwinding his long, complex point about wealth and property; he was thinking how lovely in a way that we constantly betrayed ourselves, betrayed our intention to hide with our irrepressible desire to be forthright and seen. This he thought as he asked (rhetorically) where anyone's wealth came from – answering his own question that, with hardly any exceptions, the fortunes we saw amassed today were merely the long, violent exploitation of advantage rooted in an early sin. Conquest and pillaging, fraud and theft, slavery and colonization. The lineage of the control and ownership of land traced back invariably to violence. Behind possession of any sort: *dispossession.* Today's notion that wealth testified and attached to merit – to the quality of ideas and tenacity of labor – made an attractive but thin veneer on the true store of wealth accumulated in earlier dispossessions. It was this capital, after all, that invested in the good ideas and profited from the hard work of others. We held out hands to catch the crumbs falling from the master's table and called it meritocracy. For at the moment that property rights were enshrined in law, who owned the land and how did they come by it? And if it was by tenancy and improvement that land turned into property, when colonists arrived on distant shores did they extend this definition to the people already there? (Locke said they needn't.) We like to tell the story of social history, Topel continued, as a movement away from bondage toward freedom, from the privileges of power toward the inalienable rights of the individual, but it might as easily be told as the story of power's attempt to entrench itself and disappear from view, to hide in plain sight, protected from popular reclamation by the patina of democracy and impartial law. As the movement of power inward, until the civic body self-regulated its own discontent. Meanwhile exactly what we congratulated ourselves for abhorring and abandoning in slavery, serfdom, and servitude we resurrected in less explicit form – through contracts, debt, the exploitation of market power, impossibly strong negotiating positions, insider trading, union-busting, offshoring, lobbying, the private financing of elections, you name it. And protest would be tolerated to a point. But it was no accident, Topel said, that the police were out shooting those members of society with the least share in the historical plunder and least investment, therefore, in the status quo. People made dangerous, it seemed, because after centuries of exploitation and worse we had the indecency not to buy them off. It was no accident either that our army was deployed around the globe trying to contain the chaos and danger represented by individuals who had no stake in the world order as currently constituted. People willing to die for ideas. The great threat to power. The *only* threat. Everyone else could be bought. Keynes saw what the fundamentalist defenders of ill-gotten privilege would sow. He left Versailles in a huff, remarking that the absolutions of contract were the true authors of revolution. And so perhaps there was enough money to buy off the powerful who rise from the ranks of the poor. And perhaps there would always be too few people willing to die for ideas. But Topel wouldn't count on it. Greed, he said, had never known how to stop itself – that was what made it greed – and those who loved money were all Midases: they had no idea *what* they loved and would turn every last thing to gold until it choked them.

These speeches, Topel thought. Richard had been right. If only we could wrestle one another and come up breathing hard, come up laughing. Come up brothers and sisters at last. What more did we want? We wanted to touch each other. And when we pulled away we didn't want to see that we had turned our sons and daughters to gold. What Topel had wanted to say – what he wanted to say and never could – was what it had been like meeting Jane in his twenties. He had come east from Berkeley with a few introductions from his friend Max Scherr at the *Barb*. It hadn't taken long to run into Jane, a decade older than him but a fixture in the New York scene. The image in his mind was of her holding court in the kitchen, hair done up like Hepburn, prosecuting some long point she interrupted only to take two tiny puffs from the joint someone put to her lips. How would he describe her charisma and charm? The warmth that came off her, fully realized in her smile, her laugh, and at once tempered by a sensible and bright restraint, expressed itself most readily in a formal affection that flirted with self-mockery. There was something like authenticity in her affectation. It helped that she was brilliant, smart enough to justify their revolutionary hopes within the strictures of realism – no mean feat. She taught colonial history at the New School for Social Research, lectured at CUNY's Graduate Center on Louverture and Denmark Vesey. The example and pattern of historical uprising. Lumumba's assassination was often on their lips.

Perhaps they should have been more careful, but a nervy hope ran through the alumni of Free Speech and the campus occupations. Media was still to come, but Michael Wood in *Ramparts* had blown the lid off the National Student Association's collaboration with the CIA. Cleaver was running the Panthers into the ground, but the precedent had been set. Rioting had become routine. Chicago had happened. The Eight dwindled to Seven as the trial edged further into satire. Sam Melville was planting dynamite in office buildings. Cracks showed roughly everywhere.

Jane and Sergio had married young, in the 50s, but it hardly mattered. They had married so they could live together, not because they believed in proprietary relationships between people. And God, they knew some characters. Franzie Feldman, the heiress, who'd renounced her birthright and married 'Serious' Kenneth Feldman, very funny in his dry way, a journalist in the style of Bob Scheer, never smiling at his own jokes but a happy enough audience to your amusement. Franzie and Kenneth had spent two decades in Maoist China, they had their girls there, and when Topel ran into Franzie years later, handing out pamphlets in Washington Square Park like the past quarter-century had never happened, and asked her what they had done all those years in the People's Republic, she'd said, still funny and dry herself, 'We carried things.'

It was a joke, and probably true. The crispness of inflection showed a pride behind the humor. Some things had to be carried: Did you think yourself above it? Jesus was a working man (Phil Ochs). Or: A thing of beauty is a joy forever (that was Keats). Beauty lay in the land and work – *on every morrow are we wreathing a flowery band to bind us to the earth* – as well as the noble nature's assumption of responsibility. And so what Topel would have related, if he could, was how it felt holding a rifle at the second-story window of the Village brownstone, peering down through the curtain at the street hung in still shadow below, listening to Jimmy Echevarria talk to the police officer at the door. A second cop stood by the car, two-way radio in hand, and Topel could make out the calmer voice of Loewe, the lawyer, behind Jimmy, reminding the cop that he was legally enjoined from entering. It was true, but Topel could see this play out any number of ways. With what they had in the house the Fourth Amendment wouldn't earn them much sympathy. Besides, if the city cops were there, the feds couldn't be far behind. He heard Jimmy swearing, insulting the cop – or no, insulting the commissioner, running down Lindsay, Nixon. Jimmy the Brave, but he was only reckless, irascible. Through clenched teeth, to himself, Topel told Jimmy to shut up and fell back into the dark room. The second cop kept scanning the windows. They were nervous too, Topel could feel it. He had a nose for people's fear, and this calmed him and set him on edge. Yes, he hated the police. In a deep, simple way he hated this embodied power arrayed against everything and everyone he cared for. They would unleash violence with impunity, as they always had. But he did not mistake the violence of a power structure, insinuating itself in the false consciousness of a working people, for the corruption of the individual. Those who wielded institutional violence were its victims too, maybe its worse victims since it demanded that they sacrifice their humanity in its name. The last and most fundamental act of resistance, Primo Levi said, is to refuse our consent. But for Topel, in this moment, what did it mean? *And such is too the grandeur of the dooms we have imagined* . . . The paralytic question left his breath shallow. It reminded him of a book he had read long ago that hung on the same point, the question of whether *this* was it, how you were to know when you had reached the moment of your destiny. Would this be the epistemological break, as Althusser had described it, but rather in his own life, demarcating forever a before and after? And if so, was it enough? Big enough? Imperishable vanity asked whether the sacrifice were commensurate to his promise, because – oh, he would give his life and freedom happily to the cause – but senselessly? Rashly? In the manner of Jimmy Echevarria who sought only requital for the iniquity that touched off the crimson in his Basque blood. No, recklessness helped no one. And yet, and yet . . . If you multiplied the decisions outward perhaps it was the unwillingness to budge from principle that made the difference, the unwillingness to let ideals warp under the influence of convenience, and therefore the very smallness of the sacrifices on which the fate of the world rested. Anyone could find courage when the World-Historical Spirit had selected you to enact your martyrdom on the *Six O'Clock News*. But in the shadows, in secret, unrecognized? *We carried things.*

Topel had been there because of Jane. She had explained it all so matter-of-factly, strapping a lace bra around her thin chest, putting up her auburn hair. 'They need sentries, watchmen – whatever you call it. In case of raids.' She had that prim nodding look, caught back up in plan-making before they were even dressed, like she had been sending young men into battle her whole life. Topel imagined her playing the make-believe games of childhood, ordering children about some sultry garden, among statues dressed in lichen and falling ivy. He almost thought her silly when she said, 'The Panthers were right, you know. We can't trust them to respect our rights unless they see unambiguous violence as the consequence.' Topel didn't disagree. He had a copy of *Negroes with Guns* in his rucksack. Che on guerrilla warfare. *The Wretched of the Earth*. Still, the off note in Jane's tone threatened to disclose how delicate a line it was between revolutionary ferment and playacting. But Topel was silly enough in those days himself and susceptible to the romance of it too. You never gave up the romance, frankly, because there were so few consolations in a life like his. But at twenty-nine he had not yet seen that his love for the beautiful mind of a woman had nothing to do with the struggle. They seemed as fixed and knotted as roots in hardpan. He didn't know about Jane's depressions. The days she spent in dark rooms, under blankets, falling in on herself like the timber of a house gutted by the flames of passion. Presumably only Sergio knew, and when Topel asked him about it much later – Sergio by then a thin, muted man, moving about his dusty house with the awkward precision of a long-legged spider – he said, 'The greatness of Jane's heart inspired many people, I know that, but she was dealt a bad hand.' He tapped his head. 'In the chemicals department.' They were drinking tea out of delicate scalloped china cups. A residue floated on the surface, Topel saw, a plume of oil, a speck of lint. 'You know as well as I do,' Sergio went on, 'that we need people to imagine a different world for us, to believe in it, but it's a terrible strain, isn't it? And so lonely.' The tea was bitter, as dark as rosewood, and Topel thought the great act of Sergio's life had probably just been to go on living, to live without the hope of anything else.

'Can I help you?'

Topel turned. A man held the door of the convenience store open, a set of keys dangling from the inside lock. He was roughly Richard's age, wearing an old shirt coined in oil.

'I was hoping to use your phone,' Topel said.

'No payphone. Sorry.'

'No, it isn't that. I was running . . . My knee.'

The man smiled, a trace of liquor on his breath. 'Bit old for running, aren't you?'

Topel couldn't stifle a grin at the way he hadn't meant it. 'Maybe,' he said. 'All the same.'

'Come in, come in.' Beneath his impatient, put-upon air the man didn't seem upset by the interruption. 'No cell phone, eh?'

'Never caught the bug.'

'I don't blame you. Government spies with those things. Listens in on you, keeps track of where you go.'

'My feeling exactly,' Topel said.

'Rush says –' They had passed through the small shop, into a backroom office outfitted as a tiny apartment. A coarse plaid blanket lay on the bed of a pullout sofa. A hotplate, set up on the counter by the sink, held a saucepan. On a small wood table Topel saw the unwashed dishes of the man's dinner and a few cans of beer. He smiled in grim recognition. 'Do you listen to Rush? Rush makes a lot of sense, but you know, he and I part ways on this. Sure you want the government going after terrorists, you won't hear me say otherwise. But do you trust them? Really? I figure you give them powers, let them operate in secret, they're going to abuse it. Now, Martha says . . .'

Topel had the sensation of moving into a dream, someone else's dream. The physical reality of the space was as soft and strange as the curtains on the windows. Someone had put them there. Someone had *made* those curtains, everything. None of it was an accident. And in another sense it was all an accident, the long playing out of accident. This was the cave in which lived one man's dreams. And men had been drawing their dreams on the walls of caves since they were men. Topel had spent nearly thirty years walking into rooms like this, not his own, halfway between reality and dream. Never his own room, not once. No phone. One bag for all his things. No tax receipts or bank card. No email address. A forged ID. A fake name. Not a few over the years, spinning through the carousel of safe houses. His letters posted from remote counties. Code words for the phone calls placed on his behalf. It was laughable – kids' stuff – but there he was, indoors, avoiding windows. Everyone else had moved on. China was a market economy. The Soviet wealth had been looted by strongmen dressed up as market capitalists. Castro would be dead any day now and Cuba would turn into a resort town again, an investment opportunity for criminal developers, a recreation ground for Westerners with no interest or belief in history. There had been 2,000 protest bombings in the US in 1972 alone; now if a smoke machine went off in Rittenhouse Square they would have Philly on lockdown for forty-eight hours and martial law ready in the wings. Where did the rage go? How did it get absorbed and dissipate, or transmute? What did it become? How did the character of an era come to be, how did it eclipse everything in its lurid actuality and then disappear without a trace?

'. . . a temporary situation,' the man was saying. 'More a business decision than anything. I'm spending eighty, ninety hours at the station anyway. You wouldn't believe the costs. Insurance, permitting. Franchise fees. Gas contracts. The suppliers want a cut of sales, just like the parent company. So the price of oil goes up, our margins get tighter, but it looks like sales are up because AR goes up too. Accounts receivable. Now I purchased this station ten years ago and worked it ten before that for Tom Beckerink. I don't guess you know Tom? . . . But there's something called financial responsibility regulation. The EPA, right, the government says you're responsible for leaks and spillage from the underground storage tank, the UST. But of course, how do you prove if the leaks come on my or Tom's watch? I'm the owner, though, so . . . Well, I apply for an SBA loan, which used to be not so hard to get. But after the meltdown banks are wary even with the federal backing. They want to peg the loan to demonstrated and anticipated profits. But I'm making maybe five, six cents on the gallon – nothing – just to keep pace with Sam's Club and the box stores. What kind of profit can I show? We have the highest gas taxes in the country here, you know. People are nuts. They'll drive out of their way, wait in lines, waste gas and time just to save a couple bucks on a fill-up. It's not rational. It's human behavior though. So I'm trying to do what I can, stay open late, run a free air station . . . But the longer hours means either I work more or I have to take on Joe and Sally full-time, and that's a nightmare with the tax contributions, the health benefits. Meanwhile the price of oil's up and down, bankers gambling on it with futures contracts, OPEC – biggest criminal cartel in the world – trying to gouge us for all we're worth. Russians too. They want prices as high as possible. And we've got a president— Look, I'm not one of those kooks who thinks he was born in Africa, but nobody disputes he went to a Muslim school as a kid. It's in his book. And that's got to have an impact on your worldview . . .'

It had been warm, briefly, stepping in from outside, but the room was cold and Topel felt his legs going tight. A freestanding electric heater by the sofa gave off no warmth he could discern. It seemed only to intensify a sense of the irremediable in the room. A large TV set, perched uneasily on a stand veneered in faux-wood vinyl, discharged a flow of rapidly shifting images in silence.

'. . . and you've got these Russian stations now to compete with. One way or the other they're getting some break. State subsidy or – I don't know – but Putin means to embarrass us, you can bet on that. Underselling American companies. So that's why I'm here. If I'm going to work from six in the morning to ten-thirty at night, it makes sense. You get old, though. So it's temporary, like I said. I can't do it forever. But then I look at our country and I think, What's going to change? What's going to come along? People are counting their pennies. Big retailers selling at a loss to corner the market and drive folks like me out of business. You're basically forced to hire under the table. I haven't done it, but . . . this is why people get angry about the foreigners coming in. I don't have anything against foreigners. My kid had a kid with a woman from the Philippines. Then he leaves for California, leaves her, leaves the kid. Now she's raising this kid on her own. A good, hard-working woman. More than my son deserves. And so Martha says I need to be more forgiving. But how do you decide? If you forgive everything, I guess there isn't nothing a person can do wrong. Do what you like. Whatever it is, we forgive, we forgive . . . But that's the Lord's job and not mine. I'm a father. I'm sure you're a father too. You've got to set some lines between right and wrong. This lady on TV the other day said, what if your daughter got raped? Well, I have a daughter, and maybe I'd go after the bastard that did it, but the child's done nothing wrong, see? Babies don't take some evil from their parents. That's hocus-pocus stuff. Martha says I'm angry. Says I'm letting out my anger the wrong way and to come let her know when I've calmed down. Maybe *I'd* be less angry, I said, if I took pain pills for my back three times a day . . . But I don't feel angry. It's not anger – it's worry. I'm worried. Worried all the time. I'm worried construction's going to divert traffic. Worried the vapor recovery unit's going to break down. I'm scared even, I'm not above admitting it. I'm scared, because I'm the one who's responsible trying to hold it all together. And I look out, and it looks like a world that's gray and dying. A world gone of color or solidarity. What we used to call virtue, responsibility . . .'

Topel was eyeing the phone, sitting in its cradle on the small table, by a saucer of stubbed smokes compassed in spilled ash. The residue of dinner was hardening on a plate. A quart of whiskey on the seat of a chair. The man followed Topel's eye and moved toward the phone, still talking.

'. . . I don't know what happened. We used to have some solidarity, you know what I mean? We looked out for each other. God, family, country. Up and down the line. But it's come apart. It used to be you could make enough for a family, one man working a good, hard job. But wages go down with all the workers everywhere. Lots of people out of work. And the government's taxing the rest of us to pay for them and the children of people here illegally . . . There's a revolution coming in this country, I tell you. It's no accident the government wants our guns. There's a revolution coming. At some point people will've had enough. And when the government comes to take their money and their guns, to tell them how to raise their children, who to marry – oh, they'll line up shoulder to shoulder at the edge of town, not looking for a fight, but armed – armed – and they'll say, "This is our country, sirs. This is our community, our land, and now kindly leave us be." You get enough of that, enough people rising up in enough towns and places, and maybe things change. Maybe it's the blood of patriots. I don't know. Watering the tree of liberty. Maybe things turn ugly. But injustice doesn't last. It can't last. Unjust laws, well, people stop obeying them. It's the way of history. I'll defend my family to my last breath, my kids, my station – shotgun in hand. There must be millions like me. Oh, I'll defend what's mine, don't think I won't. And if we're starving, if we're starving, don't think I'd hesitate to eat you right up.'

The look in the man's eye was wild and lonely. Topel put out his hand for the phone. 'Let's hope it doesn't come to that,' he said. ■

Courtesy of the author

SANA KRASIKOV

1979

Sana Krasikov was born in Ukraine and grew up in Georgia and the United States. Her story collection *One More Year* won a 5 Under 35 award from the National Book Foundation, was a finalist for the 2009 PEN/Hemingway Award and for the NYPL Young Lions Fiction Award. Her latest novel is *The Patriots*.

REMEMBERING WESTGATE

Sana Krasikov

'How can you write at that place?' A friend asked me this question last year while I was trying to finish my book. We were both expats in Nairobi. The place she was referring to was the Artcaffe at the Westgate Mall, or just 'Westgate', as everyone called it.

'It has good Wi-Fi,' was all I could think to tell her. (This was not a lie: at our house we could go without a signal for days, forcing my husband to climb up on the roof to install the expensive satphone his employer had lent him). But what I really believed and didn't say was something different, which was that lightning doesn't strike twice.

Both my friend and I had been in Kenya long enough so that al-Shabaab's attack on the mall in September 2013 was still a fresh memory. I had found myself in Nairobi nine months earlier, renting a house in the neighborhood of Westlands, a short drive away from the mall. It was not hard for an expat to fall in love with Nairobi – with its LA weather, its cheap childcare, the cosmopolitan mix of entrepreneurs and artists, many of them Kenyan-born and US- or UK-educated, returning to take advantage of the African markets while First World economies stagnated. That every dwelling, aside from those in slums, was nestled behind a concrete wall was a fact that I accommodated myself to in a matter of time. So much so that when my mother visited and remarked on all the unsightly barbed wire and cemented shards of glass, I realized that my eye had somehow learned to enjoy the greenery while airbrushing these details out.

The morning of the attack I had strayed from my routine by accompanying a writer friend to the Kwani Litfest of African Authors. Sitting in the audience, I felt irked by all the Kenyan Millennials fixating on their smartphones, while I, the eager foreigner, raised a hand to pose earnest questions to Teju Cole. Apparently, only the speaker and I were unaware of what was happening outside.

I was taking my son to a birthday party that afternoon. I'd gone to Westgate to buy a present the night before. My neighbor Puni had less fortunate timing. Our kids were playmates, attending the same celebration. That morning Puni had gone to the toy store on the third floor, as I might have. She was at the cash register when she heard the first shots. She escaped to the roof and found the remnants of a children's cooking competition. Somewhere among this wreckage of bodies and overturned ingredients, she crouched under a folding table to aid a pregnant woman who had been wounded. One of the terrorists soon returned and discovered them. Puni would later say that he was young, handsome even, like a boy you'd see lifting weights in the gym. He looked her in the eye, smiled and aimed a gun – shooting the yogurt containers above her head. Still grinning, he walked away. Did he miss her, or did he do it on purpose? Dripping in yogurt, she managed to wrap a tourniquet around her companion's leg, and then escaped by scaling a wall, only to find herself caught in a concrete canyon in the unused rear of the mall. She was rescued a few hours later. This, at least, is how I remember her story, which I heard along with a dozen others in the coming weeks. The random quality of the murders was, I think, by design – the terrorists wanted eyewitnesses to narrowly escape, to remember them and grow their diabolical legend.

But the images in my mind are other people's, not my own. I know this. And I know it was the reason I remained in the city, while Puni asked to be relocated, and, within months, had moved away with her family.

For the next two years I tried to finish a book, while helping to run my husband's news bureau for National Public Radio, raising one child and having another. Several times a week, when I needed to go to the grocery store or a doctor's appointment, I drove past the arsoned carapace of Westgate. I saw the scaffolds, but few actual workers. So many construction projects in Nairobi went on indefinitely. A part of me did not believe the mall would ever reopen. How could it, after what had gone on inside – people crawling for cover, families trapped together in grocery aisles or, worse, separated. The efforts of older children to calm younger ones, keep them quiet with bottled water. The bungled rescue, the looting by the army which followed, the implausible stories and cover-ups. We'd obtained a DVD of CCTV footage from the States (its distribution was forbidden in Nairobi) – it was instantly borrowed and passed around our Kenyan acquaintances, who used it to confirm their conspiracy theories. I watched only a few minutes of two young terrorists sashaying past the storefronts I knew so well – their rifles casually slung or pointed, as relaxed as if they'd been on tranquilizers, which perhaps they were. Then I turned it off.

And yet here it was one day as I pulled up. Its glass doors triumphantly open. Women in kanga skirts and hijabs were laying their purses down on the conveyor of the prim metal detector. The marble landing was no longer sentried by rail-thin Kenyan men in fatigues, but by burly plain-clothed Israelis talking into earpieces.

A twinkling fountain pool greeted me as I surfaced into the white afterlife sort of light that so many malls seem to have. Everything looked the same, only nicer. I sucked my breath in and continued on. I'd come to buy a diaper-changing pad for my infant daughter. I passed by the Artcaffe, where I'd once eaten panini with friends and revised sentences with an Americano at my elbow, and where people had tossed wallets and passports out of their bags so that, if discovered by terrorists, their nationalities might remain unknown.

I was shocked at how busy the place was. A group of Kenyan and Chinese businessmen were conducting a meeting at two pulled-together tables. The sound of crying babies filled my own breasts painfully. In a Danish accent, a woman was discussing the difficulties of obtaining foundation money with a Kenyan job applicant. Here were the young waitstaff in their black jeans, consulting with each other, carrying trays of cappuccinos with those touching leaf designs in the foam. I sat down and ordered a coffee.

It wasn't long before I was coming several times a week. My daughter was now sleeping in the spare room I'd used as an office. I chewed carrots and hummus and went through my editor's notes. My coffee was refreshed by a polite boy named Vincent, who always seated me on the upper balcony, in a dark grotto away from the music and close to the restrooms, which I employed frequently. If terrorists walked in through the front door, I reasoned, I'd be able to run into the toilets and barricade myself. I played out this scenario: was it better to be closer to an exit, or in a semi-invisible part of the restaurant with no egress? Was I going to be trapped in a corner? What if others were banging on the door, running from the attackers? I would open the door, obviously! How would I protect us from a hail of bullets coming through a plywood door? There was a metallic vase (or was it just ceramic painted silver?) poised above the toilet. Was it strong enough to withstand ammunition from a standard assault rifle?

When I wasn't in the lavatory, I was at a nearby table, trying to finish my novel about an American woman trying to escape Communist Russia with her family. And virtually every escape scenario on my mind involved crouching above a public toilet, holding a faux-metal vase.

'How can you work at that place?' It occurred to me, belatedly, that my friend had not been talking about the risks. Her question wasn't *aren't you frightened?* but *aren't you ashamed?* I asked her if that's what she'd meant and she clarified that yes, if she were a relative of someone who'd died or been injured in the attack, she would not want shoppers traipsing about the place pretending this hadn't been a crime scene. I tried to counter with something about how if we allowed ourselves to be cowed we were letting the terrorists win, but I knew I was parroting the traditional political language that congratulated us for being consumers. I remembered that President Kenyatta had crowed on TV about the mall's sales numbers on the day it reopened being the highest in history. I didn't believe the numbers but that wasn't the point; his speech was an echo of Bush's exhortation after 9/11 to go on with our lives. To 'go shopping'.

To be traumatized is to be locked in a moment without escape, stuck in a looping circuit of memories. In the weeks and months after the attack, those who'd found themselves in Westgate would insist that the attackers were still on the loose. A teenage girl, the niece of a neighbor who'd spoken in detail on tape about the shooting, later begged us not to use the tape for a story. She was terrified that the shooters (who by this time were dead) would recognize her voice and hunt her down. A man who my husband had interviewed outside the mall called us early one morning and swore that he was sitting at the same bar as his wife's murderer (by the time my husband arrived, the man had cornered the poor fellow, who was stoned and didn't understand what he was being accused of). People we had not been able to find called back months later saying they'd changed their phone numbers – because they were afraid of being trailed, if not by their attackers, then by the Kenyan authorities, who would surely punish them for promulgating their own versions of events, which did not square with the official narrative.

Who was it who said there is no distance as great as the one between the healthy and the sick? The same can be said of trauma. At the end of the day, I could pack up my laptop and leave the mall, while some part of the people who had been there on that day would always be stuck inside it.

What was I doing then, crouching on the common toilet, replaying survival scenarios that I knew were wishful thinking? I agreed with the Nairobians who said the mall was no safer now than it had been. I could not separate these lurid fantasies from the fact that I was writing about characters trapped by history. I do not typically write about myself, and so I am always hovering on the edge of other people's lives, inhabiting stories I haven't lived. For years I'd been tracking the journey of a real woman whose life my fictional story was based on, excavating it from a mountain of fragile clues. Was it the torment of other experiences I was fascinated by, or the inescapability?

I looked around the cafe. There were now new faces, new children, new adults who really did not remember the old Westgate. That made sense: it was September, the new crop had arrived. Such was the nature of global cities, these hubs of transience that made forgetting possible.

I began taking walks around the mall, looking for a plaque to the memory of those killed. There was none. No date engraved in brass. No framed bullet holes. Later, I'd learn that a plaque had been put up at the Amani Garden, in Karura Forest at the edge of the city. Which is a bit like putting a plaque to the victims of 9/11 in the Botanical Garden in the Bronx. I knew that in Kenya public outrage did not wield the same check on powerful interests that it did in the States. But even so, why such an insistent erasure? Maybe something was lost in cultural translation. What was it about aggressive forgetting that seemed both so necessary and so unseemly?

I noticed, for the first time, my old optometrist. It was Friday; he was wearing an ankle-length white jubba and a Kufi prayer cap. I had not seen him before. The eyeglass store had had a COMING SOON sign hung up for months, but now he was back, apparently reopening his business. I thought of going inside and asking if he'd been there on the morning of the attack. If so, how had he escaped?

Had his knowledge of Arabic prayers spared him from the wrath of the terrorists? But I walked on.

I knew that were I my mother, I probably would have walked in and asked him these questions. My mother asked people shockingly personal questions as a matter of course, questions which they never seemed to mind. I attributed this ability to the fact that she had been knifed in the heart on a street in Tbilisi when she was in her early thirties. Her recovery had been harrowing, and miraculous. The incident made her perpetually terrified for my safety, and blithe about trespassing into the private quarters of other people's trauma. It wasn't, I thought now, that she empathized with this trauma any more than I did. It was that she had been on the other side of that inescapability.

I've since thought about Edmund Burke's theory of the Sublime, and 'negative pain' – the rush of intense pleasure that stems from horror, fear and pain. Leslie Jamison, in *The Empathy Exams*, described it as 'the idea that a feeling of fear – paired with a sense of safety, and the ability to look away – can produce a feeling of delight'. I wonder if the only way to grasp what is terrifying and unimaginable for those of us who haven't experienced it is to feel around the contours of inescapability, the boundary of its negative space.

The images in my mind were other people's memories, not my own. But I do have one memory that I hold on to. It was of the next day when I saw Puni in the playground. She was with her five-month-old daughter, bouncing the child around on the giant trampoline. The girl was usually with the nanny because Puni worked all the time. That day she hadn't gone to work. She smiled at me, then went back to holding her daughter's hand as the girl balanced herself on the wobbly surface. She stood up and fell, stood up and fell, laughing every time she did it. Puni's face was a naked reflection of that laughter: I had never before seen anyone look so elated, so blind to everything but her happiness. Where was she, I wondered. Crossing the line and coming back, again and again? ■

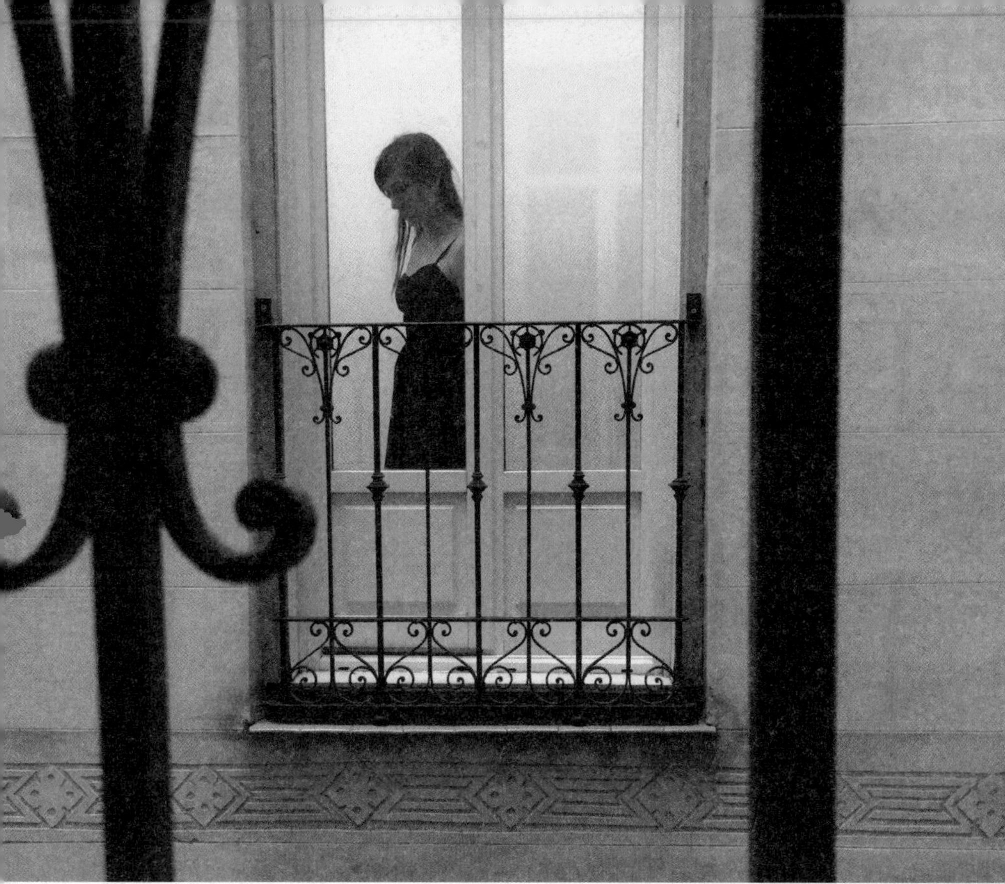

Courtesy of the author

CATHERINE LACEY

1985

Catherine Lacey is the author of *Nobody Is Ever Missing*, winner of a 2016 Whiting Award and a finalist for the NYPL Young Lions Fiction Award. It has been translated into French, Italian, Spanish, Dutch and German. Her second novel, *The Answers*, is forthcoming in June 2017, from which 'The Answers' is an extract. Her first story collection, *Certain American States*, will follow. She was born in Mississippi and is based in Chicago.

THE ANSWERS

Catherine Lacey

1

I'd run out of options. That's how these things usually happen, how a person ends up placing all her last hopes on a stranger, hoping that whatever that stranger might do to her would be the thing she needed done to her.

For so long I had been a person who needed other people to do things to me, and for so long no one had done the right thing to me, but already I'm getting ahead of myself. That's one of my problems, I'm told, getting ahead of myself, so I've been trying to find a way to get behind myself, to be slow and quiet with myself like Ed used to be. But of course I can't quite make it work, can't be exactly who Ed was to me.

There are some things that only other people can do to you.

Pneuma Adaptive Kinesthesia, PAKing – what Ed does to people – requires one person to *know* and another person (me, in this case) to lie there, not knowing. In fact, I still do not know what Pneuma Adaptive Kinesthesia really is, just that it made me (or seemed to have made me) well again. During our sessions Ed sometimes hovered his hands over my body, chanting or humming or silent while he supposedly moved or rearranged or healed invisible parts of me. He put stones and crystals on my face, my legs, sometimes pressing or twisting some part of my body in painfully pleasurable ways, and though I didn't understand how any of this could remove the various sicknesses from my body, I couldn't argue with relief.

I'd spent a year suffering undiagnosable illnesses in almost every part of me, but after only *one* session with Ed, just ninety minutes during which he barely touched me, I could almost forget I was a body. Such a luxury it was, to not be overwhelmed by decay.

Chandra had suggested PAKing, called it *feng shui for the energetic body*, *guerrilla warfare against negative vibes*, and though I was sometimes skeptical of Chandra's talk of *vibes*, this time I had to believe her. I'd been ill so long that I'd almost lost the belief I could be well again and I was afraid of what might replace that belief if it disappeared completely.

Technically, Chandra explained, *PAKing is a form of neurophysio-chi bodywork, a relatively obscure technique either on the outskirts of the forefront or the outskirts of the outskirts, depending on who you ask.*

The problem was, as always, an invisible one. The problem was money.

I needed a minimum of thirty-five PAKing sessions, at $225 each, to complete a PAK series, which meant a complete treatment would cost me the same as a half-year's rent on that poorly lit and irregularly shaped one-bedroom I'd had for many years (not because it suited me – I detested it – but because everyone said it was a steal, too good to let go). And even though my paycheck from the travel agency was decent, the monthly credit card minimums, student loan payments, and last year's onslaught of medical bills were all reducing my bank account to cents or negatives each month, while the debt always seemed to grow.

One dire morning, starving and cashless, I ate the last of my pantry for breakfast (slightly expired anchovies mixed into a tiny can of tomato paste) and I often Hare-Krishna'd for dinner, leaving my shoes and dignity at the door to praise Krishna (the god, as far as I could tell, of cafeteria-grade vegetarian fare and manic chanting).

By the fourth or fifth Love Feast, white tilaka greased on my brow, pasta wiggling around the metal plate as if independently animate, I knew that the boundless love of Krishna would never be enough for me – no matter how hungry or broke or confused I became. It was a few days later that answering that ad for an *income-generating experience* tacked to a bulletin board at a health-food store seemed like my only real option, that somehow giving away the dregs of my life might be the best way to get a real one back.

For a year I'd had no life, just symptoms. Mundane ones at first – tenacious headaches, back pain, a constantly upset stomach – but over months they became increasingly strange. Persistent dry mouth and a numb tongue. A full-body rash. My legs kept falling asleep, stranding me at the office or in a bath or at a bus stop as the M5 came and went, came and went. At some point I somehow cracked a rib in my sleep. These strange lumps began to rise and fall on my skin, like turtle heads surfacing and sinking in a pond. I could only sleep three or four hours a night, so I tried to nap through my lunch hour, forehead to desk, on the days I didn't have a doctor's appointment. I avoided mirrors and eye contact. I stopped making plans more than a week away.

There were blood tests and more blood tests, CAT scans and biopsies. There were seven specialists, three gynos, five GPs, a psychiatrist, and one grope-y chiropractor. Chandra took me to a celebrity acupuncturist, a spiritual surgeon, and a guy who sold stinking powders in the back room of a Chinatown fishmonger. There were checkups and follow-ups and throw-ups and so on.

It's just stress, someone said, but they couldn't rule out cancer or a rare autoimmune disorder or a psychic attack or pure neurosis, all in my head – *just don't worry so much – try not to think about it.*

One doctor said, *That's just bodies for you*, sighed, and clapped my shoulder, as if we were all in on the joke.

But I didn't want a punch line. I wanted an explanation. I hesitated at storefronts for palm readers and psychics. I let Chandra do my tarot a few times but the news was always bad – swords and daggers and demons and grim reapers. *I'm new at this*, she said, though I knew she wasn't. I held my spasming legs to my chest, chin to knees, and felt like a child, dwarfed by everything I didn't know.

I came close to praying a few times, but everything felt unanswered enough and I didn't want another frame for the silence.

Something in the genes or a consequence of ill choices, one might rationalize, but it could have just been a hefty stroke of bad luck – senseless or a karmic bitch slap – somehow earned. My parents would have said it was just a part of *His plan*, but to them, of course, everything was. How someone wants to explain catastrophe isn't important – that's what I know now. When shit happens, it doesn't really matter what asshole is responsible.

2

For five years, I had a life.

My childhood wasn't my life – maybe it had been Merle's life, but not mine. And the time I lived with Aunt Clara hadn't really been a life, more like rehabilitation. And college wasn't life at all, just a gestational period, four years of warning and training for this life that was coming, that future thing.

My life began on an airplane, the moment we left the ground. We ascended and I wept against Chandra's shoulder as silently as I could, and when the flight attendant came around, Chandra asked for a cup of hot water, adding her own tea bag and holding it still in the turbulence until it was the right temperature to drink, giving it to me then. She knew so much, knew all the best ways to do things. She unfurled her massive scarf, wrapped us together, and I fell asleep against her shoulder. We woke up as we were landing in London, holding hands in our sleep, and minutes later she guided us through Heathrow, a place she already knew. It wasn't that she felt like a mother to me, but I was still somehow her child.

It must have been her hundredth trip, though it was my first, a graduation present from her parents, Vivian and Oliver. Viv and Olly, she called them. I'd spent most holidays and odd weekends at their place in Montauk all through college since I had nowhere to go. The house was full of expensive things that didn't really matter to them – chipped antiques, forgotten gadgets, scratched CDs in stacks – and it wasn't uncommon to find random twenties between sofa cushions or strewn around the kitchen between candies from foreign countries. At the dinner table her family spoke loudly with their mouths full and Chandra lovingly argued with her parents about books and art. Everyone made and laughed at jokes I didn't understand, though I learned to laugh anyway. We all drank wine, even when I was nineteen and a tablespoon of it made me blithe and sleepy.

It was the two-month round-the-world ticket from Viv and Olly that began my years of compulsive travel. I saw the Galapagos birds, cherry blossoms in Japan, Egyptian pyramids, the Catacombs, Burmese snake pagodas, and that eerie neon-teal lake in New Zealand. I loved the leaving, even the 5 a.m. flights, silent subway cars rattling through desolate purple mornings, predawn airports filled with limp people. I read somewhere that the first thing you learn when traveling is that you don't exist – I didn't want to stop not existing.

At home the debts were always growing. Strangers called at all hours, spoke hatefully about what I owed them. I received serious letters with large bold numbers, each higher than the last. Other envelopes came with new credit cards, new ways out, new trips. I stopped wondering where I might go next but what would happen if I never returned. But I always returned. And each time I hit the tarmac I had this terrible feeling that the trip I'd just taken had never even happened, that I'd spent hundreds for a memory I could barely recall.

The back pain started first, which seemed innocuous enough (didn't everyone get back pain?), though I was only twenty-five or twenty-six at the time. I blamed the knotty hostel beds and kept traveling beyond my means, though in less adventurous ways after a bout of muscle spasms so strong they left me stranded on a trail in Abel Tasman for an hour until a group of hikers from Japan carried me out.

A few months later, while fighting off the first in a plague of stomach bugs, the headaches began and with the headaches came the full-body pains, pulsing and huge, pain seeming to stretch me from the inside. I was pregnant with it, labor that never ended, just ebbed. I had to stop traveling, to spend all my time and money trying to feel alive again – referrals, appointments, inconclusive results, more referrals, bills. Stern calls came from receptionists who had once seemed so kind – when would I pay, how would I pay, did I realize that missing payments came with fines? And even more calls came from debt collectors, three or four of them. They asked if I knew what I owed or they told me what I owed, more, often much more, than I thought. They told me that contrary to what some believe, it was possible to be jailed for one's debts. I said I found that surprising and they told me not to be so surprised. *It's theft, a form of theft*, one of them said, to which I said nothing. And didn't I worry about my credit score, planning for the future, home ownership, retirement, providing for my family, and I said, quickly and not kindly, *No, I didn't think of that, I never thought of that.*

Well, maybe you should, he said.

I sometimes wondered why I even answered the phone, but I guess I always had the hope that it would be someone else, some other way of life calling for me. One of the collectors spoke so fast that when I listened to him, the back of my head seemed to emanate heat through my hair, and another spoke so slow and softly I felt I was sinking or drowning, that the air had become thicker around me and would take me down if I kept breathing. It felt possible – though I know this is absurd – that the use of my own body, the only thing I really owned, had somehow been repossessed.

For a while Chandra's constant care may have been all that stood between me and the total loss of my mind or life, and looking back at that year – when I'd wake up most nights hardly able to breathe, lying there for hours, mouth hanging open like a gargoyle – well, I don't want to think about what I would have become if she hadn't been there for me, stopping me from falling out of myself. (I don't mean I wanted to kill myself – I've never had that kind of nerve – but sometimes the pain was so unfathomable and large that I wondered if I might, unintentionally, be killed by myself.)

When Chandra suggested PAKing for all the pain, and when PAKing necessitated getting a second job, I was desperate – ready to do anything for relief, no matter how expensive or ridiculous it seemed. She'd become an expert on illness and wellness, on traveling the distance between these places. Two years earlier, standing on a street corner, she'd been violently clipped by a city bus and had since been living on the settlement, devoting her time to healing herself, completely, of everything: the broken leg, twisted wrist, busted face, fear of street curbs – and the preexisting stuff – anxiety, caffeine dependence, pollen allergies, self-diagnosed chronic candida, disillusionment, thwarted intuition, commitment issues, trust issues, all her traumas and the habits they'd left. She had a herbalist, a reiki master, a Rolfer, a speech therapist, a movement therapist, an art therapist, and a therapist.

Retreats and pilgrimages took her in and out of the city for a while, but she always sent postcards. I kept them in my purse and stared at the images of oceans and temples, hoping to get some residual calm while I sat in another waiting room, clutching the part of my body that was currently killing me. First she swore by ayahuasca, then it was all about sensory deprivation chambers or MDMA, wheatgrass, body alkalinization, or a certain guru. Every day, she said, a new layer of something was removed between herself and her *self*. She was fulfilled, she said, for the first time in her life, and though I envied her, a more cynical part of me couldn't help but wonder, *Filled with what?*

When she was in town, she came over weekly with an arsenal of cures – herbs, powders, oils, bitter tinctures so powerful I had to take them by the drop. She burned sage, chanted, meditated, and sometimes – though this always embarrassed me – she'd hit a small gong or play this wooden flute. I never knew where to look or whether to suppress or release the impulse to laugh – even my embarrassment was embarrassing to me – and why couldn't I just chant with her, be at peace with her flute or that little gong? I was lucky she was there at all, that I knew at least one person who wanted to help me not because it was her job, but because she just wanted to see me healed.

The day she came back from Bali, she appeared at my door unannounced, all sleek and tan, draped in white linen.

I can tell you're suffering, she said.

Out of anyone else's mouth I'd be bothered by a statement standing in for a question, but she was always right about me. She walked through my apartment with an alluring, eerie calm, as if she were no longer interested in anything other than the slow purification of her body, other bodies, the whole world. She draped scarves over my toaster oven, alarm clock, and telephone, whispered mantras in each cardinal direction, spread a circular tapestry across the cracked hardwood in my living room, then settled into an elegant meditation posture. I tried to copy her, but my knees were too stiff and the twitching foot made it hard to keep still so I gave up and went full starfish.

I'd sold most of my furniture in a stoop sale to make rent, so lying on my floor doing nothing in particular was a habit I was all too familiar with. When she was here, I called it meditation, but I always fell half-asleep, my body exhausted by itself. I woke this time to Chandra standing over me. When she met my eyes, I noticed her face change a little, in ways I couldn't exactly explain, but could feel. Our twelve years of friendship made silence soft and easy between us, though it wasn't just the passage of time that had created this intimacy. It had somehow been there immediately, this mysterious closeness, as innate as an organ. Lying on the floor just then, the real weight of our love became palpable, pushed tears out of my head. She was all I had.

Are you still taking those medicinal fish oils?

I nodded. She crouched and wiped the tears out of my face, smoothed my hair.

And the geranium-hemp powder?

In porridge, like you told me.

Well, let's try to get your weight up.

She looked away from the little shred I was. My appetite had departed long ago; all soft parts of me followed.

First all my coworkers assumed I'd taken up yoga and commended me for it. They said I looked good, that I'd gotten into shape, asked for tips on motivation, healthy recipes. But soon they were saying I shouldn't lose any more weight, that I was *just right*, that I must be working out too much, that I needed to build muscle, put on some weight, start eating more red meat or peanut butter or full-fat grass-fed dairy. Someone gravely recommended their thyroid specialist and Meg suggested I see a hypnotist to fix my eating disorder, but when I said I didn't have an eating disorder, that I was just sick, she just said, *I know*.

When word got around of all my midday doctor appointments, everyone began speaking to me as if I had no body at all, everyone except Joe Nevins, who once interrupted our discussion about a missing invoice to say my face looked different, and when I asked what he meant by that, he wouldn't or didn't say.

Just different, he said, and went back to talking about the invoice.

I got used to it, in a way, being this sack of skin full of problems, because having a body doesn't give you the right to have one that works correctly. Having a body doesn't seem to give you any rights at all.

You'll get over this, Chandra said while unpacking the new herbs and roots she'd brought for me. *This pain is just a teacher for you.*

This was how she saw the world, that everything went according to plan, that we subconsciously made our own problems, that every cancer had been invited, every injury earned. I wasn't sure if I had the nerve to believe this, and if I did, if I really accepted I had asked for everything that had happened to me, I wasn't sure I could ever forgive myself. But thinking this way seemed to calm her. If she deserved her pain, then she deserved all the good in her life, too.

I could have used a sense of acceptance like that. I hated the pains in my body, struggled against them and cursed them so much I'd even grown to fear good feelings – a settled stomach, a relaxed back, a full night's sleep, or a whole day without crying. Even Chandra's care grew to terrify me. What if it vanished? What if she just gave up and stopped coming by?

Her kindness, as if we shared blood or history, had always been hard to accept. I was just a person who appeared in her life at random, her assigned college roommate, a homeschooled semi-orphan from a barely literate state, but she still spent hours going over financial aid and student-loan paperwork I didn't understand. She lost sleep listening to me debate the merits and demerits of what I should major in – religion, philosophy, history, or English – though she'd made up her mind from the start: theater major, marketing minor. And most crucially, she decoded the world for me, explained all the pop culture I'd never heard of, and let me evade the answer to how I'd made it to eighteen without ever hearing of Michael Jackson. I'd blame the homeschooling or say, *We were poor.* (She seemed terrified by that word: *poor.*) Once I mentioned that I'd been raised, for a time, by my aunt, a detail that stopped her questions. People like her didn't get raised by aunts.

After Chandra and I meditated, or, rather, after she meditated and I did whatever I did there on the floor, she served me maté in gourds and crudités with homemade allergen-free, vegan, sprouted pepita paste she had made, she said, while sending nourishing vibes to my astral body. It tasted grassy, felt thick in my throat.

Pepitas absorb toxins, she said, watching me eat as if watching someone parallel-park. I sat there filling myself with pepitas, as the pepitas, I imagined, filled with my toxins. Chandra took the pulse from each of my wrists and examined my tongue. She closed her eyes for a little while, then told me her spirit guides had just advised her to advise me to complete a full PAK series, as soon as possible, with Ed, her PAKer. It had something to do with past lives or future ones, or perhaps even current lives that Ed and I were somehow living in another dimension. She spoke unflinchingly, as if her spirit guides were a real group of people, a flesh-and-blood committee.

PAKing changed my life, she said. *Not just a door opening . . . but . . . a whole house of doors opening? It's going to do that for you, too. My spirit guides have never been so clear. This is your future. You just have to take it.*

I'd always been skeptical of Chandra's reports from her spirit guides, as they always seemed to have these plans for her that she couldn't explain to me yet. She'd once told me they were preparing her for incalculable fame and financial wealth, that her accident was part of a strengthening regimen for this future greatness, that she was going to eventually have her own talk show.

I didn't know you wanted a talk show, I told her, but she just smiled. *It's not about what I want. The fates are beyond desire.*

I wanted to believe that she might actually have some understanding of fate or any kind of intel on the future, because she seemed to believe in it and she also believed in me. But I also didn't want to lose her to the belief that life had a code that could be cracked, that there was some ideal way to live.

Regardless, I trusted her. Perhaps someone would say I had no choice but to trust her and perhaps that is true, but also, and I understand this now, I loved her and I loved her in that rare way, that non-possessive and accepting way that it seems people are always trying and failing to love someone, so I sipped the last of my maté through the metal straw, looked into Chandra's profoundly healed and spiritually realized eyes, and asked for Ed's number. ■

Courtesy of the author

BEN LERNER

1979

Ben Lerner was born in Topeka, Kansas. He has received fellowships from the Fulbright, Guggenheim and MacArthur Foundations, among other honors. He is the author of three books of poetry (*The Lichtenberg Figures*, *Angle of Yaw* and *Mean Free Path*) and two novels (*Leaving the Atocha Station* and *10:04*). His most recent book is the monograph *The Hatred of Poetry*.

BRIGHT CIRCLE

Ben Lerner

Things he dreamt began to show up in the bushes, the plastic figurine from a parachute firework, the small dull rusted circular saw blade he thought of as a throwing star, and he pocketed those things. His pockets were large: all year he wore one of the three pairs of army cargo pants he had purchased with his own money from the Surplus on Huntoon. Desert camouflage. Understand he had over 400 dollars in mainly twenties. He had a dozen Buck folding knives. He had in the same drawer with cash and knives a Crossman pellet gun he had often claimed to be an actual revolver and once pointed at the younger Gordon boy, which led the older Gordon boy to open a cut above his eye. The coconut smell so strong he experienced it as a taste of the young nurse who stitched that up and the very thin gold braided chain against her collarbone appeared now in his dreams, but that was OK, Doctor S said, the problem is when it goes the other way. It was like that paper TOPEKA HIGH SCHOOL banner cheerleaders held for the players to burst through when they took the field. More than to actually play that's what he'd wanted, imagined when he was a water boy in middle school. (See him in pure joy sprinting up the sideline when one of our running backs breaks away.) Now there is a hoop somewhere that held the banner between sleep and waking and things and people pass through.

He'll be at the McDonald's on Gage Avenue getting his hot water and he'll suddenly just know the man ordering in front of him is Dad, particles of windshield in his matted hair. So he walks right out head down and gets back on his Schwinn Predator and pedals full speed to the bushes of Westboro Park where he can breathe and pocket stray items from the dreams. What about the bushes makes you feel safe, Doctor S asks him every time he mentions sheltering there. Understand there is a network of tunnels under the big mass of honeysuckle and he has supplies, a plastic bag of small Snickers and PayDay for energy and some jerky lightly buried under brush in a place he will not reveal. Are there other places like the bushes? What about thinking of this place as kind of like the bushes, Dale?

Well, maybe he could do that if Doctor S didn't say at the end of every hour, Come on in, Ms Eberheart, and then Dale has to listen to his mother complain. Most recently about how he ruined the perfect job at Dillon's Grocery that Doctor S had helped arrange for him, calling in a favor. Because Dale was dishonest, unreliable, and let's not even talk about the GED. What requires Dale to slow his breathing deliberately is how her voice goes very high-pitched, almost a squeal, animal in pain, right before she starts crying, then goes deep again: I don't know how much / More of this I / can take. His lies. My diabetes. Working nights. That's when Dale feels like he is about to cry himself or choke her out but instead just looks at the clown painting on Doctor S's wall hard enough that its colors change a little. Do you like it? That is a poster of a painting by Marc Chagall.

It can't be like the bushes when that bitch is here. At first Doctor S would say we don't use words like bitch, faggot, pussy, but since he started seeing the back of his dad's head there aren't really rules. Because understand Dale is not a faggot or a pussy no matter what Gordon or Hishky or Carter or Dad said before he hit the median and went through the windshield underground. Dale had more than once confessed to killing him, at which point Doctor S said very slowly, like he was reading it off a billboard at some distance, No, Dale, you are not responsible – in any way – for your father's death. But Dale had flipped that Honda over and over in his head, pressed rewind, flipped it again. In his mind he'd sat bored and sweating through the service in the front pew of Potwin Presbyterian Church before the Highway Patrol had even called them. Feel the starched collar against his recently shaved neck.

Since he was a boy he'd have hot water in the morning to pretend along with his mom and dad that he was having coffee, here is your morning coffee, Dale, black no sugar, almost time for work. Rare shared laughter. The joke was that he was a man but now he is one, eighteen, and it's just what he does in the morning, a hot drink. At McDonald's they give you hot water for free although it can be hard to explain that you don't want to buy their Lipton tea. More than once he'd had to purchase the bag he would discard. (On Gage Avenue they gave the steaming styrofoam cup to him mostly without trouble, but the one time he'd tried on 21st someone from among the cooks he might have known said tell the retard to fuck off.) When he'd started the job at Dillon's his dad had not yet come through the tattered banner and Dale would sit in one of the red plastic swivel chairs near the glass façade and watch through his own vague reflection the traffic while he sipped it, stirred it with a plastic spoon, sipped it. And then he would rise with a purposefulness he believed the other men could sense.

If you are going to your job, the scenery organizes itself differently around your bike as you cut through it, elms and silver maples lining up respectfully to let you pass. Stacy, the friend of Doctor S, had showed him where he could lean his Predator just within the side entrance and where he could take a green apron from a hook. Tie it in the back like this. Then just ask me and I'll tell you which of the checkout lines you should help with first. Here come the heads of broccoli the box of frozen waffles the Wonder Bread the two-liter Dr Pepper slowly over the black rubber conveyor to be rung up at which point he is to put them in doubled tall paper bags and if asked to carry them or push them in the cart to the trunks of cars, beds of trucks. Often he was transporting the food of people he knew, had known, and they would speak to him, and it was fine. Eggs and milk get their own plastic bag, don't ask me why. The satisfaction of jamming the empty shopping cart into another shopping cart in the corral. Four twenty-five an hour times thirty was more money than he could imagine once you timesed thirty by however many weeks there would be in the years he planned to work. One thing for sure: he would buy Ron Waldron's silver Fiero and even let his mom use it if she followed certain rules.

But then halfway through the first month a large can of something doesn't ring up and Mike the faggot he is bagging for tells him to check the price which means first finding the aisle and then the shelf and then whatever number on whatever label corresponds to the can in question before carrying all that in his head and hands back to Mike who will have long since finished ringing up the other groceries, the customer pissed for sure. Stacy never said that pricing was his job. By the time he locates the aisle in question he already sees himself back unable to account for how the label with the price was equidistant between two similar but distinct sets of cans, or how those distinctions blurred as he looked hard, the color of the labels transitioning until he could not define a border between what costs this, what costs that. He would match the words if letters and numbers didn't go ants running across pavement twigs floating away on water as he stood there and if the other shoppers hadn't started to laugh at him until he turned to catch them. Only standing in a cold sweat before the shelves does he become aware of the muzak that's been circulating through the Dillon's all of 1995.

And then he's being told by Mrs Greiner to read aloud from *How the Grinch Stole Christmas!* in fourth grade, to sound it out, we can wait all day, the laughter, while Coach Skakel grabs him by the facemask during tryouts in seventh and throws him to the ground for being dumb as shit, ears ringing, cut-grass smell. He's also sitting in an office as Doctor Allen says to his father think nine- or ten-year-old in teenage body while being tripped up by Carter in a story about fingering Becky Reynolds some years later, do you even know what fingering means, same laughter around the fire, sparks crackling off the Osage orange. All these innumerable moments are present whenever one is, little mimic spasms around the corner of his mouth reflect that.

You have to get away from wherever those moments pool in space so he walks head down to the storeroom, hangs the apron up, and bikes the four blocks to the Surplus where he can sit far in the back latching and unlatching a .50 caliber ammo can until Cut it out Stan finally says from behind the counter without looking up. Stan, even if he is fat and wheezy, and despite the missing thumb, could cup and clap his hands over your ears like all Marines in a way that kills you or shove your nose into your brain with his palm. These and other combat skills Dale sometimes believed he had absorbed, hoped he wouldn't have to use. Likewise Dale felt that he had had a little of whatever experience Stan recounted, the way a teacher once told Dale that to smell a thing means to get some particle of it in you. So if Stan said there were whores everywhere you barely had to pay them you'd just spit on your cock for lube Dale would not exactly feel that he was lying when he told a group of middle-schoolers playing basketball on the Randolph court that he had fucked one, spat on, etc. He didn't have to pay her though he could, I have over 400 dollars. If you say a thing that when it comes out holds together, that makes it true enough, so he didn't feel that he was lying, even though he often later felt he had. His whole life his mom would demand he admit that he was lying before it was possible for anyone to know.

Yes and no the Surplus was like the bushes. Yes because no way a Gordon or a Hishky or a Carter could reach him here where Stan, who had known Dale's dad, was boss. You are free to hang around if you are quiet. Yes because this was like the bushes a dark place where Dale had tactical knowledge, even knew where locked behind the counter the antique but loaded Luger was. No because particles of Stan's anger would get in him. They all say they want nice guy sensitive types then bang the whole team is that not right Dale. I'm no racist Dale but do they not chase after them and beg for it. His name was always mixed up in these sentences when Stan was in a talking mood. The summer before freshman year they had dared him to kiss Holly Ziegler, swore she wanted to be kissed by him, was just too shy to ask, and the way she screamed and reddened and held her hands shaking out in front of her was like when a bee landed on his mom who was allergic. The laughter. He was guilty even before his open hand connected with her face and while they were showering him with blows, dirt in the mouth, he wanted to say I'm sorry, Holly, whom he'd known since kindergarten, she only lived three blocks away. They have no idea how hard it is to taste your own blood, cut-grass smell, and not go home and get your knives or gun or flip their cars over in your mind. And when Stan's anger got in him Holly just was a whore who held the hoop the others jumped through. It could be days in his mind before she wasn't.

Doctor S was not angry about the job, he had no particles of anger in him period. More than once Dale wondered if this made Doctor S a pussy. It was no trouble on my end, it's something we can try again down the line if that feels right. What concerned Doctor S was how Dale might be having at least some mild hallucinations, which isn't the same thing as telling stories. Dale, Doctor S said, Dale, until Dale looked from the painting to Doctor S's eyes, what I mean is that it kind of sounds like you're seeing things that aren't there, like your dad. Dad didn't see things that weren't there, Dale thought, gaze back on the clown in its silver frame. Although in what Dale would come to understand as drunkenness, his dad would curse people who were not present, put his fist through the basement's Sheetrock wall. Or maybe you're just telling me you *think* about your dad, that it *feels* like he's right there, but that you know he isn't, really. If you think you are seeing or for that matter hearing things that just can't be, Dale, maybe it would help to repeat to yourself, or even to say out loud, this isn't real. This isn't real. You'd be surprised how much that's helped some other people that I know.

May break my bones but words. Bounces off me sticks to you. Early in the exclusions they would equip him with weak spells to cast back against the insults. The need for the sayings disproved them and as he grew they would if anything just feed the laughter. Nice comeback, Dale. If he still sometimes said those things or other private phrases to himself, it was only to slow or interrupt the machinery of his will before it was too late and he'd set some trap for an enemy on a highway or country road. It's like there is a video game inside his head except what happens there will happen here. Recently it's been based on Spy Hunter, which is among Dale's favorites at Aladdin's Arcade in White Lakes Mall. Same electronic music. From above he sees a strip of asphalt running vertically through a simplified landscape. The image is so vague it would be difficult for Dale to say if he's picturing graphics or real terrain. But he can make out the silver Fiero that is his avatar speeding down below and he knows that if he presses a button in his mind the car will release an oil slick or smoke screen in its wake. And while it is impossible to say when Hishky or Carter or Gordon will encounter these vague but fatal hazards, understand they will, they'll go through their windshields. Once, after they'd been talking about his dad, Doctor S asked Dale if he knew how he had acquired such powers. Dale said no.

But he did know. It was at Bright Circle Montessori on Oakley Avenue when he was four, when he was still the same age as his body. It was warm for late September and the sky was cloudless as his mom dropped him off. OK, sweetheart. Dale no longer clung or cried at this point he would just walk to Mrs Coleman and hug her hello and then quietly build and knock over towers of wooden blocks and wait for Ben and Jason to arrive. Then he would follow them around and they would let him. That day they were in the sandbox in the backyard during free time and Ben said that he had a plant with special powers that he had picked from along the chain-link fence. Like poison ivy or poison oak or the way spinach makes Popeye strong this was a plant Ben rubbed between his hands until it released some kind of force. You don't have to eat it. Ben rubbed the green weeds he had picked then gave them to Jason who then gave them to Dale who got them to stain his hands a little and then buried them as Ben instructed in the sand. Then Ben said you make a wish for something to happen and it does. Dale doesn't remember what Ben or Jason wished for, or if they told him, but Dale was obsessed with tornadoes and he said he'd use his power to make one happen and then they played some other game.

The chests of fifteen toddlers rising and falling on cots in the main beige-carpeted room as poorly simulated wave noise issues from a portable stereo plugged into the corner. Mrs Coleman and her assistant Pam are preparing snack in the adjacent kitchen, small paper cups of grapes halved to minimize the risk of choking. Dale wakes to his awareness of rain falling on the school's aluminum roof. Quietly he rises and carries his stuffed rabbit to the window and parts the curtain to see unusually dark clouds he thinks are lowering. The wind throws acorns from the red oak in the school's front yard against the window and he startles. Only gradually does he realize he is looking at his work. His hands are clean now, Mrs Coleman made him scrub them before lunch, but they feel at once oversensitive and numb, like the time he touched the stove. The smell of the magic plant is still detectable beneath the artificial lemon of the soap. He hurries back to his cot and pulls the Peanuts sheets up over his head and tries to call the storm he's summoned off. To his rabbit whose name is lost he says again and again that he is sorry. And then we hear the sirens starting up.

Dale would help his neighbor Ron Waldron move things from his garage to his truck or back, mainly tools and lumber. Dale can you help me with this filled him with pride. Cody Waldron was Dale's age and while they had played together in the distant past, Cody, a quiet athlete, now looked right through him. Cody would not defend him from Carter or Hishky or Gordon types but he would do him no harm, never joined the laughter. Whatever Cody's inclination he would not defy his father who had wordlessly made it clear you do not fuck with Dale. Sometimes Cody and Dale loaded or unloaded the truck together and Dale felt a brief commonality of purpose with a peer, lift on three. If Ron and Cody were shooting baskets in the driveway Dale could park and comment or maybe dismount and rebound for them. Take a shot, Dale.

On weekend evenings Dale had biked past Ron's and seen in the yellow light of the garage Cody and his friends and girls drinking. Sometimes Ron would be there smoking a cigar, would wave to him, but never call him over. If it were summer and Dale stood in his own yard he could hear through the insect noise the radio and the laughter.

Until one Friday in November, after unloading heavy equipment until dusk, Ron said over Cody's mute objection stay and have a beer. In the garage Dale saw there was a silver keg in a rubber trash can filled with ice and he watched as Ron locked on the pump and tapped it. It's Cody's birthday and I'd just as soon they do their drinking here. He gave Dale a red plastic cup primarily of foam, then served himself and Cody. Ron indicated a stack of folding chairs and Dale unfolded one and sat beside the keg while Ron put away some tools on pegboard hooks and Cody took his cup inside, I'm showering.

To move only to drink or wipe the foam off on his sleeve and to pull down his KC Royals cap as far as possible over his eyes seemed to Dale his best strategy for sustaining this improbable inclusion. When Ron refilled his cup he refilled Dale's, but even without the alcohol Dale's anxious joy would have released into his bloodstream chemicals sufficient to prevent him from feeling through his sweatshirt the cool autumnal air. As if to mark the occasion Dale saw the streetlight on 6th and Greenwood flicker on and then around it first snow fluttered moth-like more than fell. Hear the car doors slamming shut and the voices of Carter Hishky Gordon types approaching. Ron was there so Dale did not move. No speech but surprised, unreadable smiles were addressed to Dale as the types greeted Mr Waldron, one of the cooler dads, shook Cody's hand, the latter back now in baggy jeans and licensed sports apparel. Ron must have handed Dale the stack of red plastic cups because he found himself offering them to whoever approached the keg. A job, this one without prices. You working the keg, Dale, someone said, only mainly mocking him.

When did the girls appear, Holly Ziegler among them, and how did he know she wore black jeans, a red V-neck sweater, hair pulled up tight since he absolutely would not look at her? But she said, Hi, Dale, matter-of-factly smiling lips freshly glossed and when he held the cups out to her she took one out, thank you. He knew either from his two years at THS or his previous schools the names of almost everyone in the garage although he'd rarely had occasion to speak them. Let me fill that for you, Alec Owen said, and did. Cheers, dude, let's get fucked up. The metal of the light beer on Dale's tongue.

Stan had given him a fund of anger about rap music and all those wiggers who love it now but Dale felt that what came out of the stereo had like the shopping carts or the ammo latch or one of his rare sentences that managed to hold sense over time a rightness of fit which made him feel identical to his body, now his body with the night. Dale had not moved from his chair but the brim of the hat was raised a little and he saw that some of the girls while not dancing in the cold garage were nodding or bouncing a little to the beat, the rhythmic chanting, as they milled around. The intensity of the desire this inspired in him was closer to its fulfillment than anything he had previously known. Dale in that garage, in his chair, last century, his happiness. All eyes on me, the music said.

Then Hishky was offering him cigarettes, hey man what's going on. Gordon too was there, no hard feelings about what went down last summer. Nod from Davis. Dale knew to be on guard, but when the girl named Laura said let me see your hair, removed his hat, and ran her fingers tipped with ruby through or at least across the black matted mass not recently washed or cut he was too overwhelmed by pure sensation to care about the laughter here and there. This isn't real. Others began soliciting speech from him, where did you buy those awesome boots, is that a hickey or a bruise, do you still practice martial arts. You should hang out with us more, Dale. Yeah, we're tired of the same assholes in this senior class. He just laughed whenever others laughed, kept drinking from the cup they kept refilling.

From alcohol and sheer improbability a widening delay obtained between experience and its conscience registration, Dale realizing the party had broken up only as they were coaxing him into the back of a Jeep Cherokee he had often almost flipped, Hishky driving, Laura riding shotgun, see the cherry of her Marlboro Light, Davis beside him in the back, proffering a bottle of Mad Dog 20/20 Coco Loco wine, the bass of what Hishky called his system rattling Dale's chest, all eyes on me. It's as if by the time the cold air thundering through the sunroof Hiskhy left down to let out smoke makes Dale aware they're on I-70 they have already arrived at Lake Clinton some twenty miles away, mainly upperclassman drinking around a bonfire, sparks flying off the crackling Osage orange, a few couples making out on blankets, same artist issuing from another system. Only when he rolls onto his back after puking painlessly in the grass somewhere beyond the circle of the firelight does he really hear them chanting Dale, Dale, Dale. And now he shuts his eyes he sees the stars. ■

Courtesy of the author

KARAN MAHAJAN

1984

Karan Mahajan grew up in New Delhi, India and lives in Austin, Texas. He is the author of *Family Planning* and *The Association of Small Bombs*, which was a finalist for the 2016 National Book Award for Fiction and the winner of the 2017 Bard Fiction Prize. His writing has appeared in the *New York Times*, the *New Yorker* and other publications. 'The Anthology' is the opening of an unpublished novella.

THE ANTHOLOGY

Karan Mahajan

Long before terrorism became fashionable in the West and commonplace in the East, there was a bombing at the Sovereign Center in Delhi. A major event in India, it launched six months' worth of stories in dailies across the country in every language, but it garnered next to no international attention; it appeared once in the *New York Times*, that too in a single column on the front page elbowed by an expansive story about the island-nation Nauru's failed attempt to host the Miss Universe contest.

Now, much can be made of the callousness of the West on the subject of terrorism before 9/11, but I'm of the view that the more you talk about bombings and suicide attacks and hijackings the more you encourage legions of bored, frustrated men around the world to murder their way out of anonymity; a situation that reminds me of how, ever since the beginning of the Indian culture boom, bad novelists have been fêted daily by the likes of the *Delhi Times* and *India Today*, sending thousands of other stupid men to their desks in search of their inner Ayn Rand; and so maybe the callousness of various countries towards each other is a good thing, a way to prevent the export of terror, the way Indian novelists were better off, more sincere, funnier, truer, before the world began caring about India.

I make this analogy for a reason: the bombing at the Sovereign

Center took place at a reading and so had a profound effect on the nascent literary scene in Delhi. The bombing was also a blow for the Sovereign Center, which was a decade old, and had been trying hard, with its ancient-looking architecture (monolithic brick buildings and beautiful dusty atria capped with green solar roofs) and its revolving schedule of plays, talks, readings, and screenings, to compete with the India International Center and the Gymkhana Club as the hub of intellectual life in Delhi.

For a while, it succeeded. Thousands of professionals rotting away for decades on the wait lists of the two aforementioned competing clubs rushed to join the Sovereign, and to try restaurants like the Spice Bazaar, the Purple Dragon, the Dixie Diner and even the mediocre Mediterranean Lite House, which looked out from its porthole-shaped windows at a Delhi that was so green you would be forgiven for thinking you were looking into the verdant past rather than the doomed present.

Then, in April 2000, Jeffrey Turner, a linguist, went ahead and scheduled a reading at the Sovereign.

Turner, a Kiwi who lived in a tattered colonial mansion in Lutyens' Delhi, was a famous scholar of Persian and Urdu; and because he was white and neither an insecure fiction writer nor an irrelevant poet he was able to maintain friendships with each of the tiny coteries that make up the writing world in Delhi, and to sleep with more Indian women than strictly necessary to prove his powerful hold over the scene.

I, of course, am relaying this information second-hand: I didn't know him, and wasn't among the hundreds invited for the release of his monumental study of Turkish harem guards in Delhi; in fact, I wasn't even a writer at the time; but I had read two of his books and thought him deserving of his success, and I was as bereaved as anyone else when I heard how he had died. The trouble was that I had no one to share my grief with. Everyone who mattered was at Turner's reading.

What was the event like? Readings in Delhi, particularly for famous writers, are bureaucratic affairs – bureaucracy being the preferred mode of expression in our capital city – and Turner's reading adhered to this format, which I reproduce below from the schedule handed to the fifty-odd attendees:

1. Introduction of Compere Hony. Srimati Leela Bhatt by Mini Singh, Sovereign Director
2. Introductory Speech by Compere Hony. Srimati Leela Bhatt
3. Second Introductory Speech by Sri Kapil Suri
4. Talk and Reading by Sri Jeffrey Turner
5. Questions for Sri Jeffrey Turner
6. Closing Comments by Sri Jeffrey Turner
7. Closing Remarks by Srimati Sujata Mehra
8. Vote of Thanks by Sri Deshbhakt Sawhney

Midway through item number 2, most people were sorry they had attended this boring flattery-festival; most were dead by the time item number 3 began.

I was at Patnaik and Sons Bookstore in Connaught Place, a regular stop for me, when I heard about the bombing. Mr Patnaik came up to me and said, 'I have a request. I am shutting down the bookstore early.'

'But it's not even five-thirty, sir! Can you give me one minute?'

I was shirking work at my father's soap-manufacturing company and did not want to go back.

'A bombing just happened in the Sovereign Center. My son was supposed to be there.' He explained the situation. 'Turner has come many times to our store. He's a good scholar.'

I said, 'I've read his books.' I had devoured them standing up in Patnaik and Sons, and felt guilty, but didn't say anything further. 'Is he alive?' I asked. 'Was anyone hurt?'

He said, 'I don't have news. Perhaps nothing has happened. I just heard there is a bombing. So far they haven't got any coverage on Star. I don't know why. But my wife is watching.'

I said, 'These terrorists.' Then, 'I hope your son will be okay.'

I saw, for the first time, that the man was in a daze: despite the stuffiness and heat of the bookstore, which is really a wholesaler of dust masquerading as a retailer of books, his skin was dry. He was so worried he had forgotten how to sweat. I left the bookstore and went back into the sun, which even at five-thirty was busy blaring away, and it was only outside that I realized that I had walked out with a paperback. I don't want to tell you the title of the book; I sense it will reduce my credibility as a narrator: this sort of coincidence is no longer looked upon kindly by people, who feel that the world is already wound so tight, so interlinked, enmeshed, jungled, whether by Facebook or TV or news, that to throw metaphysical meetings into the mix is only to push the limits of reality to the point of perversity.

But what if I said the coincidence is what trapped me into the wilds of this story in the first place?

What if I told you that the book I rescued from the bookstore was *Manto's Madness* by Ismail Baig – the only author to survive the Sovereign Bombing?

I almost went back inside to return the book to Mr Patnaik; then I realized how insulting such a gesture would be for a man who had possibly just lost his son.

In 1997, the Uphaar Cinema in South Delhi caught fire during the premiere of the movie *Border*; the exits were inexplicably blocked and most of the elite audience died of asphyxiation or underfoot in the stampede while the movie poured out like fine sand from the projector. A similar story was repeated in 2000 at the Sovereign Center, though it was preceded by benign confusion.

There were two bombs: one decoy, one real.

The decoy, placed at the back of the hall, made a long hissing sound and went dead in a puff of acrid smoke. Many of the audience members mistook it for a sparking fixture – a surge of electric magma from the substratum of wires that cushions our lives. Only an elderly professor sitting at a far corner was hurt by the soft shower of sparks.

Turner, speaking from the stage, said, 'It's okay. It looks like an electrical malfunction. But maybe we should all get off the stage? Better to be safe. Chalo.'

But first a couple of younger men came around to help the bleeding professor, who had been knocked down into the aisle and was moaning, a hand over his left eye and fine specks of blood on his white hair. The others started picking up their bags and standing up in the rows; you could feel their relief about the possibility of being let out. That's when the real bomb went off.

Everyone in a twenty-foot radius of the bomb was instantly killed, walloped by heat on the one hand and a hard receiving ring of burning plastic seats on the other. The roof crumbled, revealing a low-hanging nest of iron rods and cement; a broken pipe gunned water at the dying men and women below.

The rest of the audience, crippled, crawling, leaving trails of blood in their wake, reached the exits and, finding them blocked, choked to death.

Bombs always make the most of the slightest material. They don't have the tragic range of earthquakes – which pummel entire rivers into flowing backwards and crank out sudden mountains from the subsoil – but they do set roads on fire, rip concrete rinds from the façades of buildings, denude bushes and trees in an instant autumn, and turn cars into impressionistic works of art; bombs see the possibility in everything, and in this way they are like artists, brilliant improvisers, except that they happen to kill, and so isn't there a strange poetry, you ask, in a bomb that kills artists?

No.

Afterwards, the seats in the theatre were said to have looked like a garden of black singed cacti, the bomb was so hot and vituperative.

Only two men survived: a Sovereign staff member who had been at the very back, sitting on his haunches, destined to lose his legs; and

Ismail Baig who, as luck would have it, had stepped out moments before to answer his mobile.

It is remarkable to think that an entire pocket of culture can be destroyed in a single day, but that's exactly what happened on 26 April 2000. *Everyone* died: novelists (nine), critics (seven), journalists (six), poets (one – poetry was already dead), playwrights (one), historians (four), academics (three), editors (four). It was like one of Stalin's purges, but without the twenty-year foreshadowing of communism that gave the more pragmatic intellectuals pause to escape to America or work furiously before their deaths. The result of this sudden massacre of talent was that when India, in 2005, suddenly felt itself to be a world power, it had only second-rate writers like myself and established juggernauts like Salman Rushdie to show for itself. The debut writers it launched, one after the other, were so slight, so inexperienced, so full of melodrama and self-consciousness about being Indian, that they stayed in orbit for precisely one book before burning into pre-verbal nothingness.

When what should have happened is this: the men and women toiling in relative anonymity in Delhi in 2000 should have been rewarded for their work by the world's interest in India. After years of preparation, they would have been ready – with their third or fourth books – to present a national culture that was true, homegrown, brilliant, idiosyncratic; not derived from the West or pandering to it or dependent on it for acclaim and recognition.

'You're too optimistic,' friends tell me. 'Everyone sells out for the West.'

Or: 'The bombing will put great pressure on the survivors to perform and they'll write better than they would have.'

I agree that it is romantic to belong to a culture of survivors: but isn't a culture of survivors only worth celebrating if those who survived did so by dint of their wits, not a failure to land an invitation to the most overbooked literary event in Delhi?

Which is why so much depended on Ismail Baig.

What did it mean that *he* had been chosen to survive?

Not to be a conspiracy theorist, but wasn't there something perverse about the fact that he was a Kashmiri Muslim (it was a time of unrelenting militancy in the Valley) and even if he hadn't been Kashmiri, what to do with the embarrassing coincidence that his last novel, *Manto's Madness*, ended with the death of *all* the major characters in a fire?

(Sure, the book was set in an insane asylum instead of a literary event, but are the two things really that different? What if one was simply a metaphor for the other, etc.)

And then there was the historical convenience of the name Ismail: was he Call-Me-Ishmael from Melville's *Moby-Dick*, condemned to telling the story of his mates and the big white whale (Turner?) who pulled them under? Or was he living a modern recap of the Islamic myth in which Ibrahim, asked to sacrifice his son Ismail to prove his devotion to God, blindfolds himself and picks up a knife, only to peel off the blindfold to discover that he has slaughtered a ram instead of his son – Allah was Merciful?

Was the rest of the Indian literary scene simply *a goat or a ram* in God's eyes before Ismail's future authorial awesomeness?

Or was Baig, quite simply, a terrorist?

The rumor-spewing machinery of our minds worked overtime. Why, for example, did Baig think to go outside to make a call on his mobile at the very *moment* of the bombing? I personally cannot think of one Indian I have met who, when confronted with the choice between answering his mobile and preserving the solemnity of a cremation, wedding, movie, birthday party, retirement speech or press conference, would not choose the former and that too in the loudest, brashest possible style, as if to encourage the hundreds of silent others to join him; and so to have taken the time to refuse a call, get up from his seat, go out the door, and stand on the landing to return the call was so unlikely that it made one wish he had invented a better story. Which, in fact, he did as time went on: it turned out he was also smoking.

He *always* smoked and made calls at the same time. This we liked. Writers are allowed all sorts of eccentric habits (I myself always keep a cigarette cocked in the crick behind my left ear, even though I don't smoke).

Others wondered whether Turner had been sleeping with Baig's wife, whether this was the engine of the bombing . . .

But most of us writers were still too dazed to speak out or act on these suspicions. Besides, in India, it is well known that any illiberal feeling you have will be automatically picked up and amplified by either the police or the BJP or the Shiv Sena or a fringe of brand-new fundamentalists, and when these parties remained silent, blaming the ISI and Pakistan instead – perhaps they just didn't care enough about writers to hound them? – we too shut up and waited.

Then we heard Baig on TV, and everything changed.

By God, he was one of us! A Delhiite, a resident of Tara Apartments, an alumnus of the Modern School Barakhamba Road, son of a late army officer!

And now he was world-famous! The lucky cigarette-smoking bastard!

Summer couldn't subdue Baig. Once he got the attention of the press he refused to give it up.

He talked to reporters from a bed in the Sama Nursing Home near Greater Kailash. We saw it on TV. A helmet of white gauze was pulled over his head all the way down to his eyebrows. Orphaned from his forehead, his large gray eyes took on the burden of expression – closing, twitching, blinking, stopping dead to fill with fluid: few writers are so handsome. You could imagine now what the young Hemingway looked like in an Italian hospital with a nurse decoding the confounding map of shrapnel in his torso with her fingers. Baig was similarly energetic in his bed. He received many visitors. His right arm had fractured when he'd spilled down the stairs after the boom of the bomb, but that didn't keep him from gesticulating. The writing denied to him by the injury came out in swift, fluent spoken sentences.

His voice was nasal, soft, grandfatherly. 'We live, one might say, in a madhouse,' he said slowly, with a self-satisfied smile revealing teeth a tad too big for his mouth. 'The terrorists are mistaken if they think they can change anything by bringing *more* madness into the madhouse. Writing is a way to impose order on the world and my colleagues who died had done exactly that. Their good work cannot be undone and never will be.' Then he became morose. 'I don't wish to talk anymore. My business is writing. I am now trapped in a madhouse by reporters. I need space to think.'

The crankier he behaved, though, the more the press loved him, and one got the feeling that he loved the press too: why else were they perpetually in his hospital room asking questions?

The bombing had only a marginal effect on the sales of Baig's books. For a while you could see *Manto's Madness* bumped up a few notches on the bestseller shelves of Bahrisons and Full Circle and the Oxford Bookstore (Midland and Teksons took a more crass approach: building spiral towers of Baig novels), and some of my friends pretended to know his work since he was now an established locus for literary conversation. But his importance paled before that of the dead. The dead were far more romantic.

Publishers began to cash in on these forces and feelings. Having lost part of its author catalog, Penguin India responded with a marketing campaign: READING IS A RESPONSE TO TERROR. The graphics were simple (red text, white background, no border) and repeated on TV and on the front pages of newspapers, and it moved us all – but not enough to part with our money. Instead, in a final irony, all the excess sales generated by the bombing were sucked up by Turner's new book – the 1,200-page tome being fêted at the Sovereign at the moment of detonation – and the book became one of the bestselling Indian histories of all time.

In the miniature urban realms of the bookstores the Baig towers were demolished and so many tiny little Turner buildings went up that they formed their own sprawling complex.

In this way Turner continued to preside over the Indian literary scene in death as he had in life, though of course, given the timing of the bomb this made sense: he was the only deceased author to have a *new* book out and a bloody good one at that, a paean to the ugly ungrateful city of Delhi (I read it twice); and the tragedy of his life was so overwhelming, so complete – his wife and two young children were also at the reading, his was the only literary family to be wiped out – that it eclipsed all the other deaths, and one felt shame that a man like Turner (despite his sexual proclivities) had come all the way from a sheltered life in Auckland and showered so much affection on a city like Delhi only to be blown to smithereens. One wondered why it wasn't *he* who had been saved instead of Baig, who, let's be honest, *still had his best work ahead of him.*

Of course there was an anthology for the dead writers! And of course it was to be edited by Baig! And of course none of us – only the fucking living breathing *future* of fucking *Indian literature* – were invited to contribute!

No matter. We understood. Publishers must go through their motions, even though the collection – *Reading Is a Response to Terror: 35 Authors Remember'd* – seemed by virtue of its title more a monument to the botched Penguin marketing campaign than the attack. How, we wondered, did they propose to unify a bunch of squabbling authors operating on such vastly differing IQs and in so many different genres? The single apostrophe in the word 'Remember'd' also enraged us, as did the fact that our manuscripts continued to languish on the desks of editors, many of whom had also died and not yet been replaced by their eager lackeys.

So we decided to pass the time by working on an anthology of our own: *Writing Is a Response to Terror: 35 Authors Under 35 Remember.* The figure thirty-five was arbitrary but important and now we were stuck: where the hell were we going to find that many competent writers in this blasted city? Ten of us met every week in a room above Bubblez Boutique in South Ex to share our ideas and writing.

What about the rest? Should we approach the children of the dead writers? Schoolchildren? Regional, Indian-language writers? (A horrifying suggestion, this was quickly nixed.)

'We can write under pseudonyms,' someone suggested.

That was decided fast.

Then another raised the question: who would publish the book?

Rupa, Penguin, HarperCollins! – then we stopped. In 2000, there were only three major publishing houses.

And why, my good friends, would they publish rubbish by a bunch of unknown aaltu-faaltus?

We sat and considered this sad truth for a while. Then I said, 'We need an editor. Someone to introduce and give credibility to the project.'

Everyone was enthusiastic. *But who?*

We did not have to debate this long. In May 2000, in Delhi, there was only one option.

I was chosen due to family connections and the like to make the pilgrimage to entreaty Baig as he lay in a cast in Sama Nursing Home giving interviews. It turned out to be a decisive moment in both of our lives. What happened was this: *bureaucracy*. Which is to say: if the nurse at the front desk hadn't insisted on Xeroxing my license seven times (the light from the thrown-open machine passing back and forth over her face like phases of a vacillating moon) and if the man next to her with the Gandhi glasses hadn't asked me to sign a sheaf of papers worthy of an acceding monarch and if the two of them hadn't made me wait for an infuriatingly long time on a sofa in the company of the dying, sopping up staphylococci via various magazines – if none of these things had happened, I would have been in no trouble.

But bureaucracy ensured that I walked into Baig's room at *exactly* the moment that a man was strangling him.

I stood at the threshold of the door shaking my head in a knowledgeable manner. Of course. The sleeping man in the bed was Baig and the thin man with the stubble bent over Baig with his hands around his neck was a doctor in plain clothes just finishing his forty-eight-hour shift with a ritual interpretation of his patient's pulse. In my politeness I decided to wait outside the door while this operation was conducted within. The corridors were cool after the heat of May and I fiddled with the cigarette behind my ear and felt the closing and opening of every door as an affront to my privacy. That was when the screaming began. A woman – who I had not noticed when I had peered in – was wailing from the room and there was a commotion of wires and a crinkle of plastic and then the man I had assumed to be a doctor shot out and took off down the corridor at full speed, his black Keds squealing against the floor. I too must have grasped the situation for I took off after him, hollering.

I ran forever in a dream-like state: down stairs, past lobbies, waiting families, trolleys, guards, everything, and then I was out in the open on the road to the Asiad Village and the man with his long legs kept racing down the side of the road against traffic and I followed closely in the spaces that would open up every time a car or bicycle swerved out of the way to avoid him.

I remember a series of comical thoughts entered my brain at that moment, as if to distract me from the danger of the situation. One, I thought: why can't gyms be like this? I am a much better runner when giving chase. Two, isn't it interesting that the city of Delhi basically has no sidewalks and my life is essentially in God's hands? Perhaps I should become an urban planner. Three, am I running again on the insides of my feet, like a pigeon or a penguin, as my interfering gym instructor had pointed out?

The man ahead of me was hit head-on by a car. He lay sideways on the bonnet of the white Maruti 800 for ten seconds, arrogantly taking rest, and then resumed his lope through Delhi amid a medley of honks.

It was now dark and we were blinded by the high-beams of traffic. The man was fast and I was fat and after ten minutes the gap between us was too much and I gave up and stood panting on the sidewalk, alarmed by the sounds coming from my body.

There was too much sound; the cars were thundering; I felt as if an entire regiment of breathless fat men was panting through me.

When I turned around I was greeted by a corps of policemen who had rolled onto the sidewalk. One lunged at my face with a baton and I passed out.

In the Asiad police station I was accused of trying to murder Baig.

'But I am Rajesh Soni's son!' I said. 'He makes Draupadi brand soap!'

'Shut up, you fat behnchod!' said the policeman. 'Everyone saw you!'

'But Uncle –'

'Why were you running then?'

I was surprised by how this interrogation was being carried out. My shirt was mysteriously tucked in even though I could remember it rappelling out of my pants during the run. Had I been made presentable for my interview?

I was seated in a plastic chair with four legs made of arrow-sharp steel. In front of me a desk was frazzled with paperwork. Behind the desk was a man with square shoulders and the ghost of a recently shaved moustache; he was dressed in a stained white shirt and black slacks and he brought his hand down on the desk in emphatic blows.

No effort had been made to restrain me or handcuff me or throw me into a cell.

The man was curt. I would be hanged if I didn't speak. Who were my accomplices? Was I involved in the terrorist attack of 26 April 2000? Was I some sort of mentally handicapped person, giving my information at the front desk and trying to kill a man? A silly bratty, at that?

'Silly bratty? Meaning?' I asked.

This made him angrier. 'SILLY BRATTY! FAMOUS! TV!'

The ceiling sagged so low that it let out a fine drizzle of sand through several holes.

There was a knock on the door and Baig and his wife came in.

The wife was in a salwar kameez and had a pleasant long face with a big charming beak of a nose; Baig had a cast on his left arm and was taller and thinner than he appeared on TV.

I assumed he was walking slowly because of his injury, but in fact he was a deliberate man.

He came up to me and put his hands on my shoulders and said, 'Inspector-sahb, this boy is a relative of mine. We were having a family dispute. We had a disagreement and he ran out because I made an upsetting remark.'

'He doesn't look like your relative,' said the inspector, by which he meant: he has a Hindu last name; you don't.

'He is not my relative. He is Asha's relative.' He pointed to his wife.

'My nephew,' she said.

Those two words were enough to prove that she was the most classy, native-English speaker in the room: behind her accent and the word 'nephew' I sensed the Gymkhana Club, the Convent of Jesus and Mary, and Miranda House College, and I was jealous that Baig got to be married to a woman who no doubt both valued his writing and also condescended to have sex with him.

'But he tried to kill *you*, Baig-sahb,' the policeman said.

'I didn't!' I said.

'Shut up, bastard!' said the policeman.

Baig now had his arm around the policeman, who had gotten up from his chair. 'What you have witnessed is a family dispute. I would like to settle this matter on my own. Why cause unnecessary confusion?'

'Baig-sahb, you may not be aware, but we are worried for your well-being. There are a great number of miscreants out there. Second, the hospital staff says they saw two men running from the hospital. This man had an accomplice operating at his beck and call. We must locate the accomplice.'

Again I piped in. 'That's *exactly* what I said. *Another* man did it.'

'Shut up!' the policeman roared, and breaking the embrace with Baig he strode through the room and slapped me across the face.

I could feel my cheeks wobbling with pain for seconds afterward. Tears rolled down my face.

Baig grew stern. 'Enough. This is ridiculous. I am saying to you this boy is my relative and you slap him? Who is your superior officer?'

The inspector sneered. Then, shockingly, I was allowed to go.

Husband and wife couldn't have been more apologetic as we walked out of the police station. Did I need to put Dettol on the big bruise above my eye? Was there anything they could do for me? Asha explained the entire mysterious transaction with the officer once we were in the parking lot. The dust was heavy on the ground from a minor May shower, letting off the scent of oxidation and decay. From the corner of my eye I watched Baig pull a cigarette from the cool styrofoam tube of his cast and toss it into his mouth, catching it between his teeth like a dog. He trusted his classy wife so completely that he didn't interject or even appear to listen as she spoke. But surely there was some sort of telepathy at play. How else did Asha know that her husband was ready for another cigarette, offering him a light with a sweep of her arm (the delicate flame of the lighter leaving a purple arc in its wake) without ever once removing her eyes from my aching face? I got the sense then that they were a team: he was the creative talent, and she his promoter; having adopted this role, she chopped and diced at the air like a CEO racing through the terms of a questionable agreement.

I hadn't been imagining things, she explained. Someone had, in fact, been trying to strangle her husband. The reason this wasn't worrying or frightening – as both of us had thought – was that the perpetrator was Baig's schizophrenic cousin, Syed.

'It would have been pointless giving his name to the police,' she said. 'You know how the authorities treat mental people. His health is very bad, poor thing. We've taken care of him for many years.'

I found her so immensely likeable that I would have believed anything she said.

'He wasn't even strangling me,' corrected Baig, blowing cigarette smoke in a manner that can only be described as pedantic (i.e. in my face). 'He thought he was demonstrating how the *piston* of a bloody *car* works.'

First impressions are important – they are usually the last time we see a person clearly – and the thing I noticed about Baig was that he was blessed with the mannerisms of an old man. His slow, slightly pleased manner of blinking and talking and the way he laughed – with his gums showing and the chuckles coming in spiral coughs – rendered him unsexy, height notwithstanding. He had been rescued from premature senility by his alert, active wife.

I used the opportunity to do what I do best, i.e. conduct a literary interview. I asked if Syed was the reason he, Baig, wrote so knowingly about madhouses in *Manto's Madness*.

He closed his eyes and said, 'Yes, to a degree.'

'But did you get the *idea* from your cousin?'

'It could be said, yes.'

Then, knowing well that I was about to exhaust my quota of goodwill, I told him about the anthology, how my friends and I had been so moved by the bombing we had spontaneously met the next day and penned story after story in a round robin of grief, crying one minute, laughing the next, wasn't that how sadness worked, and the funny thing was that we had realized that the best response to terror was to pretend the attack hadn't even happened; yes, the stories were about the everyday lives of people in Delhi; lives in a time of innocence . . .

Baig said, 'Of course. I am happy to write the introduction.'

This, even before I had asked!

Asha must have felt they'd got off lightly, because she invited me to their house for dinner and said she wished she'd known I was a fellow writer, what had I published?

'Nothing so far,' I said.

'Well that will change!' she said.

I felt I must now act serious and not too grateful, and as they drove me home in their disgruntled-looking Maruti Esteem – a car that was so riddled with precise circular dents that one suspected it was showered with golf balls daily – I dropped the names of books and dead authors and even found occasion to bring up the Mahabharata once in relation to the traffic, suggesting that 'every day on Delhi's roads was a war on the fields of Kurukshetra'.

Then, not wishing to give them a sense of how rich I was, I begged them to drop me off by the main road.

They obliged readily; it was at this point that I blurted out the question with which I'd hoped to conclude my earlier interview: 'Do you think it means anything, as a writer, that you are the only author who lived?'

It came out sounding forced.

Baig, who was sitting in the passenger seat, smoking, thought about my question for a long time. Then he said, 'No. You can't draw meaning from violence. That would be giving it too much credit.'

But I knew from his self-satisfied tone and the way Asha stroked his thigh as he spoke that he meant precisely the opposite.

It was also hard for me to accept Baig's comment about the meaninglessness of violence because I felt that a) without the bombing I would never have had occasion to meet him and b) were it not for the strangling and the slap and the series of events that followed, he may never have agreed to provide the introduction to the anthology, thus giving a leg-up to my career: in short, being young and stupid, I believed all the violence either existed to teach me a lesson about my good fortune or to simply further that fortune, and so I came into the next meeting at Bubblez positively swaggering with news.

The looks on the faces of my writer friends when I told them the strange, funny story! The awe, the reverence, the questions!

Were we sure, one of them asked, that we wanted to get mixed up with Baig in case there was legal trouble?

'His name has been cleared, yaar,' I said. 'I could tell he was innocent. You Indians are all bloody cynics.'

And what about his reputation as a difficult and honest critic, another asked, one who had successfully alienated 90 percent of

Delhi's writers before their deaths by writing a column called 'Book Reviewing: An Experiment With Truth'?

'He won't pull that with the anthology – he owes me,' I said. 'Look at this black eye.'

Now that the doubts had been cleared, we were ready to celebrate. We drove to Flavours Restaurant and sat on fuzzy plastic chairs in the heat as friendly stray dogs circled our table, their noses pointy and mouths open and dark in a sort of imitation of my awed friends. We ordered chilled beers and drank them down with exaggerated lip-smacking relish. The girls, who had never paid me any attention before, were busy cooing over the bruises on my face and the men fêted me with jokes.

Rajesh, in particular, was on a roll: 'And then Fatso starts bloody jogging to try to catch the murderer! Hoo hoo hoo! Look at him, looking so satisfied! Now he'll never go to the gym again!' Then he stopped. 'He's drinking his beer like it's bloody high-class wine or what! Sip, sip, sip! Fatso's become a high-class detective type, wearing black pants and black shirt, eh? Oye waiter, bring another one!'

It was the best day of my life.

But that was then, when I was younger, more callow. Looking back I am surprised that neither Baig nor I nor Penguin (which eventually published the anthology) gave the title *Writing Is a Response to Terror: 35 Writers Under 35 Remember* any greater thought. After all, the anthology was born not from an earnest desire to show down terrorists but from pure opportunism, and the fact of our business instinct revealed a truism: being Indian – not a writer or a reader or whatever – is the greatest response to terror.

Saul Bellow once wrote, 'I've learned the true value of a dollar. It's about two cents.' I have recently discovered that the true value of a life in India is about 0.02 lives. We lose people so frequently in creative tragedies that we are never moved by an attack for more than three to seven days; and so it should come as no surprise that no one in the Bubblez writing group even pretended to take on the terrorists;

it was understood simply that if we didn't exploit the opportunity, someone else would; and so, in acting swiftly and without thought to the suffering of the victims, we downgraded the seriousness of the attack, we reduced it to nothing. I, for one, hardly thought about the Sovereign Bombing in the years that followed, not even when I gorged myself at the Purple Dragon or the Spice Bazaar; and judging from the conversations I have had with my fellow writers, who are all gourmands, nor did anyone else.

Then terrorism came into our lives again with a great force. ■

Courtesy of the author

ANTHONY MARRA

1984

Anthony Marra is the author of *The Tsar of Love and Techno*, a finalist for the 2015 National Book Critics Circle Award and winner of the 2016 American Academy of Arts and Letters Rosenthal Family Foundation Award, and *A Constellation of Vital Phenomena*, which won the 2013 National Book Critics Circle John Leonard Prize, the 2014 Anisfield-Wolf Book Award and the 2014 Athens Prize for Literature. He lives in Oakland, California. 'Lipari' is part of a work in progress.

LIPARI

Anthony Marra

Frank Laganà stood on the cliff suited in black, as straight as an exclamation point, poised to leap to his death once again.

When he'd set out that afternoon, he looked the part of a man on his way to a funeral. He'd ironed his shirt beneath a teakettle, polished his wingtips, and ribboned his homburg in the grosgrain of mourning. He wore his mustache trimmed, his bow tie tight, and his hair brilliantined in the patent-leather Valentino look. He was determined to meet death as he would an appointment with any of his creditors, overdressed and early. He'd even rented a three-piece suit for the occasion.

But it had taken him the better part of an hour to slog through groves of olive, manna, and carob trees, over rocks and up sheer switchbacks, and by the time he reached the top, perspiration soaked his waistcoat and the heat had wilted his bow tie. He wanted to die with grace, with gravitas, not with grime caked to his shoes. Soon enough, he supposed, the sweat and the schmutz would wash away in the rising tide below. A blast of sea breeze aerated the oppressive heat as he plodded to where the land ended. He walked until there was only one step left. Just one more and gravity would take him the rest of the way. There he stood with the dread and sobriety he brought to any important job. Frank Laganà was a confidence artist and this would be his final swindle. Today he would stiff the Fascist penal system of the nine years he still owed it.

Ahead, the half-set sun melted over blue-gray swells. Mint-green mottling garnished the receding Aeolian archipelago, each island skirted in a misty nimbus. A band of fleshy red flattened across the Tyrrhenian horizon, punctured only by the masts of swordfishing *passerelle*, from Sicily in the south to mainland Italy in the east. Not bad, as last views went. In one sense, Frank was an exile here. In another, he was nearly home. His sunburnt Calabrian complexion was the color of a half-healed bruise, matching the embroidered monogram of his pocket square. Like the handkerchief, Frank had come from Los Angeles, but he had grown up just a few dozen nautical miles from the splash of water where he would disappear.

'The Sea of Despair', that's what his *nonna* had called the Tyrrhenian, though she'd been a bleak personality. To ask her for directions was to receive a tour of her private cartography of doom. ('Left at the Vegetable Stand of Decay, straight until the Apothecary of Humiliation.') It was his *nonna*'s grim worldview, and all that had shaped it – devastating earthquakes, foreign conquest, endemic poverty, capricious gods – that Frank had tried to escape when he had immigrated to America, the land of indefensible optimism. Fifteen years he'd been there. Long enough to build enough of a life to feel trapped by. After the crash of '29, Frank had returned to Italy with a heedless scheme to sell the Fascist government rights to a Colorado gold mine that existed only in the beautiful con he had spun. Since sentenced to *confino*, he'd lived in hopelessness, in limbo, on the Sicilian island of exile: Lipari. Free to roam through the city by day, he was locked up at night in the citadel prison barracks, downwind of a colicky Neapolitan whose volition was so sapped by *confino* that he spoke only in the passive voice. Frank prayed every night for a signal or portent, something to refute his growing conviction that life was nudging him toward the door. Last week a stray ember had leaped from the end of his cigarette and incinerated his only photograph of his daughter. To a man who searched the sky for signs, who saw superstition as the only logic undergirding an irrational universe, this was an omen of cometary clarity. He had swept the photograph's ashes into the breast pocket of his shirt. Pity that his *nonna* wasn't there to make of him a cautionary tale. He had traveled halfway around the world just to drown in the same waters in which he'd learned to float.

This was to be his seventh and final attempt. The last six evenings he'd found one reason or another to turn back before reaching the edge of Lipari's tallest cliff. But here he was. The ashes in his breast pocket caught the impact of his accelerating heartbeat. The time had come. The rented suit was due back in the morning. He was ready.

Then he looked down.

Goodness.

Quite a drop.

And all those rocks! It seemed excessive, really, this much height. Wouldn't a shorter cliff do the job just as well?

While debating, he noticed two shadows scamper across the rocks. Fishermen? He walked to get a better look. They were just a couple of boys. Odd for them to have ventured so far at this hour, what with the tide coming in. He took a seat and waited for them to leave.

The two boys scaled the rocks and skipped stones on the tide pools. When the sun had finally set, they got to work assembling some kind of oblong instrument from a knapsack. When finished, one of them struck a match. The younger one flinched as his friend set the match to a fuse that dangled along his arm, ending at his hand, where the spark disappeared into the barrel of the instrument and launched it into the sky.

Then a flash and a thunderclap banged inside Frank's head.

Fronds of light unpeeled from the explosion just overhead. Sparks drizzled through the sky. A firework, Frank realized. He took a breath. One, and then another. The gloom congesting his chest leavened with each one. Hadn't he prayed to the Madonna, to the panoply of patron saints in the heavens, for any reason to persist? And here was the thundering reply. A molten asterisk to which he was the footnote.

To a man searching for signs, a firework made a compelling case. It seemed ridiculous, unfortunate, yet in the moment oddly plausible: maybe Frank Laganà wasn't meant to leap to his death in someone else's suit. Maybe he still had time.

He saw stray frames, spliced in from memory's cutting room:

- neon-tube palm trees on a nightclub wall;
- Independence Day in Los Angeles's Little Italy, when gunshots went unheard beneath the exploding sky;
- Maria rubbing her woolly socks on the parlor rug, her body a battery she slung to the bedroom where with a touch of the finger she jump-started her sleeping father to life.

He could have gone on, but down below, a wave sloshed over the shoal. It swept the younger boy's legs from under him and dragged him off. In the froth, the boy's head bobbed to the surface. His black curly hair drenched to inky moonlit lines. He windmilled his arms uselessly against the water. The older boy couldn't reach the younger one's hand. A shout emitted, fragmented by the cliff's jagged acoustics.

'Help me, help!'

A stitch popped in Frank's chest when he realized that the boy was calling for him. Only the irrevocably lost would pin hope on Frank Laganà.

The undertow dragged down the boy's head, then his elbows, and finally his waving, grasping hand.

Frank had to do something, of course, but what? An uncoiling whitecap erased the ripples where the boy had sunk. Broad shoulders of rock, epauleted with starfish, encircled the cove. The descent would take twenty hazardous minutes, and that was with a harness, heavy rope, and climbing boots. The boy would drown in, what, a minute? Minute and a half? The only way to collapse that stretch of space in such little time was to jump. Which had been Frank's original plan. It didn't bode well for the boy.

Every tendril of sanity stretched its roots through his heels, grasping at the cliff edge, but Frank felt pulled aloft by . . . what? Not courage. As a professional confidence artist, he wouldn't credit himself with much charity or compassion for strangers. Now that Frank had entertained the idea of living through the night, the thought of leaping into the ocean seemed preposterous. You couldn't save people from themselves. There had to be accountability. You horse around by the ocean, at high tide, without knowing how to swim, and lessons would be learned. It was about accepting the consequences of your choices. That's what had brought him to the cliff in the first place. He was making restitution.

And yet . . .

Look at him go.

He took two galloping steps. His feet called the shots, ignoring the distress calls he sent their way. The thought of dying heroically mortified him. He was a villain, a flimflam man, a bilker, a con. It was the only thing he had any talent for. It was downright hypocritical to pretend he could be anyone else. In three strides he'd exhausted his runway. His legs pistoned well into the leap. Fireworks for navigation lights and a mad dash toward grace. The size-eight wingtips that had carried him across vaudeville stages and picture sets, that had carried him down the front steps of his Lincoln Heights bungalow, right out of his daughter's life, still carried him, now, as he tap-danced across an abyss.

The life of Nino Rossi had thus far been one long fuse in search of a flame.

His gangly frame had never met a shirt whose shoulders it had filled. Pimples had colonized the habitable zones of his face. Once a girl told him his head was shaped like an elbow, whatever that meant. Most days, he felt marooned inside a body that betrayed him; he was a secret agent in the bowels of an enemy warship, frantically throwing switches and unscrewing valves before the whole thing blew sky-high.

'You've still got your health, haven't you?' Treating him like a moody septuagenarian was his father's idea of sympathy. His father, Stefano Rossi, was a no-nonsense Umbrian, an aficionado of bad puns and good cigars, a stony idealist still unbroken by reality's insistent chisel. Stefano followed a long line of Italian individualists, predisposed by millennia of invasion and occupation to distrust anyone in uniform, up to and including the mailman. He had still been in medical school when Mussolini marched on Rome. One of the knuckleheads on the march had been Giuseppe Oliveri, Stefano's brother-in-law and the father of the boy presently drowning.

Stefano had never seen eye to eye with his brother-in-law. The guy marched recreationally. What could you do with someone like that?

For years, Nino would wonder when his father had finally crossed the line of Giuseppe's tolerance. It might have been Stefano's habit of calibrating his moral compass by standing 180 degrees from his brother-in-law on any issue. It might have been the teasing after Giuseppe had named his firstborn Benito. It might have been this: 'I don't think much of men who parade around in military uniforms, yet missed the Great War.' Stefano had said it casually one Sunday dinner before turning the conversation to soccer. He hadn't mentioned the freshly pressed and decorated officer's uniform his brother-in-law was wearing, nor had he mentioned the ragged private's uniform stuffed in a trunk beneath his bed. If Stefano had put on his ragged private's uniform, the bullet hole through the right breast pocket would have displayed the polished nub of scar tissue that was the only war medal ever affixed to his chest, a memento of the snowy Alpine pass where alone and abandoned, with nothing but a penknife and an incomplete understanding of his own anatomy, he had performed his first surgery.

Upon receiving his medical degree, Stefano discovered that he had been assigned, at his brother-in-law's request, to a post on the newly designated *confino* island of Lipari, which by 1927 had become the main internment colony for enemies of Fascism. For an Umbrian, the moon was nearer. 'You've still got your health,' Nino would hear his father tell himself in the bathroom mirror each morning. 'You've still got your health.'

So, it was rich, Nino thought, that he should be forced to host his cousin for the summer, Benito Oliveri, the son of the man who had, in effect, sentenced the Rossi family to indefinite exile. For three weeks now, the boy had been the ball to which Nino was chained. When he learned that Benito was afraid of lightning, he felt compelled to avenge family honor by scaring the stuffing out of him with a display of the fireworks that his father had prepared for San Bartolomeo's feast day. Which is how the two boys had ended up on the shoals, past twilight, as the tide rose.

'It probably won't blow your hand off,' Nino said, optimistically.

'Then why are you making me hold it?' Benito asked.

'Because you're the guest.'

'That doesn't . . .'

Rather than brook further dissension, Nino brought the match across the strike plate. The pearly glow painted their faces in chiaroscuro. The flame ran up the fuse with the crackle of frying oil. A lurching spray of sparks singed the peach fuzz from the back of Benito's hand.

Nino watched the firework slip skyward atop a wind-socking flame. The updraft was strong enough to suction the damp shirt from his skin. The saltpeter pellets, packed from the potassium nitrate his father prescribed to asthmatics, erupted from the central cone in jets of platinum radiance. Concussive echoes batted between the cliffs. The sky was as dark as wet denim where the seams of light unstitched.

Had Nino been paying attention, he would've seen the next swell coming in a full six feet taller than the others, raggedly shorn at the crest with surf. But he was only apprised when the water slammed over the shoal. His legs swiped from under him. He scrambled over the rocks, but Benito was pulled over and under before he could reach him.

Up on the cliff, he saw a face illuminated by the falling fireworks and he shouted for help.

In the water, Benito squirmed violently against the tidal pull. Cinders pitted the surface he dropped beneath. Tiny bubbles spun off the boy's beating arms, as if his diaphragm so tightly squeezed the air in his lungs that it was exhaled through his pores. He was eight years old and his mother had said he was mature for his age. In school, he had learned the names of Roman emperors, but he had not learned how to swim.

Now the ocean in his ears amplified his thundering pulse. The telegrapher's key in his chest bashed against his breastbone; what the pulse beats relayed, what circulated in bold-faced declaration through every cubic inch of his personhood, was that he was drowning. Marcus Aurelius, he thought. Marcus Aurelius.

A tumbling shadow spread over the water.

His throat prized open.

The mute discharge of his last breath through the surface would be his final word.

The stars blinked and the sky caved in.

For one weightless moment, Frank felt entirely free.

Then the earth inhaled him.

Beige cliffs tunneled upward.

The shoals foreshortened meteorically.

The flailing man snatched at the sky.

The surface water collapsed beneath his back. A tuning-fork hum raced up his spine. Somehow he'd missed the rocky corona and plunged to a depth of twenty feet so narrowly unobstructed it felt tailor-cut to his floundering figure. Seawater singed his pupils. There, a dozen feet off, the boy lay across barnacled driftwood, arms extended, head tilted back in surrender. Balls of air rolled from his head like funny-page thought-bubbles; down here, Frank thought, the world of land and sky was no more than the dream of a drowned boy. Frank hoisted the lifeless thing over his shoulder and kicked off. The next wave stirred a sandstorm from the seafloor. He swam through the pounding blindness. Pressure built and built in his chest, poised to collapse into an eternity without weight.

Air swooped in as his face broke the water's surface. He heaved the limp body onto the shoal and hammered the boy's chest with the heel of his palm. He had never worked more fervently than he did on behalf of a stranger whose name he did not know, whose open eyes he had never seen.

He would remember himself as a B-picture villain imparting life upon the dead through the raging sorcery of his desperation. But what transpired was no cinematic conjure. There were no cameras, no special effects, just moonbeams slithering across swells, perspiration slipping down his lip, his fists malleting a steady beat against the boy's rib cage until the drum inside carried the rhythm on its own.

It startled Frank to realize that he remained a father, even now, untethered and estranged from the very child who had made him one. The day he'd left Maria, some portion of his heart was exhumed, readied for transplant, and had now found in this soaked, shivering boy a worthy host.

The boy spouted seawater in violent coughs. Frank worried he'd pop his lungs inside out like a dirty pair of socks. Beside him, the older boy kneeled. The moon glazed the water. Leggy shorebirds tottered in tide pools. The resuscitated boy tried to speak. Frank shushed him.

'Deep breaths, *picciottu*,' Frank said. 'That's it. Take your time. You have all the time in the world. You have the rest of your life.' ■

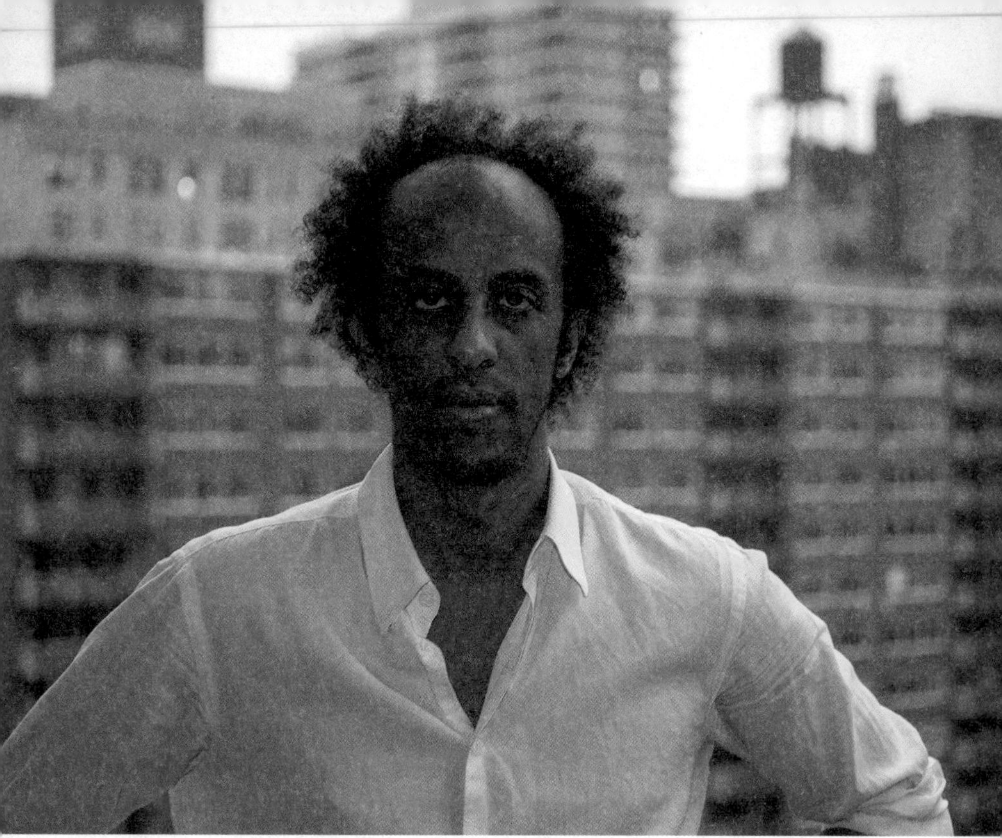

© Anne-Emmanuelle Robicquet

DINAW MENGESTU

1978

Dinaw Mengestu was born in Ethiopia and raised in Illinois. He is the author of three novels: *The Beautiful Things that Heaven Bears*, *How to Read the Air* and *All Our Names*. He is the recipient of the 2007 *Guardian* First Book Award, a 5 Under 35 award from the National Book Foundation and was included in the *New Yorker*'s 20 Under 40 selection in 2010. He was awarded a MacArthur Fellowship in 2012. His journalism and fiction have appeared in *Harper's*, *Rolling Stone*, the *New Yorker* and the *Wall Street Journal*.

THIS IS OUR DESCENT

Dinaw Mengestu

I learned of S's death two days before Christmas while standing in the doorway of my mother's new home. She lived ten minutes away from the airport in one of the suburbs south of Washington DC that had become popular with retired middle-class immigrants like her. We hadn't seen each other in five years, and yet I had insisted that I would take a taxi from the airport. It was the last chance I had to indulge the fantasy that at any moment I was going to turn around and board the next flight back to Paris. I had remained convinced until the plane lifted off that something would happen to make it impossible for me to leave. The trip was supposed to have been both family vacation and reunion, a chance for my three-year-old son to set foot on American soil and meet his American grandmother. Instead, as the cab pulled up to the address my mother had given me, my wife and son were asleep nearly 4,000 miles away in the two-bedroom apartment we had moved into when our son was born.

My mother told me of S's death as soon as I dropped my suitcase at the bottom of the half-spiral staircase that led up to the three bedrooms and two bathrooms she was so proud of. I had imagined carrying my son slowly up those steps. It would have been a deliberate attempt to demonstrate to him the grandeur of America, a two-story house many times larger than our apartment, larger than anything I had ever imagined for us as a child.

I had felt lightheaded walking up the driveway, and without my suitcase I struggled to stand straight. I might have collapsed right there had my mother not taken me in her arms and whispered, even though we were alone, 'Yenegeta, something terrible has happened to S.'

S had been like a brother to my mother, and when I was a child, something of an uncle to me. Whatever had happened to him tore through my mother's natural stoicism; she half-whispered, half-mumbled. 'Something terrible' were the only words I clearly understood, no doubt because my wife had said just that during our last argument about coming to America. We had debated whether it was safe for our son to sit in an air-pressurized cabin for so many hours, whether he would be able to bear the hour-long drive to the airport, and the hours more waiting to pass through customs and security. In the end she won by noting that because there was so much we didn't understand about our son's condition, the one certainty we had was that it was far too easy for something terrible to happen to him. 'It could be something very small,' she said, 'and for him it would be terrible. We would be far away and wouldn't know what to do.'

I didn't point out that if something terrible happened, it was likely to be in Paris, and in particular, in our immigrant-heavy quarter. When it came to our son, her defensive instincts were well-developed and all the more necessary because it was hard from the outside to see why we were so protective. Up close our son looked like any other excessively beautiful child. Over the course of the past year my wife and I had developed a habit of staring at him. Our son would discreetly turn his head to meet our gaze; or if sitting up, he would eventually grow tired and begin to slowly tilt until his body was flat against the ground. An hour could slip past during which there was hardly any movement or sound in our apartment, and I imagine from the outside it would have looked as if we were living in some abnormal state. We had to force ourselves to remember that for the first ten months of his life, he seemed primed to run, early to stand and quick to crawl. It was impossible to know when exactly that had stopped, but before his first birthday it was obvious that he was moving less and less with each passing month, as if the energy required to stand, or lift his arms above his head, were no longer worth it. We had been told by doctors in three countries to prepare for his condition worsening. They had yet to name it, but it was obvious to them that something inside him was wasting away. His legs had been the first to slow, and then his arms and upper body. A month after his second birthday, his fourth pediatrician told us it wouldn't be long before his organs followed. 'It's going to be a lung first. Or his heart, if he's lucky.'

The day before that doctor's visit, the police sealed off the metro station closest to our apartment. A device had been left somewhere in the station, but had failed to detonate. No lives were lost but just as much, if not more, terror was struck as a result. The possible death toll increased hourly, and every day that the station remained closed meant another block in our neighborhood was cordoned off. The attack was suggestive of a larger event still being scaled, and the only thing that could be done, it seemed, was to lash out in rage, or to hold our breath in fear.

Before my wife had fully committed to remaining behind, she called the airline at least a half-dozen times to ask, politely, if we could change our flight without any extra costs. On the morning of our scheduled departure, she told operators in France and in America that we would fly days, weeks, months in the future, during the darkest, coldest days of February, if only we didn't have to leave that afternoon, two days before Christmas. When her requests for a free-of-charge alternate date failed, I suggested that she find a story tragic enough to spur the sympathy of the airline agent(s) in a way a simple request never could.

'Give them a dead mother, or dying father,' I said.

I might have even offered her a crippled husband, or depressed sister without ever once mentioning our son. It had become standard practice that we no longer told strangers anything about him. He was ours, and had always been, but we grew fiercer in our territorial defense of him with each passing month. My wife once slapped a woman who had leaned over our son's stroller. I wasn't there to see it, but she insisted it was what any mother would have done if a stranger tried to touch her child. That I failed to see that served as later proof that I was the one who suggested our son play a starring role in our tragic airline story. According to my wife, like most Americans I instinctively 'sought the easiest solution to any problem' and in this case, an injured child was the most immediate path to sympathy.

'*C'est plus facile*,' she had said, 'like one of your big American hugs.'

Whatever I might have suggested, the story of a two-year-old child with a broken arm was her invention entirely. She decided on a slightly tense, borderline hostile tone to sell the story, because, according to her, 'They need to be scared, not sad.' As far as I knew, she had never acted in anything, but she believed in having convictions, and so for the duration of that conversation, she became, even to me, the mother of a two-year-old son who had fallen and fractured his arm. She described to the operator how the trauma kept him howling through the night. She avoided the disingenuous sigh most liars would have called upon, and described instead how difficult the cast made him. 'Not just difficult,' she said, 'but at times impossible,' or '*C'est just pas p-o-s-sible*' – an expression I heard daily to describe the ordinary hardships we were all subject to. My wife concluded by claiming that she was thinking above all of the other passengers – tourists, expatriates like ourselves, already tired and burdened with the long journey back to America carrying Christmas gifts that couldn't be wrapped.

'What if there's something in his cast that makes the metal detector go off?' she asked. 'Can you imagine how difficult that would be?'

It was as close to pleading as I had ever heard her come, and when she sensed that wasn't enough, she went on to describe how a two-year-old in a cast wasn't that different from a monkey with a club – both were dangerous, although you might not think so. 'He can't help it,' she said. 'He hurts people. He swings his arm and someone gets hurt.'

Her sorrow over her imaginary, injured monkey-child became real at that moment, and I'm sure had I not been in the room, a trickle of all that dammed-up grief would have found some measure of relief.

There was a brief silence, during which we both imagined that she might have won her argument for an alternate flight. Had the silence lasted five, maybe ten seconds longer, I might have seen something approaching a smile on her face, something I hadn't seen in so long that later that evening, I would imagine calling the airline back and requesting the same operator so I could tell him or her what a terrible, awful person they were for not having shut the fuck up just a little longer. What would it have cost you to say nothing? I wanted to ask.

She dropped her phone into her purse. The way she let it slip from her fingers made it seem contaminated.

'He said the airline doesn't allow animals in the main cabin.'

I knew the dangers that came with dwelling on any defeat. We had only recently come to the table of adult-sized problems laid out specifically for us. In doing so, we had learned to stop asking ourselves if we were living the lives we had imagined, if we were happy with who we had become, who we had married. Our jobs grew dull, our rent went up, but it was only after our son was born that we understood the possible range lying in wait. Six weeks earlier he had lifted himself off the ground and walked across our living room. The next morning I said I wanted us to go to America for Christmas.

Before leaving for the airport, I strapped my son to my chest so we could enjoy the oddity of having spring weather in December. His body still felt substantial suspended around my neck, but that wasn't enough now. His first steps – approximately twenty-three of them – had been made, it seemed, for no reason. Seven weeks had passed since then, and neither my wife nor I had seen him attempt to even stand.

We turned right, toward the boulevard. We reached the end of our narrow street. I wanted to show my son the soldiers who had remained a constant presence in our neighborhood since the bomb threat. I turned the back of his head slightly in their direction, and whispered into his ear, 'That's why we need you to run.'

I said goodbye to my wife and son on that same corner two hours later. I kissed my wife on the forehead and pretended to take a bite out of the band of fat roped around my son's wrist. At roughly the same time S, who I hadn't seen or spoken to in six years, and who I'd always thought of as happier than anyone else I'd known, hauled a heavy chair and a cord of rope from his living room into the basement while his family slept upstairs. ■

Courtesy of the author

OTTESSA MOSHFEGH

1981

Ottessa Moshfegh is the author of *McGlue*, *Eileen*, which was shortlisted for the 2016 Man Booker Prize, and *Homesick for Another World*. She lives in California.

BROM

Ottessa Moshfegh

I stay mostly in my bedroom chambers, examining what has found its way into my pores or the mucoid crook of my eye. I take my sister's small round mirror from her vanity and position it strategically on the floor, or hold it if I'm on all fours, and check out what may be developing on my backside, somewhere between its cracks and finally, eventually, delve deep inside where the sun don't shine, as the saying goes.

But there is light up there, for certain. Up there, so to speak, is where light goes to hide, saving itself, I imagine. I have seen this light insofar as I've seen its reflection on things.

And given the location of the light, it being up there, deep inside, such must be the thing on which the light is reflected, too – up there, deep inside. Its luster shows like a candle's soft white flicker, it saves itself that carefully.

Coaxing something up there, into the light, can take all day. I have whole conversations with myself just to remit certain muscles, frames of mind, all the while holding the mirror, and the thing, taking breaks in between to use the latrine, pick at what the servants leave for me in my study, warm myself by the fire there. This is what I do on days I have no trouble in the castle or the manor, days the village does well by the knights and the parapet is armed, no threats: I engage in myself this way, with the light up there, deep inside. If you can imagine that.

A few things I've managed to illuminate are worth noting: a small bottle of sherry, my sister's confirmation crown which I snatched from its velveteen case and hammered down straight and flat, a rabbit's foot, a brass corkscrew, an ivory penknife. When I traveled to foreign kingdoms this method was ideal for concealing jewels, sums of money, keys to containers I'd left to the proximate nosiness of my sister, her goose-neck friends, the staff.

I used to carry an occasional doodad up there during our all-too-extensible family dinners – a little wooden top from my boyhood, for example. I spun it on the cold stone floor. Now a small blond dog sits there yapping as a servant girl sweeps. Another girl scrapes the tallow drippings from the wall.

'Lord Brom,' a feeble voice follows a knock on my door. It is the servant girl Ilspeth come to take the chamber pot. I am lying in the curtained bed. I watch her shadow pass. I cough.

'Shuh,' she says, alarmed. 'I didn't hear you say "come in".'

'I could not,' I say, gasping for air.

'Are you ill, my lord?'

'Not ill, no,' I choke.

What Ilspeth doesn't know is that a certain loop of rope tied with a lovely turk's head knot does more than hold back the curtains. Occasionally I like a good strangle.

'You ate fish bones last night, my lord,' Ilspeth tells me. I hear the chamber pot slosh and watch her shadow carry it from the bedside past the windows. A hunched little wisp of a girl whom I entrust with the blood of my bowels.

'Ilspeth!' I clear my throat, wince. 'Ilspeth, tell me what time it is.'

'Past noon,' she says.

'Very well,' I say.

I untie the rope.

'Ilspeth, are you still there?'

'Yes, my lord.'

The floorboard creaks as she shifts her weight. I exhale.

'Still there?'

'Yes. Leaving now, my lord.'

I hear the door close.

I toss open the bed curtains and stuff my feet into fur-lined slippers. I see a gold streak of hay on the carpet which she must have trailed in with her from the latrine. I shuffle over, pick it up and hold it between my fingers. The hay is coated with pale brown excrement. I inhale deeply. I eat the hay.

I had a sister who didn't like me. She didn't like me, she said, because I was a bore. 'What do you even do all day?' she'd ask. 'What could you possibly be doing in there?' When we were small she'd draw pictures of pretty days – sunshine, flowers, rolling hills, with notes in Latin slipped under the door:

Obscurum est mortifer!

Procedo quod lascivio!

She was a very pretty thing, and had escaped the curse of intelligence without loss of much in the way of know-how. She could sing a fine song, sew something pretty. Whatever it is girls do. Now she was preparing for her wedding. Happily she preened about the castle with her cohorts, ladies-in-waiting juggling their tits, tapping feet, drawing pictures they'd point and laugh at and rip up and throw in the fire. I watched them with some pleasure, as one would regard a litter of kittens. 'Get a life,' I heard her say, 'think of what that means.' I take it she thought I should adhere myself to a life, my life, anybody's life, like a leech on a pig. 'Get married,' she said. I had very little respect for her.

Plus I always thought it's plain vulgar to be a lady. I'd like to meet one who can do it, be one, without making faces when she passes her reflection in the window, or who will invite you to her chambers and get finicky with the servants watching, yet have no qualms about instructing you like a whore when your head's between her thighs.

But, 'Oh,' said my sister, 'come now.' She was smiling. 'You'll marry and have children and be a father and let yourself go into the natural order of things. Have faith, Brom, there's more to life than what's in between your ears,' she said. As if she'd had an idea. There was acid in my mouth I'd have liked to spit on her.

'Bring wine,' I said to the cup bearer.

'Bring bread,' said my sister after him.

We were seated in the great hall. There was a vase of red gladioli between us. A fat-burning lamp. A rat's skull was illuminated in me, up there, not so uncomfortably that day. I had caught it, a large brown rat, in the pantry one night when I was up late, roving. My sister's dress was a fine purple silk embroidered with gold filigree and pearls. I did have love for her. She was my sister. I still can't imagine her as anyone's wife, bearing anyone's children. That seems wholly ridiculous.

She pointed down the gallery through the window past the motte. The sun was out. The crimson leaves of autumn swayed and frilled in the wind.

'It's always deathly boring and dark in the castle. Let's go for a walk,' she said. 'At the very least, Brom. It's a fine afternoon. Look.'

I rolled my eyes.

'It's our last day together before I'm married,' she said. Her chin rose, mouth parted.

'To please you, sister,' I said.

'God bless, Brom,' my sister said. 'You look like an absolute toad, besides. Fresh air, sunshine. You'll feel good. I promise.'

I held back a mouthful of vomit.

On our walk she said that she'd been to visit our mother. That there were certain disgraces which our father never wanted us to know. That I was an abomination of the family name.

I am not a knight. When I failed to impress as a squire and returned to the castle unknighted, Dad barely looked in my direction. When he traveled I tagged along in back coaches. I tried to learn the ways of the manor, but the stewards, Harlon and Rauf, had no patience. They gave me a stack of coins and smiled.

My mother went mad when my father died and was sent to live

with the nuns in the abbey. I pray God on one knee for her and for my father's memory, let it haunt me. With my cousins I go out to hunt and hawk, and riding on the horse feels good, but I can't really be cheered out of doors. The only real comfort I find is knowledge that, of all the people I've looked up into, I'm the only one who has the light up there, deep inside.

I imagine the exchange I'll have at heaven's gate:

'Who sent you, Lord Brom?'

'My father.'

And then I'll slay all three hundred angels with my sword and melt the golden gate with the touch of my finger and laugh watching the molt drip down to hell and singe all the boring souls hanging in the air between.

I recall the night of my sister's murder.

'Lord Brom,' a loud rap at my door disturbed me. I was in the curtained bed, not quite asleep.

'Sorry to wake you, my lord, but there is a matter.'

'Say it, Harlon, by God. What.' I did not and do not like Harlon.

'A madman has somehow got past the bridge guards and has been living in the buttery on your father's wing.'

'Good, Harlon. Turn him out then.'

'My lord, it's quite serious. Permit me to enter.'

I illuminated a smooth fist-sized stone I found last summer on the beach.

'The devil, having found his way to your mother's wardrobe, disguised himself with wimple and long robes and slippers. He got past the castle guards and into the motte this night. He came at Lady Fray, I'm afraid, my lord. She has died.'

'My sister?'

'I'm afraid so, Lord Brom.'

I pulled the linens over my head.

'Is she in one piece?' I asked.

Then the sound of Harlon gaping. I held back a laugh and a sob.

'Yes, my lord, she's in one piece.'

'Bury her,' I said.

'My lord.'

I heard the door close.

I keep her killer in my closet. The donjon tower is better used for storage and servants' quarters anyhow. He sleeps most of the day, hardly making a noise or stirring in there, in the dark. I let him out for meals and our weekly romp about the village at night. He is good at selecting the households with just feeble men inside. He can tell by the manner the horse is tied how strong the men are who live there. It is one of many of his gifts which I keep as my own, he himself as my own extra body. He is a man of action and few words. He will not tell me his real name.

The killer has a soft, meandrous mouth, his skin a powerful reflective sheen rendered by a thick lustrous grease. I wonder if these are the natural oils of the man or something he uses as a device, to trick us, to make us wonder at the light. I take a finger and run it across his fat brow. It's warm and my finger slides easily inside a ridge of deep wrinkle. It tastes like salt.

'Do you have a sister of your own?' I ask the killer.

'I got a sister back in Till, a big one.'

'Did you kill her as well?'

'No, I didn't kill her.'

'But you killed my sister.'

'Your sister. I did. I killed her. If I knew who she was, I wouldn't have killed her. But ha, I would of too. Who can say.'

'And when you came at her,' I ask the killer, 'What did it look like?'

'Scary because her eyes looked scary and she couldn't talk really.'

'But, when you came at her, what did you do?'

'That is between a man and a god, sir.'

'You have to tell me.'

'I have not.'

'I am going to kill you.'

'That's right.'

'Tell me what you did to her.'

'No.'

'I will have you put to death in the most painful manner known to man.'

'I am dumb on the matter, sir,' says the killer.

We are in the great hall enjoying supper. The killer's gentle mouth cradles a leg of rabbit, the meat and tendon trailing loosely around his lips. The oils glisten like stars down his chin as he chews in the candlelight. I am illuminating a dozen acorns which Ilspeth gathered for me earlier in the day. There she is now walking past the archway of the hall.

'Ilspeth!' I call out to her. 'Ilspeth, would you come here.'

'My lord.'

Ilspeth walks quickly to the heavy wooden table, curtsies and bows her head.

'This is the man who has killed my sister,' I say.

Ilspeth moves her eyes to his face and back down to the floor.

'I have a mind to let you know, Ilspeth, that he would have come at you had he encountered you in the pantry instead of my dear sister. Is that right?'

'It may be it,' says the killer.

'I wonder, Ilspeth, if you'd like to have some time alone with him. Would you like that, Ilspeth?' I say.

'No, my lord.'

'What now. You wouldn't enjoy time spent with this man?'

'No.'

'Does he scare you?'

'Yes, my lord.'

'And why is that.'

'He's a killer, my lord.'

'And you expect he'll kill you.'

'Yes, my lord.'

'Would you enjoy time alone with Harlon, or Rauf then, Ilspeth?'

'Yes, my lord.'

'So you quite like those men then, Ilspeth, do you?'

'No, my lord.'

'But do they scare you, Ilspeth?'

'No.'

'Do you expect they'll kill you?'

'No, my lord.'

'Why not?'

'They wouldn't do that.'

'Why so?' I ask.

'They're good men. They wouldn't risk their jobs.'

'Ah. I've just employed the killer here as my personal guardsman, though, Ilspeth. Won't you then spend some time alone with him now?'

'I'd rather not, my lord.'

'I'd like you to, Ilspeth.'

'Please, my lord.'

'I order you to,' I tell her.

'I beg you, my lord.'

'Do you mean to put your job at risk?'

'I don't want to die.'

'Just an hour or so, Ilspeth. As a favor to me. Your lord, abandoned by his father, mother and now his only sister, punished by God, a miserable creature in a prison of despair. For such a wretch you could do this one favor. It will not require much effort on your part. Just sit in a chair and perhaps you could explain to our killer the workings of the castle, who's who and so forth, how one day passes to the next. He'd love it. Wouldn't you?'

'It's fine,' says the killer. 'What's my wages?'

'We'll discuss that later on.'

The killer eats.

'So, then,' I say.

Ilspeth is quiet.

I was eleven when they sent me to X Castle to learn how to joust and bide God and the king and so on. I was one among six other sons of lords sent there as pages. We dutifully brushed the horses and polished swords. But I had a headache every day. Nobody believed me. One day I pulled a tick off a horse and fit it into my ear. A servant fainted watching blood drip down my jaw that night at supper. They put me to bed. They brought in a bundle of laurel and opened a window. They put a rock in my mouth. They said this would keep me from swallowing my tongue. They spent two days cutting my arms and poking my head with a branding iron. They wrapped me in raw mutton for a night. They tied a string around a wolf's tooth and had me swallow it. When it came out the other end, that's when I discovered the light. Some of the light spilled out that night, blinding my eyes in pulsing orbs of God. I didn't need a mirror then, I was a spry, soft-boned kid. My entire world revolved. I swallowed the wolf tooth again, and again the light seeped out when I pulled it out from up there, deep inside. I tried it the other way, illuminating the tooth directly. I told them, finally, on the seventh day, that my headache was gone. Harlon came to take me home. I couldn't have cared less what happened after that.

When we stake out a house in the village we come equipped with tools and weapons. There's an iron ball on a chain we throw through the window. Then one of us goes around back to kick in the door. We set fire to the manger, if there is one, or to whatever brush is around the backway. Once inside, we put down the men first. They are usually the ones to come out with a knife, a little rondel or stiletto most likely, or a club or flail or maul. The killer doesn't like to use a sword. He carries a small morning star which he fashioned himself out of wood and nails. It looks a bit like a big magic wand. And I'm armed with my father's broadsword, no shield. I have never been injured in any way which I've later regretted. Once the men and children are down, the killer takes out the great burlap sack. We put the women in there. I try, each time, to select from their mantel or chest or whatnot a trinket I think would be nicely illuminated later that night, when all is said and done and the killer and I are resting by the fire.

We keep Ilspeth now in the oubliette out in the cavalry house. We feed her horseshit and sod. We pee down into the hole. Sometimes the killer picks yellow flowers on our walks across the pasture, down the gentle hill under sunset. He plucks the petals and lets them fall between the holes in the grate of the oubliette, says he's showering her with sunshine. I have shown the killer my light inside. He says he sees nothing but black, the blind mule. When it rains the oubliette fills with water. The stink is something awful so we send the servants in with lye. Twice I threw down some of my mother's jewels, a handful of gold.

It is the anniversary of my father's death. We go to the abbey to visit my mother. The killer carries a small trunk of food: breads, honey, cheeses, wine, cherries, onions, herbs, a cake. We find the nuns in the chapel. The killer drops the trunk on the altar, making a sudden thump. The nuns gasp and rumple their robes.

'Where's my mother?' I ask. My question echoes like birdsong.

'Shhh,' goes the killer. 'You're praying here,' he whispers.

He lumbers down on his swollen knees and faces out towards the empty pews. The nuns fidget. A few of them silently walk off into the garden.

I slap the killer's head. 'Get up,' I say.

A tall, botch-faced nun comes towards us with her hands in her robes. She has a purple scar across her forehead. 'Your mother is in the infirmary,' she says. 'Follow me.'

'Get up,' I say, and slap the killer's head again.

The infirmary is behind the church and looks out at the ocean down a steep cliff of red rock. My mother's room is at the end of the dormitory hall. The nurse wears a thick white woolen shawl and covers her mouth with a rag and points. A mongol mops the floor with steaming vinegar. 'Ach,' says the killer. 'Smells like home.'

The room is dim. That's my mom in the bed, the tremulous speck of person beneath the flimsy brown linen blanket. Her hair is white and flared out on the pillow like the rays of the moon. Her face is flush and waxy and her mouth looks welded shut with spittle.

'My boy,' she says suddenly, gurgling, eyes bulging, and darts a fragile, squirm-fingered hand out towards the killer. He ignores her and sits down in the chair by the window, pulls a hunk of bread from his pocket and eats.

'It's me, Brom,' I say, taking her hand in mine. She looks at the ceiling and breathes heavily. I shed a cold tear and kneel at her bedside. I am illuminating a Lincoln scarlet scarf I found in my father's wardrobe. I cry.

'You're crying,' says the killer.

'I am not,' I say.

'My boy,' says my mother again, this time stroking my hair.

'Mom,' I say. 'How are you?'

My mother tells me all her favorite nuns are dying. She says she's watched them die, one by one, over the past ten days, and there's nothing anyone can do to stop it. Each one who comes to bring her dinner dies the next day, she says.

'There's something out there,' she says, holding my hand in hers. 'It will find you, it will hunt you down, and it will get itself into you and it will eat you up inside and you will start to rot even before you've finished dying. You will feel thirsty and you will raise your arm to lift the cup of water and your arm will break and your muscles will tear and the bones in your hand will crumble, and when you open your mouth your jaw will unhinge and your tongue will dry up and your throat will blister with fever and the water will boil as it travels down your throat and your insides will stew and it will all come out the other side, Brom, and meanwhile the flesh on your face will sink and melt and your eyes will roll backwards and your hair will turn white and you will stink, Brom, so badly nobody will want to come near you, not even to see if you're still breathing, and you won't get but a torch thrown onto your bed through a broken window and no one even closer then until it's all burned down and the light's died down, and after all that then who'll be left to sweep the ashes, because there's something out there and it can't be stopped, Brom, and I know because I can feel it down here, deep inside.' She taps on her belly making a cacophonous, huffish, hollow sound.

'Look in my mouth,' she says, and tilts her head back towards the plain pine headboard, face splayed, eyes white, leaving her lower jaw grit and grumbling where it lies on the pillow.

Inside is a gaping, vacuous infinite galaxy of black space.

There is simply no other way to save her.

I pass my sword to the killer, bend over and show him where to cut.

I let my light shine. ■

NOON

A LITERARY ANNUAL

1324 LEXINGTON AVENUE PMB 298 NEW YORK NY 10128

EDITION PRICE $12 DOMESTIC $17 FOREIGN

THE MAGAZINE OF NEW WRITING

PRINT SUBSCRIPTION REPLY FORM FOR UK, EUROPE
AND REST OF THE WORLD (includes digital and app access).
For digital-only subscriptions, please visit granta.com/subscriptions.

GUARANTEE: If I am ever dissatisfied with my *Granta* subscription, I will simply notify you, and you will send me a complete refund or credit my credit card, as applicable, for all un-mailed issues.

YOUR DETAILS

TITLE ....

NAME ....

ADDRESS ....

POSTCODE ....

EMAIL ....

☐ Please tick this box if you wish to receive special offers from *Granta*

☐ Please tick this box if you wish to receive offers from organisations selected by *Granta*

YOUR PAYMENT DETAILS

1) ☐ Pay £32 (saving £20) by direct debit.

To pay by direct debit please complete the mandate and return to the address shown below.

2) Pay by cheque or credit/debit card. Please complete below:

1 year subscription: ☐ UK: £36 ☐ Europe: £42 ☐ Rest of World: £46

3 year subscription: ☐ UK: £99 ☐ Europe: £108 ☐ Rest of World: £126

I wish to pay by ☐ CHEQUE ☐ CREDIT/DEBIT CARD

Cheque enclosed for £__________ made payable to *Granta*.

Please charge £ ________ to my: ☐ Visa ☐ MasterCard ☐ Amex ☐ Switch/Maestro

Card No. ☐☐☐☐☐☐☐☐☐☐☐☐☐☐☐☐

Valid from (*if applicable*) ☐☐ / ☐☐ Expiry Date ☐☐ / ☐☐ Issue No. ☐☐

Security No. ☐☐☐

SIGNATURE .... DATE ....

Instructions to your Bank or Building Society to pay by direct debit

BANK NAME ....

BANK ADDRESS ....

POSTCODE ....

ACCOUNT IN THE NAMES(S) OF: ....

SIGNED .... DATE ....

DIRECT Debit

Instructions to your Bank or Building Society: Please pay Granta Publications direct debits from the account detailed on this instruction subject to the safeguards assured by the direct debit guarantee. I understand that this instruction may remain with Granta and, if so, details will be passed electronically to my bank/building society. Banks and building societies may not accept direct debit instructions from some types of account.

Bank/building society account number

☐☐☐☐☐☐☐☐

Sort Code

☐☐☐☐☐☐

Originator's Identification

9 1 3 1 3 3

Please mail this order form to:

Granta Publications
12 Addison Avenue
London, W11 4QR

Call +44(0)208 955 7011

Visit GRANTA.COM/SUBSCRIPTIONS

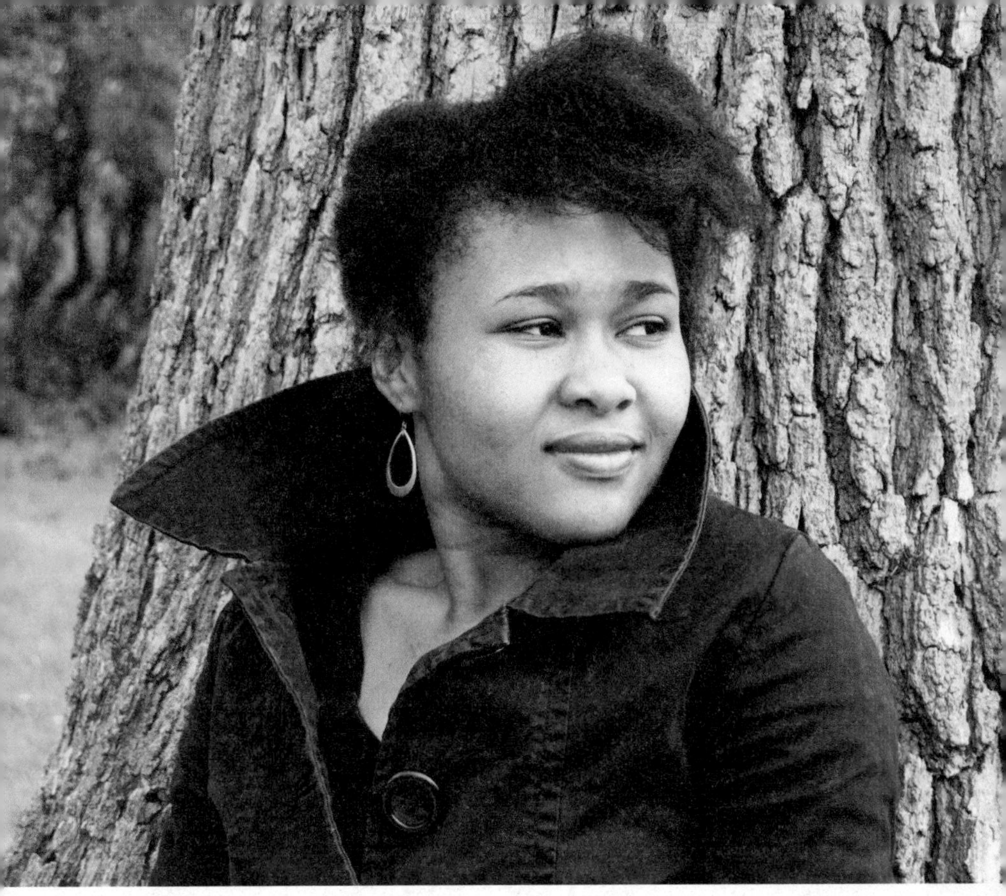

CHINELO OKPARANTA

1981

Chinelo Okparanta is the author of *Under the Udala Trees* and *Happiness, Like Water*. She is a 2014 O. Henry Award winner, and a two-time Lambda Literary Award winner. Her work was nominated for the 2016 NAACP Image Award in Fiction as well as for the 2016 Hurston/Wright Legacy Award for Fiction. Her stories have appeared in the *New Yorker*, *Tin House*, the *Kenyon Review* and elsewhere.

ALL THE CAGED THINGS

Chinelo Okparanta

'Look at them, how beautiful they are,' the girl overheard the woman say. The woman was a tall blonde wearing a sleeveless, ankle-length romper – a faded pale blue, which made her look as though she were wearing the sky. Her navy-green backpack was a blemish unto the firmament, a patch of darkening cloud. She ran her hands up and down her shoulders, across the straps of the backpack. It was a rather large bag: she could have been a hiker, or even a tourist from overseas, only her accent was nothing special, just what one would expect of an American. Every once in a while, she ran her fingers through her shoulder-length hair. She reminded the girl of Ms Abrams, her English teacher, the way the curls fell like cooked spaghetti, all creamy-looking and spirally, except fluffier, a tiny bit like yellow foam.

Another woman stood by the blonde's side, her red hair tied in a bun at the nape of her neck. She was also carrying a bag, but it was a tote, which hung down from her shoulder. She said, 'They're beautiful indeed. I just want to hold them and love them.'

The girl's favorite place to be was there, at the zoo. Washington International School was not far away, fifteen minutes via Macomb Street NW and onto Connecticut Ave NW. Twenty minutes if she walked leisurely. Of course in the winter, it was not an easy walk, but there were sidewalks recessed from the road which were always cleared of any fallen snow by the afternoon, and which made it doable even with the black ice. But it was especially doable now, in the summer.

Usually, the girl went to the zoo immediately after school at least two days a week. But this time she had left at about twenty to noon and had arrived far earlier than her usual 3.10 p.m. School was yet to let out for the year, but almost – these were the concluding two weeks of June, littered with hurried half-days when teachers were easy to outmaneuver. Leaving early was merely a matter of claiming that a parent was waiting. If she were caught, at worst she would face a detention. She was a good student. She had been admitted to Washington International on a scholarship, to her parents' delight. More punishment than detention was unlikely. Anyway, she had not yet been caught and there was no indication that she would be.

Over the course of the past school year, the girl had spent hours watching the animals and the people and wallowing in her thoughts. There was no entrance fee at the zoo, which made her frequent visits possible. As she stood with the animals, she dreamed of being one of them. She returned as often as possible for exactly that reason: because if she could not be one of the animals, she could at least be among them.

Today was not the first time she had seen these women. The first time had been last Monday, but she had not been close enough to be able to eavesdrop.

She had begun by stealing glances at them, but now she was flat-out watching them, taking in their pale and freckled faces respectively, faces that seemed both serious and sad. The way their mouths drew together in tight circles, a pair of scowls.

It was a Wednesday afternoon. Last Monday she had heard the zookeepers at the elephant yard talking about the impending arrival of two new Asian elephants. Today, the new elephants were there and stood among the others, snacking on the foliage of nearby trees. The girl stood watching them, leaning in on the barbed-wire fence that wrapped itself around the elephant yard, eavesdropping.

The blonde said, 'I had forgotten about the dried clover. Five leaves. Or was it six?'

'I can't remember,' the redhead said.

'And the key ring you gave me. I suppose I've lost them for good now. I couldn't possibly go back for them.'

'It's okay,' the redhead said. 'There'll be more clovers.' Her gaze shifted in the direction of the speckled sparrow that flitted onto a corner of the wire fence. She asked, 'What do you suppose it means when your eye twitches?' She laid a cupped palm over her right eye, then shook her head briskly, like a dog shaking off water from its coat, as if to dislodge the question, or the twitch. Now she shifted her gaze toward the elephants. 'Well,' she said. 'At least they're no longer keeping them inside. It's not much better, but still. It's a bit more freedom than being locked up in that room.'

It was true that the elephants had not always been kept outside in the yard, the girl acknowledged. For a while, they'd been kept indoors, in a sandpit of a room where they'd stood among thick cylindrical pillars and behind thick cords that reminded her of a wrestling ring. Dust from the sand rose like smoke as they stomped. Perhaps the zookeepers had moved them all outside because of the new arrivals. Maybe inside would have been too tight a fit. Whatever the case, inside or out, she wanted to be the elephants. She envied the way they were so well-taken care of, the way there was always someone to feed them, to cater to their every need, to clean up after them. She had come to the zoo enough times now that she had watched the elephants relieve themselves. Each time she watched she felt an urge to turn her eyes, in order to give the animal its privacy. But then she'd think that wasn't it one of the wonderful things about being a zoo animal? If you were a zoo animal, you wouldn't care about things like privacy! You'd be free to do whatever you wished, defecation and all, no shame involved.

In the sandpit room, there was the usual identification sign with the animal's Latin name, species, and place of origin. But above that sign was another shiny plaque, which stated:

> AN ELEPHANT PRODUCES ABOUT 200 POUNDS OF EXCREMENT PER DAY, ON AVERAGE.

She read all the signs at the zoo over and over again – each visit, another read – even though they rarely changed. Reading the signs was like a tic. Her last visit, she had tried to imagine what all of that poo would look like. How many bowls or buckets would 200 pounds be? Would it be enough to fill up a regular-size bathtub? Many bathtubs? The bathroom she shared with her parents was small, only a little bigger than a closet. Would it fill up their bathroom? She could not be sure. What she was sure of was that 200 pounds was a lot of poo, and yet there was always someone available to clean it all up for the elephants. That last visit, when they were still being kept indoors, she had thought, What a life! Like an elephant five-star hotel, complete with a skylight, the sun pouring in diagonal rays onto the indoor sandpit and the bare backs of the elephants. And a 24/7 zookeeper/maid. 'Locked up', the blonde had said. Who was to say that the animals did not enjoy being at the zoo? Who was to say that they did not see it as a long vacation? A lifetime of a vacation? Locked up was so opposite to the way the girl thought of the animals. Locked up was to be put somewhere you didn't want to be. But who did not want to be in a nice hotel with an on-call maid to serve you 24/7?

The building where she lived with her parents was in downtown Silver Spring, on Roeder Road: about a forty-five-minute ride from the zoo on the Red Line. It was an MPDU, which was the only reason they could even afford it. A one-bedroom apartment between the three of them. Her bed was in a carved-out corner of the living room, in a nook formed by a brown wooden shelf and a gray metal file cabinet. Every time she dreamed too hard and moved in her dream, she knocked against the back of the metal cabinet, and the sound was like thunder. Thunderous sleep. At first, it elicited the amusement that often accompanies novelty, but now she slept rigidly so as not to be frightened by the thundering cabinet.

Their tenth-floor apartment had a laundry room in the communal hallway and a balcony overlooking Ellsworth Place, with its bright neon-orange and red-and-blue theatre and store signs. Her mother sang praises every day for the next-door laundry room. (No longer a trip to the basement or hauling a bagful of clothes to the Laundromat across the street!) The girl would have told her mother that other people in her school had machines *inside* their homes, and housekeepers to do the laundry. No need even to fold the clothes, much less hunt for quarters each time laundry day rolled around. But to say this would be to take away her mother's joy. She didn't want to take away her mother's joy. For the past two years, every time her mother sang the laundry closet's praises, she nodded and added her own praises of the balcony, from which, in the evenings, she could look out beyond the bright lights of Ellsworth Place, beyond the tall glistening, metallic buildings and through the distant darkening sky, and imagine that she was back on Connecticut Ave NW, with the animals at the zoo.

But of course her mother would sing praises for such small miracles. Her father, too, sang praises, not for the next-door laundry room, but for the place as a whole. Even as an MPDU, there was the work they had to do to be able to afford it: cleaning in addition to the cleaning her mother and father already did, in the evenings, as janitors at Georgetown, where they were also pursuing their degrees. Sometimes – those days when their classes ran late – they did not get home until after she was already in bed. Not that their absence mattered much: her share of the cleaning work pertained to everything except the compacting: going from floor to floor, all ten of them, gathering the trash from all the large blue bins in the trash room. Throwing it all into the chute. Sweeping and cleaning the trash room with her little red mop and bucket, careful not to spill the dirty water. It wasn't the rank smell of the mop water or the tattered, fraying threads of the mop head that she hated the most. It was the glistening, cold emptiness of the room after she was finished. Once she found a doll missing a set of eyelashes in the eighth-floor trash bin. It sat at the very top of the basin, in a handmade boat created out of lined composition paper. In another place and time, in the world of flesh and blood, the boat could have been a capsized vessel, and the doll, a castaway. The girl whispered to the doll:

Like a fish coming up for air,
A fish-doll, on a pile of trash,
A fish-doll capsized,
A fish-doll heading home,
Capsized,
Coming up for air

And then she debated to herself the meaning of home for the fish-doll. Was home there in the sea, in that pile of neglected and forsaken things, or was home here in the bland, transparent, vacuous air? Was home here or there? It was certainly *there* – a memory of a place that must have been brandished in the fish-doll's mind, a place that must have seemed to have existed at least as long as she herself had existed, a simultaneous existence between body and place. Even now, when home was with her, home was still *there*, and if she had only an ocean to conquer, then one day she would surely swim back home. How long to swim back home? How long to swim across the Atlantic? Would there be dolphins or sharks to surmount?

All that thought of home gave the girl a sickly feeling, the longing of something so out of reach, something she wasn't even sure she could any longer truly remember. She folded up the paper boat and then crushed it in the middle of her palm. She buried the lashless doll deep into the edge of a trash bin.

When she was done with the trash, she cleaned out the laundry closets on all ten floors, a damp rag inside the washers and dryers.

A broom and a mop on the tiled squares. She swept and mopped all the hallways of all the floors of the building. And finally, she went down to the basement, which was adjacent to the building's garage. She made sure that all the trash bags that had come down the chute had indeed entered the dumpster. She picked up any stray bags and any stray garbage and placed them into the dumpster. It would be around 9 p.m. by then. An hour later, she knew, her parents would be back to compact it all. But not before taking care of their own janitorial duties at Georgetown.

Sometimes the girl imagined her parents pulling mops across the floors of their university buildings – shiny tiled antiseptic-looking expanses that would be neither shiny nor disinfected if not for workers like her parents. Sometimes she imagined her parents gathering and emptying trash bins, cleaning bathrooms and wiping down windows and walls. Sometimes, though, especially after rereading that elephant-poo sign, she liked to imagine them like the elephants: sitting with their feet up in a nice hotel.

She imagined her parents like the animals in the zoo now. Being an animal in a zoo meant you didn't have to worry about things like work. Being an animal in a zoo meant you could sit with your feet up and be catered to, as much catering as your heart desired. From the corner of her eye, she saw a man carrying a little boy on his shoulders. The boy pointed at something ahead of him in the distance. The girl thought: how unfair. Well, really, how lucky for him. To be able to sit on his father's shoulders, only lifting a finger, not even having to walk on his own two feet.

The sun was now very bright, and the blonde pulled out a visor from her bag. Her body was a wiry sort of thin, like a body used to moving around, getting things done. Her face was flushed, and the girl noticed now that there was something fidgety about her movements. The way her eyes darted this way and that. When the girl thought of it, this jitteriness had been there even the last time – last Monday – when she first saw the two women. It was also there at the onset of their conversation today. But it did now seem to the girl that it had grown worse.

The girl couldn't stand all that jitteriness, so she left the two women and the jitteriness at the elephant yard. Next, she would visit the Great Cats. That was her usual next stop on her visits to the zoo: the elephants and then the Great Cats.

But before she headed in the direction of the Great Cats, she sat on a rock under the shade of a tall oak tree. She had made herself a sardine sandwich earlier in the morning, knowing that she would be sneaking out of school before the lunch break. Sardine sandwiches were her favorite kind of sandwich as far back as she could remember. It was one of the things that reminded her of home, as in home-home, the one in Port Harcourt, before life and other people's dreams brought her to this whole new world. No one she knew at Washington International would ever have enjoyed a sardine sandwich. *Eeeww*, her classmates had said, the first time she had mentioned liking them. Oh well, she'd thought. Their loss.

A curly-haired toddler boy was holding his mother's hand and humming to himself a few feet away from where the girl sat under the shade of the oak tree. She observed the boy for a moment, the way his hand appeared just a fraction of the size of his mother's. The way he knelt down to the ground, cupped some sand into his palm. The way the sand dispersed below his hands like rainfall from the gaps between his small fingers.

Now, the girl took out the sandwich from her bag and unwrapped it from its aluminum foil. Just then the women passed by. The redhead said, 'Hi there, little one. How are you doing?' She spoke in a cooing voice, very affectionately, and at first the girl thought perhaps there was an animal near where she sat, and that the woman was speaking to it. It took her a moment to realize that the woman was speaking to her. The girl smiled politely, and the woman continued, carrying on as if she were an even smaller child than she was, as if she were five years old rather than twelve, as if she were a first-grader rather than an eighth-grader. Granted she was young for her grade, but that was a consequence of being smart.

'Stupid job. Stupid office. Stupid, stupid, stupid. Better this way, I guess,' the blonde said. 'I hated Marcy anyway. Worst boss ever.'

'Yeah, sounded like it,' the redhead said. 'You just didn't seem happy there.'

'Two years of utter unhappiness.'

'And the year before that, at McCormick's. Also unhappy. And the year before that at Parresia and Co. Also unhappy.'

'No good jobs out there,' the blonde said.

'Isn't she adorable?' the redhead said to the blonde. 'I could just take her home with me!' The girl only smiled and continued to eat her sandwich. What exactly could have been described as adorable about her? She was wearing her tattered pair of khaki shorts and a simple plain white T-shirt. Her canvas shoes could have been nice – an old brown-and-white-striped pair of Roxys – but the shoes were from the Salvation Army on New Hampshire Ave, and were ancient and faded and even a little dirty-looking, shoestrings fraying at the ends like old tassels. Her hair was plaited in old box braids that had the appearance of a badly pilling sweater, like hair that had not been nurtured with tenderness or time, clusters of hair bobbles all over the place.

She admitted to herself that she had her adorable days, but she was certainly not feeling very adorable at the moment, so she dismissed the women's comments and simply set her mind to savoring her sandwich – the rich taste of the fish mixed with butter, mixed with a little bit of milk. She had a pouch of Capri-Sun. Now she pierced a hole into the pouch and sipped the lukewarm drink. Fruit punch. A bit like the Ribena juice her mother used to get her from that little shop in Garrison, back in Port Harcourt.

By the time she made it to the Great Cats, she was feeling a little more energized, if not adorable.

The Great Cats – the lions and the tigers – were in the same general location, that is, on opposite sides of the same hill. Always the lions roared on their side of the hill, and very often the smaller children who came to visit mimicked their roar. The tigers simply roamed, no roaring really. The mother lion had given birth not long ago to four cubs.

'Take a look at this,' a voice she now recognized said. The sun was still strong, and the girl squinted, looked up. Her eyes landed on the redhead woman and her blonde companion.

'Can you imagine?' the blonde said. 'They actually had the nerve to put this up.' And she went on to read from the sign that was posted about halfway up the Great Cats hill:

> THE AFRICAN LION CUBS HAVE BEEN NAMED ZOE, ABBY, SHARON, AND NANCY; THE CUBS CAN ALSO BE IDENTIFIED BY THE ANIMAL CARE STAFF BY THE UNIQUE TATTOO MARKS THAT HAVE BEEN CARVED INTO THEIR HIPS AND SHOULDERS.

'This is unbelievable,' the redhead said. 'The way they carve marks onto them, as if they're property! What are we getting back to, slave days? Was that sign even there the last time we came?'

'No,' the blonde replied. 'I don't believe it was. It seems they're getting more and more out of hand. To think they'd even make such a thing public knowledge!'

If the girl were to have had any objection, she would have said, 'What kind of names are those for African lions?' There was nothing African about those names, not as far as she could tell. Not that she could speak for the whole of Africa, but still. Instead, she found herself thinking about what the blonde had said. In her social studies class, one of the books they had read was *Incidents in the Life of a Slave Girl.* There had been other books, too, that painted the horrors of slavery, the way that humans were branded as if they were livestock or pieces of furniture. The girl knew enough to know that the blonde had a point.

Well. No need for her to fixate on this tiny little unfortunate thing. She would try not to think of that aspect of the zoo and just enjoy it the way she normally did. She left the women where they were and made her way to the hogs.

Not long after she had been with the hogs, she looked up to see that the two women were there, and at it again.

'Did you hear about the virus killing pigs?' the redhead asked.

'Where did you hear it?' her friend asked.

'On the radio, this morning. Eight million pigs just dead and gone. Nobody knows where it came from.'

'It's to be expected when you lock them up in pens like these. Pigs should be allowed to be free. In the zoo or in the farm, they should be free. All animals should be free.'

Now the blonde furrowed her brow and tapped her index finger to her lips as if she had just remembered something important. Then the girl watched as the woman dug into her trouser pockets, plucked out a cell phone, dialed a number, and began speaking into it. She spoke holding the phone with her shoulder, in hushed whispers. Soon she was digging into the bag on her shoulder. She reached in and pulled out a stick – lipstick or chapstick, the girl couldn't be sure which. She twisted off the cap and dabbed it on her lips. Her lips were now a darker shade of pink. Above her the sun was a swollen orange ball and not far from her a squirrel was scurrying away with a pine cone in its mouth.

She then walked around the Great Ape House, where she met with gorillas Kojo and Bibi and Rwanda, whose names she found more fitting than those of the lions. She made a point of reading the posted signs. One of the things she read was that gorillas lived about thirty years in the wild, but significantly longer – fifty years – in zoos. She hoped that the women would see this, because surely, they would come to the Great Ape House, the way they appeared to be going to all the same exhibits to which the girl herself was going. She hoped that reading the sign might make them reconsider their stance on zoos. Perhaps they would see that zoos had their positive aspects too – this aspect of prolonging the animals' lives. The girl waited and waited, but the women did not come. Off she went to the howler monkeys.

The howler monkeys were named for the low, guttural sounds that they made at the beginning and end of the day. THEIR HOWLS HAVE

BEEN KNOWN TO TRAVEL UP TO THREE MILES, CUTTING THROUGH EVEN THE THICKEST OF FORESTLANDS. Male howlers used their sounds to guard their territories. One of them leaped from one tree branch to another, a very slow-moving leap, melancholy written all over its body. There were hardly any leaves on the tree branch. The girl watched, and she thought that perhaps the monkeys had eaten all the leaves. She wondered what else it was that the monkeys ate. Bananas, surely. But what else?

When the monkey landed on the branch, the branch gave a little. The girl moved her body in a way to compensate for the branch, or as if to try to catch the monkey if it were to fall. But she was at a bit of a distance, and there was the matter of the barrier glass; she would not have been able to save it, anyway.

Through the glass, she saw the reflection of a pair of women, and immediately she recognized them.

The blonde walked up beside the girl, then moved even closer to the glass barrier. The woman's hand curled cylindrically as it came upon the glass, like a binocular through which she now peered at the monkeys, one monkey at a time. She said, 'Can you imagine your little Baxter being kept in a zoo like this? Or even Phoebe? He would bark and she would mewl and they'd both be so miserable this way.'

It took the girl some time to realize who Baxter and Phoebe were.

The redhead walked up to her blonde friend. 'Alright, ready?' the blonde asked.

'Ready, set, go,' the redhead replied with a slight smile. 'Next stop, please!'

But they did not reach the exit, only approached it before they stopped. At one side, the blonde turned back to face the monkeys and began to dig in her backpack in a furtive sort of way, probing within the bag as if trying to locate something inside, sight unseen. Her face suddenly wore wrinkles as if her skin was now a rumpled shirt.

Now the man who had been carrying the little boy on his shoulders entered the monkey pit. The boy pointed exuberantly at the monkeys as soon as he and his father approached the glass divide. An older, gray-haired woman had already been standing near the glass, arms crossed at her front. The monkeys were squealing, like children at play.

The girl turned back to the blonde woman, who had also begun making quiet squealing sounds, a little like the monkeys' yelps, only a lot more pained. As the sounds tumbled from her, she crumbled to her knee, still rummaging in her bag.

'It's not fair,' she said. 'I've truly lost it all. That clover. Don't you remember, we found it by the marshland. How many years ago now? I've lost even that. It must have been there on the desk. I must have forgotten to take it with me.'

The girl had lost something once. Well, she'd lost many things. But this particular loss – the one that felt most like a loss of all her other losses – was a pair of brown loafers that her father had bought her just before they had traveled across the Atlantic. They had gone shopping at Mile One market. (Why was it even called Mile One?) There was nothing particularly special about the loafers, only that the fabric seemed soft, like a rabbit's pelt, and there were tiny sequins in the front that reminded her of stars. But then they'd made the trip across the ocean and the luggage in which the loafers were packed was somehow lost. Maybe it could not have been any other way. She'd seen a blackbird just before they'd left, which had eyes the color of those small sequins. The bird was pecking at something between two pieces of gravel in their old Port Harcourt driveway. And then it had noted her presence and had looked up at her. A moment that felt like a long time. Eyes locked, one small human's to a small bird's. It might have understood something about her that she had not yet understood about herself.

The woman was now sobbing. The redhead wrapped an arm around her friend. Shushed her gently, stroked her arm.

The sobbing did not subside. Though it was a soft sort of sobbing, there was a franticness in the blonde's eyes. And of course there would be. It was frantic-making to lose something so dear, the girl thought. But the way this woman was frantic made the girl's heart race. She wanted to say something to her to make her stop – a consolation that obviously had not yet occurred to her friend – but what should be said had not yet occurred to the girl either.

'We have to help them,' the blonde cried loudly now.

She now had the attention of the man with the boy on his shoulders. She also had the attention of the older woman. They all walked over to the two women, inquiring if she was alright. If everything was alright.

The monkeys had sensed the disturbance by now. As if on cue, with the word 'help' they had dispersed, as if they'd understood the woman, as if they'd understood her enough to mistrust her intentions. They leaped away to the far corners of their pit.

The blonde rose from her knees, went up to the glass barrier between the humans and the monkeys. She pounded at the glass, wailed loudly.

Her friend pulled her back. Shook her by the shoulders. 'Come on, Annette,' she said, as if pleading. 'Not here. This isn't the time or the place.'

The girl felt like running to the blonde. Holding her. Embracing her. Maybe the way she should have embraced her little lashless doll.

'Everything that drowns eventually resurfaces. Everything that drowns . . . Everything,' she whispered, something her mother once said. She should have sung it to her doll.

But then she simply did not trust the situation. She felt herself a little like the monkeys must have felt, only not so much the matter of the woman's dubious intentions, more so the dubiousness of the situation as a whole. She gathered herself and walked away, out of the monkey pit.

Outside, just seconds later, she heard sounds like gunshots. Where had the sounds come from? A louder yelping from the monkeys, sharp cries, a tumbling howl cutting through the air and her ears. Next, the beeping of an alarm. She felt a breeze in her face. She imagined the barrier of clear glass was shattering and falling and forming little stars on the ground. She saw in her mind's eye the frantic looks on the faces of those other monkey-pit visitors. Maybe the blonde had somehow managed to 'free' a howler monkey? She saw freedom clearly now. That poor monkey, plummeting to its death. A crimson pool of squandered life collecting on the sandy floor.

The girl was trotting now, cutting through the sinewy roadsides of the zoo, out the zoo gates, heading home. Have you ever seen, from the corner of your eye, clouds, like lambs in the sky? The girl looked up, eyes straight up, and she saw that the sky was full of lambs!

Just as soon, the sky turned a gauzy pale red, like a covered wound, iron-red through gossamer white cloth.

The howling of the monkeys reverberated in her ears and her mind as she ran. Had the woman forgotten about the persistence of their howls? She would surely forever be stuck with the sound. Louder and louder and louder the howling seemed, even after the girl was home. ■

Courtesy of the author

ESMÉ WEIJUN WANG

1983

Esmé Weijun Wang is an essayist, the author of the novel *The Border of Paradise*, and the recipient of the 2016 Graywolf Nonfiction Prize. Her work has appeared in *Elle*, *Catapult*, *Hazlitt*, the *Believer* and *Lenny*. She lives in San Francisco.

WHAT TERRIBLE THING IT WAS

Esmé Weijun Wang

Becky Guo, Becky Guo, won't you play with me
I can't, said Becky, I'm hanging in a tree.
Becky Guo, Becky Guo, let me braid your hair.
I can't, said Becky, I've died way over there.
Becky Guo, Becky Guo, where are you today?
I'm here, said Becky, and I'll remain until you pay.

My toes are ice-cold when I enter Wellbrook Psychiatric Hospital. I know without looking that they've gone deathly pale beneath my socks and shoes, as though shuttling blood to my vital organs will sustain me in this place that is not old enough to be quaint: stained orange carpet, cement walls, cottage-cheese ceiling. I think briefly of fleeing, and how no one would stop me because no laser-printed hospital bracelet has yet been clipped to my wrist. But I've promised to come, and I am attempting to be brave. I approach the front desk while fingering the tin milagro that dangles from my neck.

The receptionist raises her head and asks, 'Can I help you?'

'I'm Wendy Chung. I have an ECT consult at 2 p.m. with Dr Richards.'

'I see,' she says, typing. 'That you do. Well, follow me.' She leads me to a group of hulking PCs, seating me at one of them. 'You need to fill out these questionnaires before you see him. It's simple, but feel free to ask me if you have any questions.' And then: 'You know – I *love* your hair.'

I put my hand to the top of my head, as if to emphasize the location of my hair.

'I love how long and black it is,' she says. 'Just beautiful. I always find it upsetting when Asian women dye their hair.'

She goes back to her desk. I sit and look at the middle of the screen before me, which reads, in blocky green type:

> PLEASE ANSWER THE FOLLOWING QUESTIONS ABOUT THE LAST TWO WEEKS (PRESS RETURN TO CONTINUE).

I press the return key. The next screen offers me four selections.

> I DO NOT FEEL SAD.
> I FEEL SAD.
> I AM SAD ALL THE TIME AND I CAN'T SNAP OUT OF IT.
> I AM SO SAD AND UNHAPPY THAT I CAN'T STAND IT.

I glance at the receptionist as though she can help me, but she's looking at her phone. She is perhaps checking the polls, which is what I would be doing if I weren't obligated to complete an intake survey. I examine her face. Has she voted? If so, who did she vote for?

PLEASE ANSWER THE FOLLOWING QUESTIONS ABOUT THE LAST TWO WEEKS (PRESS RETURN TO CONTINUE).

The first question stymies me because I'm not here for depression, which is what THE FOLLOWING QUESTIONS are clearly meant to evaluate. Even a person without depression could answer I FEEL SAD for a galaxy of reasons. If this survey were about the election I might choose I AM SAD ALL THE TIME AND I CAN'T SNAP OUT OF IT, or even I AM SO SAD AND UNHAPPY THAT I CAN'T STAND IT, which are both interesting ways of describing inner turmoil. Who knows what we can and can't stand. In my opinion, I've been able to stand it if I'm still alive, and maybe my psychiatrist was wrong and I don't need this consultation for electroconvulsive therapy; on the other hand, perhaps I said yes to the consultation because I can no longer stand the voices and the visions.

In terms of depression, however, sadness is not so much my problem, in which case it might make the most sense to choose I DO NOT FEEL SAD. Yet it is my belief that this could never be the right answer as long as I am alive.

'Wendy?' a voice says, and I flinch so dramatically that I almost fall out of my chair. It's the doctor. He is white, like the receptionist; his glasses are John Lennon spectacles; his smile is bland. He is handsome in an unexciting way, like a bachelor on a reality television show. Out of the corner of my eye I see glossy black shoes hanging, and involuntarily I turn to look at the nothing that is there.

'I'm sorry,' I say, composing myself.

His name is Dr Richards. We shake hands with a grip. He says, 'Come with me.'

Dr Richards brings me to a messy office with pockmarked walls. The easy chair I sit in smells of bodies and terror – I imagine the others who have sat here before me. I wonder how many of them have ended up getting electricity shocked through their skulls.

'Tell me what's brought you here,' Dr Richards says.

Becky Guo, Becky Guo, won't you play with me

I've prepared for this. On the bus to the hospital I stared straight ahead and told myself that it was imperative for me to be honest about my situation, no matter how terrified I was or how many stories I'd read online about people who had permanently damaged their ability to form new memories: goldfish people, I said to Dennis, my husband, who couldn't be here because of work and is very sorry that he cannot be here to hold my hand. I'm prepared to tell Dr Richards my medical history and about the first voice I heard when I was twenty and how the election has made my stress so much worse, which has in turn escalated psychotic symptoms that have proven to be medication-resistant. And yet Dr Richards's face, which warps and flattens and suddenly seems made of plaster, sucks out all the words I had carefully constructed and lined up delicately in impeccable rows, until I am vacant; the erasure of my likes and dislikes and the hopes I harbor, leaving nothing but agitation behind, is something that terrifies me about psychosis – I cannot survive another bout of catatonia.

'I hallucinate.'

'What do you hallucinate?'

It doesn't matter, I try to say, but the words won't come out.

I'm afraid, is what I want to say.

Have you voted?

We're all going to die.

Respond; that is how to clear the river.

'I see,' he says.

When I was seventeen, Rebecca Mei-Hua Guo was found hanging from a eucalyptus tree near the outskirts of Polk Valley, where I live. To be hanged from this tree was a feat, given its size; her gleaming shoes dangled far above the heads of the two huntsmen who found her, too high for them to reach, and certainly too high for them to undo the knots that made her noose, or the rope that bound her to the branch. By the time they summoned the police and the fire brigade, she had been hanging for over fourteen hours – so said the medical examiner who evaluated her body.

I am well aware that any narrative involving a dead girl ultimately fails to animate the dead girl, who remains a corpse – or in this case, a ghost – for the duration. I do believe in ghosts. I believe that the living carry patterns of energy created by atoms and molecules and cells and organs, and that these patterns remain vibrating in the air after we die. Sometimes they disassemble and form other patterns, such as in the Buddhist belief of reincarnation, and sometimes they remain what they were before the death occurred.

As an amateur Tarot reader, I pulled a card for Becky the day her body was found, and I did not pull the World or the Wheel of Fortune. I pulled the Nine of Swords: despair, nightmares. For years I had dreams in which I was the one hanging, and that the children were singing of me while I gasped for breath, wriggling like an exotic dark-haired worm on a hook, watching the townspeople laughing from below. It could have been any of them who killed Becky. It would have been any of them. As long as the murderer was free I would not know who had sedated and then hung Becky from that high-up branch. I would not know why or how the killer had done it, and because there seemed to be no reason for the act I would have to keep my head bowed. If she had not been killed in part because of her race I could, as the saying goes, breathe easier, but I could not assure myself of that any more than I could wipe off my own face.

We, the Guo family, insist that the eucalyptus tree where our daughter Rebecca died be cut down. It is too much to bear for us to see the reminder of her terrible death, or to even know that it is there.

Mr and Mrs Guo came to me to write the letter because they wanted it to be written in perfect English, which they could not do themselves. It was the kind of thing, I knew, that they would have had Becky do, had she lived. Because I wrote this letter for them I know that they did not ask for a plaque to be installed at the site of her death; they believed without question that the town would deny them such a thing, and I too knew this and agreed with them without a word spoken.

They came to our apartment in the afternoon, when neither of my parents were home, and asked me to write this letter to the mayor of Polk Valley. I had never before seen Mr Guo so rumpled, or Mrs Guo so casual – my life had carried enough weight by then, but I'd never seen two people so heavy with sadness.

When they asked if I would please do this favor for them I was immediately embarrassed because I knew they would want me to write the letter on a computer, which my family did not have, but the couple before me was bent with such sorrow that I said yes and let them inside, mentally scanning the disarray in our tepid home. I could tell that they were trying not to see Becky in me, but that they couldn't help doing so. I look nothing like Becky – she was round-faced, had enviable double eyelids – and yet the comparison was inevitable and caused their eyes to snag on me before ripping away. I gestured to the kitchen table and asked if they wanted tea, but they were staring into emptiness. I asked again in Mandarin, and Mrs Guo's head lifted slightly.

'You can speak Mandarin?' she asked, in Mandarin.

'*Hai hao*,' I said, which was to say, 'My Mandarin is serviceable, but I'm by no means fluent.'

'We tried to teach Becky, but she only ever spoke English,' Mrs Guo said in English.

I went to the kitchen and searched for tea, vaguely aware that we had run out the day before and that I hadn't asked my parents for the money to buy some. I told the Guos with apology that we had run out of tea, but did they want some water? With enough mundane dilly-dallying my heart would stop drumming, I thought. Nor did I know why I was so afraid, though in hindsight I think it was because they emanated grief like a contagion.

Mr Guo tried to pay me after I gave him the letter, and even though I had no money and my parents were always talking about how hard they worked and how poor we were, I refused the twenty-dollar bill. But for hours after they left, the apartment smelled like death: pale and blank, dry like dead leaves. I opened all the windows and turned on all the fans for fifteen minutes, and then I went through the apartment and turned them all off, but I left the windows open. It was summer and I could hear people talking and laughing and carrying on while I went into my bedroom and did my calculus homework, and the Guos went home and, I am sure, painstakingly rewrote my letter on their computer before sending it to our mayor.

I wondered whether I should have taken the money. I decided that I was right not to.

After the crime-scene tape was removed, I would go to the eucalyptus tree and press my hands against the bark, feeling its warmth beneath my palms and knowing that it was breathing, a living thing; each time I returned I half-expected it to be nothing but a stump, but there it remained, its leaves rustling, its branches looming to remind me of all the corpses that could still hang there.

At the time there were always two or three bouquets at the base of the tree – red roses, calla lilies. I would bring flowers sometimes, when I remembered. I imagine there are no flowers left there now. I no longer go to the tree, and I avoid the Guos when I can. It seems heartless, but if I must stay and care for my mother it is important that I distance myself from Becky, because we still don't know who killed her, and if I remain too close to the situation I will corrode from fear.

'Electroconvulsive therapy,' Dr Richards says, 'is extremely effective for those with intractable depression. It has rarely been shown to work well for those with schizophrenia. I usually recommend ECT for the former, and not so much for the latter, because of the potential for undesirable side effects. Memory loss is the greatest side effect, as you've probably heard. I'm sure you've looked it up. There are those who advocate against ECT because of what they've gone through. I don't blame them for it; they are entitled to their experiences. But there are some cases of schizophrenia in which I do think ECT should be considered, and yours is one of them. ECT is most effective for people who have been diagnosed with schizophrenia and experience hallucinations – in your case, auditory and visual hallucinations – yet don't respond to the atypical antipsychotics, Clorazil, or even the older antipsychotics. For people like you, Wendy, ECT might shake up your brain enough to get things working right again.'

I am trying not to look at his face, focusing only on the words coming out of it. I am a good candidate for ECT. My health insurance would cover the treatment. I would be an inpatient at the hospital for approximately one week and receive electroconvulsive therapy each morning. They can best monitor me this way. I might be able to go back to work.

'The Wheel of Fortune is a reminder of the impermanence of life,' says a neutral voice.

'I need to talk about this with my husband before I agree to anything,' I say.

'The roots of the word "innocent" mean to be free of injury or hurt.'

'That's fine,' says Dr Richards, looking back at his computer.

The bus ride back to Polk Valley takes an hour, and the line at the polling place is long, yawning down the perimeter of the high school and around the sidewalk to the corner, across the street from a convenience store that sells cigarettes to minors and Slim Jims at the counter. I wait between a twenty-something white guy scrolling through his phone and an older white woman scuffing the toes of her red cowboy boots. I don't talk to them about who they're going to vote for; I remind myself that California always goes blue.

I can't, said Becky, I've died way over there.

I text Dennis: 'Consult went okay. Dr says I should do it. Insurance will probably cover.'

In two minutes he texts back: 'Let's talk when I get home.'

I look briefly at Twitter and see that the man I am afraid will become president has insinuated that it would be best if his supporters harassed people at the polls, particularly people of color; of course, he never says 'people of color', but we know what he means. I click on the tweet and scroll down; the woman who shared this article received fifteen misspelled and angry replies from people with names like WhiteIsRight19887 and ((Aryan Queen)). 'Muslim Obama HATES America, LOVES terrrerists!' ((Aryan Queen)) is using a photo of Taylor Swift as her avatar. My coworker at the deli used to blast *Red* while we cleaned the kitchen, singing, 'Don't you see the starlight, starlight? Don't you dream impossible things?'

When I go to sign in at the polls I see that Mrs Guo is one of the women at the table, which surprises me; I have never thought of her as someone to volunteer for anything, but perhaps I am mostly thinking of my own mother, who felt that to volunteer in Polk Valley was to extend herself too far into America. I haven't spoken to Mrs Guo in years, but she beckons me forth, a lipsticked smile blooming. Her hair is short and permed, puffy like a cloud. She says, 'Wendy-ah.'

'Hi.'

'Can I see your ID?'

'Yes.' I remove it from my wallet. She takes it and scans the names in front of her. 'Voting today. Good girl,' she says. 'You are still so beautiful.'

'Thank you.'

'Are you married yet?'

'Um,' I say, 'yes. I am.' I think of Dennis, his image slotting neatly into my mind. 'I got married last year.'

'That's good,' Mrs Guo says. She makes a mark with her pen. 'Mr Guo and I are moving to San Francisco. We're leaving in a month.'

I don't know what to say to that.

'We never forgot . . . Mr Guo and I are always grateful that you wrote that letter for us.'

'It was nothing, really.'

'No,' she says, 'it was a kindness. A true kindness.'

'I'm sorry it didn't work out,' I said.

'*Mei you guanxi.*' She gestures to an empty voting booth, and says, 'You take care, Wendy,' as I walk away.

After her body was found, and even after it was clear that suicide was an impossible explanation, there remained a contingent that insisted Becky must have killed herself. Such a strange girl, with such dark thoughts – no surprise that she had ended up dangling from a tree. And yet Becky was strange in the most conventional of ways: a Sex Pistols pin on her JanSport, a streak of hair the color of holly berries. Witchcraft or satanic practices could explain the otherwise physical impossibility of *how*, but I bristled at such associations, which only accelerated Becky's inevitable mythology. Becky could be anything, once she died, and the rest of us would have to live.

I used to avoid being in the same room as Becky. It was too much to have two Chinese girls in one place, I thought, and Becky must have felt the same way because she often entered a room, spotted me, and then backed out to find her own domain. Usually this happened at parties. Sometimes it happened at restaurants. Once at a museum: a gallery of watercolors that looked like wounds.

After she died, of course, this was no longer the case. Now I find myself wanting to talk to her. I want to ask, Are you scared, too? Even knowing that I am not alone would be its own strange balm.

Dennis and I own a television, but we use it primarily for movies and his video games, and only recently activated the free cable that comes with our internet connection. I have, till now, resisted watching the breakneck election coverage, but it is already on when I get home. I find Dennis sitting in the corduroy easy chair, checking his phone with the television glowing and muttering across the room; I kiss him and put down my bag and stretch out on the sofa, staring at the ceiling. Right now, the news anchor says, the electoral votes are 129 to 97, which seems impossible – it was not so long ago that the candidate was thought too volatile to even win a primary.

'How was the consult?' he asks.

I had almost forgotten the consult. 'It was okay.'

We are silent. Polls are now closed in forty states.

'Do you think you'll do it?'

'I'm not sure.'

He asks, 'Are you scared?' I wish I could see his face, but I imagine it: Dennis with his bespectacled eyes on his phone, performing the act of emotional multitasking. While I've been psychotic, he's been phone banking. He even went canvassing door-to-door, which sounds nightmarish to me – but Dennis is white and male and good-looking without being threatening – I never use the word *disarming*, but he is that, too.

'I read a book about ECT earlier this week. In the worst-case scenario, I won't remember major events in my life. I might even have trouble forming new memories. They don't even know *how* ECT works – a guy named Ugo Cerletti decided to use electricity on the brain because they thought epilepsy and schizophrenia were somehow antagonistic. Before ECT, they'd use camphor to induce convulsions, but camphor never became as popular as shock therapy.'

'What are the odds you'll have memory loss?'

'I don't have hard numbers. I don't know if there *are* any. It's something that might happen. I would have to make peace with that.'

'When do you have to decide?'

'Soon, I guess.' I realize I'm drawing a red X on my thigh with the nail of my right index finger. 'I know Dr Hoch wants to get me on the wait list as soon as possible, if I'm going to do it.'

Dennis says that it's my decision and that he'll support me no matter what, which is kind and supportive and the right thing to say.

I look at Twitter again. Everyone is talking about the election, about moving to Canada, about the apocalypse. A Canadian writer says, 'The grass is always greener!' The Southern Poverty Law Center is still reporting election-related hate crimes. One friend is live-tweeting her experience of watching *Casablanca* for the first time. 'Does anyone else think Humphrey Bogart looks like J.D. Salinger?' she asks. I read an article about people chanting 'Lock her up!' at a rally. I read about a Muslim schoolteacher in New York City who had her hijab torn off by a stranger in broad daylight. ('MCM LIES,' is one reply.) I read about gaslighting. I read an essay about having a younger brother with brain cancer, and I start to cry even though I don't have any siblings and no one I know is dying.

'Oh my God, Florida,' Dennis says. 'He just took Florida.'

I look at the TV through wet eyes, where his fleshy, grinning face appears with the words FLORIDA and 29 ELECTORAL VOTES. He has won. No one has conceded yet, but still, he has won.

I'm here, said Becky.

'It's over,' I say.

Dennis says, 'I think so.'

I tell him that I'm going to bed. He says something back.

In the bathroom, where I avoid looking in the mirror – an aversion to my own face is one of my latest symptoms – I turn on the tap and let the water run cool over my fingers. I stand at the sink for a long time, until I cannot remember what I am doing; I lose the next move. Suddenly, and too loudly, a girl calls my name. ■

NOTICEBOARD

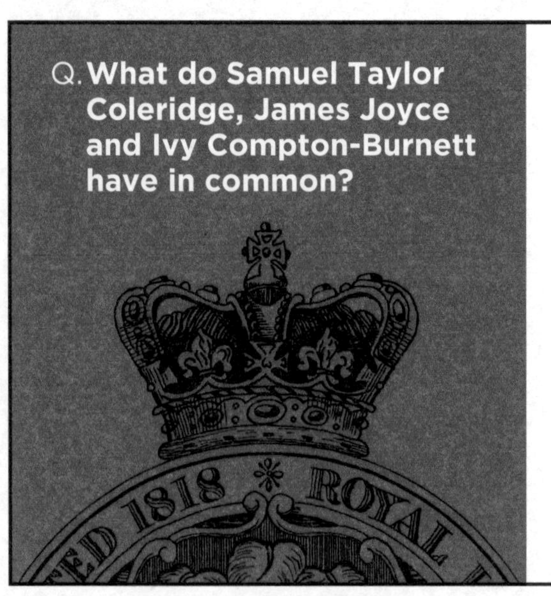

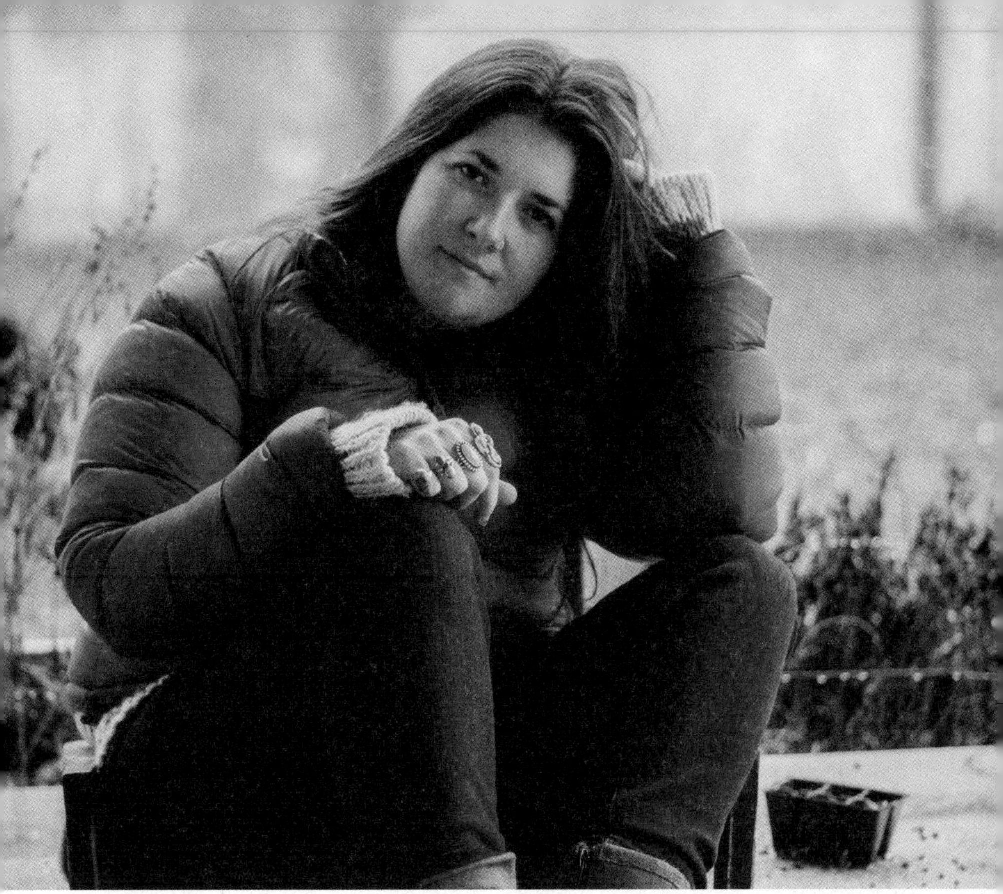

Courtesy of the author

CLAIRE VAYE WATKINS

1984

Claire Vaye Watkins is the author of *Gold Fame Citrus* and *Battleborn*, which won the 2012 Story Prize, the 2013 Dylan Thomas Prize, the 2013 NYPL Young Lions Fiction Award, the 2013 American Academy of Arts and Letters Rosenthal Family Foundation Award, and a Silver Pen Award from the Nevada Writers Hall of Fame. In 2014, she became a Guggenheim Fellow.

I LOVE YOU BUT I'VE CHOSEN DARKNESS

Claire Vaye Watkins

I spent the morning on myspace looking at pictures of my dead ex-boyfriend. The phrase *my dead ex-boyfriend* is syntactically ambiguous you can't tell from it whether this boyfriend and I were together when he died. We were not. We'd been broken up for about two years. We were together for three then apart for two then he died. He died in a car crash that's how he died.

Myspace is still with us. You could dogear this page literally or figuratively bookmark it set aside the volume or magazine or swipe to a new screen new beginning and find my myspace page or yours assuming you were aged fourteen to say twenty-five in the early oughts. The reason myspace failed isn't because it was populist or ugly or bought by news corp but because it was hard to talk about: *my myspace* is harder to say than *my facebook*. The uncooperative cadence of the phrase *my myspace page* perfectly encapsulates the awkwardness of the early oughts when our story begins.

His name was Jesse but in the years between our breakup and his death he went by Jesse Ray meaning his new friends and his new girlfriend called him Jesse Ray. I never called him Jesse Ray. No one from our old group ever called him that. We all grew up together don't talk about him much now maybe because we don't know what to call him.

I remember his body best of all because it was covered in tattoos. Not covered that's lazy. His body could not have been covered in fact because his tattoos were a secret from a few important people – his parents mainly and the people in their church. It's not that his parents didn't know him as I thought then but the him they knew was not the him I knew. There were at least three Jesses at the time of his death: Jesse, Jesse, and Jesse Ray. His parents knew one I knew another his new friends and new girlfriend knew a third. The only person who knew them all was probably his biological mom K she lived in Elko and knew everything. Jesse and I once fucked in the sacred vestibule of the Mormon Church in Ruth Nevada while his grandfather's ninetieth birthday was taking place in the multi-purpose room down the hall and she knew about that for example. K had been a waitress her whole working life she was basically omniscient.

Clothed Jesse was just a tall lean white guy. Long feminine fingers goofy mop of glossy brown curls he was vain about a stupid soul patch sometimes sometimes a mustache eyelashes of a fawn. I'm still attracted to men like him. But when he undressed he exposed torso biceps and thighs crowded with ink: a scarecrow and graffiti he photographed in the Reno railyard and his own let's say underaccomplished drawings. His collarbones read I LOVE YOU BUT I'VE CHOSEN DARKNESS. with a period as in end of discussion. We'd been friends of friends in high school where his stepmother was a biology teacher who didn't believe in evolution. I'm being unfair. She was a lot of other things too – my own sister – but the combination of her courses' difficulty and her stern piety made her stepson's secret rebellion first-rate gossip. And he'd had many of these tattoos done with an improvised apparatus built of a bic pen.

Jesse was on the football team wore eyeliner and sometimes other makeup with his jersey on home games suit on away-days. He dated evangelical girls who would only permit him anal sex another secret from his parents theirs too I assume. His father was a bearded giant a/c repairman taught karate led a Saturday night home church of his own strict eccentric doctrine. Their study was based on a code he had developed for unlocking the secret meanings of the Bible something about every seventh word or fourth word and each in their small congregation had their own three-ring binder with highlighted decryption glyphs in plastic sheaths. Jesse's father had had a shipping container buried somewhere on their property stocked with supplies to wait out the days between y2k and the rapture. All this I gathered from Jesse for though at that time I still possessed my anal virginity I was never recruited. This could be because my stepfather rocked prison tattoos on every region of his corpus including his neck and hands but was probably because my family didn't have a church. Work was our church my mother said though for most of my childhood she attended her Friday night AA meetings religiously.

I paid little attention to Jesse in high school because he was a rollerblader and I preferred skateboarders suspected him gay. I was fifteen sixteen seventeen and didn't know how to spend time with a boy who didn't want to fuck me. Then all of a sudden it was August and all the swimming pools in town gone mouth-warm so you didn't even want to swim until after sundown and Jesse was back from college and I was headed off to the same one in a few weeks. He was working a/c wrung out from crawling under trailers in 120-degree weather in long sleeves so his dad wouldn't see the markings on his arms.

We were at our friend Sean's drinking budweiser with clamato Sean's dad made us – where I come from if you work you drink, no matter that we were eighteen nineteen years old. By dusk Jesse and I were alone in Sean's parents' semi-above-ground pool. I gave him a shoulder massage – his shoulders pallid his neck and face sun-leathered save for little white hyphens at his temples where the arms of his sunglasses rested. After the massage Jesse said, in the voice of an animated luchador from a web series we all watched then, 'Maybe you want to take your top off?'

I was somewhere between willing and compliant. *Down* we called it as in *she's down* short for *down to fuck* or *DTF* which is what it said beside my name on the wall in the football locker room Jesse said. CLAIRE WATKINS = DTF. Inked as an insult but I've never taken it as one. I was indeed down to fuck. I was curious liked exploring other bodies I also liked to be liked who doesn't.

'This is why I have no respect for rapists,' Jesse said, cupping the white triangles of my boobs and glancing into the house to see whether anyone was watching at the sliding glass door. We couldn't tell didn't care.

Jesse said, 'Girls are really nice. Most of them will do whatever.'

I told him that was because he looked like white trash Ryan Phillippe.

He blushed turned the color he would ask me to dust across his cheekbones some mornings in the bathroom in the one-bedroom guesthouse we rented behind a halfway house off I-80. 'You just have to ask. That's all they want. All consent is is asking. If you can't even ask, you're a pussy.'

'You're using that word wrong,' I said lifting myself topless to the edge of the swimming pool.

'What, "pussy"?'

I pulled him close worried about my stomach rolls. I had probably been reading my mother's copy of *Our Bodies Our Selves*. 'You're using it as an insult meaning weakness,' I murmured into his neck. 'The pussy – by which I assume you mean the vagina, vulva, clitoris, cervix, uterus, and ovaries – is the strongest muscle in any body. The clitoris has twice as many nerve endings as the penis.'

Jesse had freed his from his swim trunks. 'No for real pussies are tremendous,' he nodded.

'Also,' I said, 'it's a term that belongs to a community. Like the n-word. I can say it but you can't.' I pulled the crotch of my swimsuit to the side and we kissed.

I said, 'I can use it as an insult or in reference to my anatomy. I can say, "Fuck my pussy, Jesse." Or, "Let's fuck, you pussy." '

All this was mostly fun and erotic though we rarely came but it was also my survival strategy. You could question its efficacy since it made sweet boys afraid of me so that I always ended up with the crazies but in this manner I went from being raised by a pack of coyotes to an academic year on the faculty at Princeton where I sat next to John McPhee at a dinner and we talked about rocks and he wasn't at all afraid of me.

Anyway I didn't like sweet boys. I liked filthy weirdoes who scared me a little and I still do.

Someone eventually shooed us out of Sean's pool and Jesse and I drove out to BLM land and lit off fireworks and fucked a few times in the back of his little pickup where he said, 'How do you like it?' and 'No, I'm asking' then we were boyfriend and girlfriend and then we lived together up in Reno working retail and fast food and taking night classes and Jesse quit drinking and proposed on Christmas and I reneged on New Year's and Jesse started snowboarding and going to shows and doing hard drugs and I started writing and Jesse fucked a girl in a tent up at Stampede Reservoir and another girl at the Straight Edge house and I tried to fuck a kid whose dad had an amazing cabin at Tahoe but I chickened out and in this manner Jesse and I broke up about a dozen times and eventually tacked a curtain across our living room and that became my bedroom where I would occasionally find Jesse napping in my bed because he missed my smell or on my computer without my permission doing homework or jacking off.

Jesse lived like he was dying a saccharine nugget of pinspiration terrifying to actually behold. Take it from me you do not want to room with anyone who lives like he's dying. His body was coiled with eros, anarchy and other dark sparkling energy. He looked for fights at shows or by wearing eyeliner and little boys' superhero shirts he bought at walmart to strip clubs waited for someone to call him a faggot and then he beat their ass. He had been on the club boxing team before he dropped out and snow bros in town for bachelor parties did not expect his long arms nor his gigantic martial arts father. After he went to awful awful for an awful awful or a buffet for prime rib.

He got gnarly nosebleeds all the time and our best talks happened with him in the tub letting the blood slide down his face and red the warm water. He was in the mug club at the tavern around the corner an investment he called it not because a mug club member received his beers in a grand customized stein though that was appreciated but because members could purchase another pint for a friend for a dollar which Jesse did often and then sometimes he smashed the pints on the floor to emphasize a punchline or one time into the side of a guy's head because the guy called Jesse's favorite milf waitress a cunt.

He liked to sing classic rock karaoke and uproot street signs and use them to smash too-nice cars parked in our bad neighborhood. He once shit his pants while skateboarding to work then worked his whole shift like that. He owned three skateboards two snowboards and about a dozen books in a crate beside his sleeping bag until he read *Walden* and said I don't need this crate! We had taco night at our apartment every Tuesday for all the runts and strays in our friend group and Jesse cooked the meat. He cut all the lilacs from the bushes on campus with his leatherman and piled them on my unmade bed even though we were broken up because the previous spring we'd been walking together and I guess I'd stopped and smelled them. He was very good at keeping secrets. Needless to say he became a junkie junked out on all sorts of things near the end but he was also very much alive.

One day I came home from my new job forging signatures for my butch women's studies professor at the subprime mortgage company she owned with her partner and Jesse was at my computer a piece of shit dell I'd maxed out my credit card for. He must have gotten a nosebleed during because he was jacking off covered in blood. I let him finish kissed him during then told him it was time to get the fuck out and he agreed said he would after the World Cup because we'd gone halvsies on the cable.

There is no story – he was there then he was gone. I am a dumb lump scratching my head baffled by this basicmost constant the ultimate fact: he was there then he was not.

I found out he'd died from my sister who found out on myspace. His current-now-suddenly-former girlfriend was in mourning black hair black clothes black makeup long all caps passages of pure screaming grief. No syntactic ambiguity. You want to know whether I hated her I did.

People die on the internet now really die we can watch them die in real time every gruesome frame if we like and sometimes if we don't. Periscope into dorm rooms into cars off bridges black people executed by the state unarmed fleeing autistic hands up fathers mothers children sisters star in snuff films screened in airports.

Of Jesse I have only pictures – his body on myspace. I like the selfies best you can see his gaze in them see what he thought was hardcore what he thought was punk. The last he posted before he died are of some operation he had throwing metal horns beside staples in a savage line from his sternum to his navel then around the navel a few inflamed sutures beneath the navel disrupting the outline of a new tattoo on his abdomen one I don't recognize not a very good one never to be completed.

There was a car crash someone was fucked up probably everyone though I don't know that for sure. I heard Jesse was thrown through the windshield flung into the desert off the highway on the way out to BLM land the place we first made love. I'd like to put it that way.

He kept secrets hated condoms. I watch his then-current-now-ex-online for signs and symptoms. I check his myspace and I know she does too since she is me is my own sister. We have the same thing living in our blood now. I am not doing a good job of this.

Jesse always let me be the good guy. He did not pay much attention to what I was doing and this is the version of freedom I have grown most accustomed to most protective of. He saw I was a watcher and gave me something worth watching. He was not violent but he enjoyed violence he was a vandal and a fighter but he was never mean never tolerated meanness. He was the person I called when I was afraid. He walked me anywhere I asked him to though he admitted the only time he felt unsafe on the street was anytime he had a girl with him. He always let me be the better person even though I wasn't better than anyone. He wasn't cracked up but he let me be the steady hand made me make myself feel safe. When I was with him I was always in control and this was true somehow even the night we drove to Berkeley to see radiohead and after drove a little stoned across the bridge and slept at my sister's place in the tenderloin on the living room floor because we were twenty twenty-one.

He was harmless there the street was noisy and the living room was lit orange from the soda streetlights and we collapsed into a mess of sleeping bags and yoga mats and pillows and somewhere in there my sister's cat making my eyes itch. I woke up with Jesse rolled atop me wanting sex. I was tired didn't want it he was not at all violent but also not relenting his body unyielding his long arms beefed up from snowboarding all winter and from lifting boxes in the stockroom at work. He held me down.

I remember thinking in italics. *Is this when it happens?* And then I answered myself. *That's up to you.* I decided that it wasn't it was simpler. I was determined to make it out of college unraped an actual goal I had though before I even started college I met a kid in the shoe store where I worked who invited me to a party but the party was just playing cards and so I was playing poker a tourist's game with him and some other people and drinking a corona then I woke up and it was morning and I was on the bathroom floor sore with my pants around my ankles. I walked into the master bedroom looking for this kid the kid who'd invited me whose apartment it was the only person I knew at this party. He was in bed asleep with an erection no blankets and another girl I didn't recognize naked spread eagle on the bed her hands were tied to the bedposts I think but I could be wrong. I didn't want to wake him wrote my phone number on his bathroom mirror with what I am just realizing now must have been her lipstick. This was in Los Angeles.

What's your family church? Jesse's father asked me the one time in three years I had dinner at their house. We don't have one I said or maybe I said work. Work was our church and laughter too. Farts and laughter and work and words. Rocks and photographs and dogs and TV. Breaking into houses for sale viewing things at night building materials casino decor landscaping elements once some mature water lilies and some koi. My sister my mother and me around the kitchen table bullshitting. The earth the body the sisterhood.

My husband has a dead love too. We traded them on our first date by my count the night we were the last two left at the bar and we walked to the united dairy farmers on high street for ice cream and took those to a hipper bar open later where we sat on stools playing footsie and drinking beer and eating sundaes with the ghosts and thereafter went home and dry humped without kissing in my bed where eventually Dap slept with his jeans on. This was in Ohio.

It was the first real conversation we had as intimate with another person as I've ever been. I told Dap about Jesse which was my way of telling him about my mother. Dap would not know her name for months.

Dap's love had been in grad school. She went on a research trip to South America something with biomes spores got an infection but didn't know it. She came back to the States and died in her sleep. Her roommate found her in the morning cold in her own bed. She'd had bulimia some thought and that compromised her immune system possibly.

Dap never got to see her body. I never saw Jesse never saw my mother. She was cremated while I finished my midterms. By the time I got home she was ash. We spread her in our garden at the Tecopa house the so-called Watkins Ranch on supposed Sunset Road. My sister and I put some of her ashes in the backyard at the Navajo house at the tree she planted where she'd buried her beloved hound Spike. I don't know where Jesse is now.

Jesse, I wish you were here. America is violent and queer as fuck. The snowbanks are rising and every morning I drive over a frozen river past a mosque an elementary school this week sent a letter threatening *a great time for patriotic Americans*. I pass a kid who looks like you walks like you did I pass a sculpture by Maya Lin called *Wave Field* which is like a bunch of waves made of grass covered in snow so like a bunch of bumpy snow. Pretty cool. I drive to a strip mall and smoke weed in my SUV and do rich bitch yoga with these fierce old dykes and Indian grandmas and public ivy sorority alumni and other basic traitorous cunts and for $20 each we all come out an hour later looking like we just got fucked all of them my sisters.

Maya Lin also designed the Vietnam Memorial. Ross Perot called her an eggroll remember? We were kids. Did you ever get to see the Vietnam Memorial? I don't think you did. I've seen most of the monuments in DC. I've been to New York and Paris and The Hague and Antwerp for a night and London and Toronto and the Amalfi coast in Italy and Wales twice. I've had coffee with Margaret Atwood lunch with Justice Stephen Breyer and a beer with the *Game of Thrones* bros while Anne Enright sang hymns. Once I was talking to Michael Chabon at a party and Ira Glass interrupted Chabon to talk to me and then – then! – someone cut in to talk to Ira it was Meryl Streep.

Sorry. I only have so many people I can talk to about these things.

My sister came to visit and she had this strange look on her face and I said what what and she said do you realize that our parents could not have afforded the dollhouse version of this house? I spent the morning looking for you on myspace and trying to untangle a sad mess of white cords made by slaves and this too is America.

We have electric cars sort of and any day now the tesla gigafactory outside Sparks will be the largest building in the world. We have virtual reality headsets and as you predicted people use them mostly for porn. We have HD porn. My sister knows a woman in Albuquerque who was raped repeatedly by her husband and he liked to watch porn on his VR headset during. I can't shake that.

I can't shake the pictures you posted of your body hundreds of them on myspace. In some you are Jesse Ray alive but dying actively dying looking dead choosing darkness. In none of them in an unnamed album you are finally truly dead. You are a torso beneath a sheet in the desert. There is a shattered windshield a cop car an ambulance a fire engine tilted on the soft shoulder of the highway lights blazing. The sun is rising and the mountains are indigo above you. Someone has tucked you up so none of you is showing so we don't have to see the parts of you we don't want to.

You were here then you were gone.

Jesse, Jesse, Jesse Ray, my dead ex-boyfriend, my son, my stepson, my own sister, mom, Martha Clair, I have a daughter now she knows your name. ■